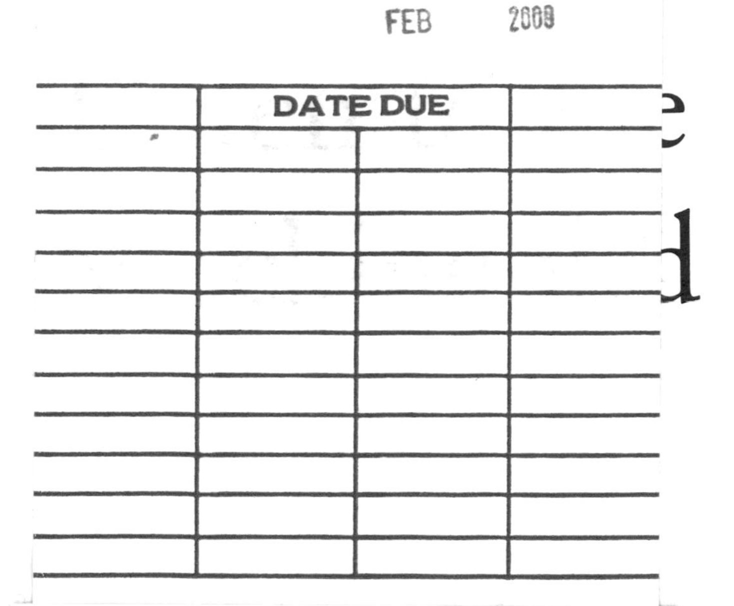

	DATE DUE		

Also by Penny Rudolph

Thicker Than Blood

Life Blood

Listen to the Mockingbird

Penny Rudolph

Poisoned Pen Press

Poisoned Pen Press

Second Edition 2007

10 9 8 7 6 5 4 3 2 1

Library of Congress Catalog Card Number: 2007924782

ISBN: 978-1-59058-348-7 Trade Paperback

Poisoned Pen Press
6962 E. First Ave., Ste. 103
Scottsdale, AZ 85251
www.poisonedpenpress.com
info@poisonedpenpress.com

Printed in the United States of America

This is for Ralph, whose steadfast confidence,
even on the darkest days, was the wind beneath my wings

Acknowledgments

The author owes much gratitude to:

Pam Williamson, for her enormously invaluable assistance with research

Bob Rich and Elizabeth K. Burton, both excellent authors in their own right, for their graceful editing

Rob Kresge, good friend and indispensable critic

Molly Murphy, author of dozens of books, for her willingness to help a beginner

Goldialu Stone, Jane Sampson, Sharon Winters, and the local Ms for their ongoing support

Betty Parker, though we've never met or spoken, for her extraordinary early review, which restored my faith in this book and in myself

Chapter One

Maybe I was a mite too pleased with myself.

By that night in April 1861, I had spent three of my thirty-four years answering to the name Matilda Summerhayes, or as most folks call me, Matty. I was getting used to it. The last thing I ever wanted was to run a horse ranch, but I reckoned I was finally getting a grasp on it. I was so full of myself I was pondering how soon I could put that ranch so far behind me it would seem no more than a puff of forgotten dust like you find under a bed.

All that day, the relentless spring wind had seemed intent on sweeping the ranch—if not the whole of New Mexico Territory—straight into the Rio Grande. But the blowing always went still at sundown, which had a way of gladdening the heart. So, I was sitting, chin in hand, at the plank table that served me well enough for a desk, gazing at the wall, imagining an orchestra. I could almost hear the trill of a piccolo.

A tremendous loud crack, like a felled tree before it hits the ground, sent me bolt upright. A bloodied face, mouth like a jagged hole in the dark beard, was staring blindly through the window. He tilted toward me and sagged slowly, his head grazing the pane, leaving a bloody smear. My heart near stopped dead inside me.

Leaping up, I snatched at the pistol on its hook on the wall only to see it clatter to the floor. Another crack thundered, then another; and something thudded to the ground so hard it rattled the house.

I plucked up the gun and on feet barely touching the ground fled down the hall to the parlor. Only once had the hands got drunk and shot things up. That awful face had been strange to me, but hands came and went. If Nacho had hired him in the past day or two I might not meet him till payday. If he was still alive.

I swallowed hard and held my breath till my head cleared. Few things terrify me more than a drunk with a gun.

Warily flattening myself against the wall, I eased open the front door. The moon was still low, the stars like chips of ice in a black lake. No sound broke the quiet. Near the barn, a huge shape sprawled in the rabbit grass like some chunk of rock flung down from the mountain. This was nothing human. Had some fool got himself mauled by a bear before he could bring it down with a bullet? Was the animal dead or only stunned?

For a long moment I fixed my eyes on the dark shape, but nary a sound or movement came from it. I grasped the pistol with both hands, thinking to shoot the beast in the eye if it rose. Feeling the earth hard and cold beneath my bare feet, I stepped toward it and was well-nigh close enough to touch it by the time I realized it was a horse, splayed out, legs every which way.

My eyes darted toward the window where the man had been, but no crumpled form lay there. My arms prickled in the chill air. Pulling my calico wrapper more tightly about me, I took a lantern from the patio and made my way back to the horse.

It was not a horse at all, but a mule. The saddle that had slued across the broad back looked trifling small. In the lantern's yellow halo, the animal was the color of coffee grounds. Except where the blood had pumped from the hole in its neck. Poor beast. I hoped it was beyond pain.

The hem of my wrapper caught on the saddle horn as I edged past. Where was the man? He hadn't seemed up to taking himself any great distance.

In the barn the air smelled of dust and dry grass. And blood. Fanny, my grey mare, poked her head over the corral gate and made a high, nervy sound. Inside, other hooves pawed the ground. George Washington was the only horse that slept with a roof over his head. He had cost an almighty sum.

Holding the lantern higher, I glimpsed something lying like a dark puddle on the straw in the corner. This shape was man-size. Like the mule, no sound, no motion came from it. My knee cracked as I dropped to the ground. The pistol felt cold in my hands as I crept in a half-crouch across the barn.

He was lying face down. A perfectly round hole the size of a copper, dark and shiny as molasses, stared at me from the back of his head. I swallowed hard and forced myself to stoop over him, struggle to roll him over. He flopped back on the straw like a sack of flour. I gulped back a cry and nearly gagged.

The eyes were wide below a gaping big breach in his brow. He looked Mexican and very young, not more than eighteen. The beard must have been a recent achievement. Now it was matted with saliva and blood.

Choking on the bile in my throat, I bolted for the barn door. The moon had climbed high above the mountains. The baked-dirt trail that led all the way to the river showed pale and empty. A jackrabbit scuttled across the patio. Nothing else seemed to stir.

Poor lad. What had brought him to where there was nothing left but to crawl into my barn and die?

"Nacho!" My voice sounded dry and quavery. I moved toward the house and threw open the door.

Herlinda was plodding into the parlor, a disapproving scowl on her sleep-swollen face. She and Nacho shared a room in the back of the house; their two sons slept in the bunkhouse with the other hands.

I touched the wall to steady myself. "Ask Nacho to come to the barn."

When she had dished up another sullen look and gone to fetch him, I grabbed a blanket from the deacon's bench, wrapped it about my shoulders and went back outside. No matter how hot the days, the night air almost always carried a bite. At the barn door, I turned back. The poor lad was a lonesome sight. I would wait for Nacho.

My eyes swept over the house. I hadn't much liked the place the first time I saw it and wasn't over-fond of it now. But that mattered little. I was just a temporary resident. Foot-thick adobe walls gave it a heavy, defensive look. The round ovens where Herlinda baked bread squatted near the patio like a pair of bears ready to spring. The ovens, like the walls, were made of mud. That's one thing we had plenty of—mud.

The living quarters had proved comfortable enough. And with some tile made by a Tortugas woman, I had fixed myself two panels, one for each side of the mud fireplace in the parlor. It was a simple thing to chip out a few adobes to make room for a small cherrywood chest. And the revolver. When the tiled panels with their painted mockingbirds were in place they seemed a natural part of the room.

The door to the house was still closed. Nacho would come in good time. To this day he is one of the best men I ever knew, but he was never hasty. The meager glow from the lard lamp on my desk was the only light inside. Oil was dear. Herlinda would likely frown at my having lit the lantern.

I brushed the heel of my hand against my cheek. Sometimes I was hard put to believe I lived here, much less that I owned nigh onto six square miles of this rude land. In all my born days I had never wanted to own a ranch. I reckon I put on a good show of it, but the more I learned, the more I met my own ignorance. There was little use for my studies at Bartholomew's Ladies Academy now.

What use were literature and sums and writing a fine hand? What good the finest head of hair in all of St. Louis, as Mama was fond of saying? Almost every day I thanked God she would never know the sordid state I had come to. She had taken such pains to show me how to part my acorn-colored hair in the middle, braid it and wind it just so. My wide-set grey eyes had come from her, but the high cheekbones and what Papa called my "noble chin" were his, as was the broad streak of willfulness that had bedeviled my poor mama no end.

Of course, the overlarge mouth had come along with the rest, and the nose that was a mite too short, and the freckles that would not go away no matter how many times I scrubbed my cheeks with soured milk. So much for that. Freckles mattered little here.

At last the door to the house swung open. Nacho Lujan ambled toward me, his gait slow and uneven from some mishap in his youth. A short, stringy man with muscles like ropes, he had a great mountain-ridge of a nose, a face like badly tanned leather and hair like coiled grey wire. His real name was Ignacio. No better man with horses was ever born.

"Que pasa, señora?" Longjohns stuck out at the wrists of his hastily donned homespun shirt. He stopped as his gaze fell on the dead mule.

I nodded and swung the lantern toward the barn's interior. Nacho followed me inside and across the hay-strewn floor.

"Madre de Dios." His face didn't change as he peered at the body. He only fastened a button on his shirt with great care. "I go to Señor Zeke?"

I blew a stream of air between my lips. Zeke was the sheriff. The village of Mesilla was nearly an hour's ride. "I reckon it can wait till morning."

He gave me a sober nod and started back to the house.

"Check that all the hands are in the bunkhouse," I called after him. "Could be the rascal who did this is a drifter or one of ours on a drunk. Either way, maybe we should post a guard."

"Sí." And he ambled toward the bunkhouse as if this sort of thing happened every night.

In the lantern light, the boy's eyes stared at me. Whatever I had endured, he had this night seen far worse. I bent to close the accusing eyes.

His shirt hadn't been washed in so long it looked the color of damp earth. The holster tied to his leg was empty. He had either used his pistol and dropped it, or someone had taken it.

I was about to leave him to his cold, hard bed when I noticed that the dirty rawhide thong around his neck led to something wedged under his left shoulder.

I pried it loose—a small leather sack, dark and stiff with dried sweat. I tugged the loop of rawhide over his head and opened the pouch. Inside was a torn piece of yellowed foolscap, cracked where it had been four times folded. Squatting next to the lantern, I peered at the odd pattern of lines and letters and arrows.

The scattered words were carefully printed in Spanish. I could make out *Arroyo, Fuente, Sinsonte,* and *Cuevas.*

Sometime in the distant past, boulders had spewed from the mountains to form, on the southwest corner of my land, the entrance to some caves. Locals called that the *cuevas.* Holding the paper closer to the lantern, I could see three scrawled lines, their spacing very like the arroyos carved across my land by rainwater coursing down from the mountains.

I had learned enough Spanish to know that *fuente* meant fountain and *sinsonte* was mockingbird. The place where Herlinda filled our clay water jugs had given the ranch its name: Mockingbird Spring. As I stared at the squiggly black lines, tiny icy feet began to creep up the back of my neck like a long-legged spider.

The cracked, yellowed paper in my hand was a map of my land.

Chapter Two

There is something about death that curdles thoughts and turns them backward. They converge in the chest like a jagged knot of ice in a winter stream gone dry.

We had left the boy as he was. Chilled, I lay awake thinking we should have granted him the dignity of a blanket and rose to do so, but found we had none to spare.

Still, sleep would not come. I thrashed about for hours puzzling over that strange bit of foolscap with its map. Was it really of my land?

In the morning, I woke late, the bedding twisted about my legs like snakes. My long legs had made me almost as tall as Papa. My skirts wanted an extra length of cloth just to reach my ankles. Mama had thought me too tall, but Nanny prized my height. With such legs, she told me, I would grow up to be stately. My legs did help me to cling to a horse as well as most men, but I doubt that's what Nanny had in mind.

Faithfully, three times a year, I penned a note to my grandmother. The months between, I made up the lies.

By the time I made my way to the kitchen, Herlinda was already clearing the dishes, banging them about in some wordless accusation that I reckoned had to do with my rising at such a late hour. Still nervy from the night before, I snapped at her. She gave no ground and shot me a withering look so I put off thoughts of breakfast and took the folded bit of foolscap from my pocket.

Nacho and his sons were dragging the dead mule from the door of the barn. "Was anyone missing last night?" I asked.

"No," Nacho grunted, dropping the mule's hind legs.

"Must have been a drifter, then."

"Arturo was *guardador*. He see nothing."

I showed him the map. He scowled at it for a long moment then dropped his eyes, twisting the strip of harness leather that seemed always in his hand. It came to me that he couldn't read, so I pointed out the springs, the cuevas, and pronounced the words. He scowled some more, then shrugged as only a Mexican can shrug—a slow movement of the shoulders that declares the matter beyond understanding.

"Never mind," I said and put the map back in my pocket. "Will you ride in to the sheriff?"

He pushed his hat back and scratched his head. "Much fence is down, *señora*. And there is need for *la sepultura*." He jabbed his chin in the direction of the boy. The local folk believe the spirit will take to mischief if the body remains long unburied. Frankly, I'm not one to say they're wrong.

I gnawed at my lower lip, wondering whether Zeke would want to come look things over before we put the poor lad in the ground. After all, he was murdered. Most likely the burying should wait until we reported it.

But the kitchen garden wanted another branch spaded out from the acequia to water it. With no hands to spare, I would have to dig the ditch myself; and the air that morning was finally still. No telling when the wind would stir up again.

"Señora?" Nacho shifted his weight from one foot to the other. I could see by the way he looked at the sky that he would as soon chance a word with Satan as with the sheriff. Mexicans got pretty shabby treatment from the law.

I glanced up at the sky myself. The days were sunny but still quite cool. "I reckon there's no harm in waiting. I'd best see to the spading today, but tomorrow I'll ride in to see Zeke myself."

Nacho was clearly relieved, but the notion did little to cheer me. I cottoned to the law even less than he. Catching his eye again, I added, "Make a good strong coffin for the boy."

His brow rose in silent surprise. No doubt he had expected to bury the body as it was. Wood was not easy to come by.

"Somewhere he has a mother," I said, not sure why the sadness had suddenly stabbed so deep. Perhaps it was because my own mother was gone, or because I would likely never be a mother myself. I cleared my throat to cover the catch in my voice. "She would want him to have a real coffin."

Folding the map, I went back to my room and opened the bottom drawer of my bureau. Another ache stole through me at the sight of my last remaining camisole, its lace yellowing. I stowed the foolscap beneath it, assuring myself that it would not be long before I could go home. Not to St. Louis, of course. That life was doubtless lost to me. But east—perhaps even to Philadelphia. I'd heard that the symphony orchestra there had admitted two ladies to its august section of violins. Might it not entertain the notion of a lady flautist?

When I finally sat down to breakfast, Herlinda had stopped making irksome noises and disappeared. The tortillas had gone tough, and I was chewing a joyless meal when I heard footsteps outside rasping toward the front of the house. One of the hands must want something. But they knew to come to the kitchen stoop.

The parlor door was thick pine stained almost black and about the edges someone had carved primitive images of birds. I opened it to a face I'd never seen before and drew back, skittish. Had the boy's killer come calling on me in broad daylight?

He was taller than I, which few men are, and reedy. His face, neither young nor old, was the color of new wood after a rain. The beard was streaked with grey. The eyes possessed a gentle intensity, and a sadness that might have been devastating if it weren't for an equal measure of humor. He did not have the look of a killer.

"Yes?" I choked, still trying to swallow a tasteless chunk of tortilla.

"Tonio Bernini." He pronounced the name carefully, as if he wanted me to remember it. "I should like to ask a favor."

I gave him a long, hard look. "Drifter?"

He returned my gaze with a softer one of his own and started to shake his head, but his eyes flicked away. "I reckon some folks might see it that way." His trousers were a blue canvas worn white in places, with rivets at the pockets.

Many's the time I've ladled up a plate of beans for a drifter, no questions asked. Might be I could feel my own heels in their worn-out boots. But I most certainly never allowed a drifter into the parlor. Once their bellies are full they like as not get rowdy. So I was shocked and even a bit annoyed to hear myself inviting him in.

A search of the kitchen produced a chunk of yellow cheese, and I boiled up a fresh pot of coffee. Our cheese making was not yet perfected—the pale slabs I set out were crumbly. "Won't win any prizes," I told him, "but it's quite edible."

"I'm sure it is," he nodded. "I'm right grateful for your hospitality."

Perching stiffly across from him at the table, I watched his hands move with a peculiar sort of grace as he ate. The fingers were narrow, not tapered; the knuckles larger than the rest. On his right hand was a ring, its edges blunted by wear but almost certainly gold. His glance at my own hands made me drop them to my lap. The nails were cracked, the skin rough and ugly.

Raising my eyes, I looked straight into his. "You spoke of a favor?"

"There's a cave near here. I hear you own the land."

That brought me up short, recalling the boy's map. "The cuevas?" I asked sharply.

The stranger nodded and said easily, "I'd like to put up there for a time."

"How did you hear of the caves?"

Two straight lines puckered over his nose as he frowned. "Can't rightly say I recall. Someone mentioned them."

"You packing a weapon?" The way I snapped the words out sounded a mite bolder than I felt.

"No, ma'am." Lifting his hands palm up, he rose slowly, as if expecting me to search his person. "You're welcome to look through my bag. It's just yonder." He started toward the door.

"Sit down," I ordered and fetched it myself, a sort of made-over saddlebag, the leather as worn and cracked as soil too long without rain. Wondering what had possessed me to accuse him but unwilling to back down before that level brown gaze, I carefully shook the contents onto the kitchen's plank floor. I could not make out all that was rolled up in bits of cloth, but nothing had near the weight of a gun.

"Beg pardon if I seem over mindful," I said gruffly, handing him the bag and sitting again at the table. "We had a shooting, just last night."

"Can't be too cautious these days," he agreed, gazing plumb straight through my eyes into my head. Then he began putting things more to his liking inside the bag. "Does that mean I cannot bide a spell at the cave?"

I sighed. There seemed nothing objectionable about him. Another day he might have found me quite hospitable. "Why are you bent on staying there?"

He seemed to think about that a moment. "Looks to be out of the wind and dry. Why not?"

"Coyotes, for one. Rattlers for another. Indians for a third. Bobcats and scorpions, I shouldn't wonder. Might even be the odd bear or two. There's only a sort of two-room cave, you know, no house, not even a lean-to. And it's a good sixteen miles from Mesilla, thirty or more from Franklin."

A smile began at one corner of Tonio Bernini's mouth and moved like a slow sunrise across the canyons. "Be that as it may, I've put up in worse places." He sat down again across from me and picked up the bit of dry tortilla left on his plate.

Suddenly curious, I asked, "How do you eat if you don't even pack a hunting rifle?"

"A goodly number of edibles grow most anywhere. Small game is easy enough with a trap, and I've a fair aim with a slingshot. That was mighty good cheese, by the way. A real treat."

I found him another chunk of it then studied his face as he ate it. His manners were a good sight neater than most. I reckoned his years might be nearing fifty. His shirt was fresh clean, faded by many washings. I wondered how he managed to stay clean if he was putting up in worse places than a cave. A rumpled bandana hung below the open collar. A hint of curl lent the thick hair a slightly unruly look. But I kept going back to the eyes. They at once beckoned one forward and bade one keep a proper distance. They seemed to conceal something, but also to warrant that the man who lived inside was no danger.

A bit of the eggshell I'd used to settle the coffee grounds floated in my cup, and I fished it out with a spoon. "In truth, I am not eager to see any stranger set up camp nearby."

He folded his hands on the table in front of his empty plate. "I give you my word I will bring no trouble. Might be I could do some service."

I couldn't halt a smile and passed my hand over my mouth as if to cover it. "You don't much have the look of a hand," I said more sharply than I intended.

Those eyes held mine longer than I liked before he gave a short nod. "I do know plants—the root that calms colic, the leaves that relieve indigestion…"

The stiffness left my limbs. "Ah, you're a healer, then."

"Of sorts." The eyes steady on mine were dark and shiny and ever so gently amused, which annoyed me again.

But Doc Adams had up and died a year before. The barber in town could patch up cuts, if they weren't too deep, and set some bones; but the closest real doctor was in Franklin, nigh a day's journey.

"How long a time are we talking here?"

He lifted one shoulder. "Like as not, I'll move on by winter."

The caves were little use to me. I tried again to read what was written behind his eyes but found that territory still well guarded. "All right," I pronounced slowly.

He got to his feet. "I do appreciate it, ma'am."

Struggling with second thoughts, I rose, too, hastening to add, "You're to remember I'm the owner here. If ever I ask it, you must move on right quickly. Before winter or no."

"Understood," he agreed solemnly. "I'll get on down there, then. Thank you kindly for the breakfast."

"You'd best feed your horse, too. There's plenty of hay and a bag of oats in the barn."

He shook his head, his eyes seeming to hint at a private jest. "I have no horse."

"You can't be on foot!" There was the odd settlement here and there, but none I would have wanted to walk to. The cuevas were a mile or so south of the house. "Where—?"

But I stopped myself. It was not my habit to ask folk where they came from. I wanted no gate open for the same to be asked of me.

Tonio Bernini nodded at his boots. They were round-toed, wide-heeled and the color of dust. "They get me where I want to go." He hoisted a pack strap over his shoulder, opened the door and stepped out, then turned back. "Reckon you don't see many strangers out this way."

"Used to be true enough, but we had two others just yesterday. One did some shooting, the other did some dying."

He cast me a glance that seemed as mournful as questioning.

"Mexican kid. Someone killed him, and his mule. We've no idea who he was."

"Sorry to hear it." My new tenant ducked his head gravely. As he turned again to leave, it occurred to me that strangers sometimes meet in saloons and such. Might be one could identify another. "Maybe you'd recognize him."

This latest stranger shook his head. "Not likely. I don't know many folk."

"You must see a few from time to time. Mind taking a look?"

He paused for a long moment as though thinking it over then nodded reluctantly and followed me to the barn.

The blade of ice pricked up again in my chest. The boy looked no better in the sunlight now slanting through the door than he had in the lantern light the night before. He seemed to take up so little space. He was, or had been, little more than a child, thin and wiry, and rather short. Catching a tense look in Tonio Bernini's eyes I saw he was even less fond of death than I.

He squatted down beside the body. With the back of his hand he touched the cheek of the narrow, hungry face below the hideous void where the forehead had been. When he stood, a look of infinite sadness seemed to hover about his eyes; then his brow went smooth. "Sorry. He's a stranger to me."

Chapter Three

The next morning Miss Feather, our roan mare, went into labor. The mare's face had put me in mind of my English mistress at Bartholomew's. Naming the horse after her had been sheer meanness, of course, but the woman wasn't apt to learn of it.

This would be the first colt from George Washington, the handsome stud Nacho had chosen at the auction. His purchase was the first time I pronounced the word stud aloud.

We had high hopes for old George. He had cost the princely sum of five hundred dollars. We pampered him with oats, and George was happy to do what was expected of him. Miss Feather was less pleased, but she had obliged.

Again, I put off going to Mesilla, this time to learn how to be midwife to a horse. That was the first birthing I tended, a quick and normal one. There was little for Nacho or me to do but stand by, watch and marvel. When Miss Feather licked away the mucus and the fine little filly wobbled her way to the mare's teats, I was purely thrilled.

With the colt suckling heartily, I saddled Fanny and got ready to ride into town to tell Zeke that an unknown Mexican boy had breathed his last in my barn.

◊◊◊

Fanny lowered her head and stretched her legs into an easy gallop. I watched the grey mane flare across the back of her neck and listened to the power of her hooves pummeling the earth like an exuberant drummer.

Mesquite stood like placid, graceful deer amid the scraggly, defiant creosote and rabbit grass. Long, thin shadows were sharp black, like iron swords stabbing the land. My first thought on seeing that land was that for vast stretches there seemed so little to hide behind. But I was growing accustomed to the emptiness.

Fanny is an Appaloosa, bred from mustangs, a handsome mottled grey with white stockings, black mane and tail. She was also a mindreader. When we slowed to a trot, she turned her ears to listen to my thoughts.

A wide brocade bag bumped at my knee. In that was my pistol. Indians hadn't given me much bother since I'd come to the Valley, but there had been a raid or two further south. And rascals were always about, sometimes local men drunk and mean as goats, sometimes drifters. No telling who might be full of himself and thinking up mischief, so it was out of the question to go about unarmed. Nonetheless, I couldn't quite bring myself to strap one on my hip. I still had my limits.

I began to wonder what had possessed me to allow a drifter to set up camp on my land and resolved to look in on him soon to be sure he wasn't brewing up some sort of devilment.

◇◇◇

Most of the buildings in Mesilla were mud, a few were wood weathered to stone grey, one or two were dusty brick. They clustered around the plaza like old women at a fountain. I looped Fanny's reins over a post. Subduing my vague uneasiness about visiting the sheriff, I strode briskly across the duckboards in front of the hotel and headed for the brick building behind the bank. I failed to notice the door of the barbershop swinging open, a man in uniform stepping out. I trod smack on his foot.

"Beg pardon." I felt the flush creep up my neck as I looked into a broad face the color of honey. A thin white scar ran along the jaw all the way to his ear.

He made a small, annoyed smile then looked me up and down, clearly trying to decide whether he should doff his hat. Desperately hoping that some tattered evidence of good breeding still remained to me, I was greatly relieved when he lifted the hat a few inches. His hair was yellow and tidy, his eyes like bright blue pebbles. "Lieutenant Beau Jenks, U.S. Army."

I apologized again, trying for the dulcet tones my voice had once learned but had now nigh forgot.

"No harm done, no harm." He marched off stiff-legged and, by the look of his back, still annoyed.

But at least he had not treated me like some strumpet out for a stroll and blinded by the daytime sun. I smoothed my hair, slowed my pace and watched where I was going.

Zeke Fountain swung his huge feet off his scarred and blackened desk when I opened the door. He was a big man with tufts of carroty hair and a neck like an ox. A dent circled his head where his hat perched. His eyes were small and set wide in the broad, fleshy face. This morning, the eyes looked vexed.

Zeke's wife had run off with a drummer the summer before, and I can't say I blamed her. He was ham-fisted and blockheaded, the sort no woman would want to be seen with.

He was more interested in the newspaper spread out on his desk than he was in my story.

"It wasn't one of my hands did it. Nacho says they were all in their bunks. Must have been some vile drifter. He even killed a mule," I finished.

Zeke grunted. "There's always some such varmint about. Like as not drunked up on tarantula juice." He brought one ham of a fist down on the newspaper. "I knew there'd be trouble. Horse breeding's no fit work for a woman on her own hook."

"It hardly has to do with me," I sputtered.

Zeke leveled his mean gaze on me. "If you was after knocking off a Mex kid, would you do it out to your place where there's nothing but a spindly Mex foreman or out to Jess Parker's?" Parker viewed everyone as a potential cattle thief and ran off anyone who so much as set the toe of a boot on his land.

"That's nonsense." I gulped back the rest of my retort and lowered my voice. "I have plenty of men about, Zeke, and they're all armed."

"Knew I shoulda kept an eye on the place." He moved his head slowly back and forth. "I knew there'd be trouble. It just weren't meant to be. Woman jefes," he snorted.

If there was anything I didn't want, it was more of Zeke's—or anyone else's—eye on me. I stared at him, and he must have taken the look for strength because he nodded stiffly and muttered, "No Mex missing I know of. Guess you just got to dig him under." He shrugged and went back to his newspaper.

Jamie O'Rourke's office was just around the corner. Jamie was the government surveyor. It was he who had told me about the ranch and sweet-talked me into buying it. I'd been a stranger to the valley with no mind to stay. I was headed for San Antonio; but truth be told, I had no idea what I would do there, either. I had thought that after everything else the rest would be easy. But I'd no more than found myself and the cherrywood chest a room at the boardinghouse for the night when I suffered a terrible attack of panic. Perhaps it had to do with calling myself Matilda Summerhayes. That was the first time. And the name did not set easy on my tongue.

My heart began to beat like that of a dying bird, my breath went from me, and my thoughts rammed into each other. I slept not a wink that night and the next morning it was fair more than I could do to get out of bed. I missed the stage for San Antonio; and when I did venture out, I learned there wouldn't be another headed in that direction for a fortnight.

As it happened, Jamie's sister-in-law was staying at the boardinghouse. A bulldog sort of woman, short and solid, with bright brown eyes that snapped sparks, Eliza O'Rourke struck up a conversation with me over supper. She had married four times and outlived them all. Her sister, Jamie's wife, had died some years before; but she had a liking for Jamie, so she'd stopped for a visit on her way to San Francisco.

Eliza insisted on introducing me to him, and it was that very day he had learned that Byron Cox had succumbed to a fever. Cox was a horse breeder, Jamie explained, with a ranch called Mockingbird Spring. Near the cuevas, he said, as if I knew where that was.

I was still not myself and didn't say much, except that I was a widow with a small estate and on my way to San Antonio. Jamie, quick as he always was, discerned that nothing much awaited me in Texas. He had a silver tongue, Jamie did; and he loved the valley with a passion contagious as the pox. He could have stood on a street corner in St. Louis and sweet-talked six folk out of ten into packing up, crossing the country and settling here. He cajoled, coaxed and coerced until I thought buying the Cox ranch a brilliant thing to do.

It would have to be done quickly, he said, before the hands up and left. The foreman, he assured me, was one of the best. Perhaps Jamie turned my head when he said the valley had too few handsome, clever women. No one had paid me a compliment in nigh onto four years. When he mentioned that in a half-dozen years I could sell the ranch for twice what I paid I realized that kind of money would be enough to see me settled back East. And I confess the name Mockingbird Spring struck a wry chord; I felt a kinship with the bird that imitates others and pretends to be something it is not.

◇◇◇

Jamie fixed me with his bright blue eyes as I slid into the chair next to his desk. The aroma of ink was thick and pungent. I pulled my skirt close about my legs, sitting primly, mindful of the smudges that lurked everywhere and wondering how Jamie always stayed so tidy.

"If you don't have the prettiest eyes I ever did see. Not blue, are they?"

"Grey," I said. Jamie's head was ear-to-ear with blarney, but he had something about him that made you believe he had your best interests at heart. In addition to his string tie and what was likely the only set of clean male fingernails in the valley, he also sported a black-and-white sense of right and wrong.

Jamie was determined to put the Mesilla Valley on the map. He had come here as land agent five or six years before, soon after the Gadsden Purchase had transferred thousands of miles of land west of the Rio Grande to the United States.

The way he told it, people weren't real pleased about the Purchase or about a land agent. Right after the war with Mexico, a lot of folks had up and moved from nearby communities to Mesilla. In the war, their hometowns had been lost to the U.S., but Mesilla still belonged to Mexico, which meant it was eligible for land grant. They had just secured one when Gadsden cut their new home away from Mexico and patched it neatly into New Mexico Territory. Now it was necessary to buy the land, which was where Jamie came in.

He was a charmer, all right. He managed to reshuffle so many papers that no one paid much. After that, there was hardly a soul within thirty miles who didn't dote on Jamie. Late last year he had decided that a thriving village needed a newspaper and launched the *Mesilla Times*.

"Confederate or Yank?" he growled at me, then grinned. His face was pink and smooth and shiny as a baby's, except for the bushy eyebrows. Greyish-brown wisps of hair clustered around his ears but had long ago deserted the top of his head. There was nothing Jamie loved so much as a good argument. Since he had printed the paper's first issue last fall, he had warmed to the task of making his opinions known. His tirades were good as any preacher's, and I'd never known him to hold a grudge against those who disagreed. He just marked them as needing a bit more instruction.

"Do I have to be one or the other?" My father had been a staunch Abolitionist, but I knew that here Anglo sentiments tilted toward Atlanta.

"Matty, you got to pay attention," he said, leaning forward in mock solicitation. "The Convention of the People of Arizona was held right here. The folks of the Mesilla Valley and the mining companies up around Piños Altos decided to send Dan Wilbur to Alabama to ask the Confederate States of America to admit us as a Territory. The line will run right below Socorro all the way to California." When he said "Confederate States of America" it sounded like the bass notes on a church organ.

"But what about Fillmore?" That Union fortress was only a few miles away.

He chuckled. "We'll give them enough mountain oysters to fry." Mountain oysters were the private parts removed from bull calves. Jamie reddened a little but didn't beg my pardon.

I ignored it, my mind beginning to paw at something. "And the Indians?"

"Dixie, luv. Dixie will protect us. Dixie will administer law and justice."

Slowly it came to me that this could mean many things—that I would be living in another country, for one. But more importantly, if there was war men would die, and no one would question that a lieutenant in the dragoons might well perish in a battle. My eyes flicked distractedly over the boxes of paper along the walls, the cans and trays that held the metal letters.

Jamie's forehead furrowed into shiny, quizzical wrinkles. "You look right flummoxed, Matty."

"It's just that you sound like a political broadside."

Laughter started deep in his throat and his eyes twinkled. "Look here." He opened the top drawer of his desk and took out a flat piece of metal. I had watched him set type once, so I knew what it was. He pushed it across the desk toward me.

There was the image of a banner waving and the words *Our Flag* backward, like in a mirror. More reversed words below were in short lines, like a poem. I raised my eyes to Jamie's.

He peered at me over the spectacles that always rested on the end of his nose. "That, there, is the Stars and Bars of the Confederate States of America. Texas pulled out of the Union. Now the Yankees have gone and fired on us. Our boys were just minding their own business, and the Yanks started shooting off cannons!" His smile was as bright as the light bouncing off his bald head. He drummed his fingers on the desk and broke into a lively whistling of "Dixie."

Mind racing, I fidgeted with the handle on my brocade bag. Did this mean that when the fighting was over I could go home? It would only require one more falsehood; and after so many, what was one more? I drew in my breath and let it out slowly. "This may be very good news, indeed."

"It is, Matty, it is."

I paused to consider it more then remembered what had brought me to his office. "You know anything about a stranger in the area?" Jamie's eyebrows rose. "A man came by to ask my leave to live in the caves. Not a ruffian. Looks Mexican but doesn't talk like it. Someone must have told him the cuevas were on my land."

Jamie shrugged. "I heard there was some priest or holy man or some such fella." My eyes must have widened because he patted my arm soothingly. "Sounds harmless enough. Hard on shoe leather, though. Walks everywhere. No horse, not even a burro. Hear tell he's a healer of some sort."

"That must be him," I said and got to my feet.

"Before you go, you hear about Joel Tolhurst?"

"What about him?" Joel was a Baptist preacher, a missionary. A good man, I suppose, but sort of stiff and disapproving; and I can't say I liked him much. His wife Isabel ran the mission school. The white women in town, their virtue as rigid as the stays in their corsets, were mighty curious about me. No doubt they thought I'd earned my money as a strumpet and planned to turn the ranch into a bordello. Isabel had tried every conceivable gambit to maneuver me into talking about my past.

"Joel's in a bad way," Jamie said. "Real bad. Ate his dinner, went into the parlor, sat down to read the Bible and never got up. Not by himself, anyway."

"He's dead?"

"Not yet, but I reckon he's good as."

I thanked him for all the news and moved toward the door, half ashamed for not telling him about the dead Mexican boy.

Jamie's intentions would have been the best, but I didn't want anyone poking about in my life.

"Mark my words," he called after me. "This will be the Confederate Territory of Arizona."

I took my leave, beginning to hope he was right. But that was Jamie. He could make you want the rope at your own hanging.

Fanny lowered her nose and watched me approach. Turning her toward the ranch, I let her have her head as soon as we were out of town. A gust of wind whipped at my face and tore the leather thong from my hair, which was now the color of rabbit grass after a rain—a red that's almost brown. I still troubled to care for it, had brushed it properly and braided it that morning; but it would be full of knots by the time I got home.

Racing into the wind, I didn't have to hide my thoughts. Surely there would be no fighting west of the Mississippi. But suppose there was. My heart leapt in my chest. I might be able to go home. Really home. To St. Louis.

I was still muttering to myself when the ranch hove in sight. The sunset was painting the organ peaks crimson. It was easy to see how the mountains had got their name; they resembled nothing so much as the massive pipes of a cathedral organ. The sight quite made my breath catch.

Fanny was anxious to get to her feed. I swung down from the saddle and followed her. She was barely inside the dim barn before she made a sharp sound and tried to turn back.

I was putting a puzzled hand on her flank to calm her when something hard slammed across my shoulders. Another blow rammed the back of my head and I sank like a stone.

Chapter Four

I opened my eyes slowly. Fanny stood above me, her breath hot on my neck. A faint ugly smell crept up my nostrils. Confounded that I must have been sleeping in the barn, I lifted my head, picked a strand of straw from my cheek. A white pain erupted behind my eyes.

The lump on my head was the size of a jay's egg. Someone had coshed me from behind. Who? How long had I been lying there?

Steeling myself against the pounding in my skull, I dragged my aching body upright and hobbled to the door. The sun was still high. A saw rasped at wood somewhere nearby but nothing untoward seemed to be stirring. Who had hit me? Was he still lurking in the barn?

I twisted my neck to look back across the barn, and a wave of dizziness lapped at my senses. Something dark swam into focus, something lying on the hay like a strewn heap of dirty laundry. It was a moment before my dazed mind recollected the dead Mexican boy. Had his killer come back for me?

The odor was ripening, and I almost retched. Then a chill pricked across my scalp. The body's chin was in the hay. I could see the blood-matted hair on the back of the head where the bullet had rammed through. But I had turned him over, hoping he somehow still lived. Nacho would not have touched him. Nor the hands. And most assuredly the boy had not turned himself back prone again. My breath seemed like a dead thing in my throat.

Why had he been carrying a map of my land? And why in a pouch tied round his neck, as if it were especially dear? A rancid fog of panic wrapped itself about my soul. I could not live like this. No lady could. I squeezed my eyes hard shut, and a salty tear drizzled down my cheek to my lips.

I steadied myself against the barn door, drew my wits about me as best I could, raised my chin and stepped outside.

Nacho and the hands had finished the coffin. They had seen no stranger hanging about. Nor had Herlinda. All were dumbfounded that someone had struck me down in the barn.

My head still pounding, I tried to puzzle it out; but my mind rebelled. I couldn't bring myself to think about it. Like as not, I had surprised a drifter in the act of stealing some tack. I sent the men back to work. The boy had to be buried as soon as possible.

In the kitchen, I ladled some water into a pan, dipped a towel in it and held it to my head. After a time the pain gave way to numbness. I gave my face a good wash and went back outside.

Fanny was munching hay, still saddled, near the barn doors. I took the reins, thrust myself onto her back and set out for the cuevas, keeping her at a slow gait to appease the ache that drummed in my head each time her hooves hit the ground.

I had ducked to peer into the cave's darkness when Tonio Bernini's face suddenly appeared around a rock, just inches from mine.

"Pardon me," I faltered, backing away.

"Good afternoon." He stepped into the sun.

I backed two more steps then drew myself up. "Have you been up to the ranch today?"

He frowned and shook his head.

"Have you seen anyone? Anyone who doesn't belong here?"

He lifted his shoulders and let them drop. "I expect I wouldn't know whether someone belonged or not. Why?"

"No matter." I leveled my gaze at him. "I've heard you are a priest."

His eyes bored into mine, then strayed above my head. "Sorry. I'm afraid you're mistaken."

I studied his face. It was full of something I could not read. "Beg pardon." I turned to go.

"Have you need of a priest?"

"The boy—I thought it fitting to have a service. Sorry to have bothered you." I moved toward where I'd left Fanny.

"As it happens, I do know the service." I turned back. His face was almost empty now. "I was in seminary once."

◇◇◇

A clod of clay thunked the top of the narrow coffin.

The flute felt cold and heavy in my hand. My lips and fingers were wooden with the weight of the time that had passed since I last held it. The casket gleaned from scraps of wood seemed unutterably apart from the group gathered around it, and the wind-scoured range a cheerless place for a spirit to begin its journey toward the next world.

Thirteen of us clustered under an old scrub oak. When I counted, the number made my skin prickle as though someone had tread on my own grave. But I shook off the feeling, not much one for superstition. Thirteen, and not one of us had known the boy alive.

My eyes rested for a moment on Nacho's bowed head. Next to him, on her knees but back straight, head thrust up, face wearing a profound sadness, was Herlinda. Mexican women have a gift for mourning. Their sons, Ruben and Julio, albeit a bit unsteady on their feet and smelling of whiskey, stood obediently, with eyes closed. The Lujan boys might have been a trifle rowdy from time to time, but they were good hands.

Homer Durkin, a rawboned man with slicked-down hair, had planted his feet apart, as if someone might try to knock him down. His head was hunched down between his shoulders, like one trying hard to show proper respect for the dead. At Homer's elbow, Eliot Turk stood as tall as his scant frame would allow, dark face held high, eyes closed, looking peaceful as a monk in chapel. Buck Mason towered over Eliot, eyes staring blankly at the coffin, a battered felt hat grasped tightly as a lifeline and held to his heart. I always thought Buck wasn't quite right in the head, but Nacho said he was strong and willing and that was good enough for me.

A small knot of Indian women clustered near, but not with, Herlinda. Two looked to have no more than twenty years between them; the third, mouth open showing absent teeth, was getting on. They swayed a little in unison, no doubt having a word with their own Great Spirit as we prayed to ours.

I glanced again at the casket, ineffably lonely perched next to its rocky grave; and once more wondered who had done this. Killings were common in these parts. Not a year went by without a dozen men meeting their Maker forthwith in a tavern brawl or a quarrel over water or grass. But most times the culprit was known. This one was like a riddle. It could be anyone, someone I knew, even someone on the ranch.

My eyes flicked back over the small group. There had been blood on that wretched face at my window, but the man had been fit enough to quickly get himself to safety.

Obviously, it could not be Nacho. Julio and Ruben shared the broad features of most Mexicans in the area, and I knew their faces too well not to recognize them. The man was dark but not Mexican. I was sure of that. Homer's hair was red, and Buck's complexion was fair. Eliot's was dark, but his nose and mouth were delicate, almost like those of a woman, more like those of the boy killed. And that awful face was bloodied from a wound somewhere about the forehead.

Just the same, I scanned the men around the grave yet again. All looked to have scoured themselves with lye soap for the funeral. All had hair combed straight back, still looking damp. No sign of a fresh scar anywhere. No, that face belonged to no one here.

But was one of them part of some scheme that had led to this?

I chewed on that for a time, but it didn't seem likely. The hands seldom left the ranch except on Saturday nights. And I'd often heard tell they wasted no time getting too drunk to do anything but lose their pay at poker. No, shootings hereabouts were done by one man in his cups or enraged to madness or a gang of outlaws bent on thieving.

Except this time.

And what about Tonio Bernini? His voice now telling the scripture was like warm, buttery rum. It half-coaxed me to believe there was a God; and that this poor, dead, unknown boy would soon be looking into His face. I could not imagine this man shooting a young boy in the back. Besides, he could hardly have expected me to search him, and I had found no gun.

At the "amen," I raised the flute, closed my eyes and breathed into it the first bars of "Lo, How a Rose." The notes were clumsy and thick. My vision blurred with tears—whether for the boy or for myself I could not say—but something seemed to ease in me and the hymn floated plaintively over the emptiness of the desert.

◇◇◇

We had just finished after-supper cleanup when a horse clattered to a halt, and I opened my front door to find a round face, cheeks pinker than ever in the lamplight, bushy eyebrows high.

"Jamie!" A kernel of alarm stirred in my innards as it always did at anything unexpected. Jamie seldom came to the ranch. I always visited him in town.

He followed me to the kitchen, where I hesitated between the coffee and tea. Tea was terribly dear at three dollars a pound, and our stock was nearly depleted; but Jamie was just about my only real friend and he had a passion for tea, so I brought out the pot. The cook-stove was still warm. I took a dried horse-pie from the gunnysack, opened the iron door and chucked it onto the embers.

"Have you heard something?" I asked him. "Will the Confederacy take us on?"

"That they will, my girl. How else can they get to the Pacific? They're in great need of a port; and our mining is no mean attraction, either. We do not go to them empty-handed. But I don't look to hear from Wilbur for another week." Jamie folded his plump hands on the plank table.

I tossed a careful measure of tea into the pot.

"Ah, Matty, I was hopin' for tea. You spoil an old man." He watched me watch the pot, and I must have looked as melancholy as I felt. "You seem glum, lass. Are things not going well?"

I told him of the murdered boy, feeling vaguely guilty that I hadn't told him earlier.

"Sure enough an unfortunate happening," Jamie said. "Wouldn't let it worry me too much, though. Like as not some fool got a snootful of whiskey and decided he had some reason to hunt that Mexican kid down."

"Zeke seemed to think it was my fault, somehow. He claims it wouldn't have happened if I was a man. Says he aims to keep a closer eye on the ranch."

"Ah, Zeke sometimes has suet for brains," Jamie sighed. "I expect he only means to give you some protection."

"He's a mean-minded dolt! The last thing in the world I want is anything he would call protection." I surprised both of us by slamming a fist onto the table, causing the teacups to jitter about in their saucers.

Jamie was eyeing me with obvious shock at my outburst. "Easy, girl," he said as if I were a half-broke horse he wanted to gentle. "Easy. What has put such a burr under that lovely saddle?"

"I'm sorry," I said, bringing the heel of my hand to my temple and holding it there. "I'm not myself today. But I don't need Zeke's help, Jamie. I'm perfectly safe...except..." I wouldn't have left it like that if the funeral that morning hadn't somehow kept me weary all day. I didn't want to think about disagreeable things any more.

"Except what?"

"That day I stopped by to see you, when I got back to the ranch someone was in the barn. He hit me over the head, knocked me clean out."

"Dear Jesus!" Jamie said, covering his mouth as if trying to prevent himself from saying more.

"No, no. It didn't amount to much. I'm all right. Really. I figure it was just a drifter stealing tack. I surprised him so he conked me and took off."

Jamie held my eyes as if trying to decide both whether that was true and whether I believed it. After bouncing the bowl of the teaspoon in front of him up and down on the table a few times, he asked, "How happy are you with this ranch, Matty?"

I stared at him. "Why?"

"It's a business proposition I have for you."

"That right?" The kettle was steaming; I got up to retrieve it.

"Fella come to see me this afternoon wants to buy your land."

The tea I was pouring into the china cup in front of Jamie sloshed past the saucer and onto the table as hope exploded inside me. If I could get enough for the ranch now…I strove to quell my eagerness, put the pot down and mopped up the spill. When I felt my voice would be steady, I asked, "At what price?"

"Now, I know it's not as much as you would like, but I promised to present it to you fair-and-square-like. He's offering about what you paid."

The hope whooshed out of me. I set the cup down.

"I know, I know. You've put a lot of work in here, Matty. I told him that. I wouldn't rule out his being willing to pay a bit more."

I ran my finger along a board in the tabletop, finding a sticky place where honey had spilled. "I couldn't possibly take less than I paid, Jamie. Fact is, I would need a good deal more."

"Understood. You give me a figure, I'll put it to him."

"I don't expect he would pay twice that. But in a few years the horses alone will be worth what I paid for the land."

"Well, that may be true enough," Jamie said, "if you aim to hold out here that long. But the fact is between now and a number of years down the road this here is a real good offer. Land values are dropping off pretty good, what with the war and all. There won't be anything sold till it's over. I'm not urging you, Matty. I just want you to understand how it is."

"I'm afraid I'll have to wait." I took a sip of tea. It was cool now and tasted like metal. "Who is it wants to buy?"

"Don't know exactly. Fella come to see me said he was from Austin, Texas. Said he was representin' a gentleman who come through here a couple months ago and saw some land he wanted to buy. Then he described your ranch, right down to the springs and the cuevas."

Choking down a rush of foreboding, I gazed into my cup. A few stubborn leaves were floating on top.

My mouth went on chatting with Jamie. When he rose and kissed me on the cheek, I forced a smile and bade him goodbye.

◇◇◇

Joel Tolhurst's coffin was dark pine shiny with shellac. Thirty or forty of us had gathered around it to give him a proper send-off. We spoke about how fine Joel looked, which he didn't.

I had brought as many wild spring blooms as I could carry wrapped in a damp bit of calico, and others had brought whatever they could find. Only old Mrs. Grady actually grew flowers with seed she got from back East; but her garden didn't bloom till early summer, so Joel had to make do with the wild varieties. He had teetered between this world and the next for many days before deciding things looked better on the other side. A second funeral and all the thinking I had done after Jamie's visit had weighted my spirits with lead.

Isabel stood across from me, small and prim, dwarfed even more by her enormous skirts, draped with black lace. Her ankles were no bigger than my wrists. This morning she had greeted me at the church looking like a toy sailboat about to capsize and asked me to pay her a visit after the burial.

I didn't know her well; but when I was new in town and still staying at the boardinghouse, she had invited me for tea and introduced me to the six or seven youngsters who lived part of the time in the long wing that had been added to her house as a dormitory for the mission school. The children were a ragtag bunch, some Indian, some Mexican. Most wore their newly learned manners like a hair shirt, but I daresay their souls were a small price to pay for three meals a day.

When the praying was over, I tied Fanny to the back of Isabel's little carriage and drove her back to her empty house. As we came to a stop, I realized she was trembling. A rivulet of tears grew to a torrent, sliding down her cheeks and spattering her lap.

"Oh, Isabel," I said, putting my arms around her. "It's awful, it must be truly awful, but the worst of it will pass. Really it will."

She just kept shaking her head, staring straight ahead while the tears dripped from her chin.

"Come," I said, helping her down from the wagon. "Will one of the boys put up your horse?" I lifted my chin in the direction of the dormitory.

"I've sent them away," she said in a monotone.

I hesitated. "Well, make me a cup of coffee, then, while I do it."

The brew was so weak it tasted like bathwater, but I wasn't about to complain and Isabel didn't seem to notice. She sat, took one sip, rose again immediately like a porcelain marionette and with quick little steps went to a black pine cabinet beside me. She withdrew a large bottle of Charlotte Fotheringill's Vegetable Compound from the drawer and poured the contents into a large goblet.

"It does help my headache," she said, not looking at me as she took up the glass. "This is the only piece of crystal I have left." She raised it to her lips and downed the entire contents, then began to pace back and forth in the parlor where Joel had been stricken. The floor of pine planks, stained almost black, bowed and creaked under her every step. "You can't know how awful it has been, Matilda."

I mouthed some awful platitude about how terrible it must be to lose someone you care for.

"No," she said woodenly, finally lighting like an ailing butterfly in a chair. The sky had been overcast all day and the room was dim as a cell. "I mean, it's not just that, not just Joel's dying and all. A missionary's wife must give her husband a life of dignity and respect, but..." Her voice trailed off, then rose plaintively again. "The heathen children. I thought I could at least help them."

"But you have. The mission school..."

Isabel swung her head away and looked at the wall. "They aren't interested in the Gospel," she said in a small, drab voice. "All they want is food. They don't want to work. They don't want to learn. And they are filthy. They have lice, Matty. Vermin!"

"Nothing a good head wash with kerosene won't cure." I tried to say it lightly, not knowing what else to say.

"I tried," she wailed. "Believe me, I tried. But they're such sly little beasts. They would pretend to be interested. Then they would steal food right out of the pantry and run off. Back, I suppose, to the lice-infested huts they came from."

"Surely you and Joel..."

Isabel rose to her feet again. For a moment I feared she might topple; but she righted herself, holding her shoulders stiffly. "It might surprise you to learn that Joel Tolhurst was not a kind man!"

The words exploded from her and hung in the empty air. I stared at her, at a loss for how to respond. The words of the womenfolk of my childhood sprang to my lips unbidden: "Men are sometimes..." I faltered. "...insensitive."

"We should have had children. But he—" She bit the sentence off, poured herself another glass of Charlotte Fotheringill, took a long draught from the goblet, sat down and leaned forward, her eyes shiny as marbles. "I have asked you here to request a favor. A very great favor."

The skin of my arms tingled. "Yes?"

"I want to live with you at Mockingbird Spring."

My gasp was audible.

She raced on. She must have rehearsed it. "I am passing good at cookery and I sew a fine seam...truly..." Her voice trailed off, eyes pleading like those of a lame bird.

Wordless, I blinked, stifling an overwhelming desire to bolt out the door, leap onto Fanny's back and keep her at a gallop till I was out of sight of Isabel's house.

She read the panic in my eyes and got to her feet, drawing herself up ramrod straight. "I understand." Her voice was bitter as vetch. "I know you think I would be a burden."

"It isn't that. It's...I have an...odd way of living," I stammered, unnerved at the thought of someone like Isabel living with me, someone who might somehow stumble across the truth about me. As I clumsily tried to cover my fright, the next words rushed out. "I don't think you would be comfortable. Surely the Baptists will help you to...to a more suitable life."

"Oh, yes, the American Baptist Home Mission Society will send me to another missionary if I give my oath to marry him." She stared at the air. "I'm sure you think I should welcome that."

I'd had no inkling of her plight, had only envied her looks and her place, if not her husband. Her pain seared me like a brand. But if I took her in, the time would come when she would ask questions; she would have visitors who asked questions. Unable to meet the agony in her eyes, I stared instead at my lap.

"Or they will send me the funds to go home," she was saying. "To a father who is—how did you put it?—who is even less sensitive than my husband is. Was." With that, Isabel composed herself, with more will than I'd thought she possessed; and the woman I had known returned: prim, superficial, courteous, dainty. She escorted me to the door.

I forced my eyes to meet hers. Feeling coarse, clumsy and cruel, I muttered, "Thank you for the coffee."

"Of course." Her smile was raw, her mouth hard.

It seemed to me that Fanny should find the weight of my guilt too much to carry. How could I abandon her like that? I, of all people? Twice I almost turned back to tell Isabel to pack her things, that we could try to make our way together if…

But the *if* was much too large.

Chapter Five

Nacho sprained his wrist wrestling with a palomino gelding that didn't take kindly to the saddle. I brought him cold water to soak the wrist, put liniment on it, bound it up in a strip of linen and told him to rest.

"But the selling day," he protested. With the auction coming up, we'd been working every hour of daylight, and I had much yet to learn; I could do little without him. All the same, he whitened with pain when he tried to use his hand, so I insisted he keep his arm in a sling and give it a chance to heal.

Suddenly, I had the day ahead and no plans for it. Restless, I swept up an armful of clean laundry from the table where Herlinda had left it and was stowing it in my bureau drawer when I saw that the leather pouch had slid out from under my camisole. Its owner clearly thought the content was valuable. Why?

I drew out the yellowed scrap of foolscap and studied the markings again. It was a map of my ranch, all right. And a little more. There was an odd series of X's above the spring. Far as I knew, there was nothing up there but rocks. Below the X's, some dim markings led like a path from where the arroyo bent as it left the mountains a little beyond the cuevas.

The morning sun was so bright it hurt my eyes. A squirrel followed me to the barn hoping for a handout. I took a pecan from my pocket and tossed it to him. He checked it over like an urchin biting a coin to be sure it's real, nodded his approval, flicked his tail like a naughty dancer and disappeared.

"Fanny!" I called to the mare in the corral. When I had saddled and cinched her and eased the bit between her teeth, I went back to the house to fetch my pistol. As an afterthought, I slipped my flute into the brocade bag next to it. After my poor performance at the boy's funeral, I had resolved to practice more, but there was so little time. I pulled myself into Fanny's saddle, fumbled at my skirt so it wouldn't bind my legs and wondered what folks would think if I sewed myself some trousers.

Along the arroyo, the junipers grew larger, and a few piñon pines wandered down the mountain to join them. Last year's yucca blooms had turned papery above the barbed spears. Here and there new waxy-white blossoms were opening. Fanny picked her way past a patch of cholla that was all angles and thorns and tall as a man.

At the cuevas, the land becomes flat, a broad, high shelf; and you can see across the entire valley to Mesilla. Fanny followed the arroyo to where the pines and junipers congregate. The sun was razor-sharp, and I was glad for the shade.

I slipped down from the mare's back. If the map was right, this was where the path—if that's what it was—began.

Beyond the trees, the sun-mottled brush was thick and matted all the way to where the bare rock rose steep and straight, like the walls of a cathedral. I inspected the area carefully. If there had ever been a path, a jumble of spiny brush had long since covered it.

On a shady rock flat enough to sit on, I assembled the flute, only to discover when I lifted it to my mouth that I remembered little of the fine music I had once played. My life had grown over it like the brush. My fingers were graceless, my wind sluggish, the tones dull and flat. Doggedly, I played what few bars of Mozart I could remember; and slowly, the sound improved.

"Very nice." A man appeared among the piñons and chucked a sack to the ground: my tenant from the cuevas, Tonio Bernini. He smiled. "I wondered if the fairies were having a party."

"It's not nice," I said. "It's awful. I've forgotten all the music I ever knew. And I don't believe in fairies. I doubt I ever did."

His beard gave him a look of patient wisdom, which for some reason vexed me. I was churlishly thinking that I owned six square miles of land and still couldn't sit down on a rock without someone spying on me.

Unabashed, he reached into his patched jacket and brought out a pipe. "Mind?"

I shrugged, which he took for acquiescence. It didn't smell like tobacco. It was dusky and sweet, like the juniper.

"What's that?" I pointed the flute to the sack at his feet.

"Leaves, last year's dried flowers, a few roots, aloe, red pepper, juniper." He sat, quite unselfconsciously, on the ground. "There's still a stand of Saint Ann's-wort up there." He gestured to a point above the springs. "I was sure it would be gone. Good for aching joints, Saint Ann's."

I leaned forward at that. "Would it cure a sprained wrist?" I told him about Nacho.

"Wouldn't cure, but I wager it would help." He opened the sack, drew out some leaves and handed them to me. "Put them in some hot water and make a poultice. If you stop by the cave I'll give you some bark for the pain."

Thanking him, I stowed the leaves in my bag. "These came from up there?" I jutted my chin toward the area about the tangle of brush. He nodded. "There's a way through the brush then?"

He gave me a sharp look then his eyes slid away. "Of sorts, but one must brave the rattlers. There's a nest of the vipers up there."

That dampened my interest in the area. "The local rattlesnakes can be awfully mean. We've lost a couple of colts to bites. You'd be safer on a horse than walking about among them. If you really have the healer's art with those herbs, I daresay you could trade your skill for enough money to buy a sturdy gelding."

"Perhaps. But I'm comfortable this way." Pairs of laugh lines appeared at the corners of his eyes and he glanced at his feet. "I wager these have carried me nigh as many miles as the circumference of the earth. Not all in one stretch, mind you."

I wondered if he was having me on. "You said you were once at seminary. Where?"

Wisps of fragrant smoke curled around him like slim strips of rain cloud. "Italy."

"Really? I've always wanted to see Rome."

He gave me a slow smile and leaned his head back against a rock. "It's full of ugly hulking buildings that cut off the air."

"Why were you in Italy?"

The sun made a bright triangle on his forehead. "I was born there."

That explained his not-quite-Spanish looks. "You don't like your homeland?"

"I don't like Rome. I was born in a village near Milan."

"And you always wanted to be a priest?"

He peered at me quizzically as if over spectacles. "Not exactly. I happened to be a third and unnecessary son, so I was sent to the Franciscans when I was nine."

"What does one do among the Franciscans? I've always imagined them just sitting about feeding birds."

He chuckled. "There's a little more to them than that. They taught me about plants. One of the brothers knew *Hildegard's Medicine* and the *Leech Book of Bald* by heart and compiled his own catalog of formulas. I became his apprentice."

"Was it very complicated?"

"A little. Sometimes a plant material's properties change if it's dried or heated. There's a root from South America that is poisonous if you eat it raw. If you boil it one hour, it is safe to eat and quite nutritious; but if you boil it for two hours, it is again poisonous."

"Eating it at all sounds a bit risky."

"So is eating nothing."

"So it is," I agreed. "Was it the Franciscans who sent you to America? Like a missionary? I'm afraid I don't know much about how the Church does such things. I shouldn't think they had even heard of New Mexico."

He gazed at the branch of piñon needles above his head. "My path was not quite so direct. I left the Franciscans to see the world. Eventually, I took passage on a ship to Mexico City and found my way to Chihuahua, where I worked with a priest in a small church until a drought killed almost everyone. I went east to Pennsylvania and lived with the Moravians for a time, but I found I missed the desert."

He fell silent, his face like that of a boy who has recounted what he ate for supper. For an odd instant I wanted to touch his cheek. How many years had it been since such an impulse had warmed me? Five? Six? I knew all too well the path that sort of feeling could set a woman's feet upon. I had survived by becoming neuter, as sexless as if I had cut off my breasts.

Discomfited, I turned my head to hide the blood rushing to my cheeks.

"There's something witching about these mountains," he said. "Once they have called to you, you can never be happy anywhere else."

Chapter Six

I watched the battle from the shelf-land near the cuevas. It was a July Sunday; and heat smothered the land like a massive feather pillow, cutting off the air. The sky was almost white, and empty save for the relentless sun, which seemed to stalk any creature foolish enough to venture out.

An hour before I had been sitting at my pine-table desk, daring to hope that I would soon be turning a profit. Our horses fetched good prices at the auction, and the mares had dropped a beautiful crop of foals. I calculated that if the war didn't interfere it truly might be only two more years before the ranch would bring enough money to set me up back East. I was adding up the figures when Nacho's son, Julio, burst into the room.

"Señora! They have attacked!"

I looked up from the papers and sniffed the air. It wasn't yet noon, and already I could smell the whiskey on his breath. "Who has attacked what?"

"*Tejanos!* They have attacked the fort."

I jumped up, knocking over some books. "How do you know?"

"Ruben, he was in town last night and he did not...ah, come home..."

Neither did you, I thought, but said nothing. The brothers always drank their way through Saturday night. As long as they could do a day's work and didn't make a nuisance of themselves, I counted it no business of mine.

"We meet the mama and papa at the church. That is where we hear the guns." Julio's voice jabbed at each word. The natives detested Texans, who tended to regard them as local wildlife, a step or two above the coyote.

I tried to think where Fort Fillmore was in relation to the church. "You're sure it's an attack on the fort?"

"Six, seven hombres come running. They say get back in the church. But Papa say to me if I can cross the river to come here pronto, so you can be warned. On the bridge are many men, so Maria and I go to the north and swim." He beamed, relishing the feat. Maria was the mare I'd given him as a year's advance pay.

I was thinking that Jamie was right about the Confederacy when it came to me that men toting firearms might bode more ill than I had reckoned if the fighting turned toward Mockingbird Spring. The other hands were still in town. Save for Julio, I was quite alone. He was still standing there full of his own daring deed.

"Thank God you didn't get yourself killed," I told him. "Will your parents be able to get back?"

"Quién sábe?" His shrug was a perfect replica of his father's.

I sent him to bring more water from the spring and set about loading every rifle and pistol we possessed. That done, I saddled up and rode out to see if any danger seemed headed our way.

The heat made the air thick and hard to move through. I didn't urge Fanny to do more than her easy lope. From the shelf-land, I could see puffs of dust exploding near Fort Fillmore. These were followed a few seconds later by a dim growl of cannon. With the action miles away, the possibility of threat here seemed remote. Despite the stifling heat, I found myself oddly fascinated by it.

I had been squinting at the scene for some time when the rumble of cannon ceased, and the puffs of dust were replaced by a great bloom of black smoke. The fort was on fire.

As the Union wasn't apt to have set its own fort ablaze, it seemed right likely that the valley, and I, had just joined the Confederacy. The fat's in the fire now, I thought. Jamie and most of the Anglos in town would be pleased. I hoped they were right.

With nothing to see now but the billows of smoke, I turned Fanny toward home.

◇◇◇

Nacho and Herlinda arrived just before dark.

"Estupido." Nacho was raving before he even got down from the wagon. The only other time I'd heard him raise his voice was when a horse broke loose from the training rope and threatened to trample him.

From his agitated report, I gathered that the fort's commander had been so incompetent he might as well have been wearing the Texans' uniform. Led by a Confederate colonel named Baylor, about three hundred men had, by some apparently audacious maneuver, attacked the fort. The garrison had put up a sloppy, halting resistance, then fled. The Texans occupied and burned the fort; and within hours, they had captured most of the Union troops.

The sun had barely topped the mountains the next morning when Ruben threw open the kitchen door and announced that two men on horseback were approaching. *"Tejanos,"* he muttered.

"How do you know?"

"They wear the hats," he said, his hand miming a pull on a small brim.

"What could they possibly want from us?"

His shrug was as eloquent as his father's and brother's.

Built as it is like a square horseshoe around the patio at its center, the house from the west looks rather like a small fort. Only two slim windows showed themselves to visitors, who usually hitched their horses at a row of posts near the barn and entered the parlor door at the corner of the horseshoe. On the tiled step in front of that door, I waited. Both the approaching men were clad in snug trousers and shirts, not standard wear in these parts but not uniforms.

They didn't ride up to the posts and dismount but turned their horses to face me.

"Morning, ma'am. Lieutenant Tyler Morris, Second Regiment, Texas Mounted Rifles." He doffed his hat. For a moment, he looked familiar, and I tried to place him.

He was one of those men whose cocksure demeanor dares women to resist him and other men to challenge him. Apparently, he had fallen asleep somewhere with his hat over his eyes because the lower half of his face was sunburnt. On his clean-shaven left cheek were various scrape marks, and above them, a jagged scar marred his temple. I decided they must be minor wounds from some other battle as they weren't fresh enough to be the result of yesterday's fighting.

Still, you would have to call him handsome. His eyes were wide-set in the squarish face; the sunburned chin bore a cleft. Dark, curly hair was pushed to the left where it almost covered the scar. No, I decided, I didn't know that face. I would well remember someone that cocksure of himself.

"This here's Corporal Isaac Cox." Lieutenant Morris nodded at his companion, a short, blond fellow with a mustache too big for his face.

"Good morning," I said evenly. "What can I do for you gentlemen?"

"I'm sure you've heard we have occupied this valley." Morris glanced over his shoulder toward the trail that led to town.

"Yes." There was nothing of the South in his voice, but Texas has a range of twangs and more than a few Texans were born-and-bred Northerners.

"We need some horses," the shorter man said with the bluntness of impatience.

I stiffened. Why hadn't I realized that an occupying army might help itself to every horse I owned? The sun was already hot, but the perspiration trickling down my neck was icy. "So you intend to rob me in the name of the Confederate Army?"

"Oh, no, ma'am." Lieutenant Morris gave me a smile that might have charmed a bobcat. "No, no, no. Not at all." He dismounted and came toward me, his face open and devoid of cunning, his eyes almost merry. He held out his hand.

I didn't offer mine. I was no bobcat.

"Come now, ma'am. Colonel John Baylor, my commanding officer, is hardly a thief. We need a few horses. We asked around and heard you had the best. We're prepared to pay for them."

Atop his horse, Isaac Cox swung his head around to stare at Morris.

"We've already sold this year's lot," I said. "We have few left beyond breeders and our own mounts."

"Ma'am, it sure would be of great assistance to the Confederate States of America…"

I eyed him, trying to conceal my fears and wondering whether I could say no. Did I have any choice or was this was just a game? "How many horses? And how much are you willing to pay?"

"Depends on the merchandise," he said with the faintest mock bow.

"An average good horse is worth a hundred and ten dollars," I said. "Ours are not average."

"So I've been told," he said. "Let's take a look."

Of course, he didn't pay anywhere near two thousand dollars for the eighteen horses he took, but I was relieved to get the fifty-one dollars apiece we settled on.

And I wasn't sorry to part with one of the mares: a palomino with three white stockings. She was a sturdy horse, and we had thought to sell her at auction; but when Nacho, using a stick as a pointer, had barely touched her chest she had gone quite wild and queered the sale. The same thing happened later in our own corral. She might have become a good breeder, but none of the hands trusted her for serious riding.

Nacho and I watched the two men ride off, our horses trailing in strings behind them, the palomino bringing up the rear. The foreboding that had risen in me like a pillar of ice did not thaw.

"Is no matter, señora. He pay more than I think. We do not need those horses."

"I just don't like not having a choice."

"Choice, señora, *es peligroso.*"

"Dangerous?" I chuckled. Nacho was not much given to philosophical notions. He divided his world into blacks and whites and proceeded accordingly. "But it's the only control we have over our lives."

"Si?" That may be the first time I ever saw amusement on his face.

"You don't think there's such a thing as choice?"

He lifted one shoulder stiffly. "If I have choice, I be *muy rico*, very rich. If Herlinda have choice she have *matrimonio.*"

I opened my mouth to explain the difference between choices and wishes, then frowned. "Herlinda is married. She has you. She has two big sons."

The shake Nacho gave his head had a hint of machismo.

"You two aren't married?"

"How can it matter, I tell her. We have sons, we have work, we have food. *Matrimonio*, it means nothing. But she say we must go to El Paso. We must find a *padre*. I tell her that would take three, four days. There is not the time." El Paso is just beyond Franklin, on the Mexican side of the river.

"But there's a priest in town."

"Padre Ramon is a fine man, but his tongue is loose at both the ends. Herlinda, she will not even do the confess."

I smiled. A short, rotund fellow with a few tufts of white hair on an otherwise bald head, Father Raymond had a perpetual sparkle in his eyes that I suspect had to do with his fondness for the communion wine. He grew the grapes and fermented the juice himself. So, Herlinda believed she was living in sin, and the padre who could remedy that could not be trusted.

"There's no other priest closer?"

Nacho shook his head. "Padre Ramon is the first. Except for the priest at the gold mine."

"You mean at Piños Altos? That's silver." Piños Altos was the mining camp at least as far to the northwest as El Paso was to the south.

"No," Nacho said. "Here. People come from Chihuahua. A padre, also. They find gold. Then they are gone. The *serpientes de cáscabeles* run them away."

"Rattlesnakes?"

He nodded. *"Muchos serpientes."*

"When was that?"

He thought for a moment. "I was a man but not old. Maybe twenty year."

"Maybe they left because they didn't find any gold."

"Si," Nacho said. "They find it. They trade little stones of it for *provisiones*, for supplies."

Chapter Seven

Not a lot seemed to change under the Texans, although I watched the road obsessively, slipping away from whatever I was doing to peer across the valley. I was sure Lieutenant Morris would return and take the rest of our horses. And this time he wouldn't pay.

The hands, once they recovered from their Saturday nights, gave whatever news they could remember, which was mostly gossip. Lieutenant-Colonel John R. Baylor seemed to be spending a good deal of time striding about the plaza surveying his kingdom. He had claimed the southern half of New Mexico Territory as the Confederate Territory of Arizona, with Mesilla as its capital, and installed himself there as military governor.

His troops had skirmished with Indians who were making raids in our valley. The local Indians, who lived in a mud-hut village and farmed the land around it, were quite peaceful. But every so often a wilder bunch—Jamie said it was Apaches—would wreak havoc on a stagecoach or an outlying ranch.

We were cut off from the old capital, Santa Fe, but the difference was hard to notice. Santa Fe, and its trails to Colorado and Kansas, was almost three hundred miles away. Our news, travelers, supplies and mail had generally arrived from Texas and the South anyway.

Jamie, as he put it, was happy as a pig in clover. So were Jeremy Neuman at Farmers and Merchants Bank and Jacob and Moses Fountain, Zeke's cousins, who owned most of the land around Mesilla.

Word was that folks were leery about the Union forces at Fort Craig, the federal post guarding what had been central New Mexico Territory. The fort sat on the Rio Grande about a hundred miles upstream from Mesilla. On the maps he sent to Atlanta, Baylor had claimed the very land Fort Craig stood on as Confederate territory. Doubtless this miffed the commanding officer, a Colonel Edward Canby.

And we had our own troubles. The ruthless summer sun was scalding a vacant sky and frying everything beneath it. The first rain usually arrived in early July, but we hadn't had a drop. It was hard for the farmers along the river to divert enough water to keep the tomatoes, corn and beans from shriveling.

At Mockingbird Spring, the only news was that I had made myself some chambray trousers. I still had not dared to wear them into town.

Here, above the valley and some cooler, it was still all we could do to keep our kitchen garden alive. To save the few acres of grain we'd planted for fodder, we had to irrigate ceaselessly. With only the early morning and evening hours fit for work, we ate supper very late, slept only five hours at night and devoted mid-day to siesta. And worrying at the edge of my mind was the fear that the spring would dry up.

In a way, I suppose I was grateful for the hardship. It swept Isabel, the murdered boy and his map out of my head along with everything else I didn't want to think about. Whoever had clubbed me on the head in the barn must have been a drifter and long gone. There was precious little time for fretting.

But one wretched afternoon, after trying to sleep but only tossing about on the bed like a drop of water on a hot griddle, I rose and went to my desk and took out a sheet of the special stationery I kept for letters to my grandmother.

I'd put off writing to her for so long she might, at the least, worry. At the worst, she might begin to feel she should come for a visit; and that, above all things, must be prevented. Because I never received whatever letters she wrote to me, I never knew when that thought might cross her mind.

Dear Nanny, I wrote. *We are making plans to go to Philadelphia as soon as this silly war is over. When I can logically claim to be a widow, I thought. All is well here, though I still find the West a rude place and long to return to the civilized world. I am weary of gowns that look like potato sacks, which are all we can get here.* Nothing I owned could be called a gown at all, I thought peevishly.

I laid down the pen and waited for the ink to dry. A single velvet dress could cost as much as five hundred dollars and all the laces for flounces might total in the thousands. To be accepted in the right circles in Philadelphia I feared I should need at least twenty dresses—not all of them velvet, of course, but the cost would be at least a hundred dollars each—not to mention dresses suitable for the horse races and yacht races, the evening robes and garden robes. I would have to sell the ranch for more than twice what I paid for it. Now it seemed even more loathsome to be living in a place where most new dresses were faded old ones made over.

I picked up the pen and dipped it into the ink. *P.S. Andrew is well and sends his love.* Writing the letter left me even more peevish. Lying about it all always did. I folded the letter and opened a bureau drawer. I couldn't very leave such a letter lying about until it could be posted. Shoving things around in my bureau drawer for a place to hide it, I saw another piece of foolscap I had squirreled away: the boy's map. I drew it out and studied it again. Poor lad. Hardly more than a child. Why had he been killed? Why here? And above all, why had he been carrying this map? The X's above the springs clearly had some meaning. But what? More hot and restless than ever, I stowed the map again and went outside.

A few clouds were building above the mountains: A good sign—I hadn't seen a cloud since Joel Tolhurst's funeral. But summer clouds can do that for weeks before we get a drop of rain.

I saddled Fanny, and we wandered slowly along the base of the mountains where the trees threw long shadows as the sun dipped closer to the horizon. Spindly ocotillo rose from the ground like lightning bolts. In spring tiny, vivid red blooms dot the barbed stems like drops of blood; the natives believe the crown of thorns was made of ocotillo. I made a note to cut some next spring. Foot-long sticks, snipped and stuck in the ground, root quickly. In a few years you have an almost impenetrable living fence.

A lone piñon stood in the niche that led to the spring. It looked beleaguered and weary of the heat, but its scent was spicy and cool. In fall, people rode up from town to collect pine nuts in the mountains. They say the trees don't bear till they're eighty years old.

My sluggishness wore off as the heat waned. Above me, a rock reared like Moby Dick frozen in stone. It marked the spring. I got down and dropped Fanny's reins on the ground in the shade of the piñon. I had trained her myself to ground-tie. She wouldn't budge from that spot until I returned.

Rounding the rock to the spring was like entering a shrine. Along the damp rock base clustered plants that grew scrawny anywhere else, but here they flung out their branches joyously. The spring, I saw, had slowed to the barest trickle.

Hoping we had enough water stowed in the big clay pots to last till the rains came, I cupped my hands and was catching enough for a sip when I noticed the trickle puddling in a small, half-oval depression in the dark bronze mud. I nudged the foliage away with my toe.

It was the print of a good-size shoe. Too big to belong to Herlinda or the Indian women who helped her haul water. Besides, when they didn't go barefoot, they wore soft-leather soles. This heel had been wide and flat. Most boots in these parts had small heels. Perhaps it was Tonio.

I had been avoiding him. Now that I thought about it, I wasn't sure why. I caught another sip of water and splashed some on my face, holding out the collar of my shirt so it could roll down my neck. I dried my hands on my trousers.

It occurred to me that the trail Tonio had said was filled with rattlesnakes would pass above here, which would put it on the other side of the giant fish-headed rock. One of the arroyos that funneled rainwater from the mountains ran along the base of that rock. I tried to remember the dead boy's map. I was sure there was a rather straight line that could have been this cleft in the earth. If there was a trail just over the rim of rock, there might be a way to reach it from the arroyo. At any rate, it would be a mite hard to get lost walking in a ditch, and I wasn't doing anything else useful, so I would trek along it for a while and see.

The arroyo floor was powdery sand and going was slow. The banks of the natural ditch got steeper quickly. By the time it bent to the right I couldn't see over them. With the sun below that high horizon, I was suddenly in dusk. The ground underfoot turned rocky as the arroyo opened into a miniature valley dotted with boulders.

I passed under the trunk of a tree that must have been uprooted in some storm and wedged between the ravine walls. Here the sun still reached the tops of the wind-etched cliffs. The bold beauty was stunning, and I had perched near one of the thick branches to admire the scene when a scraping sound came from behind me. A dozen or so rocks skittered down the wall, their clatter echoing and re-echoing.

I was turning back to the cliffs when it happened again. This time I was sure I saw something move on the arroyo rim. I watched the spot intently, but all was still. A coyote, maybe; an antelope or a wild sheep. Nothing stirred.

The sky had gone a glowering purplish-grey. This time it might actually rain. I had just completed that thought when a thundering crash careened through the canyon like some monumental god in a runaway coach.

The rain seemed to begin in mid-torrent, sluicing over the cliffs in sheets. I tried to run, angry with myself for getting caught like that. A fool of an Easterner—that's what they would call me. The rocks made running impossible.

Another thunderous clamor rang out; and the sky above me grew white, then purple, then almost black. A dull roar behind me grew, blotting out all other sound. I stumbled and turned. A wall of water— rocks and debris at its base, almost white at the top—was moving toward me so fast I only had time to leap for a boulder before it was upon me, tearing my legs from under me, pummeling my back with rocks, swamping my head, engulfing ears and nose. It could ram me against the canyon wall, bust my bones like kindling.

I had never learned to swim. If I couldn't climb on something higher, I would die.

I forced myself to turn loose of the boulder, and let the water carry me. My head broke the surface and I took a ragged gasp of air before the water lunged over me again, remorselessly dragging me, thrusting me at the arroyo wall like a battering ram.

The log, the tree that had fallen across the arroyo—if I could reach that, I might stand a chance. But I had no control at all, no way to avoid a collision of flesh and stone.

My feet hit an underwater rock and I bent my knees to absorb some of the shock, praying my limbs hadn't broken. Something clawed at my face, a branch? Yes, the tree. But the water eddied and swept me sideways, slamming my head against the stony arroyo wall.

A ball of yellow light burst behind my eyes and the world went black.

◇◇◇

Consciousness came back like a sharp stick.

My legs, still bent beneath me, were numb, my entire body sodden and bruised. It seemed so dark I kept blinking my eyes to be sure they were open. But I didn't need light to know I was snagged among the tree's dead branches and as marooned as any caterpillar on a log in a river.

Chapter Eight

In the murky dimness, the water still roiled angrily. Big drops fell from above, slapping the top of my head like wads of chewed tobacco. There was nothing to do but wait.

The moon hoisted itself above the canyon wall and peered down at me: fat, yellow, jolly and utterly uncaring about my fate. I shivered. It was so like another cruel moon. I squeezed my eyes shut against it, but my past came at me as overwhelmingly as that wall of water.

Under such a moon, I had surrendered my honor and, ultimately, my very life.

Andrew Collins and I had married three months later. I hadn't regretted forfeiting my virtue; I fairly reveled in it. Andrew only had to give me one of his little-boy droll looks, and my knees would fairly buckle.

I was the envy of every woman I knew, and I knew a substantial number of young women from the best families in St. Louis.

Very soon after we married, Andrew decided we must go West. I never asked why. Somehow, he wangled a commission in the regular army, I bade goodbye to Nanny and we joined a military train at Independence for the trek across the prairie on the Santa Fe Trail.

Most of the wives complained of boredom and discomfort. My carriage seat was hard and the days moved slowly; but I marveled at the thicket of bayonets, like the spiked head of some vast dragon, and the stream of wagons that seemed to trail all the way to the horizon. Mostly we followed rivers, and red-winged blackbirds often fluttered along with us.

Andrew was at his most gallant. I had not yet discovered that his high good spirits were owed to another kind of spirits. Before we left Missouri he bought me two wonderful gifts. One was Fanny, "bred from mustangs captured in the northwest," he told me. Just a filly then, she trailed around behind me like a puppy.

The other gift was Winona. Andrew had not actually bought Winona, or so he said. He had won her in a poker game. My conscience quibbled at owning a slave, but I told myself we were doubtless rescuing her from some cruel master. Such was the state of my ignorance.

Winona was not as friendly as Fanny. She was solemn and kept to herself, but she had already made one trek with the army as a cook and she knew exactly what supplies would be needed and how to fix decent meals on the trail.

Andrew and I had lived very well and traveled in better style than most of the officers. Giddy with love and the excitement of my new life, I didn't question that it was my papa's money that paid for it.

Not until we reached Fort Union in New Mexico Territory did the trouble begin. Soon after we arrived Andrew did a most peculiar thing: He stole a hat from the quartermaster's store.

"Why, Andrew? Why on earth would you steal when you have all those gold coins locked in your mother's chest?"

That was the first time he slapped me.

Almost immediately, his face became a map of pain. Scooping me up from the floor where I had fallen, he hugged me to him. "God, Matty! I'm sorry," he cried in a choked voice, then grabbed a hatchet from the hearth and swore to chop off the offending hand. I found myself begging him not to do so and telling him it was nothing.

He was court-martialed for the theft, but it was many months before anything came of it. And when it did, the result was far different from what I expected.

Over the next few weeks, Andrew began to antagonize his fellow officers. He flaunted authority, skating right up to the edge of disaster but not quite crossing the line.

New Mexico seemed the stony edge of civilization. The sparse landscape, the houses that seemed little more than low mud huts, were cheerless at best. Yet the blue-blue mountains seemed to possess a sort of magic. And, as I told myself daily, all of this was temporary. Andrew would soon have his proper place among the officers and be happy again. The houses were not quite so awful as they looked—ours was quite snug. And the stout mud walls provided a place to hide.

I was nursing another blackened eye and wearied of describing the fall and my own clumsiness that had caused it. Several times a week, Andrew flew into rages followed almost instantaneously by bouts of self-loathing and pleas for my forgiveness. For my part, I was both horrified and bewildered and believed that all would be well again if I could just make him happy.

He continued to drink heavily, spend grandly and give away what seemed like vast sums of money when he was in high spirits. Even when he brought me lavish gifts, which was more and more often, I began to begrudge that he was so free with the coins—money that my poor papa strove so hard to save, money that but for Andrew would be mine.

But such thoughts were futile. Only a woman who had no man to look after her—no husband, father, brother, even an uncle—had money of her own. They said we were fortunate not to have to concern ourselves with it. Certainly no married woman I knew controlled a purse of her own, except Dora Tewkesbury in St. Louis, whose father had stipulated in his will that his fortune was to be hers and hers alone. Her father had deplored his daughter's husband for a scoundrel and a wastrel; and from what I saw, he was right. My papa had never met Andrew, and I suppose the making of such a will never entered his mind. The wrongness of it all has gnawed at me to this very day.

One evening I returned from quilting with the other wives, and thinking myself alone, I burst into the bedroom eager to see my new creation on the bed. I was unfolding the quilt when from behind two hands gripped my arms just above the elbows and slammed me onto the bed.

"You told him, didn't you?" Andrew snarled.

"Told who what?" I gasped.

"Told the colonel I killed old man Peters in St. Louis and took his goddam stash of coins."

"How could I," I faltered, bringing my hands up to protect my head from the blow I knew was coming. "I never knew anyone named Peters in St. Louis."

He took hold of my bodice and ripped it chin to waist. "Don't lie to me, bitch!"

An odd, exceeding calmness came over me. It was as if all that I am retreated deep inside. I suspect much of it still resides there. At that moment, I fell silent as a piece of wood. Andrew stripped my torn clothing from me and shook me. I let nothing show on my face. Even when he fell upon me and rammed himself into me I didn't resist. Even when the pain was blinding, I just closed my eyes, hung on to the bed and thought of the mountains. His rampage didn't last long; he was too drunk.

"Oh, God, I'm sorry." He laid his head on my breast like a lost child and sobbed. "Don't leave me, Matty. I am lost. Only you can save me."

Dry-eyed, I patted his shoulder.

◇◇◇

"Who is old man Peters?" I asked Andrew the next morning at breakfast. I felt safe because Winona was there, setting biscuits and honey on the table. She had not disguised her silent inspection of the bruises on my cheek.

Andrew's eyes flicked to Winona, then back to me. "A greengrocer in St. Louis. Why?"

"Just idle curiosity," I said, amazed there was no tremor in my voice.

"Where did you hear that name?"

"Someone mentioned him yesterday," I lied. "At the quilting."

Andrew stood up peremptorily, and the conversation veered in a direction odder still. "You know voodoo, don't you, Winona?"

She looked down at the floor. "No, sir."

"I thought all darkies practice voodoo."

"No, sir. That ain't true."

"Whatever are you getting at?" I asked.

He ignored me. "I wager you could put a hex on someone if you had a mind to," he said to Winona, who did not raise her eyes.

"Andrew, surely you don't believe that nonsense?"

His eyes became small and hard. "Do not belittle what you do not know," he said slyly. "I saw a woman once, when I was a lad. A chicken got loose from the pen. A dozen people were chasing it. The darky woman just stood there holding a knife. When the others had tuckered themselves out to no avail she raised that knife and pointed it at the chicken—only pointed it, mind you—and that bird fell over dead. Yes, indeed, I do believe in voodoo."

He turned back to Winona. "I may one day tell you to put a spell on someone for me, and you'll do it, you hear?"

Winona nodded stoically and backed through the doorway.

Andrew waited until he heard the door open and close and Winona's footsteps returning to the cabin she shared with other slaves and servants. Then he leaned over me so close his nose almost touched my forehead.

"You are not to go there again," he said. A little puff of stale, hot breath hit my face with each word.

I leaned away. "Not go where?"

He grabbed both my arms above the elbows and yanked me to my feet. "Anywhere! You are not to leave this house!"

I weakly mouthed the first words that came into my head: "But...Fanny. I must see to Fanny."

Andrew was at the front door. "If you value living in this world, you will not leave the house." He left, slamming the door behind him.

And for the first time, the reality of my situation roared through my consciousness like a silent scream.

I think now that Andrew's truly dangerous side was not the cruel side but the endearing one. He could tease, his pale blue eyes sparkling with laughter. And sometimes my heart would fairly wrench inside me to see him standing, feet slightly apart, one hand on the dining room table, head tilted down so the thick shock of red-blond hair fell across his brow, those same eyes filled with such a lonely sadness. It was those times I would know that if I just tried hard enough, I could repair whatever had gone crooked inside him.

A few months after he stole that hat, Andrew received orders to report to Fort Craig. We packed and began the journey southeast with a couple dozen others. The other officers were single, so Winona and I were the only women.

Andrew had entered one of his silent periods; and interpreting this to mean he had truly changed, I set out quite happy, believing everything might be different at Fort Craig. When we reached the Rio Grande, we turned south on a well-traveled trail. One of the men rode alongside our wagon pointing out landmarks. We were on the Camino Real, he said, the road cut by the Spaniards two hundred years before; and it excited me to be seeing the same rocks, the same soil beneath our wagon wheels as those first explorers.

We camped where a second river joined ours from the north. Wanting to explore a little, I went to find Fanny. She was obviously bored with following the wagons and welcomed the saddle.

"Where do you think you're going?" Andrew's voice came from behind me. We were quite alone between the tent and the stream.

"To see what there is to see," I said. "It's lovely here. Why don't you come, too?"

"Go back to the tent. You are not to leave it."

"I won't go far."

He took a step toward me. "Get back in the tent. You're the only woman here."

"No, I'm not. There's Winona. I'll take her with me if you want." I was holding the harness, preparing to insert the strap into Fanny's mouth.

"Get back in the tent."

I turned to look him straight in the eye and kept my voice calm and low. "Please believe me. I won't go far. I only want to ride a bit."

Andrew snatched the reins from my hand, threw them about my neck and twisted. I fell to my knees unable even to gasp as my heart exploded in my ears. He twisted the straps again and I thought my head would burst. My heart near beat its way out of my chest; my lungs didn't know what to do with the air inside them. Andrew's face snarled into mine, and the world got black around the edges.

Chapter Nine

In his own good time, Andrew loosed his hold and I crumpled to the ground. After that, something inside me changed. Looking back, I confess I am puzzled by my response. I was frightened of Andrew, but I was also afraid that someone might find out. I suppose it was my pride. No one must discover my sordid circumstances. Above all, I detested the thought of becoming an object of pity.

I no longer deluded myself with the notion that I could "fix" whatever was wrong with Andrew. But instead of going to any of the two dozen men who might help me, I took great pains to hide the bruises and to appear normal. I tied a strip of flannel about my throat and feigned a cough. I was so good at this I was sure even Winona did not know.

Dazed and unresisting, I continued the trek oblivious to the landscape, to Andrew's fellow officers and, especially, to myself.

The following night, Andrew brought Fanny's reins into our tent and made me sleep with them around my neck.

Numb, dazed and exhausted, I fell into a troubled sleep until something smashed into my pillow near my ear. My eyes flew open to stare at a hatchet blade buried in the feathers inches from my cheek.

Andrew stood over me, his pale eyes like chunks of evil glass.

"Don't even think about taking my mother's cherrywood chest," he said, his voice low and deadly. "All those pretty gold pieces were not hers, but they are mine! And will always be mine. Never yours. Never. If you so much as look at that chest, I will carve you into small pieces of meat and roast you over the fire. I might even treat the men to a special banquet."

◇◇◇

For some wholly irrational reason, I looked upon our arrival at Fort Craig as an end to my ordeal. Exhausted but relieved, I unpacked. Now things would return to normal. All of this would become what it really was: a horrible dream.

The first week, I spent all my waking hours making our little mud house tidy and homey. Because Andrew still was under court-martial for the stolen hat incident, he was not assigned to active duty. He had not yet begun to chafe at that, regarding himself as quite clever to be paid for doing nothing. He was cheerful and even helped me polish my grandmother's silver.

I told Winona that Andrew had harbored some odd ailment that made him understandably ill-tempered, but he was now recovered and himself again.

Her face went deadly serious, her eyes hard at the corners. "No, Miss Matty. Do not fool yourself." And then she disappeared, leaving me with a puddle of something cold in my innards.

A few days later, I rose, dressed and prepared to do some visiting. Several of the other officer's wives had sent servants with invitations to come for tea as soon as we were settled.

Andrew had left early on some business of his own, Winona was preparing some sort of stew that had to simmer many hours and I spent the day laughing and chitchatting, and sipping tea. By late afternoon, I was feeling quite my old self and almost eager to go back to my little mud house to have dinner and exchange the day's stories with my husband.

At home, I freshened up, washed my face, braided my hair again and changed my shirtwaist. At full dark, Andrew still had not appeared. I lit two oil lamps and the fire Winona had laid. Trying to sound cheerful and unruffled, I suggested she take a big portion of stew back to her own cabin. Something unavoidable must have detained my husband. I would serve him myself when he got home.

Having dined on nothing but tea and sweets all day, I was hungry; and after another hour, I ladled some stew onto a plate and was just sitting down, carefully not thinking about what might be keeping Andrew, when the door burst open.

"I see you have disobeyed me." His words were slurred. He slammed the door behind him.

I had jumped when the door was flung open, but now the familiar false calm descended upon me like an armored cloak and I looked up at him. "Winona has made an excellent stew, Andrew. I'll get a plate for you." I started to rise but he slammed me back into the chair.

"You've told them, haven't you! That's why they won't put me on active duty."

My telling someone something was a frequent theme, and I no longer tried to understand what I was supposed to have told to whom. "No, Andrew. I've only been getting to know the ladies. Captain Blair's wife is delightful and funny and—"

I got no further because Andrew yanked me up from the chair by my hair and dragged me toward the hearth, where he pushed me to the floor.

Cold metal pressed my cheek. It took me some time to realize it was the muzzle of a pistol.

"You've told them about old man Peters and they're going to cashier me. Probably send me to prison. I didn't mean to kill him, you know; but he wouldn't get out of my way."

Numb with fright, I sat rock still. Well I knew the danger of trying to reason with him. He moved the gun to my temple and pulled back the hammer. Then he pulled the trigger.

The click-click seemed to echo endlessly. I had stopped breathing and was certain I would never breathe again.

He pulled my head back, shoved the revolver close to my face and opened the cylinder. All the chambers were empty but one. He snapped the cylinder back into the gun and pushed the muzzle into my ear. At the click of the hammer being cocked, I closed my eyes, absolutely certain I was going to die.

"If you scream," he said quietly, "you assuredly will be dead before anyone comes. And as it happens, I have several other bullets I can load in time to greet anyone who fancies himself a hero."

The click of the trigger nearly stopped my heart.

He spun the cylinder again and cocked the hammer. "Now open your mouth."

◇◇◇

That night, something hot and seething rose up inside me like a pillar of liquid iron. When it had settled and cooled, I had but one purpose: to get away.

But with Andrew still not on active duty due to the court-martial, I could never count on his being gone for a definite period of time. Day and night, I wracked my head to conceive of a way. There seemed none. My friends were back in St. Louis. I didn't know anyone there at Fort Craig; and I figured if I told anyone, they wouldn't believe me—they'd be sure to tell my husband, and then he really would kill me.

I reckon he sensed the change in me because each day his rage grew. One night he swept all the china off the table, then shouted, "What are you waiting for, you slut? Pick them up." It didn't even occur to me to resist. I bent silently to do as he demanded. He kicked my legs from under me. "That's better. On your hands and knees, like the dog you are."

He watched as I picked up every tiny chip, booting me in the ribs when I overlooked one. When I finished, he raised his pistol. I closed my eyes and waited for the end. A shot exploded, then another, and another. I felt nothing. When they ceased, I squinted beneath my lashes. A neat cluster of craters peppered the wall.

I wondered whether anyone would hear and question the shots.

"I am going to walk barefoot around the table," Andrew announced. "If I cut my foot on even one sliver of china, your head is going to look like that wall."

◇◇◇

About a week later, Andrew arrived home from an officers' meeting in a fury more towering than any before. He stalked to where I sat knitting some mindless article—a scarf, I think—in front of the fire. His eyes were enormous. They knew but one color: black.

He bade me sit on the floor and bound my wrists behind me, then spun me about by my hair until I was lying face down. Then he tied my ankles, then looped the rope about my neck. This he attached to my wrists and ankles. If I made even the slightest movement, I would choke myself.

I don't know how many hours I lay there while he prowled about the room, shouting threats then laughing and draining a bottle of whiskey in short, quick gulps. When it was empty, he flung it into a corner and took hold of my hair. Yanking my head back, he shoved the muzzle of the pistol against my cheek and drew back the hammer. This time, I prayed that he would kill me.

When the hammer fell, I jerked and the rope bit into my throat. But no bullet put me out of my misery.

Andrew disappeared and returned with a broad kitchen knife, which he waved in front of my face; and I could see my own blood spurting from my throat. Instead, he laughed and cut the ropes and lurched off into the bedroom.

A pure, distilled hatred filled every atom of my being until it seemed it would spill out and rot away the floor. I thought about finding his pistol and killing him as he slept. But the Army would waste no time seeing me hanged. Perhaps I could just steal away in the night...but I knew full well I would be quickly hunted down like a wild hare and brought back. Might I beg aid from Andrew's commanding officer? Andrew would certainly give some frightful account of what I had done to deserve it. Beating one's wife, while not encouraged, was the prerogative of any husband who found it necessary to correct unseemly behavior and preserve her virtue.

In the end, I only lay there, my cheek chafed by the braided rug, listening to his drunken snores until the sun rose.

The next few days, Andrew's demeanor seemed almost normal, and I began to hope if there had been some sort of poison in his system it had finally worked its way out. One morning I awoke to the short yips of a small dog. When I opened the kitchen door, a puppy bounded toward me nearly bending himself double with tail-wagging; and I laughed for the first time in many weeks. He was all white but for one black paw and one floppy ear. I scooped him up, fed him, made a bed of rags for him near the stove and named him Patch. Andrew grunted once about taking in a "fool dog," then ignored him.

A few nights later, Andrew came home, sank into the stuffed chair in the parlor and stared at me with tortured eyes. "They are going to arrest me for killing old man Peters."

I stiffened, and my breath went so shallow that I got dizzy waiting for his next move. But he only laid his head back against the chair. "They are watching me every minute." He was silent a long moment and I stopped breathing altogether. "I've got orders to report back to Fort Union. We're to take the stagecoach Thursday a week."

Silent relief rushed over me; I would be traveling in public.

"I requested a change in orders, but the lickspittle bastards denied it. I asked for a pass to go to Santa Fe immediately to see General Wilkinson. No. The cursed sons of Satan said no."

Still I said nothing.

Finally, he went on. "You must go to Wilkinson for me."

At first, I didn't think I heard him right. I didn't know anything about anyone named Peters. I had no idea whether Andrew had actually killed someone by that name, though he was clearly capable of such a thing. I wondered why the Army wouldn't just arrest him here if they thought him guilty. Most of all, I was absolutely certain Andrew would not allow me to leave here alone.

But the next night and the next, he talked of the same thing. "You will talk with General Wilkinson. Tell him what they have been doing to me here. You can persuade him to redress my situation and protect me. I know you can."

"Yes," I agreed. "Of course."

"On Thursday next, I will take the stagecoach. It should reach Santa Fe by nightfall Monday. Meet me there. If you have been successful we can come back home."

My mind was in such tatters that at first I couldn't think where he meant by "home"; but of course, he meant here, this house where I had seen more horror than I had dreamed existed.

I nodded, praying for time to think. "Yes. That's a good plan, Andrew."

"If General Wilkinson refuses..."

I expected some threat to me if I failed to earn the general's assistance, but Andrew peered at me earnestly and said, "I will then desert the Army. We'll have enough money. Don't you worry about that. I will bring Mother's cherrywood chest with me."

Then, as if laying out a simple plan to go to the commissary, he said, "We can't trust any of the men here. You'll have to go alone. After dark tomorrow."

I started to shake my head, still trying to gather my wits. "Will that be safe?" As if anything could be less safe than where I was at that very moment.

He swung his face toward me, eyes drilling holes in mine. "You will do exactly as I say."

I forced my voice flat. "Of course."

Andrew brought his fist down on the arm of the chair. "You've got it into your head to leave and never come back, don't you?" he shouted.

"No." The word strangled itself in my throat.

Patch chose that moment to charge at Andrew. Perhaps the poor tyke had some notion of defending me.

Andrew caught the puppy by the nape of the neck, then grasped the dog's hind legs and lurched up from his chair. Patch yelped and let out a wail.

I stood frozen, as if my shoes were nailed to the floor, knowing with perfect prescience what was going to happen.

Andrew carried the howling pup across the parlor. "If you desert me now, when I need you most, this is what I will do to you." And he smashed poor Patch hard against the fireplace.

"No!" I leapt toward Andrew, the first time I had tried to resist him in many weeks. I grabbed his arm but he flung me to the floor. With a roar part-rage, part-eerie laughter, he swung the whimpering puppy against the bricks again and again until there was nothing left of the dog's poor head but a bloody pulp.

The next morning, not two hours after Andrew had left the house, I fully understood what I would have to do.

Chapter Ten

The sheets of cascading water from the arroyo's rim had ceased, and the water that engulfed the tree was slowly but certainly diminishing. And I was alive.

I tried to think. The effort made me cough, and water sputtered from my nose. My legs were there, submerged in water to above the knee; but I couldn't seem to move them. My arms were covered with scratches and cuts that didn't look real on my eerily white flesh, but I could move them. My fingers were shriveled and puffy.

The torrent had dumped me onto the fallen tree trunk as if it were the saddle of a horse. If I could get my feet onto solid dry ground, surely the numbness would leave my legs.

I grasped the sodden branch above me and tried to pull myself up, but it was slippery and my arms were like a rag doll's. I sagged back and willed my feet to push against the log. Slowly, I crept further out of the water.

How long had I been unconscious? I had no idea. Nacho and his sons would surely have begun a search when I didn't show up for dinner. Maybe they would find Fanny. An abrupt vision of my loyal Fanny engulfed by that wall of water made me gasp. I tried to remember exactly where I had left her. Had I been stupid enough to leave her right in the path of that torrent? She would have eventually abandoned her ground-tie, of course, but would she have done so soon enough?

Squeezing my eyes shut against those thoughts, I threw my head back and tried to scream. Only a wretched rasp croaked from my throat. Even if Nacho had found Fanny and was searching nearby he'd never hear me.

"Help!" I shouted again. "I'm trapped. I need help."

Above me on the rim of the arroyo, something scraped; and a rock skittered down the wall and plunked into the water. Was someone there? I called again.

The water stirred by the falling rock lapped rhythmically just below my feet. Then the faint sound of a horse's hooves began, quickly picked up speed to a lope then faded. Perhaps whoever it was had gone for help, but something inside me gave an ugly laugh at that notion. Someone knows you're here all right, it whispered, and hopes you will drown or die of exposure.

That's ridiculous, I told myself.

The darkness above me began to change. A glow appeared above an outcropping of rock on the canyon rim. As the moon grew brighter, I gingerly lowered my legs as far as they would stretch. My toes struck solid ground, and I inched the rest of my body from the tree trunk. Water sucking at my boots, a chill raising goose bumps under my sodden clothing, I slogged to where the canyon widened. With a series of muddy niches for toeholds, I climbed the cold and slippery arroyo walls and staggered to the place I was certain I had left Fanny. It was empty.

She will have gone home, I told myself rigidly, unwilling to consider any other possibility.

I struggled on through the brush, the rocks and stubble biting into my feet through the drowned leather of my boots. The darkness began to melt with the approach of sunrise. A tree appeared, and beneath it a small, thick cross. I moved toward it, confused.

Somehow, I had wandered much farther than I had realized. This was the tree above the Mexican boy's grave. But the compact mound of rocks had been tossed aside, the coffin sat in its shallow depression, exposed. Had the water done this when it raged from the mountain?

The ground was damp, but surely this far from the arroyo the water would not have had the power to shove away the stones. Had some kin of the boy turned up, someone unable to believe he was deceased? Had his killer wanted to be certain he was dead? I squinted at the rubble, bewildered. With no apparent answer, I corrected my course and found my way home.

I lurched along the side of the house on bruised and bleeding feet that had long since gone numb again. My hand was reaching for the door when it suddenly swung wide and a voice I had never expected to hear again bellowed, "Good God, Miss Matty, it's about time you got yourself to home!"

A lively face with cheeks the color of darkest onyx peered at me. Hands gripped my shoulders, pulled me inside; and Winona engulfed me in a bear hug.

"Just where did you get yourself off to when an old friend comes callin'? Lucky for me these people you got here let me in." Light from the lard lamp lit gold flecks in her eyes.

"I..." My head spun like one of those bowls at the rodeo when they draw the name of a prizewinner. Even in my stunned state it was impossible to miss that her belly bulged with child.

She shook me gently. "Lordy, lady. You is bedraggled. You're as soppin' wet as a wad of rags in a river."

If I had been asked to choose between seeing God or Winona at that very moment, I would have picked Winona. She had seen me through more corridors in hell than I cared to remember. "This is only the road to heaven," she would say. "We ain't settin' up housekeeping till we get to the other end."

The last time I'd seen her I had stuffed a fistful of money and a handwritten paper into her pocketbook and asked her to arrange boarding for Fanny for a couple of years. I had hoped the paper would be enough to prove she was a free woman.

I stripped, rubbed my blue-white flesh with rough towels until some of the blood ventured back to pink my skin and put on fresh clothes. Figuring Winona would disapprove of the trousers—she was prim and proper about the oddest things—I donned my old calico dress.

She had already taken over the kitchen, which had not endeared her to Herlinda; and now there were biscuits and crabapple jam and strong, hot coffee on the table. I swallowed one of the biscuits almost whole and buttered another.

"You look right pert, Miss Matty. Sure enough your hair has grown. It always was the prettiest color I ever did see."

I ran my hand through my still-sodden locks. The braid had come loose, and it hung about me like Spanish moss. "However did you find me?"

"Nothing hard about it," Winona chuckled. "I knew you would as soon lose your own teeth as that horse of yours. The folks I paid to look after her—"

"Fanny!" I leaped from my chair. "Did she come back?" I started for the door.

"She come moseying in this morning at first light, just before you did."

I sank back onto the chair and wolfed down another biscuit. "How did that happen?" I nodded at Winona's belly.

"If you don't know that yet, you got to go back to school," she guffawed. "It be a couple months, more or less, afore this chil' join us."

She was quiet for a moment then related a wild tale of falling in with a small party of Indians returning to their village from a trading expedition. The village, on a hilltop some miles west of Albuquerque, was called Acoma, which meant, she said, City of the Sky. "The menfolk was fierce as bears and beautiful as bobcats. They wasn't mean—I never saw no scalps or such-like. They done a good deal of praying and talking to their gods, which must have tuckered them out, 'cause they didn't do much else.

"The womenfolk, now, our life was not so fine. We done all the work, the farming, the birthing, looking after the young ones, the fixing of food and all. It was us made the pots and stuff the men traded for knives and such. The headman had made me give over my money, so when my man got hisself killed I had to steal back as much as was left. While I was at it, I took a horse, too, 'cause I had to get pretty far pretty fast."

I told her the territory had gone Confederate. "Was there any trouble about your papers?" I had just improvised what I wrote, hoping it would be accepted as proof that she was a free woman.

"Them Texans ain't much interested in colored folk. I only run across one, and the way I was dressed and expectin' and all, he pro'bly thought I was a Injun gal who done sat in the sun too long."

I propped my chin in my hand and gazed at her, so grateful to see her I was almost afraid to ask, "You'll stay?"

"That is surely what I intend to do. I didn't come by just to make a pan of biscuits. You need some overseein' if you don't know no better than to come traipsing home at pert' near sunrise, dripping like a dunked biscuit." She narrowed an eye in an almost-wink. "Now, tell me how you happen to get you this fine ranch. I bet that is one fine story."

I was nearing the end of my tale when, with no warning at all, my eyes clouded and tears spilled down my cheeks and into the empty coffee cup in front of me.

She put her out her arms and pulled me to her ample bosom. "Lord, child, I done forgot what you just been through in that old arroyo. You get yourself to bed and rest up some."

"It isn't that," I sobbed. "I'm just so glad to see you. Strange things have been happening, Winona, and I swear I just don't know what to do."

"Strange happenings like what?"

I told her about the murdered Mexican boy and his map of my ranch, about the unknown brute who had clouted me unconscious in the barn before the boy was buried, the sheer terror I felt when someone neared the truth about me, the wrong I had done Isabel. All of it came rushing out like that water down the arroyo.

"And if the Texans take many more of my horses, I'll never get to Philadelphia."

"What you want to do that for, anyway? You got yourself a mighty fine place here."

"You can't imagine how I long to hear an orchestra, to talk of something besides fodder and foaling, to wear lace, to waltz, to read books."

She stared at me a moment. "That plan is about like nailing currant jelly to a wall. If you ever got the job done, you wouldn't want it there. And mostly all you'll do is make a mess on the floor and a hole in the wall."

Chapter Eleven

It was maybe a week later that I took the wagon into town for supplies. Herlinda had sullenly accepted Winona's presence in the kitchen. As they competed, our meals soared to standards a hotel would envy. Winona would hear of nothing less than a whole fresh collection of spices and herbs, and a trek to the general store fell to me. I took along eighteen pounds of our smoked cheese to trade.

The plaza seemed oddly empty. I left the wagon at Garza's general store and went in search of Jamie.

He stood, sleeves rolled up and secured by black garters, sorting type. His string tie looked like he'd tied it in the dark. His thick eyebrows made a solid line above his pudgy cheeks when he saw me. "Good. I thought I'd have to send someone to you."

"The plaza looks like a ghost town. Where is everyone?"

He nodded grimly. "We put out the word last night. Folks had to be told."

In my stomach, little icy stones began to click together. "Told what?"

"Canby's getting ready to march."

Canby was the Yankee colonel at Fort Craig, about a hundred miles north.

"He's called in a bunch of garrisons and militia and word is they're toting a dozen cannon. Word is, a thousand Pike's Peakers are with him."

"Pike's Peakers?"

"Colorado troops." Jamie threw a piece of type in a tray so hard it bounced. "Baylor's like an old maid, fretting and whining."

"He claimed Fort Craig as his own. Surely, he didn't figure the Yankees would tip their hats and move on without a fuss."

Jamie leveled a glance at me. "That may make sense to you and me, but Baylor's yelping that if reinforcements don't get here soon he'll have to evacuate."

"But the Yankees would waste no time taking over the valley again. What would that mean?"

"At best, they won't exactly be tickled that we welcomed Colonel Bloody Baylor," Jamie growled, fixing me with intense blue eyes. "At worst, we could be strung up as traitors."

For a moment, I could only stare at him. "We who?"

"Anyone they think gave aid to the Texans. Sure enough there are plenty of old newspapers around to braid a noose for my neck."

"What are you going to do?"

A muscle jumped along Jamie's jaw. He slung more type into a box and closed it. "I'm heading south. Everyone with fair-to-middling sense is burying their valuables and sending children and womenfolk across the border." He propped his hands on his hips and looked about the room. "I most strongly suggest you do the same."

My mouth opened but nothing came out.

"Almost forgot." He scratched at his head, leaving a black smudge on his earlobe. "There was a woman asking for you around town. A colored woman."

"She found me."

"She a slave?"

"Of course not."

"Friend of yours?"

"I knew her in St. Louis."

"If the Confederates stay, they'll be thinking you are harboring a runaway slave. And if the Union comes back, they may take a dim view of your supplying the Rebs with horses."

I opened my mouth, closed it then opened it again to sputter, "I had no choice. They could have marched on me and taken the horses."

Jamie looked down; and when he raised his eyes, they were both sad and angry. "That may be. But the exacerbating fact of the matter is you're known to be a friend of mine. And I, most certainly, am a traitor to the Union cause. Send the nigra north and pack up and get yourself to the other side of the border."

"She's with child; her time is coming soon. I can't send her away, Jamie."

He went back to his task. "Be that as it may, neither of you is safe here. "

A few people were moving like lost souls across the plaza when I crossed it the second time. Faces were grim, chins jutted out. There was no time to dawdle.

"Miss Summerhayes!"

I flicked a glance over my shoulder. It was the horse buyer, Lieutenant Morris. I nodded, waved and hurried on.

"Excuse me," he said, taking my elbow with a brash smile. He was only a little taller than I, but his frame was like iron and his eyes were so self-certain that he looked like he could wrestle a bull to the ground.

I slowed. "Sorry, I have to get to Garza's while he still has something to sell."

"Of course," Morris said. "Then I'd like to buy your lunch at the Double Eagle."

"Thanks anyway—"

"Surely you don't mean to go without lunch."

I was puzzled at his persistence, but it occurred to me that this man might be an even better source of information about the Texans' plans than Jamie. "All right," I said slowly. "Thank you kindly for the invitation. I will need some time to get the wagon loaded. I'll meet you there."

◇◇◇

The Double Eagle was a lot better place to take a meal than you'd expect to find in a town like Mesilla. Moses Fountain, like his brother, had made a good deal of money mining silver up at Piños Altos and bought up a lot of land in and around the town. When he opened the Double Eagle he said he figured it would lose money and didn't care. He had plenty of money. What he needed was class. And this was nothing if it wasn't class—as good as any dining establishment I'd seen in St. Louis.

When I got there, the dining room was almost empty. Lieutenant Morris sat at a table in the corner chatting with a man I'd never seen before. Morris saw me, got to his feet and came to meet me at the door. The other man disappeared.

Garza's store had been filled with panicky people. I'd purchased as much beans and flour and other edibles as I could and wrestled the sacks to the wagon myself. Finally, I'd seen a kid slouching in front of the saloon and gave him more money than I should have to finish the loading.

It seemed odd to sit now at a linen-covered table as if everything was normal.

"Are you Texans going to abandon us?" I asked.

"You do get down to the heart of things real fast."

He chuckled warmly and changed the subject. When we finished eating the biggest cuts of beef I'd ever seen on a plate, I asked again.

"Are your men pulling out?"

He turned a steady gaze on me, taking my measure. I took a cautious sip of tea so smooth it tasted like satin. Morris was having whiskey. He'd mixed it with water, but the color was still dark. I didn't much like whiskey. Ladies did not drink alcohol, which is not to say I had not tried some.

He leaned back in his chair and pressed a napkin to his lips. "I'm afraid there is that possibility." He folded the napkin and put it on the table. "I would like to offer my services."

"Excuse me?" He was an officer. He couldn't be asking for a job.

"You'll need help packing up."

"Thank you, but no. We won't be leaving."

"You must!" he said sharply.

I stared at him.

He dropped his eyes like a bashful schoolboy. "Sorry. It's just that I'd hate to think what might happen." He peered at me earnestly. "I hear you have a slave woman out there. You won't be able to trust her once the Yanks get here."

"Winona is not a slave. She wouldn't dream of causing me any trouble."

"Well," he cajoled smoothly, "you haven't had time to think about it properly. At least say you'll hold your decision till you've had time to give it your full consideration."

I ran my fingers around the rim of my saucer and agreed to think about it.

◊◊◊

By the time I got home, I had just about made up my mind to take Jamie's and the lieutenant's advice. But no way would I send Winona north. She would come with me to Mexico.

We couldn't bury the horses with our silverware; we would have to take them with us or lose them to Canby. A horde of rather proficient rustlers always hovered about the border, but Nacho and his sons were good hands with guns and they knew the language. We would have to risk it.

Winona met me at the door, her dark face puffed with impending motherhood. "Well, Miss Matty," she said when I had explained, "are we to turn cottontail and hip-hop off to Mexico?" Her words were flippant, but her face looked drawn.

We sat in the parlor, me in the rocking chair, Winona on a straight-back chair because her back was bothering her. It shocked me to see her looking so frail.

"You can't travel," I said flatly. "The baby's due too soon."

"I can ride in a wagon," she said. "What's there to riding in a wagon? I ain't sick. I ain't crippled. I'm just 'specting a baby."

"You want to have it on the road where we'll have to boil water over a campfire? You could die. The baby could die. No, we can't go just now. We'll stay here."

"I have read me the signs," she said, "and I truly do believe it would make no never mind where I have this baby."

I put my hand on her knee. Her dress was nearly worn through with too many washings. "If the Texans bolt and run, the Yankee army will be too busy to hunt up everyone who did business with the Confederates. If they do, we've got guns, and we know these parts better than they do. We can run them off if we have to." I wasn't at all sure that was true, but it was a chance we would have to take.

How quickly I had learned to call them Yankees and think of them as enemies—soldiers who a few short months ago I'd thought of as "ours."

◇◇◇

A couple of mornings later I was training one of the geldings on a lead in the corral when a voice called from behind me. When I turned, Lieutenant Morris grinned and saluted from atop a chestnut mare.

"Sorry. I'm rather busy," I said stiffly, but instead of turning back to my work, I tugged the gelding toward me, unfastened the lead and slapped him on the rump. Parading a fine piece of horseflesh in front of this man would be tempting fate.

Morris had tied the chestnut to a post and was strolling toward me. "Just wanted to see if you need any help."

"Thanks, I'm fine."

"I trust you've had time to think this thing through?"

"Yes." I wiped my hands on my skirt. "I take it there's still a good chance your troops will be pulling out?"

Morris nodded. "I fear so. O'Rourke is being mighty hard on Colonel Baylor, practically calling him a coward right there in print. I could direct you to a place in Mexico where you and your people might put up."

A puff of wind ruffled his hair. I settled my hat firmly on my head. Why was Morris so interested in my welfare? Did he think I'd leave the horses behind, and he could have them for the taking? "Thanks anyway. But we shall be staying."

An unpleasant look came into his eyes but was gone so quick I wasn't sure I'd seen it.

"I hope you won't be sorry." He smiled easily, replaced his hat and untied his mare.

I watched him ride off. The breeze whipped my hat from my head; and I chased it, wondering if we were in for a sandstorm.

Winona had seen us from the window. "Does that army man bring trouble?" she asked when I got back to the house.

"I don't think so, but he seems awfully anxious for us to leave." I explained who he was.

"I suspicion he thinks you be leaving your horses, and he wants to nab them quick."

"Could be," I agreed. "What did you mean when you said you had 'read the signs' and it wouldn't matter where you have this baby?"

"Just signs." Winona picked up a cleaver and set about dismembering a freshly plucked chicken. The blanched feathers lay in a mound on the table, their smell rank.

"What signs?"

"You bein' pesky, Miss Matty." She took aim and brought the cleaver down with a bang, splitting off a leg. She raised the cleaver again.

I put out my hand and stopped her arm. "What signs, Winona?"

Her mouth pulled into an annoyed line. "Wax and feathers," she said.

"What?"

"You melts wax. You puts out feathers. In the night, the loa writes a message."

"In the wax."

"Where else?"

"With the feathers."

"Yes'm, with the feathers. You think the loa carries a pot of ink?"

"Approaching motherhood has made you senile," I snapped and stalked out of the room.

She followed me into the parlor and stopped dead center of the room, a chicken leg dangling from her hand. Her body looked so huge I wondered how she could stand.

"Oh, Winona." I threw my arms about her neck; her pregnant belly pressed against mine. "I'm just so damn worried."

Wordless, she patted my shoulder and something moved against my abdomen.

I beamed at her as if I had discovered something all on my own. "He's kicking."

"She." Winona put her hand on her belly. "It's a she." Then she turned her head toward the window. "What's that smell?"

"You must have left a pot on the stove."

"I wasn't cooking." She moved to the door, sniffing.

We both saw it at the same time: A thick wad of black smoke came from the north as if someone were painting the sky with a wide brush dipped in tar.

I dashed off the doorstep, Winona on my heels. From the front of the house we could see short tongues of dark orange below the blackened sky as the flames ate their way toward us through the dry brush. Range fire travels like the wind.

And a brisk wind was blowing straight into our faces.

I darted a few steps forward, desperate to believe that what I saw was something else. Whirling, I almost collided with Winona.

"Go back to the house." I shouted the words into her face. "Tell Nacho to get everyone out here. It's still a ways away. Tell him to load the full jars on the wagon. Get every blanket we have and wet them down in the cistern. Tell Herlinda to fill the empty jars." I grabbed Winona's arms, reading her mind and shook her. "You cannot go out there."

Winona fixed me with a dark eye. "The flames is movin' mighty fast. We needs as many hands as—"

"You want to lose the child?"

Winona's jaw set, but she turned and lumbered heavily toward the house.

I raced for the barn and threw a saddle on Fanny and dunked some saddle blankets in the trough. Wet, they stank to high heaven. I tossed them over Fanny's shoulders, leapt into the saddle and dug my heels into her flanks.

Horses are terrified of fire, but Fanny stretched into a gallop straight toward it as if she knew what was at stake.

Nacho came with more sodden blankets and we beat at the flames, killing some, diverting others. Ruben and Julio brought the wagon as close as they could. The horses were balky.

Our arms and hands and faces grew black with soot. I killed one tongue of flame with my blanket only to find another licking at my boots. The smoke was so thick we kept track of each other by listening for the coughing.

Herlinda arrived with more jars of water. No one spoke. We just grunted and coughed and slapped at the ugly red mouth of the monster.

My blanket grew dry and began to smolder. I reeled and dashed toward the wagon to wet it down again.

The wind changed direction, taking the nose of the fire with it. With arms like blazing tentacles it reached for the wagon. The horse reared and lunged. The wagon's two side wheels jolted off the ground and the water jars inside sloshed wildly.

Smoke swirled like a black gauze veil of mourning. I stumbled and hit the ground hard. When I raised my head I fully expected to see the wagon slued on its side, the water lost. But the wheels seemed to have stopped in mid-air. Scrambling to my feet, I plunged into the thickening smoke. My hands struck the edge of the wagon, but it was already steady. The two straying wheels bounced back to the ground. Another pair of hands had steadied it.

I looked for a moment into the begrimed face and piercing eyes of Tonio Bernini. "The horses," he grunted.

I hurled myself toward the stocky, long-maned palomino. In his frenzy, the horse had mired himself in the traces. I pulled them free from his legs, patted his shoulder with an assurance I did not feel and led him a safe distance from the flames.

My charred and shredded blanket had become useless. I scrambled into the wagon, searching for another, but they were all in use. I yanked off my skirt, dunked it into a jar, and ran back toward the fire. When I unfurled the skirt, it snagged on a cactus, nearly jerking me from my feet. A hand caught me at the waist, steadied me then drew away quickly as if I myself were on fire. Tonio tore my skirt free from the cactus and handed the sodden mess to me.

To my right and left, blankets flailed at the fire. Arms ached and threatened to take leave of their sockets, but still we thrashed at the burning brush with the drenched and reeking blankets. I didn't see Tonio again.

Devouring brush did not slake the fire's appetite but made it hunger even more.

The hair on my arms was singed. Winona's and my argument about packing ourselves off to Mexico had been a waste of time. We not only would have to flee, we would have no belongings to bury. Nacho had turned the horses loose, of course. We'd be lucky if we could round up enough for spare mounts.

The sun began to drop toward Arizona. And the fire glowed brighter.

Then the wind stopped. It didn't slow and simmer to a breeze. It stopped. Dead. Like I hear it is in the eye of a hurricane. The fire fell back, still crackling and crunching and chewing its meal, but its appetite waned as the wind lost its driving fury.

Still I stood with the shreds of a soaked blanket poised above my head, not trusting the lull, waiting for another gust. Chunks of red glowered like a huge triangle of fiery teeth as the smoke ebbed.

We had somehow confined the fire. And without the wind, it whined and crawled to a halt. Finally, we beat and stamped out the last of it.

By the time I got back to the wagon, my head seemed four times its normal size and weight. Only Nacho seemed to notice that I stood there in soot-encrusted bloomers. He averted his eyes and posted Ruben nearby with a half-dozen jars of water, a rifle and a whistle, in case the fire rekindled its craving for dry brush.

At the house, Winona met us at the door, looking even more exhausted than I felt. "It be a deal harder to wait than to do the work," she said gruffly.

I nodded. "Go to bed. Tomorrow will be better."

She frowned at my legs, disappeared and returned with a skirt, which she pressed into my hands. I put it on, fumbling at the bone buttons with thick fingers, and went back outside.

The stench of ashes and water made me swallow hard. Herlinda was spreading the few blankets we had left over the rail that linked the hitching posts. Her squarish body looked twisted and hunched and ready to drop. I recanted every mean thought I'd had about her and touched her arm.

"Thanks. I'll finish that. Go to bed. Rest."

For me, I knew, sleep would not come easily.

I washed off as much soot as I could in a pan of water and went out to sit on the steps. I could detect no red coals glowing anywhere. Elbows propped on knees, chin in hand, I stared into the dusk toward the horror that had almost stripped me of everything.

"Señora?" Nacho approached from the barn with his stiff-legged gait.

"We're hanging by a thread, Nacho," I said, my eyes still combing the shapes on the darkening desert for some telltale tinge of red.

"Si, señora," he agreed, seeming as unruffled as ever. But he wasn't. "I wish to show you this." He thrust something into my hands—a battered and burned can about the size of a large book. "I find this out there." Nacho tilted his wizened face toward where the fire had very nearly defeated us. "Inside, I think, was oil."

Chapter Twelve

Unable to think about anything, I had barely managed to remove my filthy clothes before falling into bed. I woke to the smells of coffee brewing and bacon frying. Lazily, I rolled over, hoping Winona was baking biscuits. Herlinda's chorizos and tortillas were good, but biscuits were like being home.

Tossing back the covers, I found that my arms ached from shoulder to wrist; and reality smacked me in the face like a bucket of dirty water. But for the grace of God there would have been no house to cook breakfast in. Was Nacho right? Was the fire set deliberately?

Nanny used to say that what looks like wickedness is often just stupidity, and I knew that in this dry landscape, fires sometimes just happen. Drifters might pitch camp and build a fire even though we forbade it. No doubt they were loth to use what little water they carried to damp a fire. It was all too easy for a live ember to linger, even for days, and easier still for the wind to bring it new life. This wasn't our first fire, but it was the first to get such a start on us. One of the men might have dropped that oilcan by chance, though I couldn't fathom what he was doing with it out there.

Something sharp twisted in my middle like a splinter of broken glass. Did Lieutenant Morris want my horses badly enough to try to burn me out? Who else would want to force me off the land?

Donning my calico wrapper over my nightclothes, I made my way to the kitchen. Winona was, indeed, baking biscuits and frying slabs of freshly smoked bacon as if nothing had happened. I made my way outside to the privy. The breeze was crisp with autumn. From the privy I could see the huge patch of scorched brush lying like a fallen dragon amid the creosote and mesquite. Yesterday it had been gnashing its teeth, ready to swallow our house; but now even the acrid odor of water mixed with ashes had been scoured from the air.

I was back in my room, searching the bureau for a clean shirt, when it occurred to me that something was amiss. A remnant of my earlier life, a white silk petticoat, had lain for years at the bottom of the drawer. Now it was sitting atop the cruder underthings I wore these days—still neatly folded, but on top. Other fingers had picked through my belongings. Why, for mercy's sake, would anyone be interested in my meager stock of linen? I sorted through the items again, but nothing else seemed disturbed.

As I dressed, a sharp sudden thought bit into my mind: the map. How could I be so feeble-witted!

That Mexican boy had thought the map so valuable that he kept it where most folk on the move keep gold. Might not someone else think it valuable, too? Rifle through a drawer in search of it? Even set a fire to be sure no one was in the house to catch the culprit out?

Some less-dim part of me had known that map held import because I had concealed the foolscap in my one remaining corselet. I slid my hand into the drawer. Between the stays, my fingers struck the leather pouch. The map was still inside. I drew in a breath of relief and slipped the thong around my foolish neck.

From the pitcher on the table next to the bureau, I sloshed water into the washing bowl. Scrubbing my face and arms and neck until they were red, I recited to myself the events that seemed to be popping up like malignant corn at every turn in my life. The list seemed to go on and on, from the murdered boy, the map, the man who accosted me in my own barn to the fire, and now that bureau drawer. Even Tonio Bernini. I had trusted him on instinct, but what really had brought him here the very day after that boy was killed?

Bending my head, I pushed my hair forward till it nearly touched the floor and brushed until it felt almost clean again. Any army could take my horses with or without my leave, so why was Lieutenant Morris insisting that I decamp to Mexico? I brushed and brooded and brushed some more.

I had to allow there was little that couldn't be explained by some peculiar but blameless reason. But I kept coming back to the map—that devilish, queer map. Had my assailant in the barn merely been a drifter spooked by my return? Or had he been after that sheet of foolscap?

After breakfast I drew Herlinda aside. "Thank you for all your help yesterday."

She nodded stiffly; her usual sullenness had returned.

"Today, you should rest."

She looked at me as though she didn't understand.

"You worked very hard yesterday. Today, rest. Do nothing."

"Someone must take the *ollas* to the spring," she said, as if explaining to a child. "We are without water."

"Send Julio to fetch the water."

"He must hunt the *caballos.*"

I sighed. The horses had scattered when they were set loose, but they would most likely wander home this morning for their feed.

"Okay," I agreed, wondering why, no matter whether I was gruff or kind, Herlinda always got the upper hand. "But no housework. I'll do it myself," I told her, still determined to be considerate. "When we're full up on water, go back to bed. Rest."

Eying me as if my solicitations were somehow a threat, she backed through the kitchen door.

I helped Winona tidy up the breakfast dishes then took the broom from her. "Sit," I said. "I'll make us some tea. I need your advice."

The tea was the color of mesquite honey and mellow. I took a sip, then raised my eyes to meet Winona's questioning gaze. "Nacho found an empty oilcan out there on the range. He thinks someone set that fire. Someone may be trying to run me off my land."

Winona nodded, rocking back and forth a little in her chair. "You ain't telling me a shred of nothin' new, Miss Matty. I didn't need no oilcan to start wonderin' about that. Who you think it be?"

"I wish I knew..." I pondered it all again, this time aloud. When I finished, I brought the flat of my hand down hard on the table. "What chafes me most is that damn map."

Winona gave me the steely-eyed look she reserved for when I cussed. I ignored it and drew the pouch from the neck of my shirt. She studied the markings on the foolscap. "That be a map of this land, all right."

I stowed the paper again. The little leather sack felt rough against the flesh between my breasts. "Why did that Mexican boy have it? Did he draw it himself? I'm coming to think he didn't just happen to have that map hidden away on him when he was shot. I think he was killed because of that map."

"Mercy." Winona's deep brown eyes darkened.

"And there's something else. A few weeks back, someone tried to buy the ranch. I turned him down. Maybe he's aiming to get the land even cheaper."

"He be barking up the wrong tree if he thinks we just slink away easy-like." Winona stuck out her jaw and rocked back and forth. "What he look like, this man who wants to buy this land?"

"I don't know. Jamie brought the offer. Why?"

"Mayhap everything you're going on about is true. Hard thing is, you got nothing but your own cogitations to prove it. Now that buyer person, he got to be real, got to have a name, a face and warm blood runnin' in his veins. Seems to me that buyer person is the only real thing we got to go on."

◇◇◇

When things got back to their more customary disorder, I saddled up Fanny and rode into town, hoping to catch Jamie before he left. Surely he knew more than he had told me about that offer to buy my land. I was certain he wasn't hiding anything, but maybe he had left something out.

The office of *The Times*, when I reached it, had boards nailed across the window and a big padlock hung on the door.

Old Ben Smithers, part-time barber, part-time sawbones, part-time postmaster, poked his head out the door of the barbershop down the street and called, "Jamie's done packed up his press and gone to Mexico. Yesterday."

All the steam went out of me.

Smithers came down the street and peered at me over his spectacles. White wisps of hair stuck out where the stems went round his ears. "You'd be well advised to do the same, Miss Summerhayes," he said earnestly and loudly. Ben Smithers was hard of hearing. "Things ain't likely to be real safe here for a time. Most all the women and children are going. And like as not, a third of the men. We just don't know what might happen."

"Thanks for the news about Jamie," I shouted and turned to leave.

"Hold up a minute," Smithers said. "I nigh forgot. There's a letter for you."

"You must be mistaken," I said. "There can't be a letter for me."

"Yes, yes," Smithers said. "The express riders pay no mind to the soldiers and the soldiers do likewise, so mostly, the mail gets through. Come along."

I followed him through the barbershop to the desk and row of boxes that did duty for the mail. I hadn't meant that I doubted the mail was getting through. No one outside the valley knew where I was.

He fanned a stack of envelopes and handed me one. My name was printed across the front: *Matilda Summerhayes, Mesilla, Arizona Territory.* The Confederates had claimed half New Mexico Territory and named their half Arizona.

I tore the envelope open. Inside was a sheet of paper. At the top, black letters spelled out *V. B. Peticolas, Attorney-at-Law,* and gave a Franklin address.

Dear Miss Summerhayes, he began.

> *I am pleased to inform you that I have a client interested in purchasing your land. I don't need to tell you that what with the uncertainty that has befallen the Mesilla Valley, this is a most fortuitus offer for you.*

I noted that *fortuitous* was misspelled. And that the amount V. B. Peticolas' client offered was less than half the figure Jamie had ridden to the ranch a few short months ago to discuss. Jamie's "client" didn't offer enough, but he was far more generous. I expect that was because of the war. Or were both clients the same person?

"Where did this letter come from?" I asked Smithers.

"From?" he said. "Why I suppose it come up with the rider from Franklin."

"You suppose…?" He didn't answer. I shouted the question again.

"Well…" He cleared his throat. "It all gets tossed together, you know."

"When did it arrive?" I shouted.

"Don't rightly know," Smithers said, dipping his chin toward the letter in my hands. "That one got mixed up with the outgoing mail. Found it this morning when I was sorting. It all gets sorted out in the end, you know," he assured me.

"You mean it could have been brought to the post office here? Could have been mailed from here?"

He scratched with a pencil at the wisps of hair. "Well, I guess it could. But that ain't very likely, is it?"

"Why not?"

"People in the valley don't mail letters to each other," he said slowly, as though to a halfwit. "They hand 'em to each other. Or more likely, they ride out and sit a spell and say whatever's on their minds."

"Thanks," I said, putting the envelope in the pocket of my jacket. I could feel the frown still etched into my face when I closed the door of the barbershop behind me.

The plaza wasn't as crowded as usual; but a few horses were tied at the posts, a wagon sat at one corner, and a few people moved in and out of the doors that opened onto the wooden walks.

I took the diagonal footpath across the plaza and was mounting the boardwalk just as Isabel emerged from the bank. I felt a rush of guilt. I hadn't seen her since Joel's funeral. Behind her was Lieutenant Morris. Isabel's eyes narrowed.

"Why, Matty, are you still here?"

"I don't plan to leave."

"But Jamie O'Rourke says Colonel Baylor is going to abandon us. That he was pleased as punch to sashay in here and set himself up as governor of half the southwestern corner of the continent, but now he's turned tail and plans to run."

I wondered at the wisdom of saying that in front of Baylor's officer, but Morris only said, "Colonel Baylor is doing everything he can." He looked at me and shook his head. "O'Rourke was ill-advised to print those accusations. The colonel is not likely to pull out."

I stared at him. "But you yourself said—"

He cut me off. "I listened too much to O'Rourke myself. The man is dangerously persuasive."

Isabel nodded. "Lieutenant Morris was just telling me that Colonel Sibley is bringing reinforcements from Austin." She couldn't seem to remember which side of the argument she was on.

"Austin is a lot of miles away," I said distractedly, remembering that Jamie had mentioned Austin in connection with the offer for my land. "So, you're staying, too?"

Isabel looked down at feet too small to belong to an adult woman. The little boots were worn but polished. "The Baptists are not generous," she said. And I remembered that she was awaiting funds to return East. "They have just now wired me barely enough money to stay here another month or so. I cannot afford to take up temporary quarters in Franklin or across the border." Her face looked pinched, then she smiled and her teeth were all pointy and white.

A wave of guilt assailed me for rejecting her plea to come to Mockingbird Spring. "Yes, well, good luck." I took my leave.

"Matty," Isabel called after me. "Was there a fire out to your place the other day? We saw an awful lot of smoke."

"Yes," I called back to her, "but it didn't amount to anything."

"I hear you have a slave woman out there."

I remembered that Isabel was from Atlanta, where a lone Negro inevitably spelled runaway slave. I walked all the way back to stand in front of her and say in no uncertain terms, "Winona is not a slave. She is a free woman. She works for me."

"You pay her, then?" This from Morris. If he said one more word, I would bite him.

"Yes," I lied.

"But, Matty," Isabel went on, "I hear tell she is a witch."

"A what?"

"A witch. I reckon she likely started that fire. Best you be careful. Mighty careful." With that, Isabel turned; and I was still standing there like a fool with my feet all over the ground as the lieutenant helped her into the wagon on the corner.

Chapter Thirteen

"You must have done something to make someone think you're a witch," I said to Winona across the kitchen. She stopped her after-dinner tidy-up and fixed me with an iron stare. "That's hogswallow, Miss Matty. You know I ain't no witch. I got a mind to learn me a hex or three and give them folks something real to worry about."

"Did I imagine that talk about wax and feathers?"

She plunked fists on hips. "That ain't witchery. I'm just tryin' to understand something when I do that. Tryin' to get my loa to 'splain something."

I swallowed air. "Your what?"

"Loa."

"What the devil is a loa?"

Winona hesitated. "I guess it be a sort of spirit."

"That's witchcraft!"

"It ain't neither! It don't affect no one but me."

I expelled all the breath I'd drawn in. Through the window I could see Herlinda's dark form moving like the shadow of death toward an old hen destined for the stew pot. I shook my head at Winona. "Be that as it may, people here are suspicious of nigras. This is the Confederacy now. You have to remember that."

"But you freed me. You give me the papers."

"I couldn't prove I had the right to do it, could I? I couldn't even prove you were mine."

The indignation in her face turned to puzzlement, and I was suddenly aware of how thin her arms looked compared to the bulk of her belly. I put my arms around her. "I'm sorry. I shouldn't have yelled. I know you wouldn't do anything wrong that way. I'm edgy, is all. I just don't want anyone making trouble for you."

Something brushed against the wall behind us, and my eyes flew to the open parlor door but saw only the deepening shadows cast by the sinking sun. The kitchen door scraped open and Herlinda stepped inside, the dead chicken, wings flopping, dangled by its feet from her hand.

◇◇◇

A couple of mornings later I fumbled my way out of bed, dressed hurriedly and was making my way back from the outhouse when I saw Nacho eyeing the horizon solemnly.

"Today comes the *granizo, señora.*"

"Hail? Surely not." The sky was a deeper, clearer blue than any jewel; but in my few years' time with Nacho I had learned to respect his uncanny ability to foretell the odd turns of weather on the high desert.

In the kitchen, I paused only long enough to wrap a tortilla around a chorizo and ask Herlinda to see to some churning—the last of our butter had gone rancid.

Gnawing on my makeshift breakfast, I dashed back outside. A gust of wind with a hint of autumn in it hurled a tumbleweed toward me. Abigail, our best cow, was ambling toward the milking shed and Nacho was jerking a thumb at one of the hands and giving instructions.

A deep-throated neigh issued from the barn. George Washington had been contrary and balky ever since the fire. Only Nacho could get near him. A sound of stamping was followed by the crack of a breaking board. The stallion was the ranch's future. We couldn't risk his getting himself torn up in a tantrum.

"I'll see to the stock," I shouted to Nacho.

Fanny and I headed north where the land runs along the mountains for nigh onto three miles. There we ranged our few head of beef cattle. With autumn coming on fast, we had much to do. Yesterday had been given over to readying the smokehouse for the hogs we would butcher.

With no warning at all, my eyes began to burn with tears. Autumn had been my favorite season. In St. Louis the weather would be glorious—the air crisp as fresh cider, the trees exploding into brilliant reds and the broad river still and bright, like a strip of sky fallen to earth. Here, the smattering of cottonwoods went yellow, but there were no red leaves at all, and the river always slowed to a trickle. I dabbed at my face with my sleeve and turned Fanny toward the watering hole.

We had dammed a spring to make the pond. Six or eight head of cattle lifted their heads as I approached but I barely glanced at them. My eyes had fixed on something that lay on the other side of the pond.

The calf was on its side on the low bank, its muzzle inches from the water. It was small, born late in the year. The cow that stood over it raised her head and her moan echoed from the mountains. Before Fanny's hooves halted, I was already out of the saddle. The cow eyed me nervously, ears twitching, her head down between me and the calf. She bellowed again.

The calf squirmed, its legs jerking forward as it struggled to gain its feet. It swayed unsteadily for a moment then toppled into the pond. I seized the hindquarters and hauled the still-struggling animal from the water. When it turned toward me, I recoiled, appalled. "God in heaven!"

A pocket of raw flesh stared from where the left eye had been. At the side of the head was the hole where the bullet had entered, the angle so shallow it had missed the brain but exploded through the eye socket.

"Who did this!" The words burst from my lips, though I knew no one could hear me. "Why?" I said, this time under my breath. Why maim a poor dumb creature and leave it to a slow death? Our distance from town put us beyond the reach of most drunked-up rowdies. Was it a band of renegade Indians bent on even worse harm? But even the worst of them have a high regard for animals.

They kill only for food.

Now on flat ground, the calf was wobbling to its feet and trying to lick my fingers. Blood had caked around the wound and no more seemed to be flowing. The poor beast shivered, though the sun had warmed the air. The mother nudged at it, and it staggered a few steps. All four legs seemed to work okay.

I called Fanny, then roped the calf's feet and strove to thrust it across the mare's neck in front of the saddle. What I might do with a blind calf I didn't know, but I couldn't leave it on the range to die. Riding slowly so the cow could follow, I made my way home.

Julio was raking up droppings in the chicken yard. Steeling myself for mutterings about keeping a blind animal, I turned the calf over to him. He shot me a surprised look but took the poor beast willingly.

Only then did I notice the horse that waited patiently in front of the house. The wagon it was hitched to was quite empty. I had a caller.

My first thought was that someone had come to alert me that the Yankees had returned, but as I crossed to the house I remembered where I'd seen the wagon before.

She was sitting alone in the parlor reading a Bible so small that I wondered she could see the print. She rose and greeted me as if I were the visitor. Her clothes looked fresh-pressed. Wisps of hair were artfully arranged to dangle below the bun at the back of her neck.

I was sweaty and windblown and stank of horse and cattle and blood. I tried to force a smile. "Isabel. How nice to see you."

She opened her mouth to say something, but her eyes caught on my sweat-and-dirt-stained breeches. "Those must be very…convenient."

I wiped my hands on them, feeling like a man must feel caught out in women's clothes.

Isabel looked at the hand I held out, started to take it then drew her hand back and herself up to her full delicate height.

"Has no one given you coffee?" I faltered, hating her and myself in equal measure. "I'll put the pot on."

"I have not come to pass the time of day."

The sternness of her little-girl voice halted my progress toward the kitchen.

"You must cast out the evil in this house, Matilda." The words fairly rang out.

"Evil?"

Isabel raised her chin. "The slave woman. She is known to be a witch."

I tried to run agitated fingers through my hair and discovered it was snarled and sticking out every which way. "Winona is neither a witch nor a slave."

"I tell you truly, she will bring God's wrath upon us. She must leave here."

"She's expecting a child, Isabel, for mercy's sake! She has to remain here at least until it is born. I swear she is no witch."

Not a muscle in Isabel's face seemed to tighten, but her eyes hardened. "You must rid our valley of this ungodly woman." She marched on her absurdly small feet toward the door then turned. "Or she will be purged. I shall pray for you that God does not smite you for harboring a she-devil." Her chin seemed pointed as a dagger as she lifted it, held my eyes for a moment, then stepped outside, not bothering to close the door behind her.

I stood staring after her until Winona's voice came from behind me. "We have company calling?"

I fingered my mussed and matted hair. "A kindly Christian woman."

Winona frowned at me. "I hope she is a blind one. You looks like a four-bit gunslinger."

I watched Isabel climb into the wagon, take the reins and urge the horse toward the trail. "I wish I were one."

Winona jabbed her hands to her hips. "I means the breeches." The apron strained tight over her belly.

I looked down at my shameful attire and shrugged. "It's better for riding."

"Ain't proper."

"Nothing here is proper. Nothing. So neither am I."

Winona shook her head and made a clicking sound with her tongue.

I retired to my room to freshen up. Isabel might be het up about some notion that Winona was practicing witchcraft, but she had not shot that calf. I dawdled over my lunch wondering how I had managed to make two enemies since sunup.

Isabel would have no trouble drumming up ill will among the Baptists, who loved nothing more than railing about the godlessness of others. But the Catholics, which included most of the natives, far outnumbered the Baptists. If Isabel stirred up the Catholics against Winona there would be hell to pay, for sure. I bit my tongue at my coarse thoughts. I was becoming as wild as a bobcat myself.

A clatter began on the roof as though God had spilled a cartload of pebbles. Nacho had been right about the hail.

Chapter Fourteen

As soon as the chores were done next morning, I set out for the cuevas. I hadn't seen Tonio Bernini since the fire, and I'd been wanting to see him ever since I began putting things together that refused to add up. Had I trusted him too readily? The sinister riddle that had taken over my life began just hours before he arrived. He seemed a sensible, decent person. But was he?

He had some standing, whatever it was, with the Catholic Church. He might be willing to help me now. A visit would also give me a chance to look him over yet again, this time with a more critical eye.

I halted Fanny near the boulders and was picking my way across the stone-strewn ground toward the cave when Tonio's tall, rangy frame appeared in the rock opening. A second figure followed, a woman in a garment that had once boasted bright broad stripes but was now badly faded. The cloth stopped just above what looked like leather socks. A tiny ripple of shock ran up my spine. A native woman. Soundlessly, she glided away, melting almost immediately into the landscape. A peculiar scratchiness invaded my throat and thickened my tongue.

Tonio moved toward me, stopping a dozen feet away. "Good to see you, Matty."

So, I thought meanly, if you are a priest you are surely a fallen one. And a bold one, at that. I examined his eyes for guilt and finding none irked me even more. Steeling myself against I knew not what, I said simply, "I need your help."

With an affable nod, he waited, his face clear and innocent as a child's, while I explained.

"Winona is no witch," I finished. "I don't understand why Isabel is so bent on stirring folks up." Actually, I was afraid I did understand. Isabel was quite disposed to do this purely to spite me. "If a man of God were to tell them Winona is a good woman..."

He frowned. "You know I'm no longer associated with the church."

"Be that as it may, people seem to think you are a holy man. They would believe you."

His brow furrowed, but he did not protest further.

"Winona is heavy with child. You can see that. Her time will be soon. She's a darky. Some folks suspicion she is a runaway slave, and this is now a Confederate territory. Are you to stand by while they force her from this valley?"

Pain seemed to rake his eyes, but perhaps it was only the sun. I waited.

Finally: "What do you want me to do?"

"Do you ever go to church?"

He stared at me for a moment, as if turning over my question to seek some other meaning. "It's a bit far to walk in a day."

I felt stupid. "Of course. I'll bring the wagon Sunday, Winona with me. We can go together to Mass." I hadn't been near a church in many months; but Nacho had reported that with the Baptist house of worship empty since Joel's death, some of the Protestants had decided their immortal souls were safer with the Catholics than with no service at all.

Tonio's shoulder twitched and he shifted his weight, like a man who had found cornmeal in his bedroll. He looked down, then back at me. "All right."

A strong gust of autumn wind caught my back, and I staggered a little before getting my feet braced. I'd been so intent on persuading him I hadn't noticed the livid bruise that had crept across the sky.

He turned to examine the thick clouds that had vaulted over the mountains. "It should pass quickly. Come in. I'll make some tea. Put your horse over there." He nodded at where two huge rocks formed a sort of stone lean-to.

The cave was cozier than I had imagined possible. A low rock ledge circled the room, forming a bench on one side, a hearth on the other. A small pile of burning logs radiated warmth and a rosy glow. He offered me a blanket of sewn-together rabbit skins.

I sat near the fire where the ledge was warm.

He soon had water boiling in an iron pot and tossed in a few pinches of something from one of the tins stacked neatly against the wall.

"Is that really tea?" I asked, unable to imagine how he could afford it.

"As good as," he said, handing me a cup made from horn.

I took a sip. It was warm and smooth and left a trace of fruit after you swallowed. "It's wonderful. What is it?"

"If I told you, you could make it for yourself."

That was the first time I saw him laugh. The firelight caught his eyes, and I remembered the Indian woman and felt a surge of something that made me nervy. I dropped my gaze and took another sip of the tea.

"You look dubious," he said. "Is it too strong?"

"No." I sighed and rubbed my forehead. "I never thanked you for your help with the fire."

"It's well we halted it before it took the house and barn."

"I don't know what I would have done. It hasn't been an easy year." The muscles in my back and neck began to relax and I wondered if it was the tea. "It may be that fire was no accident." I told him of the oilcan Nacho had found in the burnt brush and watched his face for a tightened muscle, his hand for any hint of shakiness; but he showed no sign of disquiet.

His face seemed so open, his eyes so unguarded, his concern so genuine, the rest of my worries began to spill out like a dam giving way. "The Texans took some horses. They pretended to be gentlemen about it, but it was clear I had no choice but to hand over whatever they wanted. I keep wondering if they'll come back and demand more. And the Yankees may come back, which might be worse. Some Union officer could blame me for helping the Texans, could declare me a traitor. And truth be, I haven't had an easy moment since that poor Mexican boy was shot."

"Did you ever learn who he was?"

"No." The wind was whistling around the rocks outside, but not even a breeze reached the interior of the cave. I never decided to tell him, it just slid off my tongue with the rest: "There's also the matter of the map."

"The map." His face remained still. Only his eyebrows crept a bit higher.

I drew the pouch from my shirt, where I had kept it since the day after the fire, and unfolded the paper it held. "The kid with the bullet in his head had this."

A tired, haggard look crept across his face. He bent close to the paper and examined it in the firelight for a long time. Then, his features blank, he handed it back.

"It's a map of my land—or part of my land. Even the cuevas is marked."

"It does seem to be." Tonio rubbed his eyes.

"What can it possibly mean?"

He was silent a long moment. "Two things. He could have gotten this map anywhere. In a saloon. He could have won it in a poker game. He might even have been flimflammed into buying it."

"But why? Why was this map drawn? Why would anyone want it at all?"

He opened his hands as if to say he didn't know, but something in his face denied it.

An icy thought brushed the back of my neck and tingled to the top of my scalp. Was he lying? But before I could consider that, another notion flared in my head like a comet and a rush of hope nearly overwhelmed me. My words came out in a rush. "It's silver or gold or something. That map shows where it is."

Tonio had gotten up and was stirring the fire with a stick. I couldn't see his face.

"That has to be it," I said. "Doesn't it?"

He turned to me. Most of his face was in shadow, but the eyes looked unbearably sad, and strong as iron—as though they had peered at Satan and stood their ground, as though anything else was meaningless. "Perhaps," he said.

I leapt to my feet. "Don't you see? It must be. What else could it be?"

He gazed at me. "If it is, what would you do?"

"It would mean everything," I gasped, my mind darting among the possibilities. "Everything. I could leave this dreadful place. I could go…" I hesitated. "…home."

"Where is that?"

"Philadelphia," I lied.

"Why can't you go now?"

"I need more money. I'm only trying to build up the horse breeding so I can sell the ranch for enough to get out of here."

"Your land could be trampled by every ne'er-do-well in the Western Hemisphere desperate for a quick fortune. Have you not heard what happened in California?"

I sank down again on the ledge. I hadn't thought of that. "But if it is on my land…" I drew my feet up under me and leaned back against the warm stone wall, my mind addled by the possibilities of such a dose of luck. I felt like the gods must have felt when they realized they might make it rain or knock down mountains. If only it were true.

Tonio gave me a small unhappy smile. "It is not so simple as that. Men would camp on your land, some would steal your horses, there would be brawls and killings. You would need an army of guards a thousand strong just to continue your life as it is now."

We both fell silent, staring at the chunks of glowing embers, the remnants of fire-consumed wood.

We are prisoners of what we want, I thought, and murmured, "It might be wiser to live like you, warm and dry with nothing to lose."

He sat a few feet from me, his shoulders hunched together, still staring at the fire. "There is always something to lose. Always."

My mind was going feeble with the strain. I had to stop thinking about it. I folded the map, slid it back inside its leather jacket and seized on the first thought that came to mind. "Who was the woman I saw leaving?"

His eyes never left the pouch until it had disappeared inside my shirt. "A Tortugas," he said. "Her man is ailing, shaking with ague. She wanted something to slake the fever."

Of course. Why had I leapt so quick to other, shameful, conclusions? "How did she know about you?"

He shrugged. "Word travels fast as wind among the natives. They are good healers themselves, especially the women; and they're always seeking more and better ways."

"How did you learn which berries or leaves or stems to use for which ailment?"

"From a man called Mario. Brother Mario."

"At the monastery."

Tonio nodded. "He had a special house of glass where he grew hundreds of species from all over the world. I thought he was the greatest man on earth because he could relieve suffering—sometimes it seemed that he could even prevent death."

I imagined a ten-year-old Tonio contemplating such miracles and smiled. "Why did you leave, then?"

He leaned back against the stone bench. His beard, I saw, wanted a trimming. The firelight danced in his eyes as he stared at the blackened wall above the coals. "Brother Mario said there were many more plants that might be useful. When I came of age, I decided to find some of them for him."

"So your decision to leave had nothing to do with religion."

"There was a time when I wanted to be a priest," he said slowly. "But I wanted to see the world. I always intended to go back."

"Why didn't you?"

Something in his eyes seemed to drown the fire's twinkle. He looked down, and the pause that followed stretched out and became heavy. "I still send a packet of seeds to Brother

Mario now and then." His tone had shifted to that of casual tea conversation.

I wanted to touch his shoulder; but instead, I put my feet on the floor and rose. "I should be getting home." Then I remembered something. "When I showed you the map you said there were two things it could mean, but you only mentioned one. What was the second?"

"If I am not mistaken," he said solemnly, "the path marked on that map leads right through the nest I told you of. The nest of rattlesnakes. Just above that are a number of very excellent herbs."

"You're joking."

He smiled. "Of course."

Outside, the wind had swept away both clouds and rain, and the sky was blue crystal with streaks of white. I mounted Fanny and walked her along the rock.

Just before I reached the place where the rocks give way to open space, I looked back. Tonio was standing at the gap in the rocks that marked the entrance to his cave, staring after me. He raised a hand in a wave.

Something inside me stirred, something I had thought was as dead as the steer we had just butchered and hung in the smokehouse. I suddenly glimpsed myself, a tot grasping my skirts and smiling up, an infant in my arms; and on my shoulder, a hand, with fingers narrow, not tapered, the knuckles larger than the rest. Coldly, I smothered the image, aghast that my mind would conjure such a thing.

"Sunday," I called.

Fanny slowly picked her way to more level ground. We hadn't gone a hundred yards when the unmistakable bray of a burro made my eyes dart over the landscape in puzzlement. We had only one burro. Herlinda used it to fetch water from the springs. But the springs were half a mile closer to home. The burro brayed again, and I spotted two grey ears twitching behind a rock. I reined Fanny toward them.

Cisco, our burro, tossed his head as I approached. Hitched behind him was the water wagon, but there was no sign of Herlinda. I had no illusions about how she would interpret my past few hours in the cave.

Chapter Fifteen

When Winona met me at the door, I cussed myself for seven kinds of fool. She looked about eleven months pregnant. And something was drawing hard lines around her mouth and eyes. Any notion of her riding in a wagon all the way to church on Sunday evaporated like dew on a hot morning. I put my arms around her. "What's wrong?" Then, even I could feel the contraction in her belly.

Clear brown eyes held mine as one small nod answered my unvoiced question. "I was starting to think there might be two of us waiting when you got back from galivantin'."

I swallowed hard. I hadn't seen Herlinda, but I had a good idea as to her whereabouts. Should I fetch her? Winona was already padding heavily down the hall to her room. I followed, feeling wholly unprepared for the task ahead.

The bed was open, its linen fresh. Next to it sat a straw basket piled with clean rags. A sheet had been twisted and run around the foot of the bed so that the ends lay together, like reins, in the middle.

"What's that for?" I asked.

"To pull on, of course."

"I've never done this before," I faltered. "Not with—"

"I ain't exactly an old hand, myself. But I figure it must come natural." She turned, and I followed her to the kitchen, where every pot we owned was simmering on the stove.

I'd had what they called "a lady's upbringing," which sorely lacked even the merest hint about birthing. "I'll fetch Herlinda," I gulped. "She's sure to know more than I do."

"I already told that woman to stay clear." Winona's voice was thick, but her tone was adamant. "All them bad spirits peerin' over her shoulder—I don't want them in that room."

"Tonio. You said yourself he's a good healer. He may know what to do."

Winona's eyes fixed on me. They had turned a darker shade of brown. "I don't want no man around, neither. This is woman's doings. Eve knew a whole lot less than we do, and she got through it okay. If we can't do as good as a lady who didn't have nothing to wear but a fig leaf, we got no business procreatin' in the first place."

"Oh, for God's sake," I said, my voice veering toward shout. "Eve had a man there. She had Adam."

"Now you just tryin' to get out of this," Winona said quite evenly. "This is my party. And I gets to invite who I want."

"I don't know enough. What if I do something wrong?"

"You done horses," Winona cut me off, fixing me with those brown-agate eyes. "This ain't a lot different. Now, I already boiled all them rags in there and dried 'em in the sun." She waved toward the bedroom. "You just be sure that anything that touches me or the young 'un has been stuck in that boilin' water first." She had begun to pace slowly, back across the kitchen, through the parlor and down the hall, where she turned and started back along the same path. I trotted behind her.

"Like what? What do I have to stick in boiling water?"

"Like the knife to cut the cord," she said patiently, waddling past me in the opposite direction. "Now I already scrubbed myself with that new lye soap. You go scrub your hands and arms real good."

"Okay, okay, just don't you go and faint or anything. You'll have to tell me what to do."

In the kitchen, I poured a little of the hot water into a pan so it could cool enough for me to put my hands into it. "Go lie down," I called over my shoulder. "You should get off your feet."

"Nope." She had come up behind me. "It's the walkin' that drops the baby into the chute."

"You make it sound like riding a bronc," I muttered, scrubbing my hands all the way up to the elbow.

"It ain't unlike it, honey."

Winona went on pacing for another hour, with me trailing behind her, holding my hands up so they wouldn't touch anything.

"Okay," she said finally. "I got to lay me down. You bring a couple pots of water and that knife I put on the chopping table."

I was swinging one of the blackened pots from the stove when I heard a shriek, followed by a bellowed groan. I put the pot on the floor fast and ran to Winona's room.

She was lying on the bed, her eyes closed, her face greyish.

"What's wrong?" I gasped, rubbing my arm where some of the boiling water had sloshed on it.

Her eyes flickered open. "I'm just trying out the sounds to get 'em right."

I realized I was standing in a puddle of clearish fluid. My eyes flew back to hers.

"Water broke," she said.

I mopped up the fluid before it could turn the floor to mud and fetched two pots of water, the knife thrust into one like a sword. Then I washed again. My arms were beginning to redden from the lye.

A groan came from Winona—the low kind that sounds like it starts in the toes. She was rolling her head back and forth as if trying to avoid an attacker. Sweat had beaded on her temples, and the flesh around her mouth was almost white.

I patted her face dry with one of the rags, remembering when she had done the same for me. We hadn't been able to be so clean and careful then. But we had known it wouldn't matter.

"Do wish I had a birthin' chair," she grunted. Her body tightened and twisted, and she groaned again. "The pains are awful close together. Won't be long. If something…happens…you take care of her…"

"Don't say that!"

"Don't give her to no one—darky, white nor Injun. A girl with no pa got to have a good ma. You give your word?"

"You know I'd raise her like my own…how do you know it's a girl?"

"Her name's to be Zia. Z-I-A." She spelled the letters slowly. Winona could not read well, but she had learned her letters long before I knew her. "That meant something like 'sun' to her pa." She smiled weakly. "Sunshine."

She had never talked much about the baby's father, but now she said, "He was a good man, her pa. Red Coyote was smart an' brave; he was a good man."

"What happened to him?"

"Got hisself killed by another Injun. Over me. And his family wouldn't have nothin' to do with me after. If…you tell Zia her papa—" Another fierce pain cut her off. She screamed this time, and sweat made big beads on her lip. Her hands gripped the bedclothes, white at the knuckles.

"Twist up one of them rags," she grunted. I took one from the basket, twined it into a sort of rope and handed it to her. She opened her mouth and bit down on it. Her round cheeks had gone hollow.

I put pillows beneath her knees, and handed her the twisted-sheet reins she had devised. She pulled hard, the veins standing out on her temples. Then she gasped and began to pant. I wiped her face again and, having touched the top of the bed, re-scrubbed my hands. I had just finished drying them when Winona's body arched, then went rigid. She screamed, the sound muffled by the rag in her mouth. And then the blood began.

The baby was no bigger than a rabbit and covered with so much mucous I was sure it would choke. I didn't take time to cut the cord before turning it over and pounding her firmly on the back.

Zia was, indeed, a girl. And she let loose with a yell that would have put Winona, even at her most indignant, to shame.

"Nothing wrong with her mouth," Winona grunted.

Hands trembling, I mopped the infant clean and wrapped her in one of the rags. Tiny, perfect hands clasped my thumb. For a moment, longing for a child of my own swept over me. I turned back to her mother. "She is one fine piece of work. She truly is."

Big, dark smudges circled Winona's eyes. "She do seem so," she said, her voice husky.

Zia's angry cries halted when I laid her across her mother's now-shrunken belly. I slipped a bit of boiled yarn around the ropy cord that still pulsed between mother and infant. Pulling the yarn tight, I reached for the knife and severed the connection, freeing Zia to make her own way in the world. The baby stared at me unseeing, looking dubious about the whole process.

Winona gave me a glance of pained amusement. "You is not done yet." Her fists tightened, her head drew forward on the pillow, and the afterbirth arrived. By scooting Winona first to one side, then the other, I changed the sheets. The skin across my knuckles was raw.

Exhausted, I stood amid the heaps of soiled rags and wiped my hands on my bloodied apron. An intense sense of pride stole over me. For all three of us. "Well, we did it."

"Yes, ma'am, we did at that," Winona chuckled. Little bubbly sounds were coming from the basket at her side. "But you surely do make a mess, Miss Matty."

Chapter Sixteen

By the time Zia was a month old she could bewitch anyone just by gurgling. I spent hours by her basket marveling at her thick, dark eyelashes. In an often-sour world, she was sweetness itself.

Tonio brought juniper berries for Winona; and finding Zia suffering a bout of colic, he carried the baby about as though he were the father of ten and saw no mystery in the care of such a tiny being.

"Obviously, we'll have to put off what we planned," I told him.

"Perhaps it won't be necessary. These things whip up like thunderclouds one minute only to clear off the next." He pointed at the berries. "Mash them up and steep them for ten minutes or so. You have a timepiece?"

I nodded. My father had left me his pocket watch.

Winona recognized the concoction by its smell. "Injun women say this stuff sweeps the hearth clean an' lays the wood for a new fire." A grin split her face, and she swigged the liquid down.

Herlinda had prepared meals while Winona was gaining back her strength. She said little about anything, nothing about seeing me with Tonio at the cuevas.

I had urged Winona to take her time getting back to the chores, but she'd given me an arch look. "I is not rock-hard certain you is in safe hands." By the end of the first week, she had resumed her territory in the kitchen.

With winter approaching, the need to get our meat smoked, sausages stuffed and burnt fence mended swept all other thoughts from my head. We were so busy the hands even skipped their Saturday-night carousing.

Winona interrupted one of my feverish bouts with the account books to announce, "I needs a measure of fresh white muslin."

I stared at her dumbfounded. "Whatever for?"

"Land sakes, you think I'm gonna have that child christened wrapped in a rag?"

I stared at her, mouth open. "I flat forgot."

"No matter, Miss Matty. You is plum tuckered. I can take me the wagon and the basket—"

"It's too cold to take the baby out. I'll go."

"Nohow. I can wrap her up plenty good enough. She be a sight more sturdy than you think."

But I won the argument. It occurred to me that the christening would be a perfect time for Tonio to accompany us to church and allay any ill will Isabel might have stirred up toward Winona.

All thought of the Mexican boy's map had fled my mind in the wake of Zia's birth and the haste of the ranch work. But as Fanny's hooves drummed a steady rhythm on the trail to town, I began to dwell on it again. Why had it been drawn at all if not to mark the place of something valuable? Or had someone merely hornswoggled the boy? If the map was a fake, why was it so accurate about so many things?

My head still buzzing with these thoughts, I was paying scant attention to much else and heading for Garza's General Store, was half way across the plaza when I realized the square was a squirming mass of people. Folks from every settlement within thirty miles, from Las Cruces and Dona Ana and Robledos and even from Willow Bar down south, must have come to town.

"Que pasa?" I asked an old man who was leaning against the front of the general store, patiently watching the crowd. "What's going on?" I wasn't sure whether he was Mexican or Indian.

He took a gnarled wooden pipe out of his mouth and said in passable English, "You do not hear of it?"

I shook my head and anxiously eyed the crowd, but no one looked nervous or worried. They seemed more in a mood to celebrate. "It isn't the Yankees, is it?"

"No, ma'am." I could see that the pipe had fit quite comfortably in the space where two teeth were missing. The teeth that remained were as brown as the wood of the pipe. He smelled like a smokehouse smells in autumn when it's stoked up and full of fresh pig. He stuck the pipe back in his mouth. "It is the Con-fed-er-ates. The Rebs."

My spirits shot up. The fears that had driven dozens of people to hide their belongings and wait things out in Mexico could be laid to rest. Union soldiers would not storm our valley bent on punishing us for welcoming the Texans. People could come home.

The crowd was multiplying rapidly. Thinking I glimpsed Jamie across the square, I realized how sorely I had missed him: his good nature, his wisdom. Aside from Winona, he was the only person I could count a true friend.

The old man tugged at my arm. The newspaper he pushed into my hand was so smudged it looked solid grey. "Read, please," he said. "I do not."

Jamie and his press had, indeed, returned.

"'On issuing our last number,'" I read aloud, "'we concluded that it would be many a week before we issued another. The Abolitionists, we were told, well armed and uniformed, would advance upon us to wipe us from the face of the earth. Having hurriedly packed off our press to Mexico, cached our type, made our wills and prepared for the worst, we find the imminent stampede never occurred, no fight, nor even a sight of the enemy. The tears and partings and God knows what anguish, were for naught.'"

The old man nodded to me and limped off into the crowd.

I was thinking that with Jamie back in town I could ask him about the man who had tried to buy my land. At the least, he could describe the person who had asked him to bring me the offer.

The mass of milling bodies soon hemmed me in, but with my height, I could still scan a sea of faces. There was no further sign of Jamie; but a few paces to my left, I spied the cocky posture of Lieutenant Tyler Morris. With him, erect as a poker and seeming to swagger even as he stood still, was a Confederate colonel in full and perfect dress. Both were waving their arms, and Lieutenant Morris was smacking a rolled-up paper angrily against his own leg. Curious, I edged closer.

"It is an insult to your honor, sir. You must defend yourself. The man is a dangerous fool. You must have satisfaction."

The colonel was agreeing, bobbing his head like a furious banty rooster. Catching my eye, Lieutenant Morris gave a sharp nod, as if to dismiss me.

Perhaps it was just to annoy him, but I smiled and held out my hand. "A pleasure to see you again."

Morris looked away; but the colonel turned, and there was little the lieutenant could do but introduce me to his companion, so he straightened his shoulders smartly and did so. "Your governor, ma'am, Colonel John Baylor."

The colonel took my hand, and I looked into blue eyes that would have turned a pot of boiling coffee to solid ice. Here was more than enough temerity to claim the territory for the Confederacy and declare oneself governor, even if the top of one's head barely reached the height of my nose.

I dusted off my best voice. "Pleased to meet you, sir. I trust you found the horses worthy?"

The lieutenant's expression melted like warming wax.

The governor's eyes narrowed. "Horses? What horses?"

I knew I shouldn't say it, but I couldn't stop. "The ones Lieutenant Morris took for you. He was good enough to pay me almost half their value."

"What horses?" Baylor demanded again.

Lieutenant Morris looked straight into my eyes. "The horses were not for Governor Baylor." He said it so calmly I almost believed him myself. "They were needed for quite another purpose."

"We are in dire exigency of horses," Baylor insisted, sending specks of spittle to settle on his mustache.

"Indeed, sir," the Lieutenant said. "And we shall have them soon." Just then, the jabbering of the hundreds of folk who crammed the plaza died to silence. Lieutenant Morris took the governor's elbow and guided him through an opening in the crowd.

Voices buzzed again as all eyes swung toward the center of the plaza, where a man was stiffly mounting a narrow makeshift platform. "Brigadier General Henry Hopkins Sibley, Confederate States of America," someone said, and the crowd burst into cheers and whistles.

Sibley was a name I knew. He'd been a U.S. dragoon officer up north before the war. I'd heard that a number of men had resigned their commissions and joined the rebel states.

General Sibley was tall, and he stood as though a giant spike had been driven from his collar all the way to his boots. His hair was middle brown and somewhat curly. A thick mustache, darker than the rest, made a wide sweep from under his nose to his bearded jaw. Brass buttons bigger than twenty-dollar gold pieces marched in parallel lines up the front of his immaculate grey jacket toward a collar that didn't stop till it got to his chin.

I still remember that collar. It was stiff and white with a big star flanked by two smaller stars, all enclosed in a wide oval of blue, or maybe it was green. Sibley raised a white-gloved hand and the crowd fell quiet, only an occasional scuffling foot or cough breaking the stillness.

"Ladies and gentlemen." His voice had the depth and strength of an orator's. There wasn't a trace of softness in his vowels, and I surmised he had never set foot in the South.

"It is with great pride that I tell you The Army of New Mexico has arrived at Fort Bliss."

This drew a din of cheers.

"I have assumed command of all the forces of the Confederate States on the Rio Grande at and above Fort Quitman and all the Territory of New Mexico and Arizona." Fort Quitman was seventy miles or so below Franklin on the Rio Grande. I began to see the source of Governor Baylor's ill humor. His governorship was about to be usurped.

"I would have made your acquaintance sooner," Sibley continued, "but we were beset by Indians." The crowd roared happily, as if it were a fine feat to be beset by Indians.

It wasn't until later that I learned the Army of New Mexico was barely the size of a brigade—about thirty-two hundred cold, lonely, bored and fretting men. And they had not been "beset" by Indians. Under cover of night, their horse herd had been raided. They had lost some badly needed mounts, but not one soldier had been attacked.

Nonetheless, for the moment, I was as enthralled as the crowd and quite willing to welcome them as heroes.

"Given the exposed nature of Colonel Baylor's position here, I came as quickly as I could," Sibley continued smoothly, and his eyes riveted on the little man who now stood stiffly near the platform. The governor was being reminded that he was now just a colonel.

"I want you to know that I have proposed a plan to President Jefferson Davis to conquer all of New Mexico Territory. The Confederacy will reach all the way to the Pacific. There, our Navy will bring the Federals to their knees." The crowd roared its approval.

It dawned on me the Confederates had little interest in us. The Territory was merely a path to California's ports.

By the time the shouting was over and Sibley had taken his leave, it was growing dark. There was no time to hunt for Jamie. I made my way to the general store and asked to see the carefully covered bolt of white silk. Supplies had been slow coming through and barely a yard of it remained. The price, Mr. Garza told me apologetically, was sixteen dollars. I blinked and swallowed, and bought it anyway.

Winona was almost shocked into silence when she opened the package. "This here's not muslin." Then she railed at me, "Silk is terrible dear. This must have cost an eagle. You suddenly got money to burn?"

But Zia cooed her approval. I wrapped her in the silk cloth and danced her around. "Won't you be the fine lady?" I planted a kiss on the top of her head.

"You spoil that child."

"Just wait till everyone sees her at church. They'll know it's a princess come for christening."

◇◇◇

The next day, with morning chores out of the way, I downed a hurried lunch and headed Fanny back along the trail toward Mesilla to ask Jamie about his erstwhile client. Was the man who had offered to buy my land so determined to possess it that he might have set fire to it? Was there a connection between him and the map and that poor, nameless Mexican lad? Had he murdered the boy and later dug up the grave? Had this so-called client been lurking in my barn waiting to cosh me over the head? Another thought occurred to me: the boot print at the spring. Had the man been skulking on the rim of the arroyo while I was drowning at its base? Jamie wouldn't know, but surely he could tell me something.

A strong wind was whipping the scrubby vegetation, and the stalk of a yucca that had bloomed last spring startled me from my thoughts when it capsized, grazing Fanny's neck as it fell. I hunched forward in the saddle and moved my feet back in the way that urges Fanny to gallop.

My hair blew straight back. The plait loosened, and I realized I'd forgotten my hat. My hair would be an awful mess. We hadn't come far; I considered putting Fanny about to fetch it. But it felt wonderful to be thundering across the high desert, like challenging the wind to a duel. I rode on.

The plaza was as empty today as it had been jammed with people yesterday. The boardwalks were bare of boots, save for a couple of officers talking on the corner. A stagecoach pulled up to La Posta and the driver climbed down, but no passengers got out.

I anchored Fanny next to the stage and was waving to the driver when someone passed behind me on foot. A glance over my shoulder caught a burly figure and wisps of red hair.

"Jamie," I called. Had he not seen me?

The broad back was stiff, the shoulders rigid. His whole posture declared outrage. With no backward look so I could catch his attention, he plodded grimly toward the far corner of the plaza, where the soldiers were still talking. At a loss to explain his demeanor, I followed.

A third officer, a small man, obviously a dandy, almost priggish in his dress, had joined the two on the corner. When the newcomer looked toward Jamie, I saw it was Colonel Baylor.

With no further converse, Baylor jerked about and darted into the hotel. I stopped dead when he re-emerged: he was carrying a rifle, his hand on the stock, the muzzle pointed down but looking all too ready. He walked straight toward the approaching Jamie.

"Jamie," I shouted. "Wait!"

Oblivious, my friend trudged on.

A crowd began spilling from doorways, faces alert but not shocked, as though they had been expecting something. The air buzzed with talk then went utterly still, leaving only Jamie's footsteps to scratch against the silence.

Baylor planted a deliberate foot on each side of the walk. "Hold on, my man," he roared. "I want to speak with you."

Jamie halted. His right hand disappeared into a pocket; and when it reappeared, the sun glittered on a shaft of polished steel. He resumed walking.

Baylor swung his rifle up.

I flattened myself against the nearest storefront, not a dozen steps behind Jamie. The crowd of people froze.

Instead of firing, Baylor slammed the butt of the gun into Jamie's head. The leaden thwack was all the more horrifying in the quiet.

Jamie reeled and staggered but kept his feet.

"You print lies and trash," Baylor screamed into Jamie's face, his breath coming in gulps, his spit spattering Jamie's cheek. "You insinuate I lack courage. Defend yourself!"

Jamie said nothing.

Baylor threw the rifle down and pitched himself at Jamie like a charging bull. Jamie swung a fist, and both men fell. Jamie was far the heavier; but Baylor, his face the color of a ripe plum, pinned the Irishman with a knee against his throat.

"You cannot come upon me like that. I'm too much man for your sort!" Baylor roared, his face going redder still as he tried to wrestle the knife from Jamie's fingers. "You stab people, do you?"

Jamie only blinked and stared.

Baylor's face, red as blood, covered with sweat and swollen with fury, twitched. He grabbed the rifle from where he had pitched it, put the barrel to Jamie's cheek and fired.

I don't know how long I screamed before I could will my legs to run to Jamie. The blood was coming from his neck in spurts. His eyes fastened on mine, and he seemed to smile. Then he gave a soft choking sound and his eyes fixed.

Baylor stalked away. Stunned and still silent, the crowd parted to let him through.

◇◇◇

I sat numb and motionless in the saddle while Fanny took me back to the ranch. I'd seen Baylor's kind of rage before, and the memory sickened me. Images devoid of any meaning but horror ricocheted off each other in my brain.

Jamie was dead. And Baylor probably would not even be arrested.

Zeke had come and shaken his head over the scene. Jamie's hand had still clutched the knife. Plenty of people had been close enough to see that he had not threatened Baylor with the blade. He had only held it, as I told Zeke, for self-defense.

But that Jamie was armed was enough. The Mesilla Valley, having welcomed the Texans, now desperately needed them. Just yesterday, even I had shaken Baylor's hand.

The man was vile and treacherous and obviously quite mad. He had ordered my horses practically stolen from me and then denied it. Even Lieutenant Morris had denied it. Other purposes, indeed. The lieutenant had said the horses were for Baylor. Did they think I wouldn't remember?

Now Baylor had murdered my friend. I wanted to tear my hair and wail as the native women do when death strikes. But the tears would not come. I was nearly home before I realized that I would never learn what Jamie knew about the man who had tried to buy my land. With no more reason than I'd had before, I was suddenly afraid. I turned Fanny south.

The cuevas hove into view, and Tonio, standing at the cave's entrance, a pack on his back, waved. "Tea?" he called.

"Thank you, no." I didn't dismount. "I should like to ask a favor."

He ambled to Fanny's side and looked up at me, shading his eyes against the brightness of the sky. "What is it?"

I withdrew the stained pouch from my shirt and slipped the leather thong over my head. "Would you keep this for me?"

The lines around his eyes seemed to tighten.

"You know what it is?"

"I expect it's the map."

"Yes." I looked down at my fingers gripping the saddle horn so tightly they were almost white then tossed the pouch to him. "I was going to show it to Jamie O'Rourke. He was editor of the newspaper and a friend of mine. I hoped he might know something. But Jamie was killed today."

Tonio's face made sad creases about the eyes. "I'm sorry."

I swallowed against the lump that rose in my throat. "I was there. He was shot down in cold blood by the man who until yesterday was governor of this territory."

Tonio watched wordlessly while I flung my runaway hair from my eyes.

"It seems possible," I went on, "that whoever killed that Mexican boy may have set my range afire and searched my bureau while we fought the blaze—all because he wants that map. If so, he won't stop looking for it. But he won't think to look for it here."

Tonio gave a slow nod. "I will look after it."

Chapter Seventeen

For days I could not shake the gloom. Indeed, I was hard put to stir from my bedclothes. Even Zia's coming christening failed to cheer me.

Jamie surely did print blunt and scathing words about Colonel Baylor. His tongue sometimes got ahead of his brain. But to be coldly gunned down with a crowd of people looking on! And Baylor a free man. Justice seemed a strumpet, for sale to the highest bidder. But I already knew that.

On Saturday, I awoke still peckish. By mid-morning there seemed little left to go amiss.

The temperature always dips low at night, but that morning there was ice on the water in my basin. The hearth of the round adobe fireplace in the corner of my room was not only cold and empty; a stream of frigid air was streaming down the chimney and across the floor to stab at my bare ankles. I had put off sending some hands into the mountains to fetch more firewood, hoping they could bring back a Christmas tree as well. Now, with winter seeming in a rush, the fresh-cut logs would be full of sap, would pop and spit burning splinters.

Venturing to the outhouse and lowering my backside onto that icy plank used up the few shreds of courage that remained to me. I tried to wash up without touching any more of the ice water than absolutely necessary, which tended to defeat the purpose. My mirror showed a stranger's worn face.

In the barn I found Ruben and Julio mucking out and dispatched them to the hillside for wood. They were not at all sorry to leave the mucking to me.

I jabbed a pitchfork into the straw and began to toss it forward. A gust of wind swept through the barn, slapping the hay straight into my face. I was picking the stiff strands from my eyelashes when I heard horse hooves drumming, hell-bent for leather. I stepped out of the barn to find one of the men I least wanted to see in all the world reining his horse to a halt.

Lieutenant Tyler Morris had come alone this time. A chill settled in the small of my back. I didn't fancy this visit at all.

Crossing my arms, I waited until his horse settled down and stopped snorting. He had ridden the mare too fast—foam was clinging to her neck and withers, and in this cold that would do her no good. But I didn't offer a brush and blanket. A good deal of squawking came from the chicken roost where Winona was choosing a few for supper.

The lieutenant tipped his hat. "You are not a picture of Southern hospitality."

With neither the time nor the temper for idle talk, I cautioned myself not to be rude then ignored the advice. "Have you come to take more horses?"

"Come now, Miss Summerhayes. You do me a disservice. I bought eighteen horses from you. I didn't take them." He grinned and winked as if he expected me to swoon.

"You paid but half their worth."

He leaned forward and his wide-set eyes were quite earnest. "General Sibley himself sent me," he said. "He sends you his greetings."

A warning sounded in my head. This time Lieutenant Morris would take all my horses and pay nothing.

"You see, while the Army of New Mexico was making its way here, Indians raided the horse herd at night and made off with more than a hundred."

"I'm sorry to hear that, but I don't have a hundred horses. I don't have any at all to spare."

"Surely you could spare one or two. For the army that is here to protect you."

A cautious relief began to rise in me. If Tyler Morris had orders to commandeer all the horses, he wouldn't have come alone and he wouldn't be trying to cajole me with notions of patriotism. But the words were out before I could bite them back. "A colonel in that army shot a friend of mine in cold blood. And you told me the horses you took before were for Colonel Baylor, but he apparently did not receive them."

"Colonel Baylor is not a well man," Morris said quickly. "He has not been well for quite some time. Perhaps the exertions required of the governor were too great. His memory began failing him soon after we arrived. And then that most unfortunate incident—" The lieutenant's gaze bounced from me to something just beyond my left shoulder. The wide-set brown eyes widened, and blood seemed to drain from his face, leaving a greyish pallor beneath the tan. A white half-moon scar stood out on his temple.

I snatched a glance over my shoulder, expecting someone with a rifle or at least an overbold coyote; but it was only Winona, who was eyeing him quizzically, a pair of fresh-killed hens still dribbling blood dangling from her hand. She turned and went on to the kitchen.

Morris nervously turned his horse, his jaw set, his eyes so wide the white showed top and bottom. "That the slave woman? The witch?"

Now I was the nervy one. "Winona is no slave and no witch. She's never done anyone harm." I cast about for something to turn his attention. "How many horses do you need?"

The mare, sensing her rider's distress, was taking quick, agitated steps in place. He gave a sharp pull on the reins, the last thing one should do with a skittish horse. The mare's ears twitched, and she brought her front feet a few inches off the ground.

"That woman is not harmless," Morris shouted. "You're a fool if you believe she is." He jabbed his chin toward the house. "She will slaughter you in your bed!"

The reins went taut; and the mare leapt away toward the road, leaving me to watch bewildered as horse and rider became small with distance.

◇◇◇

When I finished cleaning out the barn, Winona was plucking the last of the chickens. Steam from the bucket where she had dunked the birds filled the kitchen with the sickish stench of wet feathers, but I scarcely noticed.

"The christening is tomorrow," she said.

"My brain isn't so addled that I don't know what day it is."

Ignoring my churlishness, she washed her hands, led me to the table, bade me sit and cover my eyes.

I protested, "I don't have time for nonsense." But she would have it no other way, so I obeyed.

When she commanded me to open my eyes, I could scarcely believe the bundle of cloth she was holding before them.

"You got nothing decent for the churching, so I find me a bit of calico here, a patch of muslin there."

It was a dress. The bodice and skirt were pale purple calico. Winona danced it about. In the back she had pieced together scraps of deep blue muslin over a big crescent of padding.

"A bustle?" I shouted. "Winona, is that a bustle?"

She grinned. "It do seem to me we will be the most fashionable ladies that town ever did see." She held up a similar one she had made for herself.

I flung my arms about her, unable to stop the tears.

Given those astonishing frocks, plus Tyler Morris' sudden retreat without a single horse, my spirits soared from the hollow void that had trapped them. By the next morning, I was fair looking forward to challenging Isabel's fool notions of witchcraft.

Zia, in her white silk gown, was a sight to behold, and she did know it. She would cock her head, roll those shiny brown eyes and wait for someone to look toward her. Then a smile would ignite, like the sun does when it first breaks the horizon on a clear day, full of energy and sheer delight.

Winona stood tall and proud, holding Zia as Father Raymond intoned the ritual words. I stood next to her, our pair of bustles in full view of envious parishioners. Isabel, her waist unbelievably narrow in a dark blue dress with little purple dots and at least a thousand buttons, was there behind us in the first row of pews.

Only half of me was listening to the padre; the other half was planning the small skirmish that would come as soon as we left the church. Isabel, I was certain, would not be able to resist making some remark to me about Winona. I would steer her to Tonio, introduce him as someone who had been educated at a monastery, who still had ties to the Church—he did send seed from time to time to Brother Mario. Tonio, as we had rehearsed, would say that he knew Winona to be an honorable woman, a good Catholic and certainly not a witch. I hoped God would not strike me dead for the "good Catholic" part.

On the other side of the church sat Herlinda, her squat body swathed in black as always, her face clamped in its perpetual frown. In the wagon, she had muttered a few words that brought a stream of Spanish from Nacho, and I had hoped he was telling her that an innocent babe should not have her baptismal day spoiled by a cantankerous woman.

When we set out for the cuevas to call for Tonio, Herlinda's jaws had been so tight you could see the cords in her neck. She had never mentioned seeing me that day at the cave, but I shifted nervously on my seat just the same. Still, she did regard Tonio as a holy man, and Herlinda was nothing if not devout. I was sure she would listen to what he would say about Winona. Father Raymond would be useless as an ally; but I figured if he were brought into it, his chronic befuddlement would likely not harm our cause.

People had openly inspected us as we arrived. Just about everyone who left town in fear of the Union Army had come back; the churchyard was full. Winona and Zia caused enough stir, but when Tonio descended from the wagon tongues really began clacking. I quite enjoyed it.

Father Raymond was droning on, and I wished he would get on with it. My feet ached. I hadn't worn proper shoes in months. I thought about the baptism rites and the wedding rites, and how in the depths of my misery with Andrew I had visited the Army's chaplain to beg for help. He had read to me from the Bible: "Thy desire shall be to thy husband and he shall rule over thee."

Zia was being baptized, but I hoped she would never wed.

At long last, the good padre placed his hand on her forehead. She giggled, eyes wide, face like honeyed tea. With that, a place for Zia's soul was reserved in heaven, and I had officially acquired a goddaughter.

I congratulated Winona, whispering a reminder that she should make herself scarce when church was dismissed. We turned toward the congregation. Lieutenant Morris' presence next to Isabel in the front pew gave me a start.

Outside, the sun was high and bright. I dawdled near the door waiting for Isabel. When she emerged, prim and stiffly straight, I moved toward her.

"Hello, Isabel, a pleasure to see you."

She drew herself even straighter and licked her thin, unpainted, almost-white lips. Her voice began so low I had to strain to hear, but it rose almost immediately to a harsh, defiant whine like that of a wasp. "You defile this church with the presence of that Nigra witch and her bastard child."

I paused, shocked at her harshness, but managed to answer calmly, "Zia is no bastard. Surely the Baptists would not stain a babe with such a lie. Her father is dead."

Isabel's eyes opened wide and she swayed a little. "Where?" she asked.

I wasn't sure what she meant. "Where was the child's father killed?"

Isabel's head bobbed like a bird pecking for worms.

"I don't rightly know. He was an Indian and—"

Isabel's lips made a bloodless little O. "An Indian! And her mother a witch! How dare you bring them into our church? You risk our immortal souls!"

I didn't try to point out that this wasn't her church, and that Father Raymond had been quite willing to perform the baptism. Never mind that I had paid an arm and a leg for a bottle of the finest red wine I could find to present as a gift when I had first discussed the baptism with him. Communion wine, of course.

Instead, I put my hand under her elbow ready to steer her toward Tonio, forced myself to smile and ask pleasantly, "Have you met Antonio Bernini? He lived a long time in a monastery in Italy and still has close connections to the Church. It's the Roman Church, to be sure, but so far as I know, the Romans are still quite Christian."

Isabel gave a good imitation of genuine concern for me. "My poor, dear Matty. You mean you don't know?"

"I'm sure Mr. Bernini will tell you he has talked with Winona," I carried on blithely. "He has examined her catechism"—I hoped it was possible to examine one's catechism—"and found her to be a good Catholic. And beyond any doubt, not a witch." I stopped. "Know what?"

"Your Antonio Bernini was defrocked by the Church."

I started to shake my head.

"Yes." Isabel's voice was firm as any preacher's. "Excommunicated. By the Pope. It seems the Church owned a gold mine. He was put in charge of the miners, and he stole huge amounts of gold. From the Church. Now he's come back for the rest."

"You must be mistaken."

"Yes, Matty. It was twenty or more years ago, but it did happen. When he first arrived here I heard rumors. I was so afraid for you, my dear. And as I was in frequent correspondence with the Missionary Society, I asked if they could find any information about him. And they did."

My eyes fastened on the little purple spots on Isabel's dress. They were violets. Tiny and dainty. My mind went blank of everything save that I hadn't seen a violet in many years. They reminded me of my mother. I was still trying desperately to pull myself together when a hand took firm hold of my shoulder, and I turned to look into the meaty face and mean little eyes of Sheriff Zeke Fountain.

"Just a moment, Zeke," I said distractedly, but his hand clamped my shoulder more tightly.

"'Fraid it can't wait," he growled, fair relishing the words: "I got to arrest you."

My mouth dropped open so wide it nigh dislocated my jaw. "What?"

Zeke cast his eyes to the sky then swung his blue gaze back to me. "Like I said. I got to arrest you. For the murder of a man of Mexican persuasion, found dead from gunshot on April twelve, year of our Lord 1861. In your barn. And..." The pronouncement apparently dried his throat. He cleared it then went on, "And for robbing, in March, year of our Lord 1857, the Cuthright and Dobbins Stagecoach Company."

Chapter Eighteen

To say the jail cell was cold and filthy would put too sweet a light on it. A mouthful of food had been spat on the floor—months before, by the look of it—and still lay there. The air stank of the sweat of a dozen or so past occupants. The sweat of fear.

I didn't care. I prayed for the world to end, to die in my sleep, to be hanged now, with no more ado. I railed at God. If not death, please, at least unconsciousness. I could not bear to think.

All that day and the next I don't believe I spoke a word. Neither did I eat the loathsome food Zeke brought, rattling the bars as he set it inside. At intervals, I was vaguely aware of Winona's voice somewhere in the distance but could not rouse myself from the backless, broken chair in the corner of that cell. I slept some, but it was more stupor than sleep, every inch of my being wrapped in a shroud of dull, unceasing ache.

Eventually, I could no longer sit in that awful chair. The setting sun was just extracting the last of its light from the bars of my tiny window when I rose and began to pace, like the wild mustangs sometimes do when first corralled. Mindless steps, going nowhere.

Slowly, my head began to clear.

I had not killed that piteous Mexican boy. But I could not prove it. No one else was there when he died but me. A sense of dread drenched my very soul, the same sinking, hopeless dread that had flooded over me in the office of J. Marcus Lewiston, the lawyer. I could no more prove I had not killed that boy than I could prove that Andrew threatened daily to kill me.

Why would anyone believe me? I was a convicted thief. I had, in fact, robbed the Dobbins and Cuthright Stage Coach. And I had been lying every time I answered to the name Matty Summerhayes.

I reached out to touch the cold bars; and my eyes fastened on my hands, the nails broken and chipped from mending fence. The palms ran with the same ice water that trickled down my sides, inside Winona's wonderful calico dress. All I had managed to do since my arrival was to remove the bustle to make the sitting easier.

Something skittered over my foot. I strangled a scream. A rat? One of those furry spiders as big as a man's fist, a tarantula?

A whiter haze of light began to inch into the cell. Restless now, I dragged the broken chair from the corner and climbed up to look through the window, which was little bigger than a belt buckle. The sight fair transfixed me.

A mystical trail of lights seemed to be slowly making its way from heaven to earth. Slowly, it came to me that this must be the Tortugas' Christmas pilgrimage. I knew the story from Jamie.

Converted centuries ago by Spanish padres, the Indians are intensely devoted to the Virgin of Guadalupe. Carrying her image, they wind their way up their small cone-shaped mountain gathering piles of grass and creosote along the way. Great signal fires are lit at the top, and when the Indians begin their descent after dark, they ignite each pile of brush as they pass. Jamie was right. The sight was wondrous to behold. Tears dammed up behind my cold, dry eyes broke free and surged down my cheeks.

Long after the tears were used up, I went on weeping. Between great dry shudders, I was grateful no one was around to hear me. I slept like the dead.

◇◇◇

A familiar voice called me back to the living next morning.

"Get up, Miss Matty!" Winona was saying. "You got to fight this. I brung you some clean duds. If you don't get yourself up right now and put 'em on, I'll be getting that sheriff to let me in there and I will change you like a baby. I am not leaving this jailhouse till you do as I say."

I did as I was told, pulling clothing off and on my benumbed limbs while Winona held a blanket against the bars to give some privacy.

"That feller out to the caves seems a right decent man. Is it true what they say?" she asked.

"You mean was he a priest cast out of the Church? I don't know. Can't rightly say that part bothers me much."

"Seems a mite farfetched that he stole all that gold," Winona said.

"Why would he even have had access to so much church treasure?"

Winona sniffed. "If you ask me, it's hogwash. People who steal themselves a big pile of gold don't go sleepin' in caves."

I was thinking that whatever the true story, he had hidden his past no more than I had hidden mine. And now he was exposed. Because of me.

"I got to tell you something," Winona said as I fastened the last button. "I don't want to, but I figure you would never forgive me…"

The hesitation, so unlike Winona, made me pause as I dragged my fingers through my filthy hair. The braid had completely untwined. "Well, put down that damn blanket and tell me," I said, my voice raspy with disuse. "There's nothing left that could harm me." But there was.

"There be men out to the ranch. Texas soldiers." She was watching me for a response. I gave none. "They is ridin' over the land, lookin' over the buildings." Her next words came out in a rush: "They say they aim to con…con-fis…"

"Confiscate?"

"That was it. Throw us off it, anyway." She peered around the blanket, saw me standing fully dressed and handed me a brush. "Fix that hair. You look like a madwoman."

I took the brush and began sorting out the tangles.

"That fella who come for the horses," Winona said, "he's the one in charge."

"They can't do that."

"They be sayin' they can. That you a murderess."

I thought about that while I plowed the brush through the snarls. Something still delicate but growing very fast began to stir inside me. "But I haven't been convicted. That is my land. Mine!" I shouted the last word.

"Be that as it may," she said, her voice sounding falsely calm. "There ain't a lot you can do about it while you're in here."

"Come hell or high water, they will not take it from me. They will not run my people off."

"I hope you is right, Miss Matty. I do whatever I can."

I gripped the broken chair and banged it against the bars. "Zeke!"

He appeared like a large, unsavory ghost. "Sheriff Fountain, to the likes of you," he snapped.

I drew myself up to my full height, which was nearly his own, dropped my chin and peered into his watery blue eyes. "There are Texans on my ranch. They aim to confiscate it."

Zeke gaped at me dumbly and shrugged. "Texans are runnin' the government now."

"They can't just ride out there and take my land, throw my people off it! I am innocent until proven guilty, or are the Confederates less civilized than the Federals?"

He shuffled his feet but said nothing.

"I have a right to a trial, Zeke. You know that. Maybe they could take the land if I'm convicted, but I haven't been convicted." My eyes flashed to Winona. "Go home, stand guard with a gun if you have to."

I fixed on Zeke again. "Where's the alcalde? Where's Guthrie?"

Winona stood mute while Zeke took a deep breath and twisted his thick-lipped mouth in an impatient grimace. "Guthrie ain't here. He left when the Texans came, and he ain't come back. He probably ain't alcalde anymore anyway. They'll send a judge up from Franklin, but that'll likely take a spell."

Winona left, but not before I saw a small smile that didn't match the set of her chin.

"All right, Zeke," I said, "for the time being, I'll settle for a pail of water. Two pails, as a matter of fact."

"Two pails of water!" He was so shocked at the request his voice broke.

"And some lye soap. If I send a message to the Women's Christian Union, they will be appalled at the disgusting condition of this jail."

If I had sent a message to the Women's Christian Union, they would have applauded my arrest and hoped for a hanging. But Zeke Fountain wouldn't be the first man who feared a woman's tongue more than a man's fist. His resolve began to teeter. I fixed him with my best stare.

Sheriff Zeke Fountain hitched up his pants, looked at the dust-encrusted ceiling for a while, and nodded.

◇◇◇

That night I dreamed of single-handedly horsewhipping those thieving Texans off my land. Accomplishing that quite easily, I settled myself on a rock where the land rises quick to meet the mountains and listened to the trickle of the dripping spring as the sunset painted those organ-pipe peaks crimson.

The next morning I was wakened by something brushing against my foot. Opening my eyes, I bit back a scream. A tarantula was trotting across the dirt floor toward a corner.

Seizing the back that had broken off the chair, I pursued the monster spider; but it climbed straight up the wall, its hairy grey body carried on black legs that seemed more than half a foot long. Near the low ceiling, it turned to look at me. I recalled Nacho saying that tarantulas eat insects and even an occasional mouse and decided that I could have a worse cellmate.

◇◇◇

I scrubbed myself and put on the clothing Winona had brought. Then I went to work on that jail cell. By the time I was satisfied the filth and vermin were gone it smelled of lye and my back ached, but I felt better. And I was much older than I had been a few days before.

Winona sent Julio with word that the Texans left without saying anything further. Whether they would be back she didn't know. He also brought more clothes, a clean bedroll and a big container of tamales and pinto beans, which I wolfed down. The jail food was unspeakable.

This was not my first jail cell. I was grateful my parents could not know. Papa had doted on me. My dear mother was not granted a strong constitution. News of how their only child had disgraced herself would have killed my father and sent poor Mama mad.

I had come into the world in a drafty castle near the village of Durnstein, in Austria. The castle was impossible to keep in good repair, but the farms provided us a living.

One early-spring day that had seemed like any other, Papa solemnly announced that the country was teetering on the brink of revolution—the emperor was feebleminded, the archdukes scarcely possessed the intelligence of geese and the people's only hope, the minister of foreign affairs, was becoming a cruel reactionary. Papa was resolved that we should go to America.

My mother didn't want to go, but my father believed in the New World more than he believed in God and he could charm the teeth from a snake; Mama could deny him nothing. To keep her happy, he invited her mother to accompany them.

As a girl, my grandmother had run off with a Czech stableboy. He died of a liver ailment before they could marry but not before my mother was conceived. Nanny's own parents must have been decent souls because they had welcomed her back, concocted some story and eventually left her their moderate wealth.

Unlike my mother, who doted on ribbons and lace and dressing for dinner, Nanny cared little for society, preferring to spend her time in solitary pursuits. One of these was her flute, which she taught to me. More than once she sent my mother into despair with her disregard for proper style. Nanny had a penchant for saucy, outrageous bonnets and would wear a Bonaparte hat even to visit the green grocer. When Papa announced we would all go to America, Nanny thought it was a glorious idea.

For my part I, too, was glad enough to go.

Papa, having no son, had taught me how to keep accounts, how the planting should be done, even how to settle disputes among the peasants who worked the farms. Mama was forever squabbling with him over proper activity for a lady. At fifteen, I was certain that anywhere would be better than Durnstein, where the Danube—and precious little else—paused on its way to Vienna. The cobblestone streets and wattle-and-daub houses had begun crumbling long before the Americans had declared independence. The only event of any moment had been the capture for ransom of some dotty English king in the twelfth century.

My father had heard of the plight of the Negroes in America, and that urged him on. He would purchase a farm in Missouri, would buy a few black folk from their cruel masters and help them to settle on part of his land. It didn't work out quite that way.

He did buy the land. And Mother enrolled me at Bartholomew's Ladies Academy. She fussed over my hair and hired a seamstress to make me a whole new wardrobe so I should not be out of style in such sublime company. I fought all the frippery, I was a headstrong girl, and when Mama fell ill of a wasting disease I was stricken with guilt. I began taking elaborate pains with my appearance to please her.

Two weeks after I graduated from the academy, my dear papa was struck down by a heart no one knew was ailing. Nanny and I arranged the funeral and saw him into the ground. Mother was too weak to be much aware of anything; she lingered another six months.

I had hardly begun to think straight when Nanny shocked everyone—me most of all—by announcing she was getting married. At age seventy-four, my grandmother, who had borne a child but had never wed, married the haberdasher from whom she bought her audacious hats.

I wandered about our huge house feeling gloomy and abandoned. My friends declared that a husband would make my life cheery again and insisted I attend as many parties as possible. To my dismay, I found them quite tiresome. Each month, another of my erstwhile classmates announced her engagement. I feared my mother was right: Papa had treated me too much like a son and my willful ways would never attract a suitor. I resolved to sweeten my behavior.

Crossing the street one day, I was splattered with mud by a passing carriage; and as I was trying to repair the damage, I felt a hand on my elbow and looked up into the face of Andrew Collins. His Irish dash, mixed part and part with a lost-boy manner, snatched at my heart and lodged it permanently in my throat. He was a lieutenant in the First Missouri Cavalry, and I wager you will never set eyes upon a handsomer figure in a uniform.

He smiled a wise-wistful-private-joke sort of smile that was all from the eyes. A broad forelock of red-blond hair slid slantwise across his forehead.

And I was as lost as the Isle of Atlantis.

Chapter Nineteen

I named the tarantula Evelina. Whether it was female I hadn't the slightest idea, but it was so fastidious about dispatching cockroaches I decided it must be.

Sheriff Zeke Fountain was astonished by my cleaning efforts and apparently thought I enjoyed it too much because he nattered something about not being sure such activity was allowed.

"You sound like a government man from back East," I said, which made him snort and eye me as if I might be some sort of spy. I added to his discomfort by asking, "Where in the name of God do these dreadful victuals come from?"

He cast me an insulted look.

I leveled a gaze at him. "Fetch me a small stove, Zeke. There must be an old one around somewhere."

"A stove!" He banged a thick fist against the bars that separated us. "You know I can't do that, Matty."

"Why not? It's cold in here, for one thing. I need the heat. You wouldn't want me to call the Women's Christian Union down on you for abusing a prisoner, would you? And I'm a sight better cook than whoever prepares that slop. It's not fit for pigs."

He shook his head and stomped off, muttering.

I heaved a sigh and sank onto the chair that was still minus its back, thinking Zeke probably wouldn't be sheriff if his cousins didn't own half the valley. Tomorrow, I'd badger him to bring a hammer and nails so I could fix the chair. It had been quite elegant once—mahogany, with graceful claw feet, it looked rather like the chairs I took with me from St. Louis.

◇◇◇

When Andrew continued to drink himself to madness, I slipped away one morning and took the carriage into town. There, I found J. Marcus Lewiston, attorney at law, and begged an interview.

He was a slight gentleman with narrow wrists inside white shirt cuffs starched stiff as boards. A shock of very white hair fell across a pale brow above an equally white mustache.

I explained my plight.

He listened carefully, asking a few questions.

"I did not come to this union penniless," I finished, "but my husband has taken charge of my funds."

"Of course." He rose from his desk, examined for a time the cases of books behind it then turned to me.

"Regaining your property, if any remains, might be possible. But it would be no easy matter and doubtless take considerable time. How do you propose to live during this process?"

I stared at him. "I don't know."

"Have you children, madam?"

I hesitated. "No."

"But you are with child."

I could feel a flush engulf my face. "How did you know?"

"That is when women in your circumstances seek my counsel." He held my eyes then turned his face to the window. "I regret that I have no advice for you except to endure."

"But suppose I find some source of support?" I gasped. "A divorce is not possible?" My voice wavered on the last syllables.

"Not if you wish to keep this child with you after it is born. Your husband would be its guardian."

"Even given the...way he is?"

"Could you prove that? Are there witnesses?"

I couldn't seem to shape my lips around words to answer.

"Even if you could prove it, the likelihood is very, very great that your husband still would be given guardianship. Think it over, madam. My advice is to endure."

◇◇◇

I grasped the bars of my cell and peered into Winona's face.

"You do look right pert, Miss Matty. It appears you is doing a sight better."

"Did the Confederates come back? Do they still think they can take my land?"

"Nosiree. I ain't seen hide nor hair of them buzzards. I had me some words with them, but I don't know as that's what sent them off.

"'She do got certain rights, sir,' that's what I told 'em. That lieutenant, he calls me a witch and I tells him 'If you think I got the powers of a witch, maybe you better think about that some more.'"

Zia, sleepy and untroubled, was hugging Winona's shoulder.

Zeke appeared behind Winona. "You got twenty minutes, Matty," he muttered. "I got me an errand to run." He scratched a bushy eyebrow, grunted and disappeared.

I put my hand through the bars and patted Zia, who stirred and found her mouth with her thumb. "She's twice as big as she was. She's been okay? No croup?"

"She be fine. Other things ain't so fine."

I raised my eyes to meet Winona's.

"Someone sure do think we got something, and they wants it," she said. "We was all out workin' yesterday. I made me this contraption to carry Zia on my back like the Injun women do an' I was mucking out the barn. When I got back to the house, I seen right quick someone been there. He sure to God made a mess. All them papers from your desk was throwed this way and that, clothes chucked out of bureau drawers and I don't know what all. Every room. Even onions dumped out an' rollin' around on the kitchen floor. Whosomever done it weren't particular."

"Your room, too?"

"Yes, indeedy. Like I got something worth lookin' for."

"What was taken?"

"That be the funny part. We don't know if anything's missin' from your papers or your clothes, but nothing else seems gone. Just mussed up. 'Specially your papers. And whosomever it was, I reckon he figgered he didn't make a big enough mess, 'cause he come back in the night."

I blinked. "While everyone was there?"

"Not to the house. This mornin', Nacho say someone was rootin' around in the barn last night. There was pictures all here and there. Seems like that Julio kid be fancying himself an artist."

"Julio? An artist?"

"Well, he does make pictures. An' I reckon the barn be where he keeps his stuff. Probably he's drawing when you think he's working. I got to say, though, he does a fair job at drawing. He got some real good likenesses of folks. He seemed real embarrassed to see 'em all layin' around like that."

"But what would anyone be after in the barn?"

Winona's shoulders rose and fell eloquently. "Maybe someone thinks you got a solid gold saddle. Even feed sacks was spilled all over."

I knew full well there was only one thing I had that anyone might want: the small wooden chest I'd brought with me to the Mesilla Valley. Only one person knew about the chest, and he wasn't likely ever to set foot on the ranch. Then it occurred to me that a thorough enough thief could have found it accidentally. "Were any of the walls of the house damaged? I mean the inside walls."

"Miss Matty, this place be affectin' your brain. Why would a thief mess up a…" Her voice slowed. "…a wall." She rolled her eyes and looked at me hard. "I don't want to know."

She knew about that chest and that it was full of double eagles and slugs. I had used most of the heavy, eight-sided fifty-dollar slugs to purchase the ranch.

Zia yawned and was shoving her fist into her mouth, melting my heart, when sounds of boots scuffling and men grunting came from the front of the jail. Something heavy met the floor with a thump and a clatter. She turned to stare at something I couldn't see. "What in tarnation is that?"

Zeke's voice growled irritably, "She wants a goddam stove."

A grin filled half Winona's face with gleaming white teeth. "Well, if that don't beat all." She bussed my cheek through the bars, winked at me and disappeared.

Zeke emerged from the hall mopping his head and neck with a blue rag that might once have been a bandana.

"Winona says someone broke into the house. Made a mess of things."

He nodded. "So I heard."

"Well, I don't see you getting on your horse and getting out there to see what's going on. Or did the Texans pass a law saying it's okay for thieves to ransack your neighbor's house as long as they leave yours alone?"

Zeke shook his head. "You think that's all I got to do? I heard nothing was stolen, nobody out there saw anything and nobody could tell if anything was taken."

"So you aren't even going to look into it?" Suddenly, I thought of the map I had found on the dead boy in the barn. Could whoever had searched the house have been after that?

Zeke was scratching the top of his head. "Tell you what. I'll send a deputy around to the saloons to see if anyone heard anything about it. That's about the best I can do." He opened the lock on my cell. "Now stand back so me and Murphy can get by. This fool thing ain't big, but it's sure enough heavy as a dead ox."

Scraggly, yellow-haired Murphy was big, but more than one or two of his wits were among the missing. He helped Zeke with fetch-and-carry work. They wrestled the small iron stove into a corner of the cell, grunting and groaning and complaining every inch of the way.

"Don't put it there," I said.

Zeke mopped his head, his chest heaving with the exertion. "Why not?"

I pointed to the wall beneath the tiny window. "It has to go there, and I'll need a pipe to send the smoke out."

Zeke groaned, but they moved the stove. Then he sent Murphy back to wherever he'd come from.

"Thanks—" I began, but he cut me off.

"Don't thank me. I'm sick and tired of your natterin' about my cooking. Fact is, I ain't fond of my cooking myself."

"You were doing the cooking?"

"You think we got a chef from Atlanta, maybe?"

"You mean you were eating the same food?"

"Of course, I been eatin' the same food." A sad look passed over his face, and I remembered that his wife had run off.

"What was her name?" I asked gently. "Your wife?"

"Dora," he grunted and examined the toes of his boots. When he looked up, his blue eyes were shiny. "She was a good cook, was Dora," he said in a tight voice.

"I'm sorry—" I began.

"Didn't harm me none," he muttered and stalked out, banging the cell door behind him. "I'll find you a dang stovepipe."

I didn't call out to tell him he'd forgotten to lock my cell; I just wrapped the arm of the big padlock around the two center bars and snapped it locked myself. I wasn't about to try to break out. Leastways, not right then.

I was wondering whether Dora was just a silly twit who would have run off with anyone who gave her a lace hanky or whether, like Andrew, Sheriff Zeke Fountain had an ugly side that drove her to seek any available refuge.

Chapter Twenty

When Andrew raised the notion that I should plead his case with General Wilkinson, I had my first inkling for escape. At first I thrust that idea away; my visit to the lawyer a few weeks before had been such a failure, I feared to hope for anything. But as Andrew became set upon sending me to the general on my own, I began to form a plan.

Winona, of course, had caught me trying to cover the bruises on my face. One morning, when Andrew had left the house, I went to the kitchen and told her everything.

"I knows somethin' be powerful wrong," she said. "I did not know it be that bad."

"You don't have to go with me," I told her. "I don't think he would do any harm to you."

"Sure to God you ain't that dumb, Miss Matty. He only thinks he own you. He knows he own me. He knows I can't go to nobody. He knows if I run away he could get them to set the hounds on me."

I squeezed my eyes shut against a headache that threatened to split the top of my head. "As soon as we get to Santa Fe, I'll set you free."

"That would be mighty nice. But the first thing we got to do is get there."

It didn't take long to pack. There was little I wanted beyond my mother's silver and a few clothes. There was no question of

Andrew ever relinquishing any of my own funds to me, and I could take nothing he might notice, nothing that might alert him to my plan, until I'd had time to get far enough away. I only hoped I could sell the silver for enough money to get back to St. Louis.

By the time Andrew returned in mid-afternoon, I was ready. We had hitched Fanny and a black horse to the wagon, and I had sent Winona back to the cabin she shared with four women who washed clothes for the army.

Andrew's head hung lower and lower as he ate the supper Winona had prepared, and I waited for whatever final horror I was sure he had in store.

Instead, he looked at me, and a tear drizzled down his cheek. "Please, Matty, don't desert me."

Something fluttered inside me, and I found myself reaching out to pat his arm and reassure him. But by the time I touched him, his eyes had closed and his head fell to the table. I sat stunned, staring at him, thinking him dead, feeling a peculiar mix of joy and fear and sorrow.

Then Andrew began to snore, and I realized he had doubtless spent the afternoon drinking and had merely passed out. I was carefully and quietly getting up from the table when Winona appeared in the kitchen doorway.

"We ready?"

"Sssh," I motioned then whispered, "He's asleep. It's best we don't wake him."

"He ain't gonna wake up. Not soon, anyways. I done give him enough yarrow leaves in his soup to keep him quiet a good long time."

I stared at her. "You poisoned him?"

"I sure did want to, yes, indeed. But I got to thinkin' you don't know what he has tol' folks about you. He might of told 'em you are the crazy one. He might of told 'em you're dangerous. So I just give him enough to put him good and sound asleep."

She leaned over Andrew then straightened. "Seeing as he probably had him a snoot-full of whiskey to boot, he likely gonna sleep right there till tomorrow night. He gonna feel sickish, but he wake up all right. More's the pity."

I expelled my breath all in a rush. "Thank you," I whispered, not sure whether I was thanking her for putting him to sleep or for not killing him. "Let's get on with it then."

◇◇◇

I know exactly when I conceived the most outlandish scheme a sane woman could imagine

Winona and I found the trail along the river and followed it north most of the night. The moon was plenty bright, the horses fresh; and with every mile we covered I felt a little lighter.

We stopped a few hours before dawn, threw our bedrolls on the ground and collapsed onto them. I wasn't much worried about Indians or coyotes. Perhaps any threat the desert might harbor seemed tame compared to living with Andrew. And I had brought the revolver he'd used to torment me, as well as a full flask of powder and his entire stock of caps and balls. I hadn't done any shooting in a very long time, but I knew how. My father had taught me when I was little more than a child, placing targets in the meadow behind the castle in Durnstein.

It wasn't until much later that it amused me to grasp the pistol Andrew had held so often to my own head and to use it the way I eventually did.

I curled up and fell into the first sound sleep I'd had in many months, and woke to the smell of coffee and sizzling bacon. Winona had built a fire just big enough for a kettle and a frypan. The aromas mixed with a spicy odor of some desert shrub and nothing had ever smelled so sweet. It was the smell of freedom.

"'Bout time," Winona said. "I thought maybe you was plannin' to sleep all day."

I drank my coffee, ate a day-old biscuit and gazed at a sky the color of royal robes.

A dreadful thought disturbed my relief at having escaped: even if I could sell the silver, even if I managed to return to St. Louis, Andrew would eventually look for me there. He would never let me go.

"Would it be askin' too much to know where we is goin'?" Winona asked.

"I guess we're headed for Santa Fe." But the last thing in the world I wanted to do was meet Andrew there as he had planned.

"Well, if we wait here long enough, that stage is gonna come along and your husband is gonna be on it. Seems like we best get off this here trail and find us another."

In that moment, I knew precisely what I was going to do. "No."

"What you mean, no?"

"We are going to wait for that stage." By the time I finished, a wave of giddiness was washing over me; and I barely got a few feet from the camp before I threw up.

"You is plumb crazy, Miss Matty." Winona drew herself up to her full height, crossed her arms over her chest and fixed me with a stare.

"What else am I to do? Throw myself on the mercy of General Wilkinson? And have him hand me over to Andrew with some whispered advice that he should keep a better eye on his dotty wife?"

"You is gonna get yourself killed, is what you're gonna do."

"Except for that silver, I am penniless," I flung back. "I can't go back to St. Louis because that's the first place Andrew will look for me." I didn't add that if Andrew found me nothing would stop him from taking the child I was carrying.

"If you don' get yourself shot on the spot, they catch you for sure; and then they hang you. They hang me, too, for good measure."

"If we're careful, we can do it. Yes, we can. Then we can go to Albuquerque and draw up your freedom papers." I wished my own freedom would be as easy.

Winona's head moved like a pendulum. "You is daft as a doorknob."

She was sitting on a rock next to our second night's camp; and I was making my case, pacing back and forth in the dust in front of her like a lawyer in front of a judge. "Winona, you don't understand. I have about twenty dollars and my grandmother's silver. That might get us a couple weeks lodging. Then what? Besides, I'm nigh to certain a good share of the money in that chest is mine and he stole the rest."

"That may be, but you don' want to lose your life gettin' it, neither."

I was standing there in the sun, waving my arms about, trying to persuade her to help me rob my husband, when I fainted.

Winona was holding a cup to my lips when I came to. "Lordy, Lordy," she grunted. "You coulda told me you be 'spectin' a child. I should of seen it myself, but I never set foot in that house of yours without countin' the minutes. The air was so thick and ugly and I paid no mind to anything but gettin' out of there."

"I'm okay now," I said, wiping my hand across my face.

"Course you is, honey. You is in perfect trim to go out there and rob you a stagecoach."

◇◇◇

In the end, of course, she agreed. I explained why Andrew must at all cost be kept from learning about the child.

We had almost a week to prepare. In Socorro, we purchased a pair of ready-made breeches and more powder, caps and balls. I was nervy, prepared to give the clerk a story about the son for whom I was buying these things; but he barely glanced at me except to take my carefully counted coins.

We examined dozens of places along the trail, looking for the best site from which to launch our foray into crime. Mornings and evenings, I would take a dead coal from our fire, draw a target on some rock and practice shooting. I wanted Winona to give it a try, too, but she told me my brain was made of green cheese.

"It makes me shudder just to touch a gun," she said. "I can fair feel the death in it."

I insisted on showing her the mechanics of loading and firing, but after that she would twist bits of cotton, poke them into her ears and crouch behind a rock while I tried to gouge holes in the target. One can't gain a whole lot of skill in a week's time, but I did improve.

◇◇◇

The rock was huge and orange-brown and looked like a camel kneeling for a drink. Wind had scoured the corners round and there looked to be a small hollowed-out place facing the trail. I walked around it, examining every possible angle of view.

What looked like a single rock was actually three. The space between the larger two was just wide enough for a horse to squeeze through. "This is it," I told Winona as we pitched our camp in its shadow.

We reckoned we had about four days left. We used three to rehearse. I drilled with Fanny, repeating the sequence over and over again, stopping only for another round of target practice. We had to hunt for a long time along the riverbank to find a fallen tree big enough to do the job I had in mind and small enough for us to drag.

On the last night, we feasted on a supper of beans and onions. Then I sprawled on the ground in front of the fire and watched the sky blacken while Winona chopped at my hair. "Just make it short enough to push up under the hat. With any luck, they'll be looking for a man afterwards."

"Has it entered that head of yours that you is also gonna be lookin' like a man when they're lookin' for a man?" Winona cut another handful of my hair with the big knife we had brought along for rope and bread and salt beef.

I fingered a severed lock that had cascaded over my shoulder and dropped into my lap. It would be a long time before a thick, luxurious braid would run down my back again. "They won't be expecting their man to be wearing a skirt." I turned to look at her. "You're sure you know what to do?" She nodded and went back to cutting.

Our plan was simple. From the top of the rock I could see a good way down the trail. The stage driver wouldn't see the tree across the trail until he rounded the bend a half-mile from the rock. It would take about that distance to halt the horses. I was sure this wouldn't be the first time this sort of trick had been tried, so the fellow riding shotgun would be looking to the rear, watching for someone to ride up from behind while the driver would probably be scanning the landscape to the front.

We had estimated and measured carefully. The fallen tree should bring the stage to a stop very near the split between the two rocks. I would simply step out, open the stage door, wave my gun in the passengers' faces—one of which would be Andrew's—and relieve them of their valuables.

I would have to take everyone's jewelry and timepieces and hand baggage. Andrew would doubtless have that cherrywood chest inside the coach where he could keep an eye on it, but I couldn't take only that or any fool would be able to figure out that Andrew was the target.

I would black my face with ashes and cover everything but my eyes with a bandana. And I would be wearing breeches and trying to make my movements those of a man. I would only gesture and maybe grunt. I wouldn't speak. Perhaps, in the shock of the moment, even Andrew wouldn't recognize me.

I would depart through the rock to a cleft in its backside where Fanny would be waiting next to a fresh-dug hole. I had many times rehearsed flinging my stolen goods into the hole, kicking the dirt over it and stomping it smooth. That should take no more than twenty seconds. I'd had Winona count it out. I was certain no one would expect me to leave the goods there. The cleft hid the signs of digging.

Then I would leap onto Fanny's back and in another thirty seconds I would disappear behind another outcropping of rock less than a quarter-mile upriver. Two miles further, in a thicket of squat pine and juniper trees, were more giant rocks; and in one was a small niche just big enough for me to slip inside. There, I would scrub my face, put on a dress and lie low for the rest of the day. The hour before nightfall, I would head back to the place where we had decided Winona would set up camp.

No one could follow. Even if there were horses tied behind the stage, there wouldn't be time to untie them before I vanished.

Chapter Twenty-one

I could see the puffs of dust kicked up by the stagecoach much further away than I expected. It was an hour past midday, and the heat was rising in waves. The horses were clear and sharp in the sun, but the dust became a trail of smoky haze almost concealing the coach, so it looked like the horses were trying to charge out of a fog from which they couldn't quite free themselves. There was plenty of time.

Winona and I had packed up our camp that morning and dragged the young cottonwood across the trail. It had only recently been uprooted by the wind; the leaves were still green and just beginning to wilt.

We feared someone else would come down the trail before the stagecoach and find the tree, or that the stage company had hired outriders. But there had been no sight of anyone in the four days we had camped there, and no one appeared that morning.

Winona had climbed into the wagon, picked up the reins, raised her chin and stared straight into my eyes. I expected some last-minute instructions or another attempt to talk me out of this folly, but all she said was, "I ain't met many people I liked, black or white. And I ain't about to lose one of 'em today, you hear?"

My confidence waned when she was out of sight and the full import of what I was doing descended upon me. It was all I could do not to mount Fanny and gallop after her, so I sat down to keep my feet from running.

Fully understanding how soldiers felt approaching a battlefield, I drew idly in the dirt with a stick, wondering if I'd ever see my friend again, if I would even live through the day. By noon, I had lived and relived every possible mishap twice, my every muscle so tense I near squeaked when I moved.

As the stage neared the bend, I scrambled off the rock and took up my post in the narrow passageway.

I could hear the hooves pounding, pounding. When the wheels began to screech as the driver started to saw at the reins, a clammy chill seeped down my spine to my heels and I fought off a wave of dizziness.

We had chosen the perfect place for the tree. The stage clattered to a halt directly in front of me. I could see the letters on the door: *Cuthright & Dobbins Stagecoach Co.*

Raising my chin, I stepped out from the rocks onto the trail. The driver was peering at the tree that blocked the horses. The shotgun rider was scanning the trail behind. No one was looking to the side. Five more steps, and my hand was on the coach's brass door handle.

I yanked the door open. The step was high, but I had known it would be. I didn't break stride as I stepped inside. The passengers gaped at me, still trying to register what was happening. It was then that I realized that I did not so much fear being shot or caught as I was terrified to see Andrew again.

He sat slouched against the window, his feet propped on his mother's chest. My palms began to sweat. But he only stared at me uncomprehendingly.

A dour old woman in black sat next to him, her broad face beginning to register alarm. I waved my pistol in her face and pulled her handbag from her unresisting arm.

The other passenger was a man with thinning blond hair. Without prompting, he handed me a silver pocket watch. I pointed at the strap that showed at his collar and he produced a money pouch.

I could hear the driver grumbling about delay, and the coach rocked slightly as someone got down to move the tree. No sign of panic from those in charge. Yet.

I stooped and yanked Andrew's chest from beneath his feet. It felt heavy as a ship's anchor. When I straightened, he was staring straight into my eyes all the way to my soul. I froze, my legs like trees rooted to the spot. His mouth opened and he said my name—"Matty"—in a voice that was part anger, part terror.

I turned and fled. The chest no longer seemed heavy at all. In three steps I was across the trail and between the rocks, two more and I was out the other side, where I dropped everything I was carrying except the pistol into the hole I had dug. I kicked dirt over it and, just the way I had practiced, I leapt and landed on Fanny's back. She knew the game well and within seconds was at a full gallop.

Something whined past my ear. Someone was shooting at me. I didn't turn—it didn't matter who it was. Seconds later Fanny and I sailed around the rocky outcropping and into the stand of trees, moving so fast that the leaves and trunks were a blur.

Elation rose in me like the froth on boiling milk. I hadn't been caught or injured. *I did it, did it, did it* repeated over and over in my brain. It was over.

◇◇◇

Lying still inside that tiny cave for the rest of the afternoon was one of the hardest things I ever did. I had changed clothes and cleaned myself up as best I could. Four times I checked to be sure the pistol was loaded before I stowed it in the wide canvas sack I had taken from Fanny's saddlebag. My heart would not stop its drumming in my ears, and my head and back began to ache as if I'd been flogged.

At last, the sky began to dim with dusk. I slipped out of the cave and moved toward where I had left Fanny among the trees. My senses must have been numb because I heard nothing but the insects until something struck me across the side of my head.

I teetered, and the ground seemed to rise to meet me. Wrenching my head around, I toppled. My attacker's face was twisted with rage, the whites showing full around the knotted pupils of his eyes. A piece of wood dangled from his hand like a club. The mouth was screaming, "Where is my mother's chest?"

Andrew.

Fool! I cursed myself. Why hadn't I kept the pistol in my hand?

The canvas sack had fallen beneath me. I slipped my hand inside, and my fingers closed around the revolver.

Andrew's hands twisted in what was left of my hair and jerked me upright like a marionette. I raised the gun and pointed it straight into his face. He let go and I wobbled, holding the gun as firmly as I could as I staggered backward.

His eyes lost their malevolence and took on a hunted look. "Don't, Matty," he pleaded.

Habits of the heart die very, very hard. I was drawing a shaky breath when the chunk of wood he had been holding slammed into my side. The rage had leaped again to his eyes.

I brought my left hand up to steady the gun.

"Pull the trigger," he taunted. "Shoot me. You haven't the nerve."

Even with both my hands steadying it, the revolver teetered. In that moment I wanted him dead more than I had ever wanted anything. But I couldn't pull the trigger.

He lunged at me, reaching for the revolver. I slammed it into his head sideways. Andrew hit the ground like a felled tree.

I spun around and ran. Through the trees, in the deepening dusk, I could see Fanny and, near her, a dark horse with a pale mane. No other horse. Andrew must have gotten a mount from somewhere and ridden back alone. His finding Fanny had been just a piece of luck.

I picked up a fallen cottonwood branch and swung it at the hindquarters of the dark horse as hard as I could. The horse whinnied with surprise and took off.

For the second time that day I leaped into Fanny's saddle. Feeling nothing but the wind in my face and the rapid thud of my pulse in my ears as we flew over the rocky ground, I prayed she would not stumble. Darkness was coming in.

Even when I saw the clearing where Winona was waiting I didn't slow. Finally, I toppled from Fanny's back and sagged onto Winona's shoulder. "It's done. The chest is buried." I drew back, breathless. "Andrew came after me. It was hideous."

"I hopes you kilt him."

"I wish to God I had."

Winona stiffened. "Lord, child, you is sopped."

I put my hand to my head where Andrew had hit me. It came away dark and wet.

Winona shook her head, her eyes big with worry. "That ain't the worst of it. Turn 'round." My skirt was soaked. I was trailing a river of blood. A column of hot pain shot up inside me like boiling oil, searing my innards. I teetered and fell. Through the night and late into the next day I lay on my bedroll writhing with the pain that had wrapped itself around my guts while she mopped my face with a damp cloth and held liquids to my lips, insisting that I drink. I told her we were short of water and not to waste it, but she paid no heed.

Toward noon, I must have fallen asleep. It was almost dark when I felt her hand on my brow. My eyes were like drops of lead, but I forced them open.

"It's done over with," Winona said.

I wasn't sure what she meant.

"The baby's gone," she said.

What baby? I couldn't think what she was talking about. Then it came clear. I no longer need fret about Andrew taking the child. God had seen to that.

◇◇◇

I awoke that night with the moon streaming full into my face. I closed my eyes against it and lay listening to Winona's soft gurgling snores. I hadn't thought beyond this point. What should I do now?

The next morning, Winona said I should lie in another day.

"No. We need to pack up. We need to get into Albuquerque."

She frowned. "Albuquerque? What you thinking of? We got to lay low awhile."

"I want to get it over with."

"That's good," she said. "I like to get things over with. What we talkin' about?"

"I'm going to turn myself in."

"You gone daft, child? You done got away with it. You ain't gonna do no such thing as turn yourself in now!"

"Andrew recognized me," I said slowly. "No telling who he told, but I reckon he told the people on the stagecoach." I squinted through the morning sun at her. "I don't cotton to living the rest of my life haunted and hunted and looking over my shoulder."

"I do believe you is hitching the donkey to the wrong end of the cart. Why did you go and do it all, then?"

"I'm going to draw up your freedom papers. You take Fanny and get someone to board her."

Winona threw her hands in the air, looking quite like a goose getting ready to take off.

I ignored her. "I am going to the nearest sheriff's office and return everything I took except that chest. And turn myself in."

Chapter Twenty-two

Zeke Fountain peered at me from the corridor. I must have dozed off because, for a moment, I could not think why there were bars across my room. I could not be in jail. I had turned myself in. I had done my time for the stagecoach job.

Giving everything back except that chest got me a shorter sentence. Three years, four months and six days later they set me free. And the chest was still right where I had stowed it next to that rock.

"Someone to see you," Zeke said, and Nacho, clearly uncomfortable, appeared beside him. "Looks like we may be lettin' you go soon," Zeke added, then ambled off.

Nacho was holding his hat in both hands like he does in church. "*Señora…*"

"What did he mean, they may be letting me go?"

Nacho's head bobbed up and down. His face was the color and shape of a cow's kidney, the nose broad and round. He still had a full head of wiry hair, but it had long ago gone grey. Even the little hairs that grew out of his ears were grey. Horses understood every word he said, but I was never sure that I did. "I make decision."

My outgoing breath stopped in my throat. Please don't let him say he's moving on. "I forgot your pay. I'm truly sorry. Send Winona back here, and I'll explain things to her. She will pay you immediately."

He nodded solemnly. *"Si, gracias."* He cleared his throat and said again, "I make decision."

I wanted to beg, to plead, but I knew it would do no good. And without Nacho, my hopes for building a reputation in horse breeding were as good as dead.

His eyes almost disappeared behind his cheeks as he squinted at me. "I say to Señor Fountain I know you did not kill."

The rest of my breath burst from my lungs. I was not sure I heard right. "You did what?"

Nacho nodded, his eyes holding mine the same way he looked at horses. "I tell him I see you in *la casa*, in the house, when the man fall down outside."

Bewildered, I examined his face. "How did you know that? You weren't there. You had already gone to bed." If he was there, why had he waited until now?

"Si." He looked down at his feet. "Was not me. Was Herlinda. She go to kitchen. She see you in room. She see *hombre*."

"Why didn't she say so before?" Had Herlinda been spying on me even then?

"Quién sabe? Who knows? Maybe she is afraid. I say to her 'The *señora es mujer*, is woman, but she is fair. The *señora* give to me good pay and a free way with the horses. The *señora* give to *mi familia* a good life.' Now I say to Señor Fountain that you no kill. The jail is not good, is not right."

It was the longest speech I had ever heard him make. When the full impact of it finally registered, my eyes began to sting with tears. I sniffed them back and held out both hands through the bars to him. I knew how much effort it had taken for this taciturn little man to come forward with a story that was only partly true in order to rescue me. *"Gracias,* Nacho. *Muchas gracias.* As long as I have a place, you'll have a job with me."

Nacho took my hands clumsily, nodding vigorously, then twisted his hat in his hands and gave me a detailed report on the horses. George Washington's colts were looking very good. The stud would make us the best breeders in all the Territory.

When he finished, I asked, "What about the house? Someone broke in?"

He nodded. "But they do not seem to take anything. Herlinda, she think it is the nigra."

"That's ridiculous!"

"Si, I do not believe it. But Herlinda say she know the nigra is witch."

"Believe me, Nacho—"

His eyes had fastened on something behind me. I looked over my shoulder. The tarantula was skittering down the wall.

"You're not afraid of tarantulas, are you? It was you who told me they're harmless."

He jammed his hat on his head then jerked it off again. "They do no hurt. But I would not wish to live with one. You come home soon, *señora."*

"Thanks," I said, *"Gracias."* And this time the tears did spill, which made him more uncomfortable than before.

When Nacho had gone, I called Zeke, who came lumbering to my cell. "When can I get out of here?"

"There's still the little matter of that stagecoach."

"But I served my sentence for that!" I had explained it all to him, taking great pains to dredge the right dates from my head, the name of the judge.

"I know, I know. And I believe you. But I got to get it from Albuquerque. I put a letter on the stage back when you first told me, but I ain't heard nothing yet. Folks up there might not be real happy to help us, since General Sibley done laid claim to half of New Mexico Territory and Albuquerque's in the other half."

◇◇◇

Four days later, Zeke opened my cell door and jerked his thumb over his shoulder. "Get your belongings together and come on out to the office."

Speech failed me. I could only stammer something unintelligible. In that moment, if Zeke had asked me to marry him, I would have said yes.

It didn't take me long to pack up my bedroll. It felt odd to walk out the door of that cell and sit down on the chair next to his desk.

"I got to have the deed to your ranch," Zeke said.

"You what?"

"Just for safe keeping. Just until the trial."

"Trial? I thought—"

"The judge in Albuquerque says you served your sentence, and your foreman says you couldn't have killed that Mex, but we still got to have a trial."

"Why?"

"Because the Confederate States of America says so. The Army says so."

"Are the Texans still planning to confiscate my property? They want my horses, Zeke. They want to be able to take them without paying for them."

"Matty." Zeke lowered his head and peered at me earnestly. "The Texans are the jefes now."

"Fort Fillmore didn't used to butt into territory business."

"That's no never mind. The Texans own the valley now."

I had no choice but to agree.

Zeke pushed his chair back in order to take his belly far enough away to open his desk drawer. He brought out a document and pushed it toward me. "Fact is, it may be a good long time afore a judge can get up here from Franklin. Sign there." He pointed to a blank line.

"Not until I read it."

"Matty," he said, "it ain't me. Truth be known, I wouldn't do a trial. Seems like a waste of time and money. But it ain't my say-so."

I nodded and wiped an icy palm over my forehead.

The words were fancy and pompous; but basically, the document said that I would deliver the deed to my ranch to Zeke within twenty-four hours, and if I failed to appear in court, my land would become the property of the Confederate Territory of Arizona. I frowned and looked at Zeke. "This is Arizona Territory now?"

"That's what they say. Up about to Socorro and a beeline across to California."

I heaved a sigh and wrote my name on the line.

Chapter Twenty-three

After breakfast on my first day back at home, Winona cocked her head at me and pronounced, "You look mighty peaked. Get on out there and take you a walk. We done without you this long, we can do without you one more day."

I had already checked the chest in the parlor wall. Andrew's revolver still lay on its lid and, as far as I could tell, no coins were missing. I cleaned and reloaded the pistol before putting it back. Then I gave out the pay and a twenty-dollar bonus for everyone. Herlinda looked stunned, then uneasy. I suspect she took her double eagle back to her room and bit it to be sure it was real.

Then, much as it pained me, I sent Julio to Zeke with the deed. But the truth was, I did feel a little shaky and my limbs ached from inactivity. I took Winona's advice and just walked about gazing at things I hadn't seen in weeks. I had forgotten how the land jutted up and down on its way to the mountains, the heady smell of juniper and how shaggy the horses' coats got in winter, how the yucca looked like seventeen swords rammed into the same spot, how winter sunlight and clouds dappled the land with flecks of grey. I felt quite restored.

Thanks to Nacho, the ranch had broken even for the past two years. If the trial went well and I got my deed back, if George Washington's colts were as fine as Nacho predicted, the ranch would bring a very tidy sum. I said as much to Winona when we sat in the parlor with cups of tea. She gave me a look I couldn't decipher.

"But I'm not sure Nacho will swear under oath what he said. The fact is, it's only half true. He didn't see me himself." The rocker made a rasping sound on the floor as I shifted my weight.

"An' you sure don't know if that woman of his will tell the truth, oath or no oath." She stabbed her needle into the shirt she was patching.

"I never laid eyes on that Mexican boy, Winona, until I found him in the barn. And by then he was quite dead. Before God, I swear it."

"Why you swearin' to me? Didn't I practically raise you? You weren't nothing but a silly girl when we first come to meet. I know you done some pretty miserable things since then, but I know for blazin' sure you didn't kill no half-growed Mexican."

I leaned over and tucked the blanket around Zia, who made a sound between a gurgle and a snore. Already the baby was almost too big for her basket. "The problem is, I can't prove it."

"I know that, too. So what you needs to do is find out who done that killing."

"How the hell can I do that?" I slapped the arm of the rocker so hard it stung my fingers.

She wrinkled her nose at my language and went back to her sewing. "Got to be some way to find out how that boy came by a map of this land."

"I've lain awake more nights than I can count trying to figure that out," I said, shaking my still-hurting hand.

Winona put her head back and studied the ceiling. "Got to be something about this land, all right. You got a boy shot dead and he's carrying that map, we know that for sure. And we know for right likely that somebody done set a fire on this land."

I agreed. "And the offers to buy the ranch. We know those for certain. But it stretches the imagination to understand why two people should suddenly want this ranch. Unless they think there's gold or silver here somewhere."

Winona squinted at me. "Okay, s'posin' that's it. It ever enter your mind that Mex kid might of been hooked up with whoever has such an almighty interest in your land?" She jabbed the air with her needle for emphasis.

I got up and paced to the window, trying to dispatch the tightening knot in my stomach. On the other side of the pane, the day had turned overcast and grim. "Someone shot one of my calves, too. The poor thing is blind."

"Mayhap that was just passing meanness. Gold or no gold, if we stick to what we darn certain know, it do seem that three, maybe four folks got a mighty big interest in this here ranch. Two of 'em are set on buying it; that kid is another, or why he be carryin' that map? Number four is the one likes to play with fire."

"It's also possible that numbers one, two and four are the same—whoever wanted to buy me out maybe tried to burn me out when I wouldn't sell." I turned from the window. The parlor looked so homey and safe that I could hardly believe so much horror had happened here. "On the other hand, maybe somebody out there just plain hates me." I found myself hoping it was true. Ordinary hatred is simple.

"That could be, all right." Winona made a clicking sound with her tongue. "I sure would like to think Herlinda set that fire. She be capable of a mess of plain orneriness. But she wouldn't chance burnin' up her own kin."

I thought about that for a while. "It's nigh impossible that Isabel had anything to do with the fire, either. And I can't think of anyone else I've offended."

"Ha!" Winona chortled. "You can't live an' breathe ten minutes without making some folks powerful mad. Some because of me livin' here, others 'cause you're a gal on her own hook ownin' a ranch and all. Then there's the ones who maybe don't like that you raise better horses than they do, or maybe they think you got better water. And some folk, you'll never know how come they work up to hatefulness. You an' me both be aggravatin' that Herlinda woman. Might be the good Lord know why, I sure for certain don't."

I began to pace again. "I guess that's more than half true. I offend the Union by selling horses to the Texans, and the Texans by not giving them more horses free for the asking." I ran my tongue over dry, chapped lips. "Even if I don't lose the land, I may lose the horses to one army or the other, which would be just as bad because the land alone wouldn't bring near enough money to set us up in Philadelphia."

"Why you got this Philadelphia thing on your brain all the time?"

"Winona, look at me."

"I'm looking."

"What do you see?"

"I see a mighty handsome woman with hair like an angel—when she remembers to brush it—and a durn good figger that's about to turn stringy because she ain't eatin' enough. Your bones are starting to stick out."

"Why should I care about my figure when I haven't seen bishop sleeves or a big collar in almost ten years? I was educated to appreciate Mozart and Milton, not to dig ditches and play midwife to a mare. I don't belong here."

"You sure to God don't if you want to spend all your time talkin' about sleeves. How do you Eastern gals do that? It sure enough would bore me to tears."

It struck me that I was never fond of such talk myself. I couldn't think why I had brought it up now. But I wasn't about to admit it and was trying to think up a smart answer when a tap-tapping sound came from a box made of twigs that sat beneath the window. The box rocked a little.

Winona chuckled and pointed at it. "That Ruben thinks you be crazy asking him to make a box for a tarantula. What you plan to do with that critter, anyway?"

"Set her free, I guess. She'll like it better out here than in the jail."

"Herlinda will like having that there spider around. Yes, ma'am, she sure will like that."

"There are lots of tarantulas around here. She's seen plenty of them." I turned back to Winona, who had finished patching the skirt and was stowing her thread in Zia's basket. "Did Herlinda give you any trouble? Isabel didn't come back, did she?"

"You getting yourself arrested plumb took people's minds off me."

"Have you seen Tonio?" Suddenly, just thinking of him set my mind on edge. Why had he wanted to stay at the caves? He had never really answered that question. In fact, he seemed to avoid answering it. How could I have been so dull-witted as to trust him with the map?

I had to get it back as soon as possible.

Winona had her eyes on her sewing and didn't notice my consternation. "Once he give Nacho something for Ruben's hand when he crunch it with a hammer."

"Has there been any more talk about him stealing gold from the Church?"

"I reckon that was just some ugly rumor." She tossed her hand in a disdainful arc. "This whole place be about as full of rumors as an eggshell is full of egg."

"The map the boy was carrying—I think maybe it marks the location of some sort of treasure. Maybe someone buried something there."

She snorted, "First time I seen that map, I figured that was a might be."

"Why didn't you say so?"

"'Cause there's something about it don't smell right." Winona picked up Zia's basket and left me to my deepening fear.

◇◇◇

The glowering clouds were spinning up a storm the way an old woman spins wool. Tonio came out of the cave while I was climbing down from Fanny's saddle. I had forgotten how the weather had burned its lines into his face like a brand. He looked thinner and a little weary, but the light still flickered behind his eyes. The rush of blood to my cheeks took me aback, and I busied myself securing Fanny's reins to a mesquite tree until I got hold of myself.

"Welcome home." His smile was as wide and warm as a sheepskin in winter.

I decided I wouldn't mention what Isabel had said. All I wanted was the map. If he was a disgraced priest, it was of no consequence to me.

He clasped both my hands in his then let them go. "Eliot Turk was over this way yesterday. He said you were home. I was about to walk over."

"You should have a horse."

"I have enough trouble feeding myself." He ushered me into the cave, where a pot of water was on the fire. "So, you are now free?"

"More or less." I sank onto the rock ledge across from the fire. "Nacho told Zeke he saw me inside the house when that boy got shot. But I still have to stand trial when the judge gets here. I had to put the land up for bail."

Tonio was pouring boiling water into shiny bright-green cups. He handed me one. The tea smelled spicy, a little like juniper. I took a sip. It was strong and radiated warmth all the way down. I looked up at him. "I've come to get the map I left with you."

"Oh?" He busied himself with the pot of water.

"The best way to prove I didn't kill that boy is to find out who did, and I don't know anything about him except that he had that map."

Tonio still faced the fire, his back to me.

I took another sip of the tea and babbled on, as if trying to fill up the silence. "I was trying to remember the exact markings." I waited.

His shoulders seemed to fold into his body.

"Maybe I could take a look at it now."

He did not turn, but spoke his words to the flames. "I don't have it."

"What?" I bolted up from my seat on the ledge, the tea sloshing from my green cup, burning my fingers.

Still he didn't move. Anger filled my throat like gorge, no more for him than for myself. Only a slack-jawed moron would have trusted him as easily as I had. "What do you mean you don't have it?"

He turned. His eyes met mine then skidded away. He carefully settled himself on the floor near my feet and looked up into my face. "I burned it."

My mouth froze open. It could hardly form the word, "Why?" Then exasperation exploded from me. "Are you mad? You had no right! For God's sake, why?"

"You know that someone searched the house?"

The calm of his voice infuriated me. "Of course I know that!"

"What do you think they were looking for?"

"Anything, I suppose. A drifter might have—"

"They say nothing was taken. If a drifter was risking getting himself shot for thieving, I assure you he would have taken everything he could lay his hands on."

I had to admit that was likely true.

"It didn't seem very safe for me to have that map lying around here. Not safe for me, not safe for the map."

His words made sense but there was something wrong with the whole thing, something wrong with the way he again avoided my eyes. Anger and doubt came together in my chest like thunder and lightning. "You just burned it? You didn't even study it and memorize it first?"

"I well know every mark on it," he said, his voice oddly quiet.

"Then draw it for me."

"I have no paper."

I made to leave. "I'll find something for you to draw it on."

Tonio was on his feet. "No."

"Why?"

"Because I won't draw it."

"Why not?"

He held my eyes for a long time before he sat down again, his long legs folding up like sticks with hinges. He was still looking full into my face. "Because the map is dangerous."

I shouted the words into his face. "There may be a gold mine marked on that map!"

"That," he said without blinking, "is why it is dangerous."

My anger hung in the silent air. Tonio's face showed a deep slash of pain, but he didn't look away. He looked like a man about to undergo torture by a master of the art of eliciting truth, and his face showed a saint's determination not to tell it.

I wilted back onto my seat. My hands were like ice in spite of the fire. I said slowly, "You know more about this than you've told me."

"Yes," he nodded. "I reckon I do."

Chapter Twenty-four

The fire snapped and shot a burning bit of coal past the hearth to a spot near Tonio's feet, but neither of us moved. Shadows seemed to hover on the walls like carrion-eaters waiting for the moment of death.

"Why?" I said finally, my voice the color of disbelief. "Why did you pretend to know nothing?"

He didn't answer.

"Have you been trying to buy my ranch or run me off it?"

"No!" he said sharply. "No." He turned to stare into the fire with a sort of infinite sadness. I knew that look. I'd seen it once before: that first night, when he had bent over the body that lay on the straw in my barn.

"You knew that Mexican kid, didn't you?"

He nodded, his eyes fixed on the fire. "Yes. His name was Diego Ramirez. He was only a year old the last time I saw him, but he looked exactly like his father."

I could tell he was trying to decide precisely what and how much to tell me. I said nothing and let him puzzle it out. I wanted to know what he would tell me of his own accord before I started asking questions. It was a full minute before he went on.

"Diego was born here. His mother was Rosita. She and his father were from Chihuahua, a Church parish in Chihuahua."

"A Church parish." I was remembering what Isabel had said.

He looked me full in the eyes. "Everything I told you was true. I was never a priest." He swallowed, looked down, then went on. "I was helping the priest. By the time I happened to stop there, a drought had wiped out most of the little farms. People were desperate. So I stayed on. We tried to help them. We petitioned the Church in Mexico City for assistance. We dug the water wells deeper. But people began to die of hunger."

"Didn't the Church help?"

Tonio's eyes became hard and hot enough to scorch. "No." He surrounded the word with silence like a tiny island in an angry sea. Finally, "Padre Francisco was an old man. He was dying of a wasting sickness. Just before he drew his last breath, he asked me to take the people north. He said a man had told him where there was gold, and I was to take his ragged little band of parishioners there. He said he was violating the confessional by telling me, but that it would save their lives and he said God would understand."

"So you took them there?"

"I brought them here."

The statement hit me in the chest, knocking the breath from me. Outside, the wind had come up. It was snuffling at the rock entrance to the cave like a hound on the scent. The firelight played over the planes of Tonio's face as he gazed into it. I remembered Nacho's story of a priest and a gold mine.

When I recovered my voice, I asked the obvious. "Where is this mine?"

Tonio put his hand to his lips as if to be certain they would not betray him.

I waited, but he said nothing. Finally, I asked, "How long were you here?"

He drew in a breath, and I didn't think he was going to answer. Then, "A little less than two years."

"And you found gold." Nacho had said the people traded nuggets for food.

After a long moment, Tonio nodded.

"Then why did you leave?"

He drew a deep breath and the rest of it came from him in a stream:

"At first I thought Padre Francisco's words were the imaginings of a dying man; but when we had buried him, I found a map among his belongings and, with it, some writing. I kept these, but I said nothing. It was coming on spring, and perhaps the drought was over. But that summer, our meager little stream dried up. They begged me to perform the Mass. I told them I could not. They knew I was not a priest, but they kept asking anyway. They had some notion I could appease God, could bring the rain. And they knew it might be a year or more before the Church sent another priest.

"A few months later, a child died, and then an old man. From hunger. I performed the rituals. It meant so much to them, how could I not? Even I began to believe I must try to talk to God. I began to say Mass. But the dying went on. The ninth was an old woman. She just crumpled over in the field.

"I called together those who were left and told them of the map and the supposed mine. I warned them the map might not lead us anywhere, that we all might die seeking this gold. And even if we somehow found ore, the work would be heavy and hard and dangerous. I asked them if they wanted to risk their lives to try this."

"And they did," I said to urge him on.

Tonio's chin dipped twice. "Twenty men and fourteen women. We had three ox-drawn carts, but that was for supplies. We walked. For twelve days. It was not so bad once we reached the Rio Grande, for then at least we had water. In the villages we passed through, we heard tales of Indians who, it was said, lived in the mountains like wolves and viciously slaughtered travelers. But perhaps our little band looked too poor to be worth the trouble. We saw no Indians at all.

"The writing mentioned a place called Spirit Springs and the *cuevas de vegas*, the caves of the meadows, at the foot of a high cliff."

Involuntarily, I sucked in my breath. "That's here. Right here."

Tonio went on as if he hadn't heard me. "They gathered at the spring and someone laughed. I hadn't heard laughter in so many months I had forgotten the sound of it. Exhausted as they were, they would not wait. We left the carts and climbed over rocks and branches, debris that had washed from the mountain. We found ourselves on the rim of a small bowl and at the bottom a lone cottonwood tree seemed to grow from the rock. This, too, was on the map. And three days later, not far from that cottonwood, we found the first nuggets of milk-white quartz."

"Quartz?"

"It is often found with silver and gold, or so we believed; and it must be true because a week or so later, in one of the canyons that ran from the basin, we found the mine. It was probably dug by the Spaniards or perhaps by Indians. There were ruins of rock ore-crushers. The smelters were adobe; they had almost washed away. We rebuilt these. We hollowed out the entrance to the mine and slept there. Knowing full well that it wasn't just Indians who might attack us, we always posted a guard. But it never occurred to me..."

He seemed lost in some recollection. I said nothing; and eventually, he went on.

"I continued to say Mass. I even heard confessions. I knew it was wrong, but the people expected..." His voice faded away.

"If there is a God," I said, "I can't imagine he would care much who leads his worship."

"It was more than just the Mass," Tonio said. "I tried to live both ways. I took a woman. I was both priest and layman." His voice faltered.

The words stabbed at me in an odd way. "But you took no vow of celibacy."

He didn't seem to hear me. His voice stumbled on. "By the following spring, she was with child; and in midwinter she bore me a son. We named him Carlos."

This time, his silence was so long I thought he might have forgotten me. After a time, I said, "What happened to him?"

"One day when I was in the village for supplies I was told a stranger was looking for me. I was astounded. Who could possibly look for me here? I went to the inn where this man was said to be staying, a Señor Pablo Rivas. He was a layman, he said, but a close friend of the Bishop in Mexico City. When the Church authorities stopped hearing from Padre Francisco, they had eventually sent this man to Chihuahua. Ultimately, he had traced us here.

"He told me he had been amazed to hear we had discovered gold. I did not confirm this, I only stared at him appalled and tried to think what to say. Señor Rivas demanded, in the name of the Church, that I deliver possession of the mine and all gold to him."

I could hardly contain myself. "He what?"

"More precisely, he told me I would be excommunicated for impersonating a priest and ordered me to deliver everything to him as a representative of the Holy Roman Church."

"Surely you didn't…"

"I told him no. He was very angry when I left him. I didn't really believe the Church could do much, but I was alarmed. We had built little huts for ourselves from the rocks we had taken from the mine. That night I insisted everyone return to sleeping in the mine entrance as we had when we first arrived. I posted three guards. Nothing happened. No one approached us. A few days later, one of the women came to see me with her son, a child about the same age as my own. He had been restless and ill for weeks. I had tried every possible remedy of my own, but still the boy ailed. She had heard there was a doctor staying in the village. She wanted to take the boy to him. So, I took them into town. I was curious as to whether Señor Rivas was still there.

"When we returned just after twilight, I knew something was wrong. The guards at the mine entrance always kept a fire going. It had burned so low I could hardly see it until I reached the clearing. Then I was horrified. A dozen ponies were grazing there. Indian ponies. I sent the woman and the boy back to the cart and approached the entrance. Nothing moved. I stepped inside. My people were strewn across the floor like kindling. They had been slaughtered."

I gasped my own shock aloud.

Tonio's voice, and his eyes, became hard as glass in the firelight. "Their throats had been cut, the men's heads were bloody pulp where the scalps had been sliced away. I had never seen this before." His voice began to shake. "It was like you skin an animal."

"What did you do?" My own voice had grown unsteady and hoarse.

"The Indians had obviously gone into the mine. Their horses were still there in the clearing. We had used dynamite for the mining, of course, and a good many sticks of it were piled in a stone hut we built for that purpose. I set the explosives." He stopped, his eyes riveted on the fire as if seeing it all again, there in the flames.

"The sound was like Judgment Day," he went on. "The dust and debris blotted out the rising moon. I gave what little gold I had to the woman and put her and her son on a stagecoach south."

For a time, I was too mesmerized by his tale to say anything. "Your woman, your son?"

"Dead."

"The woman and the boy?"

"Rosita Ramirez. She had named the boy Diego..."

"It was her son who was killed in my barn?"

"I think so, yes."

"But where did he come from? How did he get there?"

"I don't know."

"The map?"

"Before we set out from Chihuahua, I made several copies of the map. That was one of them." And Tonio began to weep.

Chapter Twenty-five

Feeling helpless against such agony, I reached for Tonio and clung to him until his shoulders stopped shaking with the dry rasping sobs. My own face was wet with the bitter tears of my own horrors. Surely the world was meant to be a better place than this.

Finally, he drew back and sat numbly against the wall. His eyes seemed barely focused. The wind was again snarling at the entrance.

"Rivas," I said. "The man from Mexico City. Was he in town that day?"

Tonio shook his head. "No. They said he had left for El Paso del Norte the day before."

"Did he...Do you think..."

"Yes, I think he did. I think he had me followed after I talked with him. I think he had some allies among the Apaches—there are Catholics among them. I think this representative of the Church to which I had devoted my entire life sent them to slaughter us. I think he then intended to take the mine for himself."

"Did he ever find it?"

"I don't know. There wasn't much left to show for it."

I reached for his hand. "What you did was not wrong. This was hideous, voracious greed. Rivas' own greed. The Church would never have sanctioned that."

"That is what I believed. Until I returned to Mexico City and learned that I had been excommunicated."

I closed my eyes against the pain I felt in him. Isabel's sources had told her true. "Well, it certainly was not some vengeance from God. Surely, you don't think that."

Tonio made a small, weary smile. "No, of course not."

I realized I was holding his hand and started to draw mine away. He tightened his fingers and drew me toward him. Slowly, very slowly, his mouth descended onto mine, and some ember I thought had died long ago ignited inside me. His beard tasted of salt and spice.

He cupped my face in his hands. Eyes like two dark daubs peered into mine. "I have been half mad with wanting you," he said. "Sometimes it has taken more strength than I thought I possessed to stay away." He lifted my chin and kissed my nose, my cheeks, my mouth.

I raised my head, my eyes searching his for his soul as my hands moved to his shirtfront and I began to undo the buttons.

A shudder ran through him.

The fire felt warm on my skin as we shucked our clothes and tossed them in a jumbled pile. Half-sitting, half-lying against the wall where it joined the hearth, he pulled me toward him and the flames warmed my left side as he stroked my shoulders, my arms, my belly.

"Even I did not guess you were this beautiful," he said, brushing the palms of his hands across my breasts as if he were a sculptor in awe of his own work.

His thumbs brushed like feathers over my nipples, then his fingers closed and tugged. I gasped and arched my back as he swelled beneath me.

The fire muttered to itself about the wind.

We lay tangled and spent, watching the red-and-yellow tongues of flame lick at what was left of the wood in the niche behind the hearth.

I turned to look at Tonio. Dark, curly hair made a mat across his chest. And the reflected fire danced in his eyes. "Why did you stay away?" I asked.

He gave me a puzzled look, one eyebrow at half-mast.

"You said you deliberately stayed away from me."

"Ah." He lay back. "I suppose I thought you had little need of a weary old man with a hopelessly twisted history. You seemed like pure fire, devouring every difficulty with such spirit."

I stared at him. "Surely you're jesting."

He sat up and looked at me again. "I suppose I was a little like you once, the quintessential adventurer, with a future mapped out and a detailed plan of how to get there."

"You make it sound so simple. I wish it were true. I truly do."

Tonio rolled over and propped his chin in his hand. "That is my persuasion, but I confess I know practically nothing of your history." He chuckled. "The rumors are rampant. They even say you robbed a stagecoach."

I dipped my chin to my chest and peered at him somberly. "I did. I also served time in jail for it."

Tonio was watching my face. I could see him struggle to cover his surprise. "You needn't talk about it if you don't want to."

I looked down at my hands. They looked old. I was old. My youth had fled sometime when I was busy elsewhere. "There's no secret about it anymore." I drew up my knees, hugged them to my chin and told him the rest.

When I finished, Tonio drew me into his arms. I buried my wet face in his chest and asked the question that had obsessed me those many years: "Why did it happen? Why did Andrew become such a fiend, a monster? Why?"

Tonio looked down into my face and said gently, "Even if you could have answered that question, you could not have changed him."

I held my fingertips to my eyes and willed myself calmer.

"And you are still wed to this man?"

I had not permitted that thought to enter my mind for many years, and the truth of it overwhelmed me. "In strictest sense, I suppose I am."

◇◇◇

At some point we dressed; and Tonio replenished the fire and from a pot, doled some red chile stew into bowls. And at some point we undressed again and slept there, in front of the fire, welded to each other as though resenting that our skin was a barrier between us.

When I woke, the fire had gone out but the hearth was still warm. Tonio snored softly beside me. Half in a dream, half out, I hugged him to me. A cold wave crested and swept into my consciousness.

I eased my arm from under his shoulder and stood. What was I thinking of?

"What are you doing?" Tonio asked sleepily.

"Dressing," I whispered, as if someone might hear. "I have to get home. Winona has probably called out a search party. The rest of them will think I'm a brazen strumpet."

"You are," Tonio chuckled.

I knelt and kissed his eyelids.

"Uh-uh," he grunted, rolling over and getting to his feet. "I will see you to the door." And we both laughed, choking it back like a secret too good to tell.

◇◇◇

Poor Fanny had not had her oats. She raised her head and nickered when she saw me. The moon was lopsided, as though some animal nibbled at it. I made sure to give her an extra measure of feed when I left her in the barn.

I had closed the kitchen door behind me and was waiting for my eyes to adjust to the absence of the crooked moon when something at the kitchen table moved, then grew taller.

A scream rose in my throat, but I smothered it there. Through the gloom I saw Winona, drawn up to her full height, arms crossed over her bosom, chin down, foot giving a little tap. "I done worry myself into apple-plexy."

The implications of my absence dawned on me. "Oh, Winona. I am truly sorry. You didn't...the men aren't searching for me, are they?"

"I just happens to take me a ride for a look-see, and there be that horse of yours, down by the cuevas. So I tells everybody that of a sudden, you got to go into town."

I gave a soft chuckle and threw my arms around her.

"Go on, now, get yourself to bed," she growled.

I hastily prepared to dive into bed, yanking off my clothes for the third or fourth time since I'd dressed in that room the morning before. I was taking off my shoes when something caught my eye, some movement or some shadow beyond the tiny window.

I rose and walked across the room. It was dark; I hadn't lit a candle, but the crooked moon was still bright. Sometimes the hands went that way toward the bunkhouse, as did Nacho and Herlinda to reach their quarters at the back of the house. But all of them would have retired much earlier. Nothing outside seemed out of place, although I shuddered a little remembering peering through that other window just as the boy fell against it.

But tonight there was no bloodied face, no dying mule slued across the door to the barn. All seemed still. I decided I must have imagined it.

I was turning back to the bed when the corner of my eye caught movement to the left. A coyote aiming to try his craft at the chicken roost? They usually didn't venture so near to the house. I leaned my head against the window to see better. A shadow was rounding the corner of the house. It seemed too short and squat to be a man—but far too tall to be a coyote. It might have been a woman, but that was ridiculous. No woman would be out and about at this hour.

I picked up the pistol and made for the door, but two wary circlings of the house revealed nothing.

The next morning I woke up full of contrary bits and pieces that tugged and shoved at each other like a litter of kittens with one ball of yarn. Tonio's story had been so full of pain, his grief so real, that his determination to rid the world of that map, to erase that mine from human knowledge, was indisputable. I was not willing to try to coerce him to redraw the map for me.

On the other hand, I did need to know more about Diego Ramirez, the boy who had fallen against my window and died in my barn. It seemed clear now that the killing had to do with the map. Whoever had shot Diego may well have seen the map, had maybe been with Diego at some point. His killer might very well be the same person who was trying to buy, burn me out or run me off my land.

While I was dawdling over a breakfast of biscuits and honey, I remembered something Winona had said. I braved Herlinda's scowl, left my plate unwashed and saddled Fanny.

It was Julio's turn to tend the cattle. I found him on the mesa near the windmill that pumped water from the well to the cow pond. The wind of the night before had given way to a sun as sharp as a newly honed knife. A yearling calf stumbled, seeming startled by my approach.

Julio looked like he would have welcomed a visit from Satan himself more than mine, but he yanked off his hat and nodded. *"Señora."*

"Put on your hat, Julio," I said gruffly. "The sun will scald your head."

He nodded cautiously, as if I had asked him to stand on his head, and clapped the filthy, wide-brimmed thing back over his hair. He was seventeen or eighteen and swarthy, built like a young boar hog, legs a little spindly and short body solid as a barrel. For no particular reason other than that I often smelled liquor on him, I had always reckoned he was pretty stupid. I can, at times, be stunningly arrogant.

"My name is Matty," I said carefully, consciously trying for the first time to combine the roles of female and jefe and finding I was no more comfortable with it than he was. "I want you to call me Matty."

He nodded, wordless.

Just then, the calf stumbled again. "What's wrong with it?" I asked.

"She is the blind one, sen—Miss Matty. The one you find last year."

I peered at the calf more closely. One of the eye sockets was puckered and white. "So she survived."

Julio nodded. "I think at first it would be better to shoot her. But she is only blind in the one eye. The other, it heal up real good."

"You've been the one seeing to her?"

"Si," he said warily. I could see him considering whether he was going to be scolded for feeding the calf too much or too little.

"Thanks."

"De nada," he mumbled.

"Julio," I said, fiddling with Fanny's saddle horn, "I hear you do drawings. Pictures."

He started to deny it.

"No," I said, "I think that's good. It's a fine talent to have."

We sat there in the sun atop our horses as he struggled to figure out where the high ground was. *"Si,"* he said finally, cautiously. "I do the drawings. Sometimes. After the work is finished."

"Good. I'd like you to draw something for me."

He just stared at me, eyes puzzled.

"You remember that kid who was killed here last year?" Julio nodded. "Could you draw a picture of him for me?"

The furrow above his nose deepened. Suddenly it dawned on me that Julio knew I'd been arrested for the kid's murder, and that the boy had been a Mexican about his own age. "Look," I said, "I don't know what you've been told, but I did not kill that boy."

"Si," Julio said. "Papa, he say that. But already I know it. I know it is impossible that you kill."

I half smiled at what seemed like a lame attempt to curry favor. "Why not?"

"You bring in calf that cannot see," he said, returning the half-smile.

I felt like a jackass. "Thank you for knowing that."

He nodded, less wary now.

"I need a picture of that boy so I can show it to people and ask them if they saw him. I think I know his name now, and I sure need to find out who did kill him."

Julio looked at the calf, then back at me. *"Si."*

In the barn, I watched the stubby fingers, gripping an equally stubby lump of charred wood, moving quickly over a tattered bit of white cloth he had nailed to a board. Paper, Julio had explained, was hard to come by and tore easily. Soaking the cloth in oil, then letting it dry in the shade, made it much better than paper.

On the cloth, a narrow face was emerging the way clouds sometimes make images. Suddenly there it was. "That's him," I said, "at least that's very close."

Grinning happily, Julio deepened some of the lines, made the nose shorter, darkened the area around the eyes and drew in the hair and the scraggly, half-grown adolescent beard.

"You are really good." My awe was genuine.

He shrugged, still adding lines. "Mama, Papa, Ruben, they say is *estupido.*"

"Dumb! Not at all! It's very good, a wonderful talent."

He flashed a sheepish grin, his mouth overflowing with very white teeth. "Good for what?" He was still busy with the charcoal.

"You could make money with that."

He gave me a patient, disbelieving look.

"With a newspaper, for one thing." I wished for the hundredth time that Jamie were alive. Photographs were still a novelty.

"I do not believe they buy from a *Méxicano."* He lifted the charcoal from the drawing. "I should put the place of the bullet?"

"No. I want him to look like he would have looked if he met someone in the plaza."

Julio made a few more marks and turned the board toward me, propping it on his knee.

I gaped at the drawing, my words of praise dried up in my throat. This was as good a sketch of the boy who had died in my barn as I could ever expect to see. It also was not the face of the bloodied man who had stumbled against my window that night.

This face was rounder. The boy's neck had been short, as Julio drew it. The man at the window had a longer neck. I realized now that man was also older, five or ten years older than the boy we found in the barn. And he had been bleeding from a wound at the temple. How could I have been so mistaken?

"Do you remember any blood here?" I pointed at place above the left eye.

Julio puzzled for a moment. "No. Only here." He made a circular motion above the center of the forehead.

The wound on the man who had fallen against my window might have come from a bullet, but one that only grazed the flesh, not one that killed. Or it might have come from hitting the head on something hard—a board, a rock, even a fist.

I expelled my breath slowly, feeling my heartbeat quicken.

"It is not right?" Julio asked.

"No, no. It's very right. Very good." I took the board from him and peered at it intently. "You are a fine artist, Julio." I took from my pocket the twenty-dollar gold piece I had taken from the chest that morning. At the time I had thought twenty dollars was far too much. Now I thought it was too little. I held it out.

"No," Julio said, standing up. He brushed his hands on his trousers and grinned. "No pay. Is gift."

I looked up at him, realizing I had never thought about the owner of the pair of hands and strong arms I paid wages to. I had hardly even thought of him by name, but only as Nacho's son. I discovered now that I quite liked him.

"Take it," I said softly. "I want you to have it. You have earned it. You are an excellent artist. As soon as I have time, I will talk to some people in town about you."

He hesitated, then: *"Gracias."* He took the coin and, with his slow, deliberate pace, left the barn.

I turned back to the drawing. How could I have thought this was the same face that had fallen against my window? The eyes in that face had not been so far apart. Now that I looked at the sketch, the two faces seemed hardly alike at all.

I had barely looked at the dead boy's face that night. I had wanted to avoid seeing it. And since the face at my window and the dead boy in the barn had happened together quickly, my brain had decided they were one and the same. There was a slight resemblance, yes—the beard, the dark hair. But the boy's beard had been that of a boy, scraggly, not full grown. And the face at my window had worn the thick beard of a man.

I wished fervently that I could describe that other face well enough for Julio to draw it. I was certain now that it was the face of the boy's killer.

Chapter Twenty-six

Zeke looked up, surprise written across his broad face, when I strode into his office. Then he smiled. "The room and board so good here you decided to move back?"

I was feeling dead serious; but this was the first time I'd ever heard him attempt a joke, so I laughed. "Nope, Zeke," I said, sliding into the chair next to his desk, "I want to ask you something."

"Uh-huh," he nodded. "You just want me to hire you as a cook."

"I daresay I figured you must have starved without me here to cook for you," I retorted.

That obviously called for another laugh before I could unroll the cloth on his desk and show him the sketch. His eyebrows pulled down in a perplexed line. "Who's that?"

"The boy I am supposed to have killed. Kid on the ranch saw him after he was dead, drew him from memory."

Zeke examined the sketch. "Why you showing this to me?"

"You ever happen to see him?"

After a long perusal of the cloth, Zeke's pale blue eyes looked up. "Can't say I ever did."

"His name was Diego Ramirez."

Zeke frowned and shook his head. "Don't know, Matty. One Mex name sounds like another, if you know what I mean. How d'you know his name if you never talked to him? And why you askin' me about him?"

I skipped the first question. "I'm thinking my best chance to get out of this free and clear, with my land still belonging to me, is to see if I can find whoever did kill this kid. Zeke, there was someone else out there the night the boy was killed. I saw him. For a long time, I thought it was the boy I saw, before he died. But it wasn't. So I'm trying to find out where this kid was before he got himself shot and whether anyone was with him. And anything else that might help."

Zeke gave me a look that said only a woman would think of such a peculiar approach. "Good luck," he said.

◇◇◇

At Smithers' barbershop, Simon Trujillo gave me a startled, embarrassed look, as though I had walked into an outhouse full of men. He did most of the barbering for old Ben Smithers. Simon was a thin, nervous fellow; he almost dropped his scissors. I didn't recognize the man lying in the chair with a towel over the lower part of his face, but the eyes rolled toward Simon as if my presence were the barber's fault.

"I wonder if you gentlemen would mind taking a look at this picture?"

Simon finally stopped staring, and his head bobbed twice. The man in the chair sat up with an ill-tempered jerk and I recognized Jonathon Mapes, who ran sheep over near Doña Ana. His square face was red where the towel had been softening up his beard for a shave. His hair was the color of rusted iron, wiry curls with a lot of grey. His chin was split by a cleft. There was a sullen look about the jaw; but at sixty-something, he was still handsome.

I unrolled the cloth and laid it in Mapes' lap.

"Looks like a Mex," he growled. "What about it?"

"This kid died in my barn last spring," I said. "I'm trying to find out if anyone knew him."

"Not likely," he fumed. Then his eyes sharpened and ran over my face like knives. "I heard tell it was you killed him."

"No," I said, trying to keep the rush of anger out of my voice. "I certainly did not kill him. Apparently, someone thinks I did because I was arrested for it; but my foreman told Zeke that he saw me in the house about the same time this boy was shot, so Zeke knows I couldn't have done it." I hoped Zeke in fact did believe Nacho.

"So, what do you care whether anyone saw him?" Mapes growled.

"Seems to me it would be best all around if we found out who did kill him."

Mapes flung himself back down in the chair and clamped the towel over his face. Then he jerked the towel away again and pitched it toward the sink behind Simon. "Dratted thing's cold now." He fixed me with a stare. "Never saw him. And I don't want you botherin' my boys. They ain't seen him, neither, and they got work to do. Anybody comes to my spread uninvited gets a bead drawn on 'em."

"That's right friendly," I said. I knew a lot of folks didn't much like Mapes, but it wasn't just his mean mouth. A creek ran through his land and he had dammed it. The creek only ran summers and didn't carry much water even then, but the air was often still in summer, too still to stir a windmill. Then, ranchers without springs like mine had to depend on creeks. Anybody below Mapes' land had nothing to rely on except whatever water they had pumped up in the winds of February. One of Mapes' men might have seen the kid in town or stopped him on the road, but I decided I'd head out his way only as a last resort.

I turned to Simon. "How about you?" The little man was obviously intimidated by his customer and probably wished I were on the moon—or anywhere but there. His eyes flicked back to the sketch. I took it from Mapes' lap and held it out. "Please," I said. "Take a good look. Did you see him? It would have been in January or early February. Did he come in for a haircut or a shave? Or did you happen to see him around town?"

"I think maybe I see him," Simon said slowly, still staring at the sketch. "But I am not sure."

"Where?"

"Not here. That I would remember. In the plaza. By Garza's." The general store.

"Please. Think carefully. Was he coming out of the store? Was anyone with him? What was he doing?"

Simon thought about that. "He was coming from the bank. Or maybe the saloon. I notice him because he was walking very fast. The heel of his boot, I think it come off and he almost fall."

"Was anyone with him?"

"There was another man, yes. Not with him, but I think maybe he try to catch up with this one." Simon pointed to the sketch.

"Did he catch up with him?"

Simon nodded. "When this one fall, he take his arm."

"What did the second man look like?"

Simon thought about this a long time. Finally, he shook his head. "I do not know. I do not remember. I am not even sure the other is the same as this one." He jabbed the drawing. "It is a long time ago. We have many strangers in town since then."

"Just the goddam Confederate army," Mapes grunted. "Hot up that damn towel, Simon, and let's get on with it."

Simon hurried to do as he was bid; and I, knowing my welcome was wearing mighty thin, at least with Mapes, thanked both men and left.

◇◇◇

In front of the bank, thick vigas supported a roof that extended all the way to the hitching posts. The building, like most of the others that lined the plaza, resembled a squat, heavy-browed peasant peering toward the dusty square in the center. The single window was barred but the bars were wood, and anyone with a good saw could have cut through them in minutes.

Jeremy Neuman was a rather stodgy fellow with closely cropped pale-brown hair and a chin as free of stubble as a baby's. I'd seen him a few times around town; but as I didn't trust banks much, I'd put no money with him.

He wore the only starched shirt I had seen in some time and a neat little string tie at the collar. He looked up and blinked watery blue eyes at me from behind the lenses of his little round spectacles. He had the look of a man who was born at about the age of forty-six and never aged further.

"Ma'am?" He managed to make the single word sound remotely suspicious.

I unrolled Julio's cloth drawing. Neuman frowned and recoiled as if I'd drawn a pistol. "It's just a picture, Mr. Neuman. Have you ever seen this man?"

He didn't bother to look at it closely. "Mexicans do not generally use banks," he said coldly.

"But I've seen Mr. Garza coming from here, and Mr. Castillo." There were several Mexican merchants in Mesilla.

"They are older," Neuman said frostily, as if age transcended race. "That is obviously a young Mexican. I don't believe a young Mexican fellow has ever set foot in this bank."

"Okay." I rolled up the drawing and left, doubly certain that I had been wise to keep my money at home.

◇◇◇

The general store had the smell of a brand-new barn, before the odors of dust and aging fodder overcome the aroma of wood and leather. Wooden buckets stacked in towers flanked one side of the door, a table full of bright yellow Mexican dishes stood on the other. A man who looked like he needed a bath more than he needed one of the tin cups he was examining seemed to be the only customer.

Garza was sitting on an upended barrel next to the counter where people paid for their purchases. I picked my way around sacks of cornmeal and wooden boxes of nails. He stood as I approached, a mere wisp of a man, probably wiry and quick when he was young but now stooped at the shoulders so that he had to cock his head sideways to look at me. Bushy eyebrows seemed about to take over his face.

Garza and his brother had opened the store the same year people had come to Mesilla in hopes of a land grant. The brother had up and disappeared with their serving woman sometime before I arrived in the valley. Or so I had heard.

There was another, smaller general store in Doña Ana; but sooner or later, most anyone who spent any time at all in the Mesilla Valley came to Garza's for supplies.

"Good morning," I sang out cheerily.

"Si, si, it is, it is," he agreed in a gravelly voice and waited. Long years of dealing with people had given him the patience of Job.

I unrolled the cloth and asked my well-rehearsed questions. He left his perch on the barrel. Despite his spine, which seemed to have fused stiffly at the shoulders, his movements were quick. His hand darted out and took the sketch from me.

"Ah," he said. "This *hombre*, he is from *México."* He pronounced it *Meh-he-co*, with the accent on the first syllable.

"You know him?" I asked quickly.

"No." He shook his head, the bushy eyebrows drawn down around the beak of a nose. "He come in the store and we talk a little, I think."

"When?"

"Many month ago, I think." Then he shook his head. "No. He was not from *México.* His mama and papa come from *México.* He say he was born here. He come back."

"From where?"

Garza cocked his head at an odd angle and studied the dusty vigas, the round rafters that held up the roof of his store. "Texas, I think. San Antonio, maybe."

"Was he with someone?" I asked and held my breath.

"I see no one."

So much for that. I thanked him and turned to go. I'd already opened the door when I remembered something and turned back, but the old geezer who had been examining the tin cups was in my path. He smelled as bad as he looked.

"Yo're huntin' someone?" he asked.

Trying to stay out of the path of his breath, which reeked of onions and whiskey, I showed him the sketch.

He nodded. His face was so filthy the grime seemed to crack when he moved. Wisps of greasy dark hair stood out at all angles from his head. He jabbed a dirty finger at the drawing. "That's the kid was staying at San Juan. Sure enough, it is."

"Where is San Juan?"

The old man raised a bony shoulder. "Tortugas, San Juan. Where them Injuns is." He poked the sketch again. "I seen him. Said him and his friend had a fallin' out an' he was puttin' up there."

I leaped at his words. "Friend?" I asked urgently. "What did the friend look like?"

"Dunno," the codger grunted. "Just he said there was two of 'em."

Garza had returned to his post by the cash register. I walked back and stood in front of him. "Did he buy anything, Mr. Garza? The boy who said he was born here?"

"Si." Garza's head gave several stiff little bobs. "He buy a money bag. No, no," he said to my stunned expression. "A little bag. To wear here." He pointed to his throat.

Behind me, the door opened, and I turned to see who had entered but glimpsed instead the disappearing figure of a woman. I frowned. I hadn't thought anyone else was in the store. "Was that Isabel Tolhurst?"

Garcia's head was bobbing; his face bore a look of tolerant concern. *"Si.* Señora Tolhurst wishes for new dishes. But she has not the money."

Chapter Twenty-seven

The village of Tortugas—or San Juan or whatever they called it—looked like an uneven honeycomb that had been shaped from mud then propped on its side in a field of cotton seedlings. A separate, squared-off triangular structure was flanked by a cross that gleamed brilliant white even in the shade of a cottonwood. An acequia, an irrigation canal, snaked off to the left toward the river.

The wagon lurched when I pulled the horse to a stop; and on the plank seat next to me, Winona raised her free hand to shade her eyes. In her other arm, a wide-awake Zia was blowing spit bubbles.

Now that we were here, I was getting nervy. "You think we'll be safe?" My knowledge of Indians was limited. The women who worked with Herlinda were taciturn and cheerless, but they worked like oxen. And the occasional redskins I saw in town seemed harmless. But Tonio was not the only one with a tale of savagery. Since Winona had lived among them for a time, I was glad to have her along.

"One bunch of Injuns is as different from another as cow's milk and rat poison," she said, eyeing the cluster of buildings warily. "Even the good ones can go along nice and easy like for a time then of a sudden hit the warpath. I don't know much about these here Injuns, but I hear tell they is Christian. And I see they got the cross to prove it."

I had forgotten the Tortugas' Christmas pilgrimage. "Yes. They're very religious." I released the breath I realized I'd been holding. "That's comforting."

"Might be. Then again, might not. I hear tell some of 'em take the faith so serious they crucify folk."

I swallowed hard, wondering if it might be wiser to forget our notion about talking with them. An occasional Indian here and there was one thing, but a village of nothing but Indians was quite another. Nacho had said the people of San Juan de Dios were a peaceful sort and that they mostly kept to themselves. I fervently hoped he was right.

Naked children who were playing in the sun-baked area in front of the disorderly tiers of dwellings had vanished before our wagon stopped, and now the place seemed deserted. Hoping the adults would at least be wearing loincloths, I started to get down from the plank seat; but Winona's hand stopped me.

"Somebody will come," she said.

Sure enough, a figure appeared at one of the ground-level doorways. Ladders led to the upper tiers. The man who approached was neither naked nor did he wear a loincloth.

Bristling grey hair had been tied back and a sleeveless vest hung open on his hairless, shirtless chest. His legs were clad in the same sort of trousers you'd see on any ranch hand. He was built sturdy and close to the ground. His face looked like Adam's must have looked when God was fashioning him from clay. The nose was like wax that has softened in the sun, the mouth seemed not quite finished. But the deep-set eyes were like sharp bits of glass. He stopped next to me and waited.

"Ingles?" Winona asked. He shook his head and she said something in halting Spanish. He nodded, turned and shouted in guttural tones toward the dwellings. A woman's head poked from one of the upper doorways. He called more words I couldn't understand. She nodded and descended a ladder as gracefully as a caterpillar.

She was small, dark and pretty, with black eyes set over high cheekbones. Her dress was simpler than ours—a single length of cloth sewn up at the sides with openings for the arms and tied at the waist with a sort of rope. Around the neck little figures had been made with thread, like embroidery. A zigzag design at the bottom of the skirt had been made the same way. Her feet were bare.

She stopped next to the man and looked up at me, shielding her eyes against the sun. "Yes?"

"I am seeking information," I said slowly and clearly, "about a boy."

"At fifteen, sixteen, Injuns be men," Winona said in a low voice.

I corrected myself. "A man, then."

"Yes." Two rows of very white teeth flashed between the girl's lips.

"He would have been here about a year ago."

"Yes?"

"Pintura," Winona piped up. "Show her the picture."

"Ah," the girl nodded, as though this made sense.

"Yes," I said, "I have a picture of someone. And I wonder if...I would like to know if anyone here has seen him."

The girl nodded profusely and waited. I reached into the bag near my feet, found Julio's drawing, unrolled it and held it out.

The girl and the man both rose to their toes and peered intently at the sketch. Then they returned their weight to their heels and began to jabber at each other. The guttural tones sounded sharp and angry, and alarm began to creep across my shoulders. But the girl looked up and smiled again. "You are hungry?"

I started to shake my head, but Winona jabbed me in the ribs with her elbow. "They ask you to eat," she grunted, "you got to do it. That be a big thing with them."

So, I put on the most gracious face I could muster and thanked both man and girl.

The man strode away toward the dwellings. A barefoot and quite naked boy of about nine appeared and took the horse's reins. Winona and I stepped down from the wagon and followed the girl around the bank of dwellings to what seemed to be a small, rudely made castle of adobe bricks. There were even eight narrow towers, like little turrets. The entrance was low and perfectly square.

"La Casa del Pueblo," the girl said, smiling solemnly.

I hesitated, hoping it wasn't where they boiled their enemies in oil or some such thing.

Winona nudged me. "Town hall."

We entered the low doorway and found ourselves in complete darkness. Another naked child entered behind us carrying a torch. Now we could see the many vigas that crossed the ceiling and, below them, the rows of mud benches. The girl led us to seats. I cast about for something to say.

"Your English is good."

"Thank you," she smiled. "I learn at the missionary school."

"What is your name?"

"Catarina Torres." She held out her hand. "I take the picture, yes?"

I glanced at Winona, who shrugged; so I handed it over, and the girl disappeared. The boy with the torch still stood just inside the doorway.

I whispered to Winona, "Can't they just say they have seen him or they haven't seen him?"

"They got to do things exact, like they always done it for maybe a million years," Winona said in a normal voice. "Things happen quicker and easier if you just go along with them. Might be this will take some extra time. I do believe they is flummoxed because we is women and we is black and white."

Zia was becoming restless, and I took her to bounce on my knee. "Think what you can tell your grandchildren," I told her. "You visited with wild Indians. You'll be in Philadelphia by then, of course, and everyone will think you very brave and bold."

Zia laughed. Winona said, "I hope you're not countin' on that."

"On what?" I asked, but the girl returned and Winona didn't answer.

The girl brought two clay plates that held what looked like small chicken legs, little balls of meat and corncakes. She handed us the plates, sat down across from us and ducked her head twice, urging us to eat. The meat was not warm, but the flavor was quite good.

"The legs are a mite small, but the chicken is right tasty," I said.

Winona was placidly chewing. She swallowed and shook her head. "Ain't chicken. It's lizard."

It was all I could do not to spit out what was in my mouth. She had given Zia one of the hard corncakes and the baby was happily gumming it.

The man appeared in the doorway, muttered something to the girl, handed her my cloth sketch and left.

When we finished, the girl stood. "Now I will tell you about the picture," she said. "We know of that man." She paused as if that was the full answer to the question I had asked.

I leaned forward. "Please tell me everything you know about him."

The girl nodded, as though she understood perfectly, but then she moved gracefully toward the doorway and disappeared again.

I looked at Winona. "What...?"

Winona shrugged. "She answer your first question, now you done asked another. She got to get leave from the headman. He can't come in here 'cause we is two women. But she can only say what he says is okay."

We sat for some time with only the boy with the torch for company. He kept shifting his weight from one foot to the other and the torch smoke was beginning to fill the room.

Zia, past her nursing time, was getting cranky. I took the baby from Winona and tickled her. When she gurgled with laughter a sadness shot through me. This child was probably the closest I would come to being a mother.

Finally, the girl appeared again and, standing straight in front of us but looking over our heads, began to recite, "The man in the *pintura,* he come to us eleven month ago. He was in bad fight and was hurted from a knife." She pointed to her left side. "We put him in a bed and make him well again. Then he pay us and leave us and we never see him again." With the last sentence, she brought her eyes down to my face.

"Did he say who had hurt him with the knife?"

"He say it was friend. Friend who now bad. Man he come from Texas with. He was happy to stay here because he say the man would get tired looking for him and go away."

"Did he say why they had the fight?"

She shook her head.

I thanked her, praised her people's hospitality; and we joined the man, who had remained outside near the doorway. They escorted us back to our wagon. We mounted to the seats, and I took the reins from the naked boy, who had apparently stood there in the dust the whole time.

"Well, that's that," I muttered to Winona. "It's not a deal of help, but they were very civil. Should I offer them some money?"

"Don't know. Maybe."

I found a coin in my bag and held it out to the girl. She peered at it then shook her head. "No, *señora,* I cannot take money for words."

I smiled then realized she had not asked me for my name. "I am Matilda Summerhayes. I own a ranch near the cuevas, by the springs."

"Si, I know."

I looked at her in surprise, but she offered nothing more. "If I can ever be of help to you or your people, please let me know."

"Gracias, señora." She darted a look at the man, who gave the barest nod.

When both only continued to gaze at me, I thanked them again and turned the horse in a tight circle, trying not to trample the cotton plants. Looking back over my shoulder I could see the girl still standing there, shielding her eyes from the sun. I handed Winona the reins, stood up and called, "Catarina?"

The girl came trotting to the wagon, lithe as an antelope.

"You said he paid?"

She nodded.

"What did he pay you with?"

"Gold."

"Coins?" I asked. "Like this?" I held out the one in my hand.

She shook her head. "No." She pantomimed with her hands. "A...stone of gold."

Diego had been a mere infant when Tonio had blown up the mine, too young to remember its location. Either he had found it again, or he had kept a nugget all these many years.

Chapter Twenty-eight

Franklin was not at all as I expected. Texas was a full-fledged state, whereas New Mexico—or Arizona, as we were called now—was merely a territory; so I had thought to find a good-size town, if not a city. Certainly I reckoned it bigger than Mesilla. I hesitated to alight from the Butterfield Trail stage, thinking this could not be the right place; but the driver assured me it was and that another coach would be departing northward the following morning.

It had been helpful to learn from the Tortugas that Diego Ramirez spent some time with them; but when it came down to it, that really didn't tell us much. It wasn't Diego I was pursuing. I knew where he was: under a pile of earth and rocks on my land. It was his killer I had to find.

Winona had pointed out again that a strange lot of folks seemed real interested in my land. I understood now why poor Diego had that map. The boy's killer might be another. And two unknown men had sought to purchase the ranch. Did they know about the map? Did one—or both of them—kill Diego? I could learn nothing more about the man whose offer Jamie had brought me, but the letter from the attorney had borne an address in Franklin.

The sudden brightness made me squint after the dark of the stagecoach. The public square was not a square at all, just an L-shaped line of dusty, disheveled, low mud buildings baking in the sun. Only the huge wooden platform in the heel of the

L hinted that the public ever gathered here. No huge, graceful cottonwoods shaded this plaza as in Mesilla. Here the sun owned all.

The mountains that rose behind the buildings were handsome, but they had none of the heart-stopping beauty of my own organ-piped ridge. A few shrubs labored to grow in the unyielding clay of the vast open space. Shading my eyes, I made my way quickly toward the line of shops. As in Mesilla, a roof extended almost to the hitching posts to ward off the sun.

In the dry goods store I inquired about V.B. Peticolas, attorney at law. The clerk, a short, spindly fellow with a deep gouge along one cheek, nodded and pointed. Then he touched his face with his pointing finger. "Bobcat," he said. "When I was a young 'un."

"Imagine that," I said in shocked tones that seemed to please him.

The lawyer's office was behind a sort of ironmonger's shop, sandwiched between the smithy and a boarding house. I tried the door and found it open. Inside, the room was tiny, sterile and dark. It smelled of vanilla. I had imagined books and papers, but there was only a barren desk and three empty chairs. On the desk was what appeared to be a jar of very long, very black snap beans.

I cleared my throat, coughed and finally called, thinking there must be a back room where the normal disarray of work was kept. No one responded, so I returned to the heat outside. I had just closed the door behind me when a dapper little man in a round, small-brimmed hat, white shirt and suspenders with shiny brass fastenings came toward me on feet as light and careful as a cat's. The hat looked something like an inverted chamber pot.

He nodded to me so formally it was almost a bow.

"Mr. Peticolas?" I could see the dust on his hat brim but not his face.

He bowed again then cocked his head like a dog waiting for a bone. When I explained that I had received a letter from him, he invited me into his office and ushered me to a chair.

A black wisp of smoke rose from the lamp he lit and he fiddled with the wick until it stopped. "It does char the ceiling," he said confidentially. His accent was that of the deep South. His eyes slid to my bosom. I had worn the calico dress, its bustle refurbished after my spell in jail.

I ignored the leer and agreed that the whiteness of a ceiling was a most important consideration. Then I got down to business. "I'm Matilda Summerhayes from the Mesilla Valley. You wrote me this letter." I pulled it from my bag and held it out.

He took a pair of spectacles from his desk and put them on just long enough to glance at the letter and once more at my bosom. Franklin women must be very flat-chested. "Ah, yes," he said. "You have decided to sell. Very wise of you, very wise."

"No. I've come to ask you who made this offer."

He blinked at me with something like shock. "Why, I can't tell you that. I certainly cannot."

"Why not?"

"Because the gentleman wished his name withheld. That is a client's privilege."

I looked at the undeniably soot-free ceiling and willed away the tears that had suddenly threatened. I hadn't realized how much I was counting on this. There were no other possibilities to pursue. "You can tell me nothing?"

His head moved from side to side. "Surely you would not wish me to betray a client's trust?"

I wanted to reach over and shake him, to shout that was exactly what I wanted him to do. Instead, I stuffed the letter back into my bag. Would it do any good to explain why I needed to know his client's identity? I decided it wouldn't, and it was best not to risk his mentioning those reasons to his client.

I rose. "I have wasted my journey, then." I had also run out of all possibility of learning who had tried to buy my land.

"You like the aroma?" he asked, and I couldn't imagine what he was talking about. "Vanilla." He pointed at the jar of beans. "They grow in Mexico. I've always been fond of vanilla." He reached for the jar. "Would you like to take a few? Wrap them in your kerchief. They're quite marvelous."

Like a wooden doll, I handed him my handkerchief and watched as he gingerly extracted two beans, wrapped them carefully and handed it back. "Are you alone in town, Miss Summerhayes? Would you care to have dinner with me? The hotel sets a fine table..."

I stared at him aghast, my hand tingling with the desire to slap the jabbering fool. "No, thank you." I dabbed at my face with the corner of the handkerchief. "I'm afraid I don't feel very well, and it will be another long journey tomorrow."

As I turned to open the door, it occurred to me that I might yet overcome his principles. Turning back, I smiled as brightly as I could and simpered, "Thank you so very much for your time, Mr. Peticolas." I gestured to the nameplate on his desk. "Whatever do the initials stand for?"

He raised his head proudly. "Victor Bernard."

"Victor," I said, in what I hoped was a gentle, mellifluous voice. "I am feeling much better. Perhaps I could have dinner this evening."

He smiled and shook himself like a rewarded herd dog. "Ah, that is excellent, excellent. We will have a most amusing time."

My dinner with Victor Bernard Peticolas was anything but amusing. Between furtive glances at my neckline, he took great pains to explain the profound importance of professional ethics.

Idly, I stirred my rather watery bean soup. "Surely you can tell me where your client is from, his business, something?"

He blinked at that for a few moments. "I suppose there would be no harm in telling you he is a Union officer."

I hid my excitement by attacking the soup with relish. The information wasn't much but at least it narrowed the possibilities. "But, sir," I said, "if he is with the Union..."

Peticolas twittered something to the effect that his professional ethics transcended a mere war. The fact that his client was an enemy officer was quite beside the point.

Gently, I cut him off. "I must make a confession."

At that, he looked quite eager.

"You have been so kind. And I fear that I have shamefully hidden something from you. The fact is, I have, indeed, decided to sell my ranch."

He mopped at his mouth with a napkin. "That is excellent, Miss Summerhayes."

"Do call me Matilda." I watched his eyes light up as though someone had touched a match to them. "Yes, I have decided to return east to Philadelphia, and of course, I will need to sell my property here."

"Yes, yes?"

"But there is a condition. I will deal only with the gentleman who proposes to purchase the ranch. You must put me in touch with him."

"I fear I cannot do that."

"Then I will sell to someone else. I have had another offer."

Peticolas looked as crestfallen as a wet bantam rooster.

"Why, if I do wish to sell, can you not arrange a meeting?"

"Because the gentleman left very specific instructions in the event such a situation arose. He said I was to tell you he is traveling and cannot be reached."

"But if he is with the Union Army, he must be in the territory."

"I do not know, Miss Summerhayes."

Angry, I jumped up, almost spilling the soup. "Then the offer was not in good faith."

The little man gazed at me looking quite forlorn. "I must abide by my instructions," he said doggedly.

I summoned the haughtiest tone I could. "Don't trouble yourself to get up, I can find my way quite well."

◇◇◇

The hotel displayed pots of red flowers in every window. In the morning, I discovered the flowers were made of paper.

There was time for a stroll before the stage was slated to depart, so I wandered, trying to fit a Union officer into my other slim bits of information. I could make no sense of it. And for all I knew, the man could have borrowed or stolen a uniform and not be a military officer at all.

When I returned from my mental meandering, the sun was quite high; and I realized that time was short, but I wasn't sure how to retrace my steps to the public square.

Ahead was an imposing building with bricked arches, tall windows with many rectangles of panes, and even a few large, if sickly looking, trees. I quickened my step, resolving to ask directions there. A man on crutches was emerging from the shade beneath the arches. His leg had been severed at the knee, but he managed to tip his hat and smile.

"Sorry to see you've had such an unfortunate accident," I said, when he'd pointed the way with his crutch.

His face was thin and pale and all nose, like that of a young bird. "No accident," he said. "This was quite on purpose." He chuckled at my frown. "This here's the hospital." He shifted his weight on his remaining foot and pointed at the arches. "Confederate States of America army hospital. I run into a minie ball early on, but we will have ours. Yes, we will."

I hoped he was right. At least I hoped the Confederates would accomplish one thing in battle: eliminate one Union lieutenant. For only then would I be truly free.

◇◇◇

I reached the stagecoach just before it departed, disembarked at La Posta in Mesilla some seven hours later, claimed my horse and wagon from the livery stable and headed home. I was still two or three miles from the ranch when I saw the lights. Every window of the house was aglow. A tingle of dread rattled in my innards. What had happened?

I prodded the horse on; and not pausing to put up the wagon, I moved anxiously to the front door. The parlor was ablaze with light. Ribbons of dark smoke drifted upward from the lanterns.

Everyone but Nacho seemed to be milling about in the brightness. All heads had swung to the door when I flung it open. From across the room, Julio held out his hand and announced, "Señora. The army has won at Glorieta."

In the relief that flooded me, it didn't seem to matter that I wasn't sure which army Julio was talking about.

Chapter Twenty-nine

The next morning, a tense excitement seemed to ooze from every corner of the house. By the time I waked from a fitful sleep and washed and dressed, the decision had been made without me. But I was quick to agree. Julio would remain to look after the ranch. The rest of us would take a well-earned breather and go into town for a full report of the victory.

It was of course the Confederates who had won at Glorieta, as they had won at Valverde two months before, so the retribution we had feared from a returning Union army seemed unlikely.

Herlinda's peculiar fear of Winona was still festering. She refused to share the wagon seat, preferring to sit in the back with her feet hanging over the dust. Ruben and the other hands rode in on their own. Zia was crowing a tune of her own devising; and I handed the reins to Winona, took the baby onto my lap and kissed every inch of her face.

I had slipped Julio's drawing of the Mexican kid into my bag. Perhaps today I would find someone who could tell me more. Surely someone had seen him with his companion, the man who must have, ultimately, killed him.

The plaza was as thronged with people as it had been the day General Sibley made his speech. Confederate flags bobbed here and there in the crowd. The Stars and Bars still looked odd to me. Some people had improvised their own flags, so they didn't all match.

The air seemed to quiver with energy and excitement, and I felt myself swept up in it. I didn't care a tinker's damn for the Rebels or the Federals, but it sure was a fine thing to have something to celebrate. Herlinda and Winona went their separate ways, but I stayed in the plaza drinking in the crowd's exhilaration.

Three men with fresh-scrubbed faces under straw hats sat on a bench strumming banjos, their chins all cocked at the same angle as they concentrated on producing the right notes. I looked about for mariachis. There's something about the strolling Mexican players that warms the heart. But there were none, and I remembered that most of the valley's Mexicans probably would have preferred a Union victory.

I found myself elbow to elbow with Mac MacPherson, who ran the blacksmith shop and livery. Mac must have been nearly fifty, but he hadn't run to fat. His fists were the size of a lamb's hindquarters; his arms, all muscle, were thick as my waist. White hair fell over his ruddy face, and his eyes sparkled with good humor.

"Exactly what happened?" I asked, raising my voice above the buzz of the crowd. "I only heard that there was victory at Glorieta."

"Aye, that there was," said Mac. "My little brother was with 'em." He had a good twenty years on his brother. "He come acrost a messenger and sent back word," he went on. "The Abs wouldn't come out to meet us, so we marched right to their camp to give battle." Confederate troops called the Union Army "Abs" which was short, I supposed, for Abolitionists.

Mac took a piece of paper from his shirt pocket and unfolded it as carefully as if it had been the Declaration of Independence. The paper had been ruled by hand, the writing was carefully neat. He waved it as he talked. "Brian says we pushed them right down into a valley and gave them a proper hiding. Even the Pike's Peakers turnt tail and run. I reckon we knocked them all into a cocked hat," he said happily, as if he had done it himself, single-handed.

"It does seem that way," I said brightly.

Mac's meaty brows knitted in a scowl. "The scoundrels got off with their own cannon and train, though. Then they sent a detachment round through the mountain and took and burnt our train."

Since all the supplies were carried by the wagon train, that seemed to me like a sorry state of affairs for "our" men. It didn't sound like victory.

But Mac was poking a thick finger at the letter. "We showed them a trick or two, though." He pushed the letter toward me. "Could you read it, ma'am? Could you read it out loud?"

It dawned on me that Mac couldn't read, that he had memorized someone else's reading of the letter. I looked at the sentence he was stabbing at and read, "The battle lasted five hours. We had kilt, wounded. They had kilt and wounded," brother Brian had written in his careful script. Mac was repeating my words, committing them to memory.

The Union had suffered casualties. It is a terrible thing to pray that someone you know was among them.

"Don't he write good, though?" Mac said proudly.

I solemnly agreed, then opened my bag, took out Julio's drawing and showed it to him. "Have you ever seen this man? Do you know anything about him?"

"Can't say I do."

"What you got there, sister?" someone shouted, and someone else jostled my arm. A man I'd never seen before was leering at me. He was short and hatless with ears big as jug handles; one of his front teeth was missing. He snatched at the drawing.

"It's just a picture," I said. "Nothing to do with the battle."

"Pitcher o' what?" he demanded, lisping around the missing tooth.

"Just a drawing of a Mexican boy. Ever seen him?" I turned the drawing toward him.

He eyed the paper. "Who made it?" he snapped.

"Julio Lujan. He's an excellent artist; the likeness is good. Have you ever seen—?" But the churlish little man had grabbed the picture from my hand.

Mac lunged at him, but the fellow was gone quick as a bobcat with a fresh kill.

Just then a thin-shouldered man climbed the steps to the platform in the center of the plaza and rose above the crowd. He held out his hand, palm down.

I put my hand on Mac's arm. "Never mind, it wasn't important." Julio could make another drawing for me.

A man in a pale grey uniform was mounting the platform. The crowd applauded wildly. Someone threw torn-up paper into the air. The man nodded, and the hand clapping faded.

"Major Trevanion Teel," Mac said into my ear, pronouncing it *Tree-vane-eon*. "He come in the stable this morning to get his horse shod."

Major Teel obviously had been to the barber recently, too. His red-gold beard had been closely trimmed and his mustache made a perfect angle under his nose.

"Ladies and gentlemen," he said, and the crowd twittered like birds.

"Our soldiers have given another evidence of the daring courage and heroic endurance which actuate them in this great struggle for the independence of your country. The battle of Glorieta—where for six long hours they steadily drove before them a foe of twice their numbers—will take its place upon the roll of this country's triumphs. It will not be long until not a single soldier of the United States will be left on the soil of New Mexico."

Major Teel stretched out both arms like a priest bestowing a blessing, and the crowd broke into cheers.

The rest of the day was more celebration than I ever expect to see again. The Fountain brothers had ordered a whole pig and a couple of goats cooked slowly in a pit dug into the ground.

Isabel Tolhurst, all decked out in a gingham dress and a straw hat, was among the women handing out platters of food. I tried to avoid her. After I was arrested she apparently had not attempted to make good on her threat to run Winona from the Mesilla Valley. I didn't want to revive those thoughts now. But as luck would have it, I found myself face to face with her.

She raised her head and fixed me with eyes as round and hard as the balls for a pistol. "I reckon that slave of yours is not too happy with this turn of events."

"Isabel, truly. Winona is not a slave. She's a free woman."

"A nigra who casts spells is a threat to us all," she intoned and spun away to someone else before I could answer.

Two of the washerwomen left behind by the army were Negresses, and Winona happily reported she had known the cousin of one of them. Even Herlinda was in good spirits, nodding and smiling and chatting with the Mexican women who had clustered at one corner of the plaza. They may have had little reason to relish a Confederate victory, but a good party is hard to resist.

Nacho and the rest of the hands were still enjoying the revelry when the two women and I headed home, exhausted and stuffed. Herlinda had even ceased to eye Winona with dark suspicion. The day's jubilation felt like some kind of gentle fluid running in the veins, warm and tingly. The wind was blowing my hair, and the sunset behind us was dying the organ-pipe mountains deep red. I lifted my face to the wind and let the horses have their heads.

The sky had darkened enough that I couldn't see the house, but I knew exactly the place on the road where I should see lantern light in the parlor window. Whenever anyone was returning after dark, we always lit the lantern in the parlor. Always. Even though Herlinda grumbled about it. I pinched my eyes shut then looked again, but ahead was only darkness. I told myself that Julio had probably fallen asleep.

With no reminder from the reins, the horses clattered to a stop in front of the barn. No light came from the house at all, not even the slight blush from a lard lamp. The air was still as a grave. Fear began to prickle at the back of my neck.

Winona and Herlinda were easing themselves from the seat, faces placid and undisturbed. I forced myself to walk calmly to the back door and threw it open.

"Julio?" I called. "Why isn't the lantern lit?" The house was utterly still.

I moved quickly through the dark kitchen to the parlor and struck a match to light the lantern. Neither Herlinda nor Winona seemed to think anything was amiss. I lit another lantern and told them I would put up the horses.

From the patio I could see the low shadowy line of the bunk-house. It, too, was dark. The horses, still in harness, were restive. I unhitched them from the wagon and saw to their feed.

Not until I was about to leave the barn did I glance up toward the roof.

Gorge rose in my throat as I stared through the lantern light at what swung from a viga on the far side of the barn. A dark form dangled limply, almost directly over the spot where the Mexican boy had died. I lurched closer.

It was Julio.

Chapter Thirty

I could not seem to make a sound. It was as though a boulder had smacked into my chest, knocking the wind from me forever. When I did scream, it sounded like it was coming from someone else.

The face of the poor body that hung above me was horribly twisted. The fingers were bloody where Julio had clawed desperately at the rope.

In the shadows beyond that pitiful form, a dark hulk sprawled as if it had been thrown there. I lifted the lantern and moved forward, then sucked in my breath. In the straw lay my hope for the future. George Washington would sire no more fine colts.

My eyes searched his flank, his sides, his neck for the bullet hole that had to be there, but the huge and handsome body seemed unmarked. The legs were bent, as if he had died fighting. Then my lantern light reached the head.

The bullet had entered the left eye and torn the skull asunder.

A screech like that of a banshee came from behind me. I whipped around. Herlinda threw herself to the straw beneath Julio's dangling feet and began to tear her hair.

I choked out, "Oh, God, Herlinda." Struggling for some way to live through the next moment with my own despair, I knew hers must be greater than anything I could imagine. I leaned over her, touched her shoulder. She flinched away. "This won't help him," I said.

She flailed at me with her fists, a horrible wrenching sound coming from her throat.

Backing away, I felt hands close on each of my arms near the shoulder. "Mercy, mercy, mercy," Winona breathed. "Did he do this hisself?"

I shook my head. "No," I said shakily. "This wasn't by his own hand. Look." I raised the lantern toward the slain stallion.

Winona drew in a deep breath. "Lord have mercy. Who done this?"

"Get a knife," I rasped, my voice like sandpaper. "A sharp one. We can't let the boy hang there."

Winona blinked at me, then backed out of the barn.

I peered into the shadows beyond Herlinda. Julio must have been forced to stand on something to be hanged. But there was no chair, no table that could have been yanked away in the final moment. Whoever had done it had tidied up.

Why? The word glanced off the walls of my mind like a metal ball in a metal box. I wanted to throw myself on the floor with Herlinda and tear at my own hair.

I cut Julio down. Standing on a table, I hacked at the rope with a cleaver.

"Get Herlinda out of the way. He'll fall on her." But Herlinda hissed and spit and kicked when Winona tried to move her.

My knees began to go to wobbly as the table teetered.

"Wha—?" Someone had come into the barn. I whirled, grasping the cleaver as a weapon.

Ruben was staring at the body of his brother as it swung in the lamplight next to me. *"Jesús, Maria y Josef,"* he whispered as he sagged to his knees and crossed himself.

"Please," I said after a moment, and realized I was whispering. I cleared my throat and tried to speak normally. "Get your mother out of here."

Digging his knuckles into his eyes, he nodded, then rose, crossed the barn and picked up Herlinda as if she were a child. She hammered at his chest with her fists. *"Bruja,"* she hissed over

Ruben's shoulder at Winona. "You kill *mi hijo.*" Big, strangling, choking sobs tore from her throat.

I heard those sobs all night long. Not in my sleep—my eyes would not close.

Hours after Herlinda's keening wails had become hoarse and finally ground to a ragged halt, I paced the house, eyes scratchy, as if sand had gathered beneath the lids.

I could not have been more guilty of Julio's death if I had held the noose. It was I who had shown that horrid little man in the plaza the drawing and told him the name of the artist. The man had seemed mean, even wicked, but not clever enough for this sort of killing. Perhaps he had passed the information to someone else. Someone who was frightfully cunning.

Julio's killer had wanted to make certain there would be no more drawings, but he wanted to serve a warning to me. Else why would he also slaughter my prize stud, shoot him through the eye, much the same way that calf I found at the reservoir last year had been shot?

The next morning, Herlinda had Ruben lay Julio on the dining room table, and there she bathed and dressed him. To erase some of the agony from his distorted face, she wadded up some cloth and pushed it into his mouth to give his cheeks a little roundness. Then she wrapped him carefully from head to toe in a bolt of pale muslin. She made almost no sound at all, but tears streamed down her cheeks to spatter the cloth with little circles of dampness.

She refused my help, but I stood like a pillar of ice in the corner, watching. Only when she was finished did I realize my hand was covering my mouth as if to still any sounds that might leak out.

All of us were like swimmers who had ventured too far from shore, unable to do more than tread water, struggling to stay afloat. Winona's face was set in a fearsome scowl. Ruben was so drunk that when I sent him in the wagon for Tonio he could barely guide the horse. The other hands wore an air of disbelief. Nacho's eyes held a dreadful look. Aside from the Indian women, who seemed on better terms with death than we, Herlinda, with her doleful task, appeared the calmest of us all.

That afternoon, we laid Julio in the second grave in that corner of the ranch. Death seemed to hover on the wind that stirred the leaves of the gnarled cottonwood overhead. It had struck two youths who had not yet reached their twentieth year, and something in me feared it might not have done with us yet.

Winona knelt behind me murmuring prayers in an odd and rhythmic language. I hoped Julio's mother could not hear her, that she would not mistake this for some sort of spell.

The notion that Julio had been killed because of me went on gnawing at the already frayed corners of my mind. He had died because someone wanted my land. And the days of simply turning down offers to buy it were over.

Tonio said some words I don't remember and I tried to play the flute, but the notes quavered and died. When the men began to shovel the clods of clay into the grave, a cry burst from Herlinda, and she flung herself onto the coffin. The moans that came from her throat were sounds I hope I never hear again.

Ruben and two others dragged her away. Mournfully, he pinned her to the ground while the others filled the hollow and we covered the broken earth with rocks to ward off coyotes.

She was still keening, thrashing and tearing her hair when it was over. The others returned to the house. I sat down next to Ruben, and we tended his mother until she finally seemed to have purged the worst of her pain.

We buried George Washington the following day. I could not shake the numbness that had settled over me that night in the barn when I cut Julio down. For the next few weeks I found it nearly impossible to get up in the morning; and once I was out of bed, nothing seemed worth the doing. I could manage little more than putting one foot in front of the other, attending to one chore after another.

I was certain the same vicious person had slain both boys, destroyed the stallion and probably set fire to the range and maimed that calf as well. Very likely he had also made two offers to purchase my land at a price far below value. But for the life of me, I could think of no reason an officer in the Union Army should do these things, nor could I think of a way to smoke him out.

We had our hands full with horses to be tended, the rest of the garden to plant, hides to be tanned, butter churned. Eleven hens that had stopped laying had to be dispatched and plucked, a fence needed mending, the small stand of winter wheat was ready for cutting and milling.

And it somehow became my task to see to it that Winona and Herlinda were never together in the same room. That effort alone left me bone-tired at the end of a day.

I couldn't bear the thought of riding into town so I sent Ruben to report his brother's murder and the killing of our stallion. He returned with a message that Sheriff Zeke wanted me to stop by the next time I came to town.

Given the second inexplicable murder at my ranch, I didn't like to consider why Zeke might ask to see me.

A pall of sadness still hung over Nacho, and I urged him to take some time off; but when one of the mares was about to foal he went out to the barn and, in a rusty voice, insisted on seeing to her himself.

The foal, when it came, was a sturdy little fellow and I couldn't help but smile at his dignity as he stood while his mother licked him clean. This one, Nacho said, we would not geld, but it would be a couple of years before we would know if he would make a fit stud. I told myself the healthy little colt was a start. Perhaps we could buy a few gravid mares at the next auction.

But at best, the slaying of George Washington had set back any hope of selling the ranch for at least two additional years, four more years in all.

It turned hot the following afternoon and everyone retired for siesta. When I was sure I was alone, I went out to the barn and took a pistol from the wall where the guns hung with the tack. I loaded it, then went into the parlor, got down on my knees to the left of the fireplace and pressed on the bottom row of tiles where the painted mockingbird raised its wings.

The tile panel scraped and came away from the adobe wall. I slid the heavy panel to the side and reached in to unlock the chest that sat in the niche behind it. The wall was more than a foot thick. Andrew would have been happy to know that his "mother's" chest was quite safe.

I pulled out a sack of coins and winced a little at how slim it had grown. Still, there was nearly two thousand dollars left. I counted it carefully. Enough to buy another stud. Enough to pay the hands, enough to be able to hang on for at least another few years. If nothing dreadful happened.

I put the sack back, closed the chest; and on top of it, I laid the pistol. Then I meticulously replaced the tile panel.

I was just getting to my feet when the shot exploded somewhere in the back of the house, followed by the sound of several pairs of running feet. I turned to start for the hall, but my feet seemed nailed to the floor.

"My God, woman, you've done kilt her!" The voice belonged to Jed Riley, one of the hands. He had apparently come through one of the doors from the patio.

His shout was followed by a shriek. Herlinda.

I dashed down the hall toward Winona's room, fearing I would find her with her brains splattered over her pillow. I shouldered my way past the three men who had gathered in the doorway.

Herlinda was cowering belligerently in a corner. Winona lay on the bed, eyes wide and shiny in a pasty grey face, mouth open in a small O. Zia, tucked under her left arm and apparently unscathed, had begun an angry squalling. Sucking in my breath, my eyes darted over Winona. Maybe it wasn't too late. Where was the wound?

She turned her head slowly to look at me and I saw where the bullet had landed. Next to her face was a mound of feathers that had burst from a round hole in her pillow. A scant inch above it, Winona's earlobe dripped blood into the feathers.

I shooed everyone from the room, ordered Herlinda to wait for me in my office and closed the door. Then I went to the bed, picked up the hiccoughing Zia, took Winona's hand in mine and looked into her face. "Are you all right?"

She blinked at me thoughtfully as if taking inventory of her various and sundry parts, then nodded slowly. "I appears to be okay, but I sure enough ain't amused."

Balancing Zia in one arm, I tended to Winona's ear with a drop of whiskey, and she screwed her face into such a fierce expression that I almost laughed. "It could have been worse," I told her. "A lot worse."

"Could have been a mite better, too," she grumbled, pushing my hand away and getting out of bed to stomp across the room to the bureau. She stabbed her finger at the door. "I tell you true, for myself, I can put up with most anything. But if that woman harm my chil', I break her in halfs and use her for kindling."

Herlinda sat sullenly in my office while I spoke to her blank face. "You are a fool. You could be put in jail. Winona is no *bruja*. You cannot blame her for…" My voice hitched. "For God's sake! She was in town with us that day." I almost choked on the memory of Julio. "If you have to blame someone, blame me. If you can't live here peaceably, leave. Leave now."

All the while, I was praying she would not leave. I knew full well that Nacho would not let her go off alone, and I needed him desperately. No one had his art with horses. She stared at me woodenly until, in exasperation, I sent her back to the kitchen.

That night I sent for Nacho. Perhaps he could talk some sense into her.

"Señora?" he said from the doorway. He was pale and haggard, and there was an awful look about his eyes that shot a knife of panic through me.

He took two staggering steps and wilted to the floor. His old sweat-stained hat rolled drunkenly toward the stove.

Chapter Thirty-one

Winona and I reached Nacho at the same time. "Holy God," I said, rolling him over, searching for the bullet hole, praying it wouldn't be in the chest or the gut. But there was no blood, no wound.

Winona touched his face with her fingers and drew in a sharp breath.

"What is it?"

"He be on fire. He burning up."

I laid my hand across his forehead. The flesh was dry and papery and hotter than caliche in the worst heat of July. "My God." I stared into Winona's eyes. "What is it?"

"Don't know. Maybe the pox."

I tried to unbutton his shirt with fingers gone thick and wooden.

Winona shoved my hands away. "You back off, now. I had me the pox when I was a little gal."

We both knew no one got the pox twice. If you lived through it, you were safe from it forever. She undid the buttons one at a time. It was all I could do not to tear the shirt open.

But no telltale blisters dotted his chest.

Nacho moaned and his head lolled to the side. He began to shake with an ague the like of which I'd never seen. He pulled his arms across his chest, and his whole body twitched with shudders.

"Herlinda," I called, fearing he would die on the spot. "Herlinda!"

Something in my voice must have told her not to dally because she appeared in the doorway almost immediately and, seeing Nacho's shaking body, threw herself across his chest, as if his cure lay in keeping him pinned to the floor. A howl, like that of an animal when first the trap springs, filled the room. Her head lolled from side to side, her black eyes like death itself.

But he was not dead. Not yet. Death may command resignation; illness is something to pit oneself against.

"Stop it." I bent over her, clasped her shoulder. "Get him to bed," I said gently but firmly, as to a frantic child. "Keep him warm." I straightened and headed for the door. "Herlinda, you cannot move him by yourself. You must allow Winona to help you. Do you hear? You must do as I say. I'm going for Tonio."

Listening to Fanny's hoofs beat along the path to the cuevas, I didn't know my breaths were coming so shallow until my head began to feel full of feathers and I had to grab the horn to keep myself from pitching from the saddle. I was less sure there was any hope in pitting myself against this horrible disease, whatever it was. Tonio was wise in the ways of medicines, but he could not perform miracles. I well knew I couldn't run the ranch without Nacho, and that without his steadying influence I even feared Herlinda a little.

But all that aside, with Jamie gone, other than Winona, Nacho was my only real friend. And I was frightened not only for him but for myself.

Faithless as I knew I was, I prayed, *Please, God, deliver this good man from such a fate as this.*

◇◇◇

They were not able to get Nacho into a bed. When I returned with Tonio he was thrashing about on the floor where he had fallen. Herlinda and Winona were desperately trying to keep him covered him with blankets; but as soon as they wrapped one around him, he kicked it away. His eyes were tight shut, his hands defensive in front of his greyish face, like a small child trying to protect itself from an attacker.

I turned in wordless bewilderment to Tonio, who stood in the doorway taking in the scene. Winona was trying to sponge Nacho's face with water from a dented cooking pot, but he knocked the towel from her hand, groaning, "No, no. Papa. No. *El verdugo.* Nooo…" His voice became a shriek and he writhed as if in combat with Satan himself. *"Ahorcarse!"* he screamed. Then he repeated the same word in a voice of utter desolation.

Herlinda's eyes widened with horror, and she stared at Winona. Then she reached across Nacho's writhing body, grabbed the straps of Winona's apron and shook her like a rag doll.

"Bruja!" she screamed. *"Bruja!"* She threw herself at Winona.

By the time I could cover the few feet that separated us, the straps of the apron had torn and Herlinda was wrapping them around Winona's throat.

"Stop!" I shouted, wrestling with her. With the brute strength of the demented, she gouged my face with her fingernails. Then her hands, fingers still rigid, were moving away.

Tonio had grasped her by the forearms and pulled her to her feet, where he held her immobile until she stopped struggling. Then he pulled her to his chest, crooning something in comforting tones; and she sagged to her knees, made the sign of the cross, fingered the rosary she always wore around her neck and began to pray. Tears spilled down her face and dripped on the floor.

Winona had returned to mopping Nacho's face with the towel. The poor man tried to twist his head away. He opened his eyes then covered them with his hands.

"La luz," he groaned. The light. I understood the word but couldn't fathom the meaning. He opened his mouth, and a greenish bile spilled down his chin. Then his body went still, and I screamed.

Tonio probed Nacho's neck then put his ear to Nacho's chest. I closed my eyes against the certainty that he would find no pulse, hear no heartbeat.

Tonio's head remained that way for a long time, the silence broken only by the murmur of Herlinda's prayers and the little splash of water each time Winona's towel returned to the pot.

Gently, Tonio pulled away the shirt and raised Nacho's arm. Winona and I stared. The lump in the armpit seemed as big, the flesh as red and tight, as an over-ripe crabapple.

Tonio was staring, too, his eyes narrowed to slits.

"Is he dead?" I whispered.

He shook his head, then gathered Nacho in his arms as one picks up a child. "Get a bed ready," he said, rising to his feet.

Herlinda looked up at him fearfully then scurried ahead of us to the room she shared with Nacho.

◇◇◇

Tonio and I sat in the kitchen with cups of bad coffee trying to regain some sense of normality. I had taken him in the wagon to the cuevas, where he collected a half-dozen packets of herbs and powders. At my cook-stove, he'd prepared some concoctions that he forced between Nacho's lips. Most had rolled down the leathery chin, and Winona mopped it away while Herlinda's frantic eyes darted from face to face. She had seemed on the very verge of trying to stop us, but she didn't.

I daresay Tonio's certainty, his command of the situation, lent all of us a scrap of security. He had given firm orders that no one was to leave the sickroom without scrubbing hands and arms with lye soap. When the bedclothes were removed, they were to be burned. Herlinda had gasped at that, but the look on Tonio's face brooked no argument.

A knife, fork, spoon, cup and plate were to be set aside to feed Nacho and boiled in hot water for the better part of an hour immediately after he finished. And we were all to eat as much garlic as we could get down.

Now Herlinda and her son were with Nacho, Winona was seeing to Zia and Tonio and I sat mute and weary on the slat-backed chairs in the kitchen, sipping coffee neither of us wanted.

There was death in the air. I could fairly smell its bitter scent.

"What in the name of God is it?" I asked dully, wondering if we would all die of this awful sickness. Putting a name to it might somehow put it in our grasp, make it manageable. "It can't be pox."

Tonio shook his head and stared at the ceiling. His bleak brown eyes traveled slowly to mine.

I waited. Then, "What is it? For God's sake, tell me!"

"Plague," he said. "It is bubonic plague."

Chapter Thirty-two

I insisted that Tonio take one of the horses; and after making me promise to fetch him if there was any change, he departed for the cuevas riding clumsily, a little too stiff-legged but well enough.

None of us slept that night. We moved about the rooms slowly and very quietly, speaking little and only in whispers, as if death were asleep nearby and we feared to rouse him.

We spelled each other at the bedside. Herlinda had refused to leave Winona alone with Nacho, but she was so exhausted she fainted and Ruben carried her to the parlor.

Tonio was back at dawn with more herbal mixtures. He listened long at Nacho's chest then announced softly, "The lungs are clear."

Nacho continued half-awake, half-asleep, delirious. Whenever he opened his eyes, he muttered *"la luz"* in such distress that we finally understood that any but the dimmest light hurt his eyes. He did no more shouting. He was too weak.

Herlinda and I were at the cook-stove preparing tortillas when Winona wandered into the kitchen with Zia. Herlinda stiffened. I put my hand on her arm. "She is a good woman. Believe me. She is no witch, no *bruja."*

Herlinda dropped the spatula she was using to turn the tortillas and began to weep. She drew up the skirt of her apron and hid her face. *"Estára,"* she sobbed. *"Estára."*

I put my arms around her and she clung to me like a frightened child. I led her to a chair. "Why?" I asked. "Why must Winona be a witch?"

"Only *bruja* make him speak of *el padre.*"

"I don't understand."

"His father, he hang. They say he was horse thief. Ignacio, he was there. He see it. *Un niño.* A child. *La bruja* make him see it again. *La bruja* make him see *el verdugo.* The hangman!"

Herlinda gasped and burst into fresh tears. *"Señora,"* she wailed. *"El favor de usted.* You would not send us away for this thing?"

"Send you away because Nacho is ill?"

"Because the father was horse thief," Herlinda wailed between sobs.

"Good heavens, of course not! Nacho is the best man with horses I've ever laid eyes on. I don't care what his father did. If he taught Nacho about horses, I'm even grateful to him." I tried to keep my voice calm and cheerful despite the bitterness that rose in me. How could God make a man wracked with illness relive such a nightmare?

◇◇◇

On the third day, Nacho's fever fell. Still, he barely clung to consciousness. Tonio arrived just as the sun sent its first slanting rays down the mountain. He sent everyone from the sickroom and bade us rest. We all scrubbed our arms and hands raw and tried to nap.

I was asleep as soon as my body touched the mattress. When I woke the window was already beginning to dim with dusk. Tonio was standing over me. His cheeks were hollow with shadow, but his eyes were bright.

"He will live," he said softly. "The worst is past."

Relief was like gravity, drawing me closer to the earth. I put my hand over my eyes to let the news absorb slowly, to be sure it was real. "Thank God."

Tonio stretched out his hands to me; and I rose, feeling light now from the empty spaces in my being where the fear had been. His arms opened, and I laid my head against his chest. His beard smelled of wood smoke mixed with something faintly like verbena.

"Sorry I woke you," he said. "I just wanted you to know as soon as I was sure."

I tightened my arms around him. "Thank you."

"Herlinda is with Nacho, Winona spelled me earlier." The creases at the corners of his eyes deepened. "She does have a way with her, your Winona."

I frowned. "You didn't let her do anything…odd…did you?"

He chuckled. "It would have been worth my life to stop her."

"Like what? What did she do?" I asked cautiously.

"Nothing harmful. A wax doll near his lips. To draw the demon, I suppose. Herlinda was asleep," he said to the look on my face. "I didn't leave the doll there." He opened his hand, and a small dark lump gleamed on his palm. The doll seemed to be all misshapen head with many legs bent at the knees. It looked quite like Evelina, my tarantula.

No one else had appreciated the spider's company, so I had taken her outside, had a solemn talk with her and bade her goodbye. Whenever I saw a tarantula scurrying around a corner of the house I was always convinced it was Evelina still hanging about to keep me company.

I shook my head at Tonio. "You've had years of Christian training. How could you let her do that?"

His shoulders lifted, and a smile tried to happen around his mouth. "What possible harm could it do? Besides, there's something to be said for hedging one's bet." He peered at me in the pale light. "What's wrong?"

A chill had passed over me. I struggled to smile. "Someone walking on my grave, I suppose. What of the rest of us? Will we catch it?"

Tonio stepped back. His shoulders sagged, and he shook his head. "I don't know."

"We did exactly as you said. I made sure no one left Nacho's room without washing. We burned his clothes; we'll burn his sheets and nightshirt. We've eaten so much of garlic, I'm sure they can smell us in town. But is that enough? I know so little about plague."

"I've seen a few cases. Doctors who have treated it say people who are meticulous about those things won't catch it from each other. They believe it's spread by insects. Fleas."

I looked at him in dismay. "We haven't had a flea problem recently, but we have so many animals..."

"That's why we are eating so much garlic. No one is certain, of course, but those who consume a goodly measure of the stuff don't seem to sicken with plague."

"Garlic cures the plague?"

"It doesn't cure. But it does seem to prevent. Perhaps fleas don't like the taste of garlic eaters."

I was about to say that couldn't be true because the Mexicans use a lot of garlic when I remembered Herlinda preparing Nacho's meals separately the past few weeks because spicy food was troubling his stomach.

Tonio moved toward the door. "You can go back to sleep if you like. Nothing needs doing. We could use more water, but I'll take the wagon and fetch some. I rested a bit earlier."

I didn't want to sleep. Nacho was going to live. Death was no longer camped on my doorstep. I wanted to celebrate. "Let's both go."

◇◇◇

By the time we reached the spring the sun had sunk into the ground, but the moon was putting out so much light it seemed to have gone quite lopsided with the effort. A fair rivulet was sloshing down the rock. I maneuvered the wagon as close to the spring as I could, as the jars weigh a good deal when full.

"How do you haul your own water?" I asked Tonio, thinking the cuevas was a ways to walk from here if one was carrying anything heavy.

"I have a flat jug that fits in a sort of harness on my back." He handed me two of the empty jars. "I learned that from an Indian woman. Never did learn to carry anything on my head, though. Haven't the neck for it, I suppose. The harness works well. I can carry enough for two or three days."

"I haven't been here in a long time," I said. "Last year, the arroyo over there flooded, and I was trapped. I was certain I was going to drown."

"Mmmm," he nodded. "Soon after I got here."

"You must have been at the spring just before the flood. I saw a man's boot prints."

"I don't remember." He handed me another jar.

Glancing at his feet, I saw his boots had almost no heel at all—the sort worn by those who don't spend much time in a saddle. Certainly, someone had been at the spring; and I'd been convinced that someone was nearby, close enough to hear me shouting. But none of that seemed to matter now. The deepening night was filled with the sound of splashing and the wonderful smell of damp earth.

The clay jars filled quickly. When the last was done, I scooped up a handful of water and lifted it to my face, letting it run down my neck till it made me shiver. Tonio had turned to watch. The past days had written deep lines into his face. I scooped up more water and tossed it at him.

A smile fluttered at one corner of his mouth. He stood stock still for a moment, his face damp in the moonlight, then nudged me aside and flung a handful of water on me. I giggled and pushed him away to fill my own hands again. Laughing, he dodged and ran, with me after him hell-bent for mud.

Tonio, much faster than I, disappeared into the shadows of an old oak so bent it almost touched the ground. By the time I reached the tree there was no sign of him at all. I drew up and stooped to peer beneath the lowest limbs and found myself looking straight into his face. He'd stuck out his tongue, put his thumbs in his ears and was waggling his fingers. When I folded up with laughter, he sprang up and wrestled me to the ground, his baritone laugh booming while I yelped with fury.

I dug my fingers into his ribs, and we rolled beneath the tree. He circled my ankle with one hand, made short work of my shoe and tickled my feet until tears trickled down my cheeks.

"Enough?" he yelled.

"Yes," I squealed, still writhing but quite helpless. He released my ankle, caught my face between his hands and looked into my eyes until I was certain he could see my soul. I realized I had never heard him laugh before. Chuckle, yes, but not really laugh. And lately, I'd done precious little laughing myself.

Without releasing my eyes from his, he dropped his fingers to my collar and began to undo my blouse.

Never before or since has it been quite like that for me, like a celebration of all that's right in the world. When he raised himself above me in the final thrust, exquisite waves of joy thrummed over me.

We lay lazy and spent, arms and legs woven together like the reeds of a half-finished basket. When he finally rolled away, an acute emptiness swept over me, a sense of profound loss.

He tossed my blouse over my face; and when I pulled it down to my chin, his eyes moved slowly from mine to my nose then my mouth. His smile was like an ember from some somber hearth deep within him. Suddenly self-conscious, I turned my back to dress.

Chapter Thirty-three

The afternoon was unseasonably warm. The land was dry, and dust devils were twisting here and there. It wasn't likely to rain again till midsummer. Fanny shifted her weight and snorted as I mopped my brow with a kerchief that still smelled of vanilla and gave chase yet again to a stubborn horse.

The week before, I had made my first purchases at the stock auction without Nacho at my elbow. He had wanted to come along, but he still looked gaunt and was a little unsteady on his feet; so I bit the bullet alone and bought a couple dozen head of new horses. Nacho looked them over when they arrived, and his approving nod meant more to me than the money I'd spent.

But one of the new arrivals, a black gelding with a white blaze, had run off. The colts would need another dozen months of feeding before they had much value and I wouldn't begin to clear my expenses for at least another year, so I wasn't about to lose that ornery black.

Neck outstretched and running like the wind, he seemed determined to leave the territory. Already, I had chased him for miles. Along the way I had picked up a stray mule.

The gelding was quick and clever, and I had lost my last bit of patience an hour before. I was getting better with a riata, having practiced on the calves; but cattle tend to run in a straighter line while horses dart from side to side as quick as squirrels. Four times I had swung my rope and missed. Mules are even cleverer than horses, and this one seemed to be enjoying a game of his own devising in which he nipped the horse on the rump to goad it on. I'd had about enough of it.

The black flounced into an arroyo, and the thick brush swallowed him. No, you don't, I thought, urging Fanny down the slope after him. But there was no movement at the bottom at all. The rogue was smart enough to keep still. I rode into the brush and scanned every bit of scrub big enough to hide him. Nothing. But at least it was cool enough here for lunch. The black couldn't get far without my hearing him.

Not bothering to dismount, in case that consarned gelding took off again, I fumbled at the saddlebag and took out a chunk of cheese and some dry bread. Intent on detecting sounds from the horse inside the arroyo, I heard no sounds from above; and when I glanced up to the rim, the two men, clear and sharp against the sky, startled me.

They both were mounted; both wore hats with broad brims. With the sun behind them, they looked like black cutouts on horseback.

Both men seemed jittery. The smaller of the two was jabbing a finger at a paper he held. Every few seconds one of them would nervously twist his head around to scan the landscape. I sat there in plain sight, but neither saw me. The wind was carrying their voices away, and for a time I could make no sense of what they were saying; but some primal wariness stilled my urge to call out to them.

Then the wind changed, and their words became quite clear.

"...know damn well that woman has the map," one of them was saying.

I froze. Somewhere, I had heard that voice before. Where? Who was it? Both men had turned their backs to the arroyo, so I couldn't even tell which was speaking. Hunching down in the saddle, I pressed a trembling hand against Fanny's shoulder and, terrified she would choose that moment to snort or paw the ground, slowly backed her into the thick shadows.

"How could you be such a goddamn fool as to lose it?"

"That jo-fired, lickspittle idiot shot at me. Grazed my head. When she come running out, toting a pistol, I had to hide, didn't I? When I went to check the body it was gone."

"She don't know what the map means, does she?"

"No. But the bitch isn't stupid. She knows it means something."

"If she doesn't understand that map, why wouldn't she sell?"

Still poking at it with his forefinger, the shorter man handed over the paper. Both men nodded in quick little jerks.

The high-pitched neigh of a startled horse came from behind me, and the stray black gelding burst from the scrub with the mule close behind. I stopped breathing, prepared to bolt. Fanny shifted her weight, but the sound was lost in the gelding's commotion. A bead of perspiration ran down my forehead and burned my eye with its salt.

The larger man peered into the arroyo. I glimpsed sun-whitened hair, a broad, squarish face of sun-darkened skin. He spotted the gelding, and a thin white scar running from jaw to ear flashed white in the dark face.

He turned back to his companion, gestured at something; and they turned their horses. The movement shifted the one nearest me out of its own shadow. I didn't recognize the men, but I recognized that horse: a palomino mare with three white stockings. She had been among the group I had handed over to the Confederacy.

Both riders disappeared from view. I waited a good long time in the arroyo before digging my heels gently into Fanny's side and urging her to take me home.

When I reached the corral, I was still deep in thought. Fanny stopped and patiently waited. I squeezed my eyes shut and chewed my lower lip, still trying to place the voice and the face. Two things were dead certain: at least one of those men was a murderer, and somewhere, some time, I had heard the voice of, had probably met, one of them.

"You going to stand there till the devil comes walking up and taps you on the shoulder?" Winona shouted from the house. "You looks like a statute."

◇◇◇

"You should be in town this very minute telling that sheriff." Winona was sitting at the kitchen table, arms crossed stubbornly across her chest, staring at me while I dried my hair.

I had sweat so much and was so covered with dust that I'd filled a basin, dunked my head in the cool water and given it a good scrubbing. "I knew the voice of one of them, but for the life of me I can't think who it was. I only saw the face of one, and I don't know if he was the one with the voice."

Pressing the towel into my eyes, I tried to see him again; but the image in my head was blurry and wouldn't come clear. "I have to think."

Winona set her chin. "Think! A body what's got a snake in her bedroll don't sit there and think. You going to worry that question back and forth till it's limp. You wait long enough, that dad-blasted bastard will come gunning for you sure as a jackrabbit's got ears. You get yourself into town and tell someone."

The following day, I took her advice and rode in to see Zeke. I needed to see him about Julio, anyway. The six wagons I met heading out of town as I was heading in told me something was up.

In the plaza, men and women with young ones in tow were dashing back and forth across the square. I hitched Fanny to a post and strode straightaway toward the jail. A little boy with tears sliding down apple cheeks careened into me in his haste. I grabbed his chubby arm, bent over and peered into his face.

"What's your name?" I asked the overflowing blue eyes.

"'Nezer," he said between sobs.

"Where are you going? Have you lost your mama?"

He nodded to the last question and didn't seem to know the answer to the first. But he did know why. "Yankees are coming an' they'll git me," he bawled.

"Yankees? What Yankees? The Yankees are gone."

"No." He shook his head vigorously. "They coming back."

"Ebenezer!" A woman had stopped in front of the bank. "Get over here, or you'll be left behind!" The child ran to her side.

Yankees? I wheeled and ran to Zeke's office. Inside, it was block and block with a dozen men or more jabbering at each other. I elbowed my way among them.

"Matty," someone called. "You best make tracks yourself. You gave the Rebs horses. That amounts to succorin' the enemy."

"I could say with a straight face that they stole those horses," I retorted hotly. "It was pretty clear I didn't have a lot of choice in the deal." But no one was listening. The chair behind Zeke's desk was empty.

A beefy man with a thick neck and a red face folded his arms across his considerable belly and said with disgust, "Sibley's got himself beat by the Abs. Canby's on his way here."

Buck McCurry, who owned a ranch to the north, threw his big-knuckled hands up in frustration. "What are we gonna do now?"

"But we won at Glorieta," someone piped.

"They damn well pumped that battle up to bigger'n it was, and then they damn well frittered it away." This from Jonathon Mapes, the rude sheepman from Doña Ana. He shoved a finger in the direction of the fellow with the thick neck. "Ask Sam. He was sutlerin', following the army with whiskey and such afore they turnt tail and run."

Sam nodded and thumbed his hat. "It was supplies done them in, too. After the hardest fighting it's ever been my lot to witness, those Abs done sent a detachment of cavalry 'round the mountains and took an' burnt our train. The whole eighty wagons. Then Sibley give the order to bury cannon and howitzers and run. I left my wagon there—it was plumb empty anyhow—an' rode on down ahead of them."

Mapes gave a disgusted guffaw. "Sibley don't give a fart what them Abs might do to us. All he cares about now is saving his own skin."

Mac MacPherson was pushing his way into the room. He reached through the men and handed me a folded piece of paper. "My brother sent a letter with the Express. Read it for them, Miss Matty."

The men opened a path so I could get to a window to see better. Much of Brian MacPherson's letter confirmed what Sam had said. "Sibley is much despised by every man in the brigade. He don't care about the wounded, he don't know nothing about being a general and he's a yellow-bellied coward. He has got room in his wagons for plenty of Mexican whores to ride, but the private soldier who done the fighting is thrown out to die on the way."

The crowd erupted in angry epithets.

Zeke was elbowing his way from the door to his desk. "Okay, okay, you boys know as much as I do. It ain't gonna do you much good to stand around here and jaw." He nodded at me. "You stay here a minute, Matty. The rest of you, git."

The men milled about, glowering and muttering for a few moments, then filed out of Zeke's office. So, the Union troops would be returning. Would they be vindictive, as the town feared? If it came down to that, Mesilla had done more than help the Union's enemy: Jamie and some of the others had sent to Atlanta asking to join the Confederacy.

Zeke took off his hat and rubbed his head. "I hear another Mexican kid got hisself killed out to your place."

"I'm afraid that's right. Julio Lujan, my foreman's son. I would have come in sooner, but we've had some serious illness."

"Sorry to hear that. Now tell me what happened."

I described the scene in the barn. I hadn't let myself think about it since and my voice trembled as I recollected. "I wasn't even there when it happened," I finished.

"Well, it don't look so good. Two of 'em. Even if they was only Mexes."

"That's what I came to see you about, Zeke. The man who probably killed both of them was out there yesterday."

◇◇◇

I leaned against a rock near the cuevas and told Tonio, "Zeke made no more sense of it all than I did."

For the second time that day, I recounted every detail I could remember seeing or hearing from the arroyo the afternoon before. Something still gnawed at me. I knotted my hands in my skirt, which now seemed infernally hot and heavy. I hadn't the boldness to wear breeches into town.

My hair had come down, and now it was blowing across my face. I combed it back with my fingers and began to braid it. "Have you got something to tie this with?"

He disappeared into the cave and returned with a strip of cloth.

"They were talking about that map. They killed those two boys." I pulled the braid so tight it hurt.

Sadness darted about Tonio's eyes. "You must promise me not to go anywhere alone."

"They won't kill me. They want that map. They think I have it. And killing a white woman might get a posse out hunting them."

"Granted. Presumably, that is why they tried to buy you out."

Something flickered in my memory like a guttering candle. One of those men. The head was in silhouette against the sun, but I had seen that jawline somewhere before. In the plaza? Here on the ranch? Like the merest wisp of mist, the image was gone. I let go of the braid and it unwound. Jamming my knuckles into my eyes, I almost wept with frustrated fury.

Tonio put his arms around me. "No sense tormenting yourself."

"The voice of one. I reckon I've heard it more times than one…" I peered again into my mind. Again I found nothing to help me remember.

"If that lawyer gentleman in Franklin was right…"

I felt my eyes growing round as double eagles. "How would they know I'd refused to sell the ranch unless one of them had tried to buy it? If it's the same man who went to Peticolas, he's a Union officer. Or said he was."

"But the Union Army has not yet arrived." Tonio rose, walked around my rock and began braiding my stubborn hair.

"What does that mean?"

His fingers on my hair had stilled. He didn't answer. I twisted my head around to look at him. He was gazing toward the setting sun. A long cloud of dust was moving like a fat, fluffy worm along the trail from town toward my ranch. I stood up and stared. There were perhaps a dozen wagons and many more people on horseback.

I bolted for my own wagon. Tonio clambered onto the seat next to me. "Who is it?" he asked sharply.

"I don't know." I turned the horses and prodded them toward the house.

We got home in time for me to station myself in front of the house, a Sharp's rifle against the wall behind me, the stock hidden behind my skirts. Nacho and the hands were far out on the range. I'd have to handle this myself. The Sharp's was powerful enough to stop a charging bull.

To Herlinda and Winona I had snapped orders to stay inside. The other women, Herlinda said, looking nervy as a cat, were at the spring. I asked Tonio to bring three more rifles from the wall of the barn and bade him stand just inside the parlor door.

"I suspicion that what's coming is like to wake snakes," Winona opined.

There were eleven wagons in all. I was hard-pressed to stand still and watch them arrive. They held about as many women as men. Most of the faces were strange to me, though I did recognize Josephine Dent, the wheelwright's wife, and Amanda Coolidge, the cooper's daughter. I had met them at a tea during my first few months in the valley. It struck me as odd that one of the wagons was full of Indians, all of them young.

The only face I recognized among the men was Jonathan Mapes, the rancher from Doña Ana, who rode with three other men apart from the others. There may have been others that I knew, but I was facing directly into the sinking sun and couldn't discern them.

Almost all the faces bore a surly look. I swallowed and tried to will my pulse to slow. Had they come to lynch me for the death of that poor Mexican kid? Or was it because of Julio's murder? Had Ruben done something awful the last time he'd been to town? Were they after him?

I had never seen a lynching party. I didn't think women participated in something like that.

Mexican faces peered from two of the wagons. What could have brought all these people together? Indians, Mexicans and Anglos with one intense purpose? Even if the Anglos truly believed I had killed one or both of those boys, it seemed unlikely that this many would be determined to avenge a Mexican.

Behind me I could hear a long wail from Zia followed by Winona's shushings. My heart drumming in my ears, I stood very still, ramrod straight and silent while the last wagon pulled up behind the others.

When its wheels had stopped, I folded my hands in front of me to keep them from trembling and counted out the seconds of a full minute. Then I stepped forward.

The air fairly hissed with angry murmurs, but I caught no clear words. Only a few people had got out of their wagons; and I noticed that the men on horseback stayed back, out of the range of the rifle hidden behind me.

"Good evening," I called, with as much calm as I could muster. "What can I do for you?"

The air erupted with more angry sounds. I began to feel lightheaded and feared I might faint. "Please state your business," I shouted.

The mob turned almost as one toward the last wagon that had arrived. There, a woman had risen to her feet. The crowd went suddenly silent. She was blackened by the sun behind her. I couldn't see who it was.

The woman raised her hand and stabbed the air with it like a gospel preacher. "We have come for the witch!"

The voice was that of Isabel Tolhurst.

Chapter Thirty-four

The increased scuffling behind me was followed by a thud inside the house and another wail from Zia. "Deliver her to us," Isabel was saying, "or we will be forced to burn this house that shelters this hex." The mob nodded and shuffled about angrily.

"See here!" someone shouted. "In the past week, four families have come down with typhus, two with pox!"

Another voice called, "The widow Norton spoke with the witch one day in town, and the next mornin' her hands was covered with warts."

"My sweet baby was hale and happy one night," whined a woman's voice. "The next morning she was dead!"

"Deliver her to us, Matilda," Isabel shouted.

I began to understand the presence of the Indians. They must be the former students at the school set up by Isabel and her husband. Perhaps she had called in a debt or somehow riled or coerced them.

I called Isabel's name, making my voice as strong and sharp as I could. "Surely to God you cannot possibly believe this...this ridiculous rumor that Winona is a witch."

"It is no rumor," Isabel cried. "She bears the devil's hoof-mark. It may not be visible to all, but I can see it plain. I can see it," she repeated, hitting each word. The mob began to move forward.

One of them stopped, pointing at something on the ground behind me. "Look there!"

I ventured a glance over my shoulder and almost wept with consternation. A tarantula was marching slowly toward the door.

"Evelina, scat!"

The tarantula stopped and seemed to look at me.

"It is the witch woman's beast!" someone yelled.

"It's only a damn spider, and it's mine, not hers," I said loudly.

The mob drew back, whether at my brazen use of the word damn or my claiming ownership of the tarantula or something else, I didn't know. You may get yourself burned at the stake this night or hanged alongside Winona, I told myself.

The crowd began to churn forward again, like the waves of an angry sea.

"Wait!" I shouted, striding a couple of steps forward. The crowd eddied and swirled, but came no further. "Isabel! You are a religious woman. Your husband was a Baptist preacher. You are yourself a Baptist missionary. For God's sake and your own, you cannot do this thing!"

"God tells us we must cast down Satan's spawn."

The blood beat in my ears so that I could hardly hear. "The woman Winona has a child, a little girl not yet six months on this earth. You cannot take her mother from—"

The crowd roared, cutting me off, and the blood near froze in my veins. I should not have mentioned Zia. They would kill her, too. Isabel said nothing. I prayed that this had given her pause and that she would somehow be able to still this mob she had incited to such wrongful acts.

"The devil's spawn is in our midst," some woman in the crowd screamed. "She must be cast down to hell, where the fire will purge her of her hideous deeds."

"Stone her, stone her!" someone cried. "She has brought the pox upon us." There was a scent of wild animal on the air.

Another yelled, "Mary Lukins bore a child with six fingers after talking with the witch."

Isabel's voice rose above the others. "The nigra child may not yet be tainted with her mother's evil. I will take the baby and raise her to heed God's word. If she does not give evidence of the devil's work she may live." The crowd roared its approval. Isabel raised both arms and the crowd stilled. "But you must deliver the witch to the Hand of God. Now!"

"Deliver her, deliver her," the mob chanted and began to press toward me. Involuntarily, I backed away. A terrible weariness surged over me, and the earth seemed to sway beneath my feet. Tonio was immediately beside me, his hand at my elbow steadying me. A rifle hung over his other arm, the barrel open, at right angle to the stock, but ready enough to close and shoot if need be.

The mob stopped like a dull-witted animal trying to assess the situation.

Tonio plunged into the interval. Handing me the rifle, he stepped forward. The mob buzzed louder, then quieted. Some were sure to have heard tales of his healing powers. And the rumor that he was a priest was still widespread.

"You are all the children of God," he said; and the crowd quieted even more, seemingly reassured that he would not berate them.

"The woman Winona is also a child of God."

"Never!" a woman shrilled.

"She has put her hand upon you," Isabel said. "She has blinded you!"

Tonio didn't pause. "A man here fell ill, and the woman Winona ministered to him day and night. She did not rest. She barely ate. I was here. I know."

The Mexicans and Indians had been still as stones, watching. But now they were nodding. "My little boy, *mal,* very ailing. The *padre,* he make *mi niño* healthy again," a voice called.

"Sí. Curandéro," another said. Medicine man.

I began to breathe more easily. Tonio seemed to have the mob in hand. It would soon be over. I watched his tall frame, bent a little at the shoulders, as he raised his arms to them again and the darker faces were looking up to him with reverence. Many Anglo chins were against their chests, so I could not see their reaction; but at least they were only shuffling their feet.

"The woman Winona—"

"No!" The voice that cut Tonio off came from behind me.

Dozens of hands pointed. I swung around. Winona, clutching Zia to her chest, was moving slowly out of the house. Her face was the color of mud. Behind her was Herlinda, prodding her with the barrel of a rifle.

"Brúja!" Herlinda howled. "She kill my son!" Herlinda jabbed the rifle barrel toward Tonio. *"No padre.* Maybe one time. *No mas.* He take *mujér.* This woman." She pointed to me. *"Durmiendos. Júntos.* I see it. They bed together."

A rumbling roar rose from the mob. Whether at me or at Tonio or Winona, I did not know; but in that moment I believed we were doomed.

"Herlinda!" A voice to my right penetrated the din. Nacho rounded the corner of the house. He had lost much weight and had not yet gained it back. He looked spindly and weak, but the crowd paused to stare at him.

Nacho was shaking his head; and in the last light of the sun, his eyes looked old as God's. *"Es no verdád, mujér.* This is not truth." His voice was very low, and I was afraid no one would hear him; but tongues seemed to hush for that very reason.

He went over to Herlinda, said something to her that I could not hear and put his arm about her. She seemed to collapse onto his shoulder.

"We are wasting time!" Isabel's voice leapt into the void that followed as Nacho led the sobbing Herlinda into the house. "The witch stands before you! Gather the stones!"

The crowd flowed forward again, and a pebble thrown from somewhere thunked into the wall of the house, spraying little chunks of mud.

In that moment I realized that they thought Nacho was telling them that Tonio and I were not sleeping together. Perhaps Tonio and I were alone in knowing that Herlinda had uttered only one falsehood: that Winona was a witch. Another stone whizzed past my ear.

The crowd began to mill about. There were plenty of rocks scattered over the land, but they would have to search out those small enough to cast. And the sun was ebbing fast.

Four men carried a rock the size of a watermelon forward, staggering under its weight. Surely they could not think they would throw that. Three more, grunting with the exertion, brought another. I peered up at Isabel for an explanation.

She stood, arms spread wide against the sunset. "The witch will be staked to lie on the ground. The heaviest rocks found will be laid upon her."

"You aim to crush her?" My voice rose to a shriek and broke.

"If she is truly a child of God, if she is not a witch, God will make the rocks like air upon her body." Isabel's voice took on a note of crazed ecstasy.

I moved forward again. I could see Tonio watching me. I did not raise my voice. I had learned from Nacho that the crowd would quiet to hear me.

"Wait."

I prayed that I was right. Perhaps they thought they had already heard everything I had to say. But the angry mutters and scuffling feet subsided.

"You believe this woman is a witch? You believe the devil is in her?"

"Yes!" They began to stir again.

"Listen!" I said it sharply, but kept my voice low. The noise abated again. "Then you must believe that Satan can be forced to abandon her."

At this, the mob fell completely silent. Dozens of eyes fixed on my face. Isabel spread out her arms again, preparing to say something.

I cut her off. "The Virgin is hovering above you." My words shocked me as much as anyone, but I tossed my hand dramatically toward a point in the air just over their heads. They turned to look. "Can you see her?"

The Anglo men began to mutter angrily, but the women and all the Mexicans and Indians were murmuring.

"The Virgin is telling you that if this woman called Winona has allowed the devil into her soul—"

A few cries came from the crowd. I raised my voice a little. "Mind you, the Virgin says if this is so, Satan can be driven out."

Now there was silence again.

"The Virgin is telling you this." I lifted my head as I had seen preachers do. "Surely you can hear her." With a pang, I realized that the power of the Virgin was mostly a Catholic belief and the Anglos here were probably Protestant. But it was too late to go back. "Surely," I implored them, "surely you are devout enough and pure enough to hear her?"

At this, heads began to nod hesitantly.

"The Virgin says that you must all help in this exorcism. Say it. Say 'exorcism.'" I repeated it again.

"Ex-or-cism," came the chant.

I almost had them now, but I needed more drama. "There are torches in the barn," I whispered to Tonio. "Get them.

"Say it again," I told the crowd. If I could involve them, I might keep them.

"Exorcism, exorcism," they crooned.

"Come, Winona." I held out my hand toward her, and she stared at me as if I had begun to glow in the dark. Very slowly, her face a mix of fear, disbelief and trust, she crossed the space between us.

Tonio returned with the torches. There were six. "Light them and hand them out." Whatever surprise he felt, he throttled it.

"You, with the torches," I called as Tonio distributed them. "Come forward. Form a circle. The never-ending circle of the Trinity."

When the six torchbearers had done as I asked, I drew Winona forward, into the circle. "Gather 'round now," I called, bringing as much fervor to my voice as I could. The torchlight helped, giving the faces of the crowd an almost eerie look.

"Kneel, Winona, child of God," I intoned. "Kneel before the Virgin." I couldn't very well ask her to kneel before me.

With both arms hugging Zia to her breast, she knelt.

I would need something to prove that the exorcism was successful. I began to sway my body from side to side. How could I prove it? Peering from side to side, I sought Tonio. He was there near the corner of the house, watching me. I beckoned and he came forward.

"There is a candle and a Bible on the table in the parlor," I intoned loudly. "Do the Virgin's bidding; fetch them." I dropped my voice to a whisper. "There is no Bible, only one of my account books, but it will have to do. And bring at least three matches."

Nodding, he disappeared.

I swayed. My badly braided hair thumped at my shoulders as I swung my head. I was no dancer. It occurred to me that I must look clumsy and ridiculous, but the crowd was watching me, swaying, too.

Tonio returned and pressed a thick tallow candle and four wooden matches into my hand. I hoped it was the right candle. I squeezed it between my fingers. It was. This was the last of the badly constituted candles I had made during my first year here. The tallow was too soft.

I brought both hands to my chest, using the "Bible" to shield the candle from the crowd. I raised my face to the sky, hoping they would do the same, fumbled one of the matches into position and pressed it hard, down into the tallow next to the wick. Pain shot through my thumb. The match wouldn't pierce the tallow deep enough.

Praying no one would see what I was doing, or that the "Bible" was only an account book, I carefully worked the match stick out, broke it in two, and shoved it back into the tallow.

The crowd had not seen. But they were becoming restive.

"Sister Winona, child of God," I intoned again.

Winona looked up at me, frowning her get-on-with-it look.

"Yes, Lord. Yes, Lord." The voice came from the back of the crowd. The people took up the chant and their disquietude disappeared.

I sang out, "I will press the Bible to this woman's head. If the devil is there, he will not be able to bear that. He will leave."

"Yes, Lord. Yes, Lord," the crowd sang back.

"There is an ancient sign of purity," I called. "I am lighting this candle." I did so, then held it high so no one would see the match next to the wick. I thanked the God I was blaspheming that He had made me a tall woman. With the candle lit, my seconds were numbered. The timing must be exact.

"If the devil is not there..." I intoned.

"Yes, Lord. Yes, Lord."

"...or when he has departed, the purity of this woman will flow through me to the candle and brighten its light."

"Yes, Lord..."

I placed the book against Winona's head.

The crowd was absolutely silent, watching the candle I still held high in my other hand.

I truly prayed, with more seriousness than I have ever devoted to the task. Then I waved the candle, causing its flame to lean.

There was a collective gasp, and then "Hallelujah!"

I looked up. The flame had caught the head of the match and it was flaring brightly. Then, the sulfur gone, it dimmed. I lifted both arms to the sky, keeping the candle high. "Mine eyes have seen the glory of the coming of the Lord..." I sang slowly. I had only heard the hymn twice. Now I realized I didn't know all the words.

But the people who stood around me did. They raised their faces to the darkened sky and opened their mouths. "He is trampling out the vineyard where the grapes of wrath are stored."

And while they sang, I lowered the candle, snuffed it out, pulled the match from the tallow, put it in my mouth, bit it in pieces and swallowed it.

Zia, who had not made a sound through the worst of it, bounced now in her mother's arms, her eyes shining in the torchlight like those of a saint. Enchanted by the music, she raised her arms over her head like I had and bounced in time to the rhythm.

I did not learn until much later that I had chosen a Yankee battle hymn. The people, at least half of them Confederate sympathizers, didn't seem to know it either. Their voices swelled.

"His truth goes marching on..."

Chapter Thirty-five

I sat in my nightdress at my desk in the dark, my heels tucked under me, my arms around my knees, trying to sort things out. My pistol lay on the desk in front of me, and it was loaded. I didn't think there was a need for it, but I wanted it within reach just the same.

The crowd had finished singing and quietly melted into the night. No one had said much, not even Isabel. I insisted that Tonio take one of the wagons. Winona had retired and so had I, but I was too exhausted to sleep. The deluge of events had drowned me, and I had to give them some sort of order or stay at the bottom of the sea forever. But I wasn't doing much sorting—more like chasing colliding thoughts through an ever more bewildering maze.

I gazed blankly at the window, which was just a slightly brighter patch in the dark wall. The moon had been brighter the night that face had fallen against that window.

My mind bounced to Isabel. What had driven her to do such a thing? Would she really have seen Winona crushed until her bones broke, her ribs gave way? A gut-deep shudder ran through me.

And what of Herlinda? Would she persuade Nacho to take her away from the woman who fornicated with a priest and consorted with a witch? What more—

"Git up, real slow like!" The hammer of a gun clicked.

The doorway showed a hazy glow of something white. I grasped my pistol and moved slowly toward it.

"Lord have mercy! Miss Matty, what you doing in here at this hour?"

This time the voice registered. "Winona, for God's sake." I set the pistol back on the desk. "I couldn't sleep, you no-account fool. You scared the peewadden out of me! I dang near shot you!"

She padded over to me in bare feet and leaned the rifle against the wall. "Well I be go-to-heaven," she said. "I be thinking one of them folk got herself halfway to home and then it come on her that you don't never go to church much so it ain't real likely you would know how to cast the devil out of some poor helpless soul. Sleep ain't rightly coming to me this night, either."

She fumbled in the dark for a chair and sat down. "If you ain't something. I sure enough thought I was a going to meet my Maker this very night. How you make that candle rise up?"

I explained about the match.

"Honey, you was touched by the hand of God Hisself. Why you almost made me believe I was all pure as fresh-picked cotton inside. Where you learn that stuff?"

"I made it up as I went along. I cheated and I lied."

"It do not bear thinking about, what they do to me if you wasn't such a fine cheater and liar."

◇◇◇

News from town filtered back with the hands who always rode in on Saturdays about noon to drink themselves stupid and lose their pay at poker. I might as well have issued their pay to Martin Dance, the card sharp who lay about in the boardinghouse all week living on his Saturday night winnings.

Without Homer Durkin and Eliot Turk, who was no more than five-foot-three with his boots on but wiry and tough as a coyote, I would not have heard much. Nacho was his old self again, but he had scant interest in army news. Ruben was seldom sober long enough these days to remember anything, and Herlinda had scarcely spoken to anyone since the day she tried to kill Winona.

I had just settled down to do my accounts when I looked up to find Homer standing in the doorway. He must have just been to the barber because there was precious little of his curly carrot-top left and his ears stood out like jug handles.

"Thought you might want to know, ma'am, General Canby took over the fort last week."

I motioned to a chair; but he just rocked from foot to foot, twisting his hat in his big raw-boned, fresh-scrubbed hands. Homer was never one to feel comfortable in a house.

"Thank you. Anything else?"

"Not rightly, ma'am." Homer fiddled with his hat some more. There was a big dent in his head where it had sat. "Except they say that this Canby seems a right decent feller. At the field hospital in Socorro, a lot of Texans there had been pretty well fixed up by the doc. Dang if Canby didn't parole them. Turned them all loose with six days' rations. They say he went down to Franklin with a flag of truce and told Sibley to get his sick and wounded out of New Mexico as there's no provisions for them." His face flushed with the effort of such a long speech.

I thanked him again; and when he'd shuffled off, I went back to the accounts, but my thoughts wouldn't focus on the figures. Here in the valley was the man in charge of all the federal troops in New Mexico Territory. Might he have a roster of Union officers who had been in the area when the offer on my land was made?

A knock on at the front door disturbed my thoughts. I opened it to find Homer, who snatched off his hat again.

"Forgot to say one thing, ma'am. The bartender at the Silver Spur said someone had been asking around town for you."

"Oh?" The hair on my arms began to prickle. "Who?"

"He didn't remember the name, ma'am. He just said it was some Union officer."

◇◇◇

The following morning, I put on my blue dress with the tucked bodice and the bone buttons, asked Homer to hitch Fanny to the wagon and was on my way to Fort Fillmore by noon.

Brigadier General Canby rolled his cigar to the corner of his mouth. The cigar wasn't lit, and it had the look of something that had been chewed upon for many days. He was a big, fine-looking man with features chiseled on a rock of a face—and the carver had carefully notched the clean-shaven chin. Standing at least six-foot-three, he towered over even me. He neither sat nor stood still, but there wasn't a black hair out of place in his beard or on his head save one small forelock that dared to jut over his right eye.

That hair, a flat black without a single grey hair, no variation in color at all, puzzled me. His years could hardly be called advanced, but he was surely nearing fifty. When it came to me that he used hair dye, I had to close my mouth tight lest the titter in my throat get loose.

Despite this vanity, I daresay he was a tough taskmaster, quick to make decisions and quick to change them. He looked every inch the gentleman, though at this particular moment he was a mite annoyed. "I do not have the time, Miss Summerhayes, to—"

"I do well understand that, sir," I cut in. "I congratulate you on your success. And I do hope this horrid war will soon be over."

"You have not the slightest notion," he shot at me, "how difficult or how horrid it is."

I drew myself up and looked him square in the eye. "I grant that I may not know war, sir, but there are things as devastating to me as war is to you. I would not be here if I did not deem it important enough to take some of your invaluable time. However, as you think my question a frivolous one, I regret having wasted my own time..." I paused to draw my breath.

Canby was staring at me, his brown eyes puzzled. "Have you no husband, madam? No father? No man to shoulder whatever burdens you?"

In a tone with as much iron as I could inject into it, I retorted: "My husband, sir, was a Union officer who nearly beat me to death, so I left him. Thank you for your help." I turned to leave.

"Just a moment, Miss Summerhayes."

I turned back and discovered my chin was so high my glare sailed right over his head.

"Sit, sit." He pointed to a fine Hitchcock chair near his desk.

Stiffly, I lowered myself to the cane seat.

Canby rolled the cigar around in his mouth and strode to his desk as though he needed it for cover. "Since Christmas, more than a thousand men have died because of my decisions. I have precious few moments to think things through, and you believe I should give some of that time to you."

"I ask it because two boys have died, and I believe it is because of what I aim to tell you."

The bedraggled cigar bobbed very slowly and deliberately as the general examined my face, then, gruffly, "All right. Tell me."

I made it as brief and to the point as I could. "I only wondered if there is a list of officers who were at Fort Fillmore last summer," I concluded.

"I know of no roster."

My shoulders slumped. "Thank you, sir." I rose to take my leave.

"Ah…some of the officers with me now were here then. It is the dinner hour. Perhaps you would accompany me to the officers' mess and I will ask."

"Thank you, sir. Thank you very much."

He offered his arm, and we stepped from his quarters into the dazzling sunlight. "Will there be more fighting here?" I asked.

"Depends upon the Confederates. Four or five hundred were left at Fort Bliss. I am told they still regard this valley as theirs."

The fort had been partially rebuilt by the Texans after they burnt the Union troops out of it, and Canby's men were busy trying to finish the reconstruction. Crossing the parade grounds amid the screeching of saws and the pounding of hammers, we passed a dozen men on stretchers. Many more hobbled about on crutches. I counted nineteen with no legs at all and at the sight of one poor fellow who had neither arms nor legs, I swallowed and had to turn away.

The general was smiling and nodding to them as if they were whole. "It is a terrible thing what minie balls and bayonets can do to a man," he said quietly to me. "But these are the fortunate ones. And I do not refer to those who died on the field. Disease is a far more malicious enemy than the graybacks."

I had not imagined things to be quite this squalid.

Judging from the scent of food riding on the warm air, I decided that the mess halls must be the pair of low mud-covered structures just ahead. A few officers were disappearing into the one on the left; common soldiers were filing into the other.

A low-built, square-set, plain-old-farmer sort moved to Canby's side. His shoulder-length hair was thin and receding.

"There is a message." The man's voice was slow and quiet with almost no inflection. Nor did he show any formal deference to the general. "They are fourteen hundred in number. Three days march to the west."

Canby turned sharply to the newcomer, said a few words I couldn't hear and turned back to me. "Matilda Summerhayes, Colonel Christopher Carson. A few months ago, Colonel Carson's regiment of New Mexico volunteers were the only well-trained men we had."

I nodded politely. They resumed their discussion; and I gazed about the parade ground, determined not to flinch at the missing limbs. A soldier was moving past me. He looked quite unscathed.

"Could you tell me the hour?" I called.

He turned and his features knit together in such a look of pain that I wanted to reach out and comfort him. I watched bewildered as he shuffled on to the mess.

Another man drew up in front of me. "It is nigh one o'clock, ma'am." He jerked his head in the direction of the first man. "Old Faraday, there, he couldn't say. He took a pistol ball in the mouth an' his tongue was near shot out. He pulled out a part of it that was hanging ragged to the edge and cut it off with his own knife, then went on fighting. That was at Valverde, it was."

"My God," I stammered. The man ambled off.

Colonel Carson was departing. Canby called after him, "How many men did you say, Kit?"

Carson shaded his eyes against the mid-day sun and took time to think about the question, then drawled, "Twelve, fourteen hundred."

The general turned back to me in a new and obviously better humor. "To answer your earlier question more precisely," he said, "there will be no more fighting here in the foreseeable future. A column of men has marched across the desert from the Pacific to aid our cause. Johnny Reb has his spies, of course, and we are seeing to it that they know." He winked at me. "Unless I miss my guess, they will clear out of Fort Bliss. They sure enough will do just that."

"You know who the spies are?"

He laughed as if I had asked a childish question. "Certainly, madam. We have the best spy company in the territories, if not in the entire Union. Have you not heard of Paddy Graydon?"

I said I had not.

"You will." He escorted me up the single step and into the officers' mess, which seemed dark indeed after the bright sun.

I hesitated on the threshold, unable to see much in the instant gloom. There was only one window. Next to it, a man with dark hair and a beard that made his face seem even rounder than it was spoke intently to someone whose back was to me. The hair began to rise on the back of my neck and goose bumps crept up my arms, as if someone had tread on my grave.

He was clad not in a uniform but in dungarees and a deerskin jacket. Without pausing the flow of words to his companion, the man flicked a glance at the door where I stood with General Canby.

Heat traveled up my neck to my ears, and I willed the muscles in my face to show no change. "Excuse me, sir," I said, backing slowly through the doorway. "I fear I feel a bit faint."

I was terrified the general would make some sound or summon aid for me; but he only followed me through the door, a look of concern on his chiseled features. His hair looked black as iron in the bright sun, and some inane part of me realized he must use bootblack to dye it.

"I'm all right. Just a bit all-overish. I only need a breath of air." I paused, watching the doorway behind him, then added, "I have changed my mind. I do not want you to make that announcement. Please, I must get home. Could you see me to my wagon?"

Chapter Thirty-six

I flicked the reins across Fanny's back, exhorting her to a pace that nearly upended the wagon. My hat flew off and tumbled to the floorboards, the brocade bag that held my pistol jounced from the seat. It seemed a decade before I got to the bridge. Once across it, I forced myself to slow the horse to a steady trot.

I tried to think; but my mind, less obedient than Fanny, refused to slow its pace.

I had seen before the face of the man who was sitting near the window in the officers' mess. More than a year ago, trickling blood from the left temple, it had fallen against my window. The man sitting calmly at a table in the Union officers' mess had killed Diego and probably Julio. I was sure he had set the range fire that nearly swallowed my house and had made at least one of the offers for my land. For the first time, I wondered why he had not, months ago, simply killed me. I rode so often alone it would not have been difficult to shoot me out of the saddle.

I should have told General Canby on the spot. I should have seen the bastard in the stockade before I left the fort. Instead, I had bolted and run like a silly schoolgirl. Now I nearly wept with frustrated fury.

I reined Fanny to a stop next to a pale-green mesquite tree heavy with bean pods and rescued my hat and bag. Should I turn back? Tell the general? I gazed unseeing at the horizon. Behind my eyes, the face swam into focus again. The beard...

My breath turned solid in my throat. I had seen that man more times than one… Something glimmered in my memory like the merest wisp of mist and was gone. I peered into my mind. Finding no quick answer, I jammed my knuckles into my eyes. Something was not right about it. A Union Army officers' mess was not the proper setting for that face. That face. Clean-shaven. Charming. No, rude. Clean-shaven. No week's growth of beard.

"Afternoon."

I drew in my breath so sharply I almost choked. A palomino mare with three white stockings was moving toward me from behind the rock. On her back was a man in dungarees and a deerskin jacket.

The curtain of fog across my mind lifted. The newly grown beard had hidden the chin and clouded my remembrance; but it did not conceal the eyes, the nose, the breadth of the cheekbones.

"Lieutenant Tyler Morris," I said softly. And with that knowledge came the realization that many, if not all, of the conclusions I had drawn over the past year had been wrong.

"At your service, ma'am," he said, his broad smile confirming my thoughts. "The general said you were ill, asked me to follow you to be sure you got home safely."

"How kind of him." I yanked hard on the reins, startling Fanny. She reared, straining the traces and nearly overturning the wagon. The palomino whinnied and shied, unseating Morris. Fanny bolted into an instant gallop, throwing me to the floorboards and loosing my grip on the reins. Clinging to the wooden slats, I frantically struggled to regain my seat as the buckboard jounced over the hard ground.

Daring a glance over my shoulder, I saw Morris had regained control of the palomino. I flicked the reins, and Fanny surged into full gallop. The wagon teetered, slinging me from the seat again. I prepared myself to be thrown, but it righted itself. Kneeling on the floorboards, I tried to melt myself into the wagon box. There, I was safer but could see nothing but Fanny's hindquarters. I would have to trust the direction to her.

A bullet whizzed over my shoulder so close I could feel the air it stirred against my cheek.

I groped for the brocade bag; but it skittered across the floorboards, carrying the pistol it held beyond my reach. The thudding of hooves behind me announced that Morris was closing in.

Fanny's speed was astonishing, but she would be no match for an unfettered horse.

The crack of a rifle frightened her, and she lurched to the right as a little spray of dust leaped up to my left where the bullet hit. The pounding hooves and my own blood thundering in my ears began to make me lightheaded. The earth turned sandy. Fanny staggered, and I felt myself begin to pitch helplessly forward. If I were flung that direction, I would surely be trampled. Fanny snorted and swung to the right, catapulting me upward then flinging me back onto the hard seat.

The wind swept toward us in gusts, and I almost choked on it. The ranch was miles away and the wind was against us. Fanny was laboring against it when the unrelenting gale began to twist, digging into the ground like a spinning spade, kicking up as much dirt and dust as a stick of dynamite. The air was so thick with debris I could see nothing.

Sand bit at my flesh. I hadn't noticed the sky darkening; but rain began to come now, not in drops but in sheets, as though a river were plunging over some cliff in the sky. Fanny was gasping for air; and I clung to the wagon seat like a burr, eyes squeezed shut, hair and clothes now sodden.

Something hard thumped my back, then another, then a dozen more, like a handful of stones. Bullets. Dear Lord. I squeezed my eyes shut even tighter waiting for the inevitable throe that would be the last thing I felt on earth.

It didn't come. The stings on my back didn't erupt into blazing pain. I opened my eyes to see big white pebbles striking the ground and bouncing. Hail.

I forced myself upright and twisted to peer behind me. The rain, leaden with hailstones, was still coming in torrents. I could see little. The storm must have slowed Morris. Fanny's gait had become ragged, and now she made a high-pitched sound of fright and reared. The reins, slick with rain, began to slip from my fingers. Fanny's forelegs plunged back to the ground, and she shot through the downpour as if possessed, the wagon lurching drunkenly behind her.

If I risked a stop I could whisk the traces from Fanny. I'd have to ride bareback in a skirt but leaving the wagon behind would even the odds. Was Morris far enough behind to give me time?

Ahead and to the right, my barely open eyes saw a formation of wet red rock. With that for cover, I might shed the wagon. There was even the possibility that Morris, blinded by the storm, might dash on by.

As we neared the rock, I sawed at the reins to turn Fanny; but the moment she veered toward it I knew I'd made a mistake.

Just beyond was the mouth of an arroyo, flooded and awash with debris and small rocks. Fanny careened away sharply; the wagon jackknifed, tilted and flung me through rain and hail to the ground. Just before the buckboard broke its skid and crashed atop me, a narrow strip cleared in the purplish fog.

Bearing down on me across the rain-swept mesa was the palomino.

◇◇◇

An icy metal rod prodded at my rain-slick cheek. My eyes fluttered open only to be blinded by a searing pain in my head.

"That's better," a voice said. I didn't have to see him to know it was Morris.

Heart hammering, every breath rasping at my throat, arms aching, hair dripping, nerves stretched to the cracking point, I waited. Rain slapped into my face and ran from my chin.

"Can you sit up?" His tone was almost kindly.

"I don't know." I could see him now, his rifle barrel down but ready.

"Perhaps you might try. It's very damp here."

I bent my legs and pushed myself into a sitting position. It seemed to take a very long time.

"That's better."

Flopped on its side next to me was the wagon. Rain sluiced from the two upturned wheels. There was no sign of Fanny.

"I cut her loose and tipped that off you." He pointed at the wagon. "You were lucky, you know. Could have broken your neck."

I gazed at him, silent. Even if I could somehow escape, where could I go?

"Come now, you might be a bit grateful." He scrunched himself under the side of the wagon. "Move over here. Get out of the rain."

I tried to gather my wits. He had killed Diego and Julio. Why hadn't he simply killed me?

"Haven't you the sense to get out of the weather, woman? Do as I say." He motioned to a sheltered space under the edge of the wagon.

I scrambled toward it, knees slipping on the wet mud, and settled myself warily.

"I don't suppose you have it with you."

"Beg pardon?"

"The map."

The realization came like white light. That's why he hadn't killed me. Morris had stood that day on the edge of the arroyo with another man, speaking of the map. He had killed others and he might aim to buy the land from me cheap, or run me off it, but he needed that map. And he believed I had it.

I gave my head the barest shake. "What are you talking about?"

Morris leaned back against the wagon, brought the rifle to rest across his legs and crossed his arms. "Going to play coy, are we?"

My arms and hands were rimed with mud. I wiped them on my sodden skirt, which was torn straight up the front, nearly to the waist. My elbow brushed something just beneath the wagon. I made to look at my hands and slid my eyes toward it. The knitting bag, the color gone black with the wet. Inside it was my pistol. But it was between us. I lifted the torn skirt to cover it and inched my fingers toward it.

"I told the general, you know," I lied. "I told him you killed those two boys." I wished with all my heart I had done just that.

Morris gave an ugly chuckle. "If he has not already learned that you're a convicted thief yourself, awaiting trial for one of those murders, I will have the satisfaction of telling him that myself." Morris spit into a puddle next to him. "The Mex kid had a map on him. Where is it?"

"Why did you kill him?" My hand closed on the brocade bag. Beyond the lieutenant, I saw Fanny. She had found some shelter beneath an old mesquite. The palomino stood next to the wagon in the still-cascading rain.

Morris' eyes held mine, and he fingered the butt of the rifle. Then he slapped his leg. "Why not? A real gentleman, that kid. When we found out you had bought the land, he thought we had to cut you in. I told him there was no woman in the world we couldn't run off that land, but he wouldn't listen. Next he would've been cutting in the tinker, the tailor, the candlestick maker."

"And Julio?"

Morris frowned. "Who is Julio?"

I tried to hold his eyes. "The boy who worked for me." The bag was too tight under the side of the wagon. I couldn't open it. I tried to wrest it from its trap, but if I pulled too hard Morris would see. My knuckles scraped on a chunk of rock and I winced.

But he was looking elsewhere. When he looked back, his smile was lopsided and ugly. "The kid who fancied himself an artist? Surely you can guess." He moved his hand toward his jacket pocket, and I realized he was not in uniform. He withdrew a length of rope from the pocket and my throat seemed to fill with broken glass as I recalled Julio dangling from the víga in the barn. Why was Morris not in uniform? But of course—he was not a Union officer; he was a Confederate.

The bag would not come free. I forced down my panic and pulled again. It was wedged tight. My hand brushed again across the rock. I could throw that, but the odds for injuring Morris with it were practically nil.

"I give you my word, I won't harm you. I regret, however, that it is necessary to bind you," Morris was saying. "I can't have you flitting off, can I? As soon as I have the map I'll set you free."

I knew there wasn't a whit of truth in that. He must think me a great fool and easy to hoodwink. Then I remembered something. In as normal a voice as I could muster, I said, "I gave it to someone."

"Who?"

"Jamie O'Rourke." I pried at the rock.

"Bullshit! He's dead."

"I gave it to him as soon as I found it, before..." The rock came loose. My fingers closed around it.

Morris' eyes fell to where my wrist disappeared beneath my skirt. "What are you doing?" He grabbed for the rifle.

Whisking my hand from its cover, I hurled the rock, hitting the palomino on the chest. Instantly, she reared. I threw myself away from the wagon just as her hooves toppled it, throwing Morris face first into the mud.

Skirts hiked to the thigh, I ran, my shoes skidding on the mud. Fanny raised her head and watched me come. Twice I tried to mount her; but with no saddle, no stirrups, I slid helplessly to the ground.

I darted a look back at the wagon. The palomino was still rearing and kicking, but nothing else moved. I tore off my petticoat, tied the torn pieces of my skirt about my waist to free my legs and tried again. This time I succeeded. With only my knees and hands to guide her, I steered Fanny back toward the fort.

The rain had halted suddenly, as if its wide ribbons had been severed by some cleaver. The mist began to lift.

I would go straight to Canby. He would have the lieutenant apprehended. Whether he believed me about the murders mattered little because I would tell him something of great consequence to Canby himself.

Tyler Morris wore the faded shirt and trousers of a ranch hand. But after eavesdropping on him and his companion that day on the mesa, I knew that he was a Confederate officer. Fillmore was now a Union fort, Canby a Union General. Lieutenant Morris was not only a murderer, he was a traitor, a spy.

◇◇◇

Quite a sight I must have made tearing up to the fort clinging to Fanny's mane, face streaked with mud, shredded skirt tied about my middle, legs clad in mud-begrimed white pantalets gripping my horse so tight my knees ached.

"Here, here!" shouted one of the guards as I whizzed past unable to rein Fanny and praying they would not fire.

When the mare finally halted, a dozen men surrounded us, weapons raised. I attempted a haughty shout but managed little better than a croak: "I am Matilda Summerhayes. I was the general's guest earlier, and I must see him again, posthaste."

I leapt to the ground and dashed for the door I knew led to Canby's office. The soldiers grabbed my arms and shoulders. I stopped, shook them loose and said with as much dignity as I could marshal, "I must see the general. He will not take it kindly if you delay me."

"She's not armed," muttered one.

"She's not even dressed," murmured another.

In the end, they escorted me to the office.

"Shall I announce you?" someone asked.

"Don't be ridiculous," I said, and pushed open the door.

Canby and Colonel Carson were bent over a table examining something spread upon it. The general scowled. "My word! Miss Summerhayes!"

"I have urgent information for you," I said. He straightened and started to say something, but I cut him off. "One of your officers, Lieutenant Tyler Morris, is a spy!"

Canby removed the dead cigar from his mouth. The silence stretched and darkened like a thunderhead. "Indeed, he is—I saw to his training myself."

I exhaled, my words about the murders dead in my throat.

The general gazed at me, displeasure written all over his face. "Perhaps you would like to cover yourself."

◇◇◇

"It is utterly hopeless," I wailed to Winona, rocking back and forth on a chair at my kitchen table and raking my fingers through my hair.

After my unseemly display, Canby had brusquely sent for an escort to see me home.

"You done told the general this Morris kilt those boys?"

"Of course, I told him; but he only surveyed me standing there in my underwear, drenched to the skin and dripping all over his floor, and said he would look into it. Morris won't waste a moment telling him I am a known thief and an accused killer myself."

"If that man still be on the loose, you ain't safe, nohow. Not by a jugful." Winona rose from her chair and set some water to boil. "If you so much as set foot out of this house, he up and grab you and torment you about that map."

"And I won't live ten minutes past the time he learns the map is gone, that Tonio destroyed it." A thought burst to the surface of my mind. I leapt up and headed for the door.

Winona followed me. "You be more fool than I take you for if you go out there."

"I have to warn Tonio. What if Morris finds out that Tonio knows every mark on that map? That he's the one who drew it?"

"Send someone else," Winona said firmly. "You got to stay inside these here walls, with one of them men to guard you."

"I will do no such thing."

But, of course, I had no choice.

I sent Homer to fetch Tonio, who received my news solemnly. I described Morris in detail. "You must arm yourself. And if you see this man you must shoot to kill, or he will surely kill you. You have a gun?"

Tonio nodded gravely and promised to be exceeding wary.

"You must pile together some brush inside a trench. If you see this man, you must set fire to it, and I will arm myself and send someone to you."

He agreed. "And you must do the same. You must promise to set a fire if there is danger."

"I promise."

◇◇◇

For nearly a week I remained a prisoner in my own home with the guard on my own payroll while the ranch work fell further and further behind. I tried to write Nanny, but could not seem to fashion the right lies. Even music could not cheer me. My flute had moldered many months in my bureau; but with a few days of steady practice, the tones were coming clear. I should have been gladdened. Instead, I quickly became impatient at sitting about the house with naught to do but twiddle my fingers and blow into a silver pipe.

By the seventh morning, I was half-crazed with shut-in fever. I dressed and prepared to go out.

Winona blocked my way.

"I cannot live like this," I shouted at her.

"You be going out there, you maybe have a very short life."

The argument was cut short by the sound of a horse arriving. Winona and I peered out the window. A soldier in Yankee uniform was dismounting. I opened the door and stepped outside. "May I help you?"

"Matilda Summerhayes?"

I nodded.

"The general requests that you accompany me to see him."

Chapter Thirty-seven

The general looked up from the papers he was signing as I was shown into his office. Rising, he removed a pair of small round spectacles and rubbed his nose.

Acutely aware of the sorry state in which he had last seen me, I tried to stand very straight. I had badgered my escort with questions but had got no answers.

"You wished to see me, sir?"

"Do be seated, Miss Summerhayes."

I perched stiffly on the Hitchcock chair and waited with chill resolve for Canby to say he had learned that I myself stood accused of the very murder I claimed Morris had committed. Why else would he have sent for me?

The general folded his spectacles and began to pace. "I owe you an apology and a measure of deep gratitude."

"Beg pardon?"

Canby tapped the frame of the spectacles against his teeth then turned to face me directly. "I have confronted Mr. Morris as well as his contact here with us—separately, of course. I also have spoken with their superior, Captain Paddy Graydon. Mr. Morris brought us a good deal of valuable information. But it seems that you were correct. He also betrayed us. As did his contact, who elected to tell me everything in exchange for his life. They are both in the guardhouse."

It was as though I had put every ounce of strength I possessed into ramming a door and, just as my shoulder touched it, the door opened. I was racing headlong past my target unable to stop. I opened my mouth to speak but could find no words at all.

"What is it?" he asked kindly.

"I wonder," I said when I found myself. "Would it be possible for me to see Morris?"

"For mercy's sake, why?"

Still quite giddy with relief, I ventured a small smile. "There have been so many dreadful happenings, I should like to understand."

The general chewed on the stem of his spectacles; I wondered what had become of his cigar. "I'm sorry, no. Mr. Morris is with a padre, preparing himself."

"He will be...?"

"Executed, yes. I take a dim view of betrayal. A very dim view, indeed. He was responsible for the deaths of eight of my men. But it would not be seemly to interrupt his prayers."

I looked at my hands, gripped tightly in my lap. "You said there is another man. Morris' contact. Could I speak with him?"

The general clearly could not understand this hankering of mine to converse with criminals, but finally he agreed. "That might be arranged."

General Canby's aide, a man with a sour face and a drooping mustache, saw me to the guardhouse and showed me to a bleak and rather dirty room. The shaft of sunlight from the small window did little to brighten the gloom. A plank bench was brought for me and I had just settled myself upon it when the door opened and a man was pushed inside.

He took three steps into the room, his leg-irons making a dismal clanking. For a long moment, the only sound was the creak of my escort's boots as he shifted his weight where he stood against the wall.

I could see little of the prisoner in the dark room save that he was large, his clothes disheveled, his hair unkempt and his stance as belligerent as his circumstances would allow.

"You were a friend of Lieutenant Tyler Morris?"

The quaver in my voice annoyed me, and I cleared my throat. When he didn't answer, I repeated my question.

His reply was so low, I had to strain to hear. "I knew him."

"I would take it as a kindness if you would tell me what you knew of his activities regarding the ranch called Mockingbird Spring."

He spat on the floor. "I would take it as a kindness if you would piss off."

Involuntarily, I jerked back, then studied my hands in silence. Was I to be cowed by a prisoner in chains? I bade myself to rise, drew myself to my full height, strode toward him and peered into his face. What I found there surprised me, but I did not draw back.

"I know nothing of Mockingbird Spring." His eyes were small and hard, like those of a dog biding its time before an attack. "Never heard of it."

I turned away from him and walked to the window. "But you have. You stood on that ranch not a month ago, on the edge of an arroyo—about noon, it was—and spoke with Tyler Morris about a map of that land."

The face I had gazed into was broad and square below dirty pale hair. The stubble of a week's growth of beard did not hide the scar that might have been drawn with white ink on the sun-darkened cheek. This time, I recognized that face. This was the officer whose foot I had trod on in clumsy haste in the plaza the day after Diego had died in my barn. "You are Lieutenant Beauregard Jenks, are you not?"

"No longer lieutenant, as you well know," he snarled. "They have stripped me of that."

"That had naught to do with me. It was because of Morris. You were a good officer before he tempted you with talk of gold. It was he who ruined you."

"He did that, all right."

"Some time ago, I trod on your foot in clumsy haste in the plaza. Do you remember that? Why were you in the plaza that day?"

"Because the bloody fool had got himself shot. A bullet had grazed his damn face. I couldn't take him to the fort. No one was to know that he was with us. I had to fetch some salve from the barber."

"Did you know he took that bullet while killing a boy on my ranch?"

"A Mex kid."

"The boy had a map."

Jenks' eyes narrowed to slits. He said nothing.

"I gave that map to someone," I said quickly. "Someone who is now dead." Jenks might be in prison now, but there was no guarantee he would stay there. "I do not know what became of the map."

"James O'Rourke."

I blinked away the tears that rose at the name of my lost friend.

"Morris blundered there. He was to rile O'Rourke to kill Baylor, but it turned the other way." Jenks paused. "He didn't know that dolt of an editor had the map. He reckoned you had it. He knew it wasn't on the kid's body. He dug up the coffin."

I sighed silent relief that Jenks had accepted my story. "Why did Morris try to buy my land?"

Jenks gave a dry laugh. "That wasn't Morris. That was me. I had a little put aside. I thought it would be so much cleaner, easier, if we just bought it."

"Cleaner and easier than what?"

"Than burning you off it. Running you off it. He even ruffled up that preacher's woman about that nigra of yours. He was a good riler, was Morris. I tried to tell him we could find that gold without the map, but Morris wanted things the easy way. He wanted that map."

"How did he know Diego Ramirez?

Jenks snorted. "Morris had just linked up with us. We sent him to San Antone to join the Texans. He just happened to sit down next to that Mex kid in a saloon. The kid had a story of a mine. Sure enough, he had a nugget and a map to prove it, but he'd run out of money. He couldn't even get himself out of Texas without cashing in that bit of gold, and he was almighty fond of that nugget."

"Why did Lieutenant Morris tell you about the map, about the boy?"

"Morris didn't have any money. He lost just about every three-cent piece he laid hands on before it got to his pocket. Poker. Three times I had to give him the money to get himself elected lieutenant."

"Was he a good spy?"

"Oh, he was that. He gave us the territory. He told us exactly where that Reb wagon train would be after Glorieta. But he was also feeding the graybacks and using our spoon to do it."

"Why?"

"Money, of course. He was into that blackguard of a gambler in Mesilla for hundreds."

"You knew that?"

"Of course, I didn't know it. I would have been tickled pretty to turn him in. You would have sold that land eventually, and I would have me a gold mine all to myself." Jenks spit on the floor again in contempt.

"But General Canby thinks you did know."

"I should have known. When I put all the bits and pieces together, it was obvious. But Canby's a hard man. He said it mattered not whether I was a knowing party to it; it was my responsibility to put those pieces together sooner."

"You told the general everything?"

"If I hadn't I would be standing out there next to Morris, looking into the next world from behind a blindfold."

I was about to ask if he had told Canby about their interest in my land when a soldier stepped through the still-open door. "The general requests your presence, ma'am."

◇◇◇

Canby was leaning against his desk, arms folded across his chest.

"Did you learn what you wanted to know?"

"Yes, sir."

"I shall arrange for the charges against you to be dropped, although that may take a little time because I cannot divulge my full knowledge to the civil authorities."

I had not expected so much luck on a single day. "Thank you." Giddy with relief, I thanked him twice more.

"Also, I have a proposal for you."

"Yes?"

"I understand you own the horse ranch called Mockingbird Spring. I should like to purchase it. I will give you a very good price."

And he named a figure more than twice what I had paid for it.

My mouth dropped open, and I fear I may have drooled like an idiot.

"Come, come," he said to my wordless stare. "The price is not fair?"

"It is very fair, sir."

"I am a horseman, you know. In my native Kentucky there is no higher calling than breeding horses. I find this valley quite to my liking, and your horses are said to be very fine."

My head was still whirling.

"I am told you work the ranch only from necessity," he said gruffly, "not from any liking of it. After all, it is hardly a fit occupation for a woman."

An odd sense of impending loss stirred within me. Almost everyone believed I did not belong on a horse ranch, not least of all myself. But suddenly I was loath to sever myself from this "unseemly" occupation.

"Well?" the general rumbled.

A series of distant cracking sounds interrupted my spinning thoughts. "Forgive me. I fear I'm too stunned to answer just now. I'm sure you will allow me to think it over?"

Just then the door opened. A tall, lean captain marched in, saluted, gave a sharp nod and departed. Morris would no longer trouble me.

I turned to leave but at the door turned back. "Beg pardon, sir."

"Yes?"

"Did Lieutenant Jenks tell you anything about my ranch?"

"Jenks? What would he know to tell me?"

"Nothing, sir."

◇◇◇

At home, I danced through the parlor toward Winona, unable to contain myself. Frowning, she listened silently while I related the events of my journey to Fort Fillmore.

"Even my fondest hopes," I finished, "were that I might—might, mind you—get that much money for the ranch after three or four more years, and then only if the breeding business prospered. But now we might as well start packing for Philadelphia."

"That is mighty good news, Miss Matty." I hardly noticed that she didn't smile.

The next day and the one after I did not go out to do the chores. Instead, I set about mending my dresses and babbling about bonnets and bustles.

Winona muttered at me, "You done told the general you take his offer?"

"Not yet. I'll take the carriage in tomorrow. But this time I want to look right. I want him to know I'm a proper lady. I have to get this awful dress sewn up first."

"That be a right fine buckboard, but it ain't no carriage."

"I'll buy all the silk Mr. Garza has in stock. I don't suppose he has any pongee or linen or Swiss muslin. I wonder if there's a good seamstress in town. You and I and Zia will have twenty new gowns."

"Zia needs diapers, not gowns. And a muslin frock be plenty good enough for me."

Her straight face and set jaw baffled me. "Whatever has annoyed you, Winona?"

"Nothing," she said sulkily and stomped out of the room.

I went back to my sewing. Whatever it was would right itself as soon as we were on our way to Philadelphia. I was sure of that. I made a mental note to buy a bolt of cloth for petticoats as well.

The following morning, being Saturday, Ruben and the other hands took off for town. Since I no longer needed a bodyguard, I let them go early. Nacho and Herlinda had gone to Doña Ana for a few days to visit his sister, who was ill. Herlinda had been strongly affected by the exorcism I had so brazenly staged. The air had finally stopped squirming with sullen looks, and she and Winona had become almost cordial.

I was so intent on what I would say to Canby that I heard no horse approaching. The thumping on the door startled me. I hadn't finished dressing, so I stuck my head into the hall. "Winona?"

She didn't answer.

I hastily donned the waist I had laid out and was still fastening the long line of buttons as I made my way to the parlor.

Winona was at the door, her shoulders stiff the way they get when her mind is boggled.

"Who is it?" I asked.

She didn't turn. "I ain't sure."

Then I heard the voice, and every drop of blood in me congealed.

"This is my house, you damn nigra bitch, and I'll not be kept waiting at the door."

Somehow, as though slogging through mud, I moved forward and nudged Winona aside.

The door swung open a few inches to reveal a man, tall and slender and fine-looking in his Union lieutenant's uniform. His flesh looked a little pale and there were half moons of darkness beneath his eyes, but otherwise he looked much the same. The forelock of red-blond hair still swung jauntily above his eye.

"Ah, the fair Matilda in the flesh!" He smiled into my eyes, for all the world as if we were friends. "As I have been explaining to this slave here, she belongs to me. I own her, same as I own this ranch. I am the master here. You do realize that? Of course, you do. A married woman owns nothing in her own right. That is the law. And I am your husband."

Andrew smiled again and stepped inside.

Chapter Thirty-eight

"You did me grievous harm, my dear. But I am prepared to overlook it." The statement slipped from Andrew's lips like drops of honeyed hemlock.

"Get out." I ground out the words through clenched teeth. Now I could smell the whiskey on his breath and see the drunkard's web of fine red lines that had claimed his nose and cheeks. Still, he looked quite dapper in his freshly pressed uniform.

"Your countenance is exceeding fine, Matilda. You are still the most handsome woman I have ever laid eyes upon." His tone was caressing.

"How—?"

"Did I find you? I came down from Craig with Colonel Carson, though I admit to little liking for the man nor him for me. So, he left me here. I've asked for you in every town I passed through, though I did reckon you had gone back to St. Louis. Imagine my amazement when the saloonkeeper was acquainted with you. Now, if you please, stand aside."

"I do not please."

Andrew put his hand gently on my shoulder and stroked it. Then, he shoved.

I staggered backward, and he stepped inside. His eyes, shiny as new buttons, seized mine. He crossed the parlor then turned back, wanting me to see him run his gaze slowly over the fireplace, the walls, the furniture. "First-rate house, from the look of it. You invested my money well."

He ambled back to me as casually as if he had just returned home from a day's journey and leaned forward, his breath brushing my cheek. I recoiled. He pulled me to him and squeezed my breast. "Did I interrupt your morning primping?"

As if it were no part of me, my hand flew toward his jaw. My palm stung as if it had touched acid.

Laughing, he danced away. "You robbed me, Matilda. I found it most difficult to believe that you had such mettle. I'm sure the sheriff here would like to hear about it."

"I turned myself in. Served my time in jail."

"Did you now? That must have been congenial. Did you fuck every guard or just the ones you liked?"

"Get out!"

Winona had remained riveted to the spot, watching. Now she threw the door wide.

"Oh, come now, Matilda." Andrew gazed through the doorway. "This surely is a fine spread. How much land do we have here?"

I took a step forward, thinking, I suppose, to flail at him with my bare fists. But just then, in the back of the house, Zia waked from her nap and let out a howl.

Andrew's eyes fixed on mine and a puzzled look spread over his face. "A child?"

The words came calmly, as if rehearsed without my knowing. "My son."

Andrew tried to read my face. "You…"

"Yes."

Andrew was drawing himself up with the new thought. Winona was staring at me. I looked down at my hands, then back at Andrew, trying to make my eyes soft. "I suppose he is that, Andrew. Perhaps I was wrong, keeping a son from his father. Would you like to see him?"

His eyes held mine as he nodded.

"I will fetch him for you." I strove not to break into a run as I left the room.

Zia gurgled when she saw me and held out her arms to be picked up.

Despite his vanity that he had fathered a son and his slightly drunken state, Andrew was not so stupid that he would not soon recognize the cry of a baby less than a year old and realize that any son of his by me would have to be at least six.

I gave Zia the rag doll she had thrown from her crib and took a piece of horehound candy from the bag on Winona's bureau; she was teething and liked to bite on the hard candy. Cooing happily, she reached sticky hands to my shirtwaist and tried to unbutton it. She adored buttons. I took it off and gave it to her. She drooled her appreciation but when I started to move away, she began to whimper.

I grasped her chubby arms and looked into her huge eyes. "You must be very, very still," I whispered, and she must have understood because she didn't make a sound as I left the room and slipped down the hall to my office.

I lifted the pistol from its hook above my desk and walked as quietly as I could down the hall, my hand on the trigger and ready. Stepping fast into the parlor, I propped my legs apart, held the gun as steady as I could with two trembling hands and aimed the barrel straight at Andrew's chest. "Get out. Now!"

He had been standing at the door, looking out. Now he stared at me, his jaw slack and open. Winona stood, stone still, a few feet from him.

"Do not doubt for one moment that I will kill you, Andrew," I said, wondering whether I really could.

He whirled and grabbed Winona. "Then kill your precious nigger!"

She squealed and jerked away; he pulled her back. I slackened my finger on the trigger. Kicking at him, pummeling his chest with her fists, Winona brought up her knee. He yowled as he doubled over, and she spun out of the way.

I moved toward him, the pistol aimed, my hands more steady now.

He straightened and backed toward the door, hands involuntarily rising as the barrel of the gun approached.

My gun still at the ready, I followed him outside to the wagon that had brought him. Andrew was never one to sit long in a saddle.

Without a word, he climbed into the seat, took up the reins and turned the horse toward town. Then he stopped, looked down at me and said quite conversationally, "I will be back. You are my wife. This is my land."

I watched the wagon move along the trail until it all but disappeared. Then I dropped the gun to my side, and my stomach began to roll.

In the doorway, Winona was shaking her head. "That be one mean somabitch. Good riddance."

A wave of weariness stole over me; my body seemed made of granite and older than the mountains. My feet lurched unsteadily and my head ached as though a minie ball had roosted there. "He will come back, Winona."

She saw me to a chair and brought a damp cloth for my head. "You get yourself to that fort and tell that general."

"No," I said dully.

"What you mean, no? He got a viper right there in his vest pocket and it dang near bite you and you say no? That general maybe can help."

"Andrew is my legal husband, Winona. He's right. He owns Mockingbird Spring. And you. And me. The general can't do anything about that. For that matter, he may realize he can simply purchase the ranch from Andrew."

"You can beat that wagon on the horse of yours. Sell it to the general before he get there!"

"It would hardly be right for me to sell the ranch to General Canby when one of his own men has a better claim to it than I."

We both considered the bleak facts.

"He knows you helped me, Winona. He might have killed you—"

"At least he be nursing his nether place a good long time!"

I tried to laugh but the sound twisted in my throat like a rope.

◇◇◇

I devoted the entire afternoon to staring at a smudge on the parlor wall, unable to muster the energy to walk down the hall.

Winona made many sojourns through the parlor, pretending to be cleaning; but I knew she was checking on me. Perhaps she thought I might take a gun and swallow the barrel. I do own that I considered it.

She mopped her brow with a kerchief. "Heat come mighty early this year."

For myself, I felt chill clear to the bone.

She was polishing an already spotless window. "I bet a pound of gold to a goose feather he not just crazy from whiskey," she said over her shoulder.

"Of course, it's whiskey," I snapped. "It's always been whiskey. But nothing changes the fact that he's right. That's the law. The godforsaken law. He can take everything, and there's nothing I can do to stop him. I reckon all he has to do is take our marriage paper to the alcalde, and he and Zeke will be out here to enforce it."

"That Andrew be dosing hisself with something. You see them eyes?"

"I didn't notice."

"The blacks of his eyes are real big. Injuns drink something that do that. It makes them all het up and mean when they go on the warpath."

"That's a merry thought."

Chapter Thirty-nine

Winona fried up some chicken for supper, and I was doing my best to eat it, though it tasted like sawdust. Zia was in fine fettle, gurgling and drooling and banging her spoon on the table from her perch on the box Homer had built for her.

I was still chewing my first bite of chicken, trying to get it to go down, when a tiny puff of breeze slid over the back of my neck. A faint stench of stale whiskey and something sweet and rancid hung in the air. I darted a glance over my shoulder. My jaw went slack, and the food I had swallowed turned to stone.

Andrew was slouching in the doorway. The air was utterly still.

"I do hate to interrupt your supper." A small smile played about his lips as he savored our shock. He had replaced his uniform with a velvet waistcoat, a cravat of blue satin and a narrow-brim hat. He would have seemed quite the dandy if the eyes above it all had not been those of a coyote sighting on a hare. "I have come for my son. Where is he?"

"You have no son." The words rasped in my dry throat. "Your son is dead."

His eyes narrowed to slits. "You take me for a fool? I heard him."

My body felt like beeswax that had got too near a fire. "You heard Zia."

Andrew's gaze took in Winona, still rooted to her chair, her eyes like saucers. He shifted his stare to Zia.

"That's no son of mine. That's a nigger baby. You fucking niggers now?" He grasped both my arms and lifted me from my chair. "Where is my son?" he bellowed, shaking me. The chair crashed to the floor. Andrew ignored it. "Get him. I will not have him grow up with a pack of whores and a nigger brat."

I willed myself numb. "Andrew, I lied to you. It's true I was expecting when I left, but I lost the baby."

He reared back and squinted at me, as though he was having trouble seeing, then slapped me hard across the face. Pain bloomed in my cheek like an evil flower.

"I own this land and I want you off it," he roared, hammering my shoulders with his fists until I lost my balance and fell.

He watched as I struggled to rise, then swaggered away. Before I could think what he meant to do, he had snatched Zia from her makeshift chair. She sensed the peril; she barely whimpered.

Winona pitched herself at Andrew like a human catapult, but he caught her face with the flat of his hand and slammed her backward.

"I shall teach you to keep your knees together," he hissed at her. Then his voice turned chillingly soft: "Why should my son die and this nigger baby live?"

Grasping Zia by the shoulder in the careless way a child holds a rag doll, Andrew stalked into the parlor.

Winona and I dashed after him but pulled up short just inside the doorway.

He was leaning against the wall. A small, prideful smile fit his face like a mask. His blue evening coat showed two streaks where the baby had drooled.

A horrible vision of the puppy, his head dashed against that other wall, swam into my head.

"It's a chilly evening," Andrew announced. "We need a fire."

"It too hot…" Winona's voice started thin and trailed off.

His eyes were fixed on me. "Perhaps you didn't hear me. I said I want a fire."

My legs moved toward the fireplace as if they were walking under water. The log box next to the tile panel still held plenty of wood. My quaking fingers laid waste to five matches, but at last the tinder flamed.

I stood and turned to him. A gush of gorge rose in my throat and I swayed on my feet, but my voice was like a ship becalmed. "That's a handsome coat, Andrew. You always cut such a fine figure."

He tilted his head and studied me with a sly look. Zia's eyes were huge and dark. She had nearly swallowed her thumb trying to find some comfort in it.

"I've not seen the like of that coat in all these years," I went on. "You do us an honor to dress so finely for your visit."

"I would not squander a pair of filthy dungarees on such swill as you have become. I intended to attend a reception for the general's wife."

"Did you send your regrets? Did you tell Mrs. Canby you would be visiting me instead?"

"Of course not." He seemed to puzzle over my question and find no sense in it. "There is ample time yet to present myself." His piercing gaze raked over me. "Your hair, there by the fire, is outlined with gold. Your hair was what I loved most about you."

I drew a breath, and the sound of it seemed deafening.

"Yes," he said, as if thinking it over and agreeing with himself. "Your hair is, indeed, your finest feature. It has a fire of its own, doesn't it, Winona?" He turned to her; and very slowly, she nodded. "Get over there by your mistress."

Winona blinked but didn't move.

"I said, get over there."

She seemed frozen to the spot, her eyes glassy. Andrew jerked Zia's arm, and the baby began to scream. Winona scurried to my side.

"That's better," Andrew nodded approvingly. "Now take that stick, Winona, that bit of kindling there on the left, under the log."

She held his eyes, motionless as a mountain.

"Take the stick." He shook Zia. The baby howled, and he shook her harder. Her head wobbled.

Horrified that her neck might break, I lunged at him. He blocked my assault with his knee and pitched me to the rag rug on the floor. A scream rose from Zia then halted as suddenly as if it had been chopped through with a knife.

Winona snatched up the stick. The logs in the fireplace toppled with a sound like a muffled drum roll.

The wand of wood in Winona's hand flamed, beginning to consume itself.

"Bring it here." Now Andrew's tone was smooth, cajoling.

Ever so slowly, she did as she was bid; but when she reached him, he shook his head. "Hold it to your mistress' hair," he crooned, the words rolling gently from his lips.

Winona's eyes and mouth were enormous dark circles in her face. Finally, her mouth moved. "No, sir, no. You not do this."

"But I'm not going to do it. You are."

Winona's mouth worked, but no sound came out. Her head jerked right then left.

Andrew grasped Zia's shoulders and held her high, then began to swing her headfirst toward the floor. I half leapt toward him, but his arm had already stopped mid-arc. He nodded at Winona.

I could almost hear her muscles tightening to the bursting point. A strangled-animal moan came from her lips.

He nodded again, sharply. "Do as I tell you."

Slowly, she moved the stick toward me. I willed myself utterly still. The stench of burning hair filled my nostrils. The fire flared, the heat searing my neck. My heart beat like a wild thing in my chest; my brain ordered me to scream but I clenched my jaw shut, knowing Andrew's cruelty thrived on screams.

Something hit the front door, first tentatively, then louder. An anxious voice rose behind it. "Matty! Why the fire? What's going on?"

I had forgotten our pact to build a fire if something boded danger. I had meant a brush fire outdoors, but the chimney smoke on a warm night must have brought Tonio on the horse I had left with him.

Andrew gaped at the door as if he were slow-witted.

"Tonio!" I rasped, my voice dry as tinder. "Go! Go away!" Then the fire reached my scalp, and I shrieked.

A crack of splitting boards sounded, the door gave way and Tonio hurled into the room.

"Sweet Jesus!" He did not pause to take in the full scene. Buttons bounced on the floor as he ripped his shirt open, threw himself over me, wrapped my head in the shirt, pummeled my head with his hands.

When he pulled away the shirt, I rolled into a crouch and swung my face toward Andrew. Tonio followed my gaze.

Andrew's eyes had narrowed to surly slits. The click of a pistol hammer seemed to echo in the silent room, the barrel like an eye, fixed on Tonio.

"You havin' this sweet white body between your sheets, my frien'?" The liquor slurred Andrew's words. "You'll like get the French pox from her. She's prob'ly warmed every bed in the territory. Or chilled it, more's the like."

I tried to breathe, but my lungs wouldn't open.

Ever so slowly, Andrew took aim and pulled the trigger. Tonio seemed to rise into the air, then fold up as he sank to the floor.

I tried to rise, but my legs turned to jelly and went out from under me.

Zia, quiet for so long, began to scream—long, terrified, sobbing screams. Andrew grabbed her by one arm. She slipped out of his hand. Hiccoughing between short shrill bleats, she tried to crawl away. In her panic, she struck her head on the leg of the table that stood next to the wood-box. Framed by the table's legs was a row of mockingbirds on a tile panel.

Andrew's eyes went flat. He swept Zia up and stuck the end of the pistol into her ear. Her cries rose then dwindled to whimpers. He drew the hammer back. She gave a high-pitched shriek. He jerked the gun in anger. She grabbed her ear where the muzzle had rammed it; when she drew her hand away I could see the round, red mark the metal had made.

Like someone whose mind is dead but whose body lives on, Winona began to lumber past Tonio's crumpled body toward Andrew.

I lurched toward the table, hooking its leg with my foot. The table flew to the side, and I pitched to the floor. Andrew was watching me. Above the gun, his eyes glittered.

Winona dropped to the floor like sack of meal tossed from a wagon. Her shoulders toppled forward until her forehead struck the floor. Then she raised her body slowly, her face still down. When she had raised it high enough, I gasped.

Her eyes had rolled in her head until no pupil, no color showed at all. Only a milky white, made whiter still by the light of the fire and the darkness of her face, filled the space between the fringe of lashes.

"Gabara," she said in a single high tone, drawing out the final syllable. *"Gabara, candombla, obea, ewa, flimani kokuwata, mawu."*

Andrew jerked back, terror written in the lines of his face. His eyes bulged, fixed on Winona. "Stop that!"

I edged closer to the wall, intent on the row of mockingbirds.

Winona's voice rose. *"De wo afikpa! Me le bubu de tefea no oh!"*

Another wrathful shout from Andrew was followed by a muffled thud. But I could not spare the time to turn.

I pushed at the mockingbird's wing, thrust the loosened panel of tile aside and seized the pistol that lay on the chest inside the niche. I swung the gun around.

Andrew had dropped Zia. Winona was scooping her up. Gripping the revolver with both hands, I brought up my thumb and yanked back the hammer.

Andrew's eyes flicked to mine, his face a deadly white, and I remembered the last time I had leveled a gun at him. My hands began to quiver. Only then did I realize that the front of my shirt was clinging to me, wet with blood. Tonio's blood.

Winona was still on her knees, Zia clinging to her neck.

His face an icy mask, Andrew raised his own revolver.

"Drop the gun," I said, my voice as cold as his eyes.

Something dull scraped against the floor. A moan, a muffled grunt. Tonio's shoulders rose clumsily and swayed as he fought to focus on the scene.

Andrew's gun jerked in an arc, stuttered past Tonio and stopped a few feet from Winona. I tensed my finger.

A very long time seemed to pass before my pistol bucked.

I watched Andrew's eyes roll white and his body crumple ever so slowly to the floor, blood spurting from a jagged hole in his throat.

Chapter Forty

Tonio was in much pain, but the ball had passed clean through his chest near the shoulder. He bade me burn the places where it entered and exited. The wrenching shouts it wrung from him and the odor of burning flesh will never leave my memory.

The man I loathed more than anything in all the world did acquire a portion of the land he intended to claim as his. But his allotment was not large.

Winona and I wrapped Andrew in a sheet. Under a black, moonless sky, I hitched Fanny to the wagon and toted him to a far corner where the hands were unlikely to roam. Even the earth was loath to yield him that small patch: its clay was like iron. Winona and I had to hack at it with an axe before the spade could gain purchase. We dug as deep as we could. When we had filled it in again, she insisted on wrestling heavy rocks atop the broken earth.

"I don't give a stump if a coyote digs him up for breakfast," she grunted, "but this spirit not rest easy. We got to keep it down there."

I touched my hand to my head; and chunks of charred hair broke off, cascaded down my face. I wiped them away with a filthy hand. "The last thing I'm worried about is a spirit. Do you really believe all that?"

"He believe it."

"I reckon he did at that." It was growing dark. A coyote yipped in a far off canyon. I leaned on the spade. "You were mortally persuasive. Did you make up those words?"

"I do own I conjure up some of them words myself."

"What does 'gabara' mean?"

"She be the goddess of love."

"You called on a goddess of love?"

"No other come to mind. Gabara not be the best—she drink rum and smoke a pipe and get herself up in fancy smells—but she be easy to call on."

"What were the other words?"

"They not matter."

"They don't matter? Or you won't tell me?"

Winona heaved a sigh. "I say, 'take off shoes, you be messin' up the place of voodoo.'"

"That's all?"

"I only seen one real spell-casting, and that be a mighty long time ago."

I fit another rock into place. "I warrant that's enough to keep his spirit here."

"Maybe that's no never mind to you."

"Why?"

"You can just up and leave this place now. You can send to the general and do your deal. You can go to your Philadelphia."

I gaped at her, the reality dawning. "I could even go back to St. Louis." I dropped my eyes. "But it won't be anytime soon."

"Why so?"

I touched a finger to my hair.

◇◇◇

By the next evening, when Homer and Ruben and the other hands traipsed back from their carousing and Nacho and Herlinda arrived home from his sister's, Tonio was installed on a bedroll in a corner of the office.

He had slept fitfully. In his waking stretches, he directed me to fetch some herbs from the cuevas and make a poultice. That done, the three of us had concocted our story.

Winona had scrubbed my head till all the burnt bits of hair came away, and I was very nearly bald. She rubbed a broken lobe of aloe into the raw places. The thickness of my hair had kept the burns from going deep, but a quick look in a mirror quite sickened me. I did not want to contemplate what might have happened if Tonio had not arrived when he did. Winona tied a big bandana around my head to hide the mess and keep the burns clean.

The three of us told our shocked listeners of an outlaw drifter who had burst in on us at suppertime, who had flung me against the open stove when I tried to stop him from ravaging our belongings. Tonio had run the man off but had taken a ball through his chest for his trouble.

Canby was busy running the rebels all the way to the border. He did not press me for an answer.

In a fortnight, Tonio was well enough to return to the caves.

Despite the urgency of the never-ending chores, I found myself snatching moments in the early morning quiet to sit on a rock and ponder the future. For the first time in a lot of years I actually had a real future to think on, and it looked oddly different from the pretend one.

So much rain had fallen that year there were daubs of color everywhere, as though the desert were a fairytale princess waking from a twenty-year sleep. Just beyond the house the mountains rise quick to become as furrowed and craggy, as full of strength and beauty as the face of God. When you sit very still, beyond the silence you can hear the water. The mountain spreads its apron to catch the rain, and the water burrows through the rock to seep out in little splashes, to make a dripping spring.

Somewhere beyond that ridge was a gold mine.

I sometimes mused on the ripples of change in my own life loosed the night that Lieutenant Tyler Morris killed Diego Ramirez.

Now and again I would return to that rock when the sunset was painting the organ peaks crimson. Sometimes a mockingbird would perch on a branch of mesquite, twitch its white-striped tail, open its slender bill and pour out its stolen songs. A scrappy little critter, it was not a foot long; but I've heard tell they will fiercely defend their territory, even against a bobcat.

It was on that rock I discovered that it was not having been in a dark place but leaving it that matters.

Winona found me there one dusk. "You be wanting to pack up soon?"

I gazed at her, not comprehending.

"St. Louis."

I didn't answer for a moment, then, "No."

"It still be Philadelphia, then?"

I shook my head. "There's something witching about those mountains, Winona. When they pull you to them, they don't let you go."

Winona's face split in a dazzling grin. "I got to say you takes your own sweet time learning that."

When I got back to the barn, Nacho was waiting.

"Tomorrow the walls," he said. "New mud is needed."

"All right."

"Es verdad, señora?" he asked. "Is true? You stay?"

I nodded.

Nacho gazed at me a moment, then, *"Muy bien."* Very good. For him, it was almost a shout.

"Thank you," I said, touched. "But you could have found other work. Better work."

"Other, yes. Better, no." He ducked his head and ambled into the barn.

◇◇◇

Tonio, his arm in a sling made from an old quilt, found me mixing straw into a big basin of mud. For the walls.

"So, you will stay on," he said.

"I suppose I shall. I reckon that after all this I'm not fit for much else."

"You will not pine for the orchestra?"

I stirred the mud with a hoe. "I expect I will, some." The loss of that dream had left a little hollow place.

"You would not be happy there, with naught to think of but petticoats and pretty music."

I glanced at him.

"They do say that the further east one journeys, the fewer the wildcats." He chuckled. "Nacho seems pleased. Even Herlinda smiled when I asked for you."

I put the hoe down. "You could marry them. Nacho and Herlinda."

He flashed me a look of exasperation. "You still think I'm a priest."

"Why can't monks perform marriages?"

"I'm no monk, either. I was excommunicated."

"People know nothing more of that than some half-remembered rumor."

"You mean I should lie to them?"

I finished smoothing the mud with a board. "At bottom, what difference does it make? Does God himself bestow the right to join a man and a woman in marriage?"

"That is what they say."

"Do you believe it?"

He shrugged.

"Then do it. Surely, it's harmless enough. Give Herlinda something she has wanted these many years."

He slipped his good arm around me and brought his lips down on mine. His damp beard smelled of spring water and damp earth.

◇◇◇

In the end, Tonio agreed.

I could hardly wait to tell Herlinda. She denied any importance to the matter, but I did not miss the flash of joy in her eyes. Together, we planned the wedding.

She slaughtered one of the pigs herself and dug the pit to roast it in. Then she busied herself in the kitchen boiling pinto beans and peeling chiles. She even taught Winona how to make tamales. A couple of drifters caught a whiff of the aroma and offered a week's work if they could just have some of those vittles.

At the spring, where the water slips between the rocks to feed the chaparral, under the scrub oaks that crowd round the little pool, we held the ceremony. Herlinda's lace gown had browned with age. Except for two new panels of bleached muslin, the dress was her mother's, she told me proudly; she had kept it for nearly forty years.

I played the flute. My fingers were stiff on the keys, but no one seemed to notice.

To the steady drip-drip-drip of the springs, Tonio spoke the words of the ritual he had no right to perform. Nacho stood arrow-straight with his hand in Herlinda's. He had scrubbed his face so hard it was still red. Ruben stood with them, holding a silver ring the blacksmith had fashioned.

Winona had baked a big teacake drizzled with honey and applejack. Zia blew bubbles and stole everyone's attention by taking her very first steps and nearly walking out of her diaper. The wine we opened was not quite ripe, and I daresay we all drank a mite more than we should have.

When the sky was purpling and we had talked and laughed ourselves hoarse, the others made their way back to the house, leaving Tonio and me to dismantle the makeshift altar.

"I'll be moving on soon," he said.

I stared at him over the cloth I was folding. Somehow, it had never entered my mind that he would ever not be there. "Is it the cave? We could build you a house, we could—"

"It's time for me to go," he cut in quietly.

"But why?"

"It's many years since I've lived long in one place."

I licked at dry lips. "But where...where will you go?"

"California, I reckon. I have yet to see the Pacific. And the trees, as I hear it, are nigh as high as this mountain."

"But I...What will I...?"

For a long moment, he was silent. "It would only be a matter of time, Matty, before you would want me to take you to the mine. Already you have persuaded me to conduct a dubious ceremony for a marriage I had no sanction to perform."

"No, I—"

"You're an ambitious, capable woman who scarcely knows how many wildcats she can whip." He gave a dry chuckle. "Do you deny you've thought of the mine?"

"I own to thinking of it, yes, but you must have a surpassingly low opinion of me to think I would—"

He stopped my mouth with his own.

◇◇◇

I sent word to Canby that I would not be selling the ranch. The general sent back a message that my decision perplexed him, but he wished me the best. He appended a warning about Indian trouble: the night Mrs. Canby had arrived to join him an officer had gone missing and hadn't been seen since.

Not long after that he departed the Mesilla Valley, taking the war with him. It was a long time before it was over, but we saw no more of it ourselves.

Isabel agreed to marry a Baptist missionary she had never met and was sent to Oregon. There was no more trouble over Winona's so-called witchcraft.

Zeke rode out to the ranch and, taking swipes at his head with a crumpled bandana, told me the charges against me had been dropped.

So far as I know, no one ever took note of Andrew's seven-by-four-foot piece of land.

My hair grew out very slowly. It was many months before I could bear the sight of myself without the bandana.

After the livestock auction, which brought us nearly three times the profit I had expected, I wrote again to Nanny. I didn't own up to the whole truth, but I did tell her about the ranch and that I wouldn't be going to Philadelphia—or anywhere else for that matter. I even suggested that when the war was done she and the haberdasher might like to come for a visit.

I went often to my rock. Once or twice I rehearsed little speeches to Tonio, giving him my solemn oath I would never so much as mention the mine, asking him—maybe even imploring him—to stay. If I could say that much, could he say no? I asked the mountains, but they wouldn't answer.

I suppose the Organos had got their name because they put some early Spaniard in mind of organ pipes. But for me, it was not their look. It was the way the sight of them makes your breath catch, makes the hair lift along your arms and your spine tingle all the way to the top of your head like it does when the bass notes of an organ swell and you believe you are in the presence of God.

◇◇◇

When the first sharpness of autumn was in the air, Tonio appeared one early morning at my door, the worn old knapsack strapped to his shoulders.

"There's a desert to cross," he said. "This time would be the best."

"So soon?" I gaped at him, the earth seeming to turn under me. "You are wrong," I said when I finally came to myself. "I might try to find the mine on my own, but I would not ask that of you."

He gave me a sideways glance. "Remember the rattlers. The nest on the trail grows bigger each season."

I swore again I would not be tempted and tried to say the rest, but the words would not leave my throat. Instead, I insisted he take one of the horses, but he refused.

I took his hand. "Come back this way. Promise it."

He held my eyes for a long time, then moved his head in a motion I took for a nod. From the corral, I watched his steady gait carry him away from the mountains, toward the river until he was only a black dot. Perhaps Tonio was not designed to be a violin in a sea of strings, but an oboe, reedy and alone. Perchance I had been fashioned by the same design.

For months after I would take Fanny and ride to the place near the cuevas where I could see the entire valley, hoping to spot a dark speck growing slowly larger, a figure on foot returning.

To receive a free catalog of Poisoned Pen Press titles, please contact us in one of the following ways:

Phone: 1-800-421-3976
Facsimile: 1-480-949-1707
Email: info@poisonedpenpress.com
Website: www.poisonedpenpress.com

Poisoned Pen Press
6962 E. First Ave. Ste. 103
Scottsdale, AZ 85251